HOLIDAY OF THE DEAD

A Zombie Anthology

A Wild Wolf Publication

Published by Wild Wolf Publishing in 2011

Copyright © 2011 with Individual Authors

First print

ISBN: 978-1-907954-05-4

www.wildwolfpublishing.com

Other Zombie Titles From
Wild Wolf Publishing

Dead Beat (2010) by Remy Porter

Rise & Walk (2011) by Gregory Solis

Written works by the contributors to this anthology include; Night of the Living Dead, Pontypool, Necropolis Rising, Dead Fall, The Kult, Domain of the Dead, The War of the Worlds: Aftermath, Sinema, The Killing Moon, the Joe Hunter thrillers, Turn of the Sentry, Unlikely Killer, Lucky Stiff, Down the Road, The Zombie's Survival Guide, Santa Claws is Coming to Town, The Estuary, the Vampire Apocalypse novels, The Invasion, Island Life, Night Fighters, Apocalypse of the Dead, Dead City, Quarantined, Flesh Eaters, Drop Dead Gorgeous, Flu, Dead Beat, Undead World trilogy, World War of the Dead, Bigfoot War, Maneater, Zombie Britannica and Prey to name just a few.

Special thanks to Peter Fussey for the amazing cover artwork.

FOREWORD

Wild Wolf Publishing has gathered together the most comprehensive assemblage of emerging and established authors in the zombie sub-genre. From legends like Night of the Living Dead co-writer, John Russo to exciting new talents like Remy Porter and widely respected established talents such as Shaun Jeffrey, David Dunwoody, Joe McKinney, Rod Glenn and A P Fuchs, this anthology really does have them all!

WE'VE all probably had a holiday from hell at some point in our lives, be it the brochure neglecting to mention the hotel was a building site, or the all-you-can-eat buffet made you live on the toilet that was just a hole in the floor for three days, while a six-packed Spanish dive instructor seduced your wife on a boat half a mile off the coast. Obviously I'm not still bitter, and this was purely a made up example.

For me, possibly the one bad thing that hasn't happened on one holiday or another is a zombie apocalypse. This is unfortunate in some respects as then I'd actually be able to score a poolside deckchair off certain non-specific European holiday makers for once*.

But joking xenophobia aside, and back in the reality that my psychiatrist has worked hard with a cocktail of drugs to maintain, I know that zombies on holiday may not happen in my lifetime. In the meantime, this collection of stunningly original zombie stories from an array of old hands and fresh talent will have to do.

This is an Anglo-American zombie collection of epic proportions. If you want the best undead stories of the year you have them here. This is the quintessential holiday read.

Remy Porter, February 2011
* Don't mention the war

CONTENTS

7

Seahouses Slaughterhouse
By Rod Glenn

A special bonus short story by Night of the Living Dead co-writer, John Russo 'The Walk-In'

An exclusive excerpt from the screenplay for the forthcoming film sequel to Pontypool written by Tony Burgess

DARK INSIDE
By
Shaun Jeffrey

I once thought dying was the worst that could happen.
Then I came back ...

10.15am – July 18

Stood on the bow of the cruise ship, Silver Surf, I performed my best impression of Leonardo DiCaprio from the film, Titanic.

"I'm the king of the world," I shouted, much to my little brother's amusement. He covered his mouth with his hand and giggled. The sea breeze animated his mop of sandy coloured hair like a strange sea anemone. I think it amused him more because I'm his sister; everything I do makes him laugh.

I liked making him laugh.

A couple of passengers looked at me with distaste, perhaps thinking my reference to a film concerning an ill-fated liner inappropriate, but they could go swivel.

The wind had messed my long blond hair, and as I stepped away from the bow I brushed a strand out of my eyes and hooked it behind my ear. The sea breeze had made my eyes water slightly and the ship's structure offered only relative protection.

If the truth be told, I hadn't been looking forward to the holiday. It was my parents' idea; I imagined the ship would be like an old people's home. But luckily my preconceptions had been wrong as there were a number of young people onboard and to my surprise and relief I had enjoyed it so far. There was plenty to do. The ship had two showrooms, a sports court, four swimming pools, library, pizzeria, steakhouse, casino, hamburger grill and shops galore. A floating town, inhabited by 1,950 passengers and crew.

Out of the passengers, one boy in particular had caught my eye. Tanned and sporty with short brown hair, he looked drop-dead gorgeous and I felt sure he would pluck up the courage to speak to me – if he didn't, then I would have to make the first move. Life's too short to miss out.

11

"What's that?" Jake asked, bringing me out of my reverie.

I looked where he was pointing and saw a small boat floating in our path. Although difficult to see clearly from our position and distance, it looked abandoned.

Noticing a steward nearby, I called him over and pointed the boat out. He thanked me for my keen eye, and hurried away to report the vessel.

Even though I knew it took a mile to stop the ship, it wasn't long before I felt us slowing, and I watched as they launched a boat to investigate Jake's sighting.

10.57am

The unscheduled slowing of the ship generated a lot of interest, and by the time the launch returned, towing the small boat, a number of people had gathered on the deck to watch.

Hard to see clearly from where we stood, I grabbed Jake's hand and led him through the crowd and down to where I imagined they would dock (I had seen hatches in the lower decks that were used to ferry supplies from the islands). In the back of my mind, I remembered something about a person who saves property at sea being entitled to a reward, and as Jake spotted it first, I felt any reward should come his way.

11.24am

When we arrived, a great deal of commotion came from the men gathered around the boat. I don't know why, but my heart felt like a punch bag under attack.

"Hey, what do you kids think you're doing here?"

I turned to face a gruff looking man with a bald head and a pockmarked face. Being called a kid really annoyed me. I'm sixteen, but I think I look older. My figure often draws admiring glances, and the bikini top I wore today only just covered my breasts.

"It was my brother and me that spotted the boat," I said. As I spoke, I noticed the gaze of his grey eyes stray toward my bosom, and then quickly realign with my face.

"Well, you're not meant to be down here. It's dangerous."

Before I had a chance to reply, someone shouted and we all turned to look at the boat that had been dragged aboard.

Another shout rang out. People fell back, stumbling over one another, and what looked like a black blanket suddenly flowed over the side of the boat.

I frowned, and then opened my mouth in shock as I realised that it was a plague of rats … and they were running toward me. They scurried quickly across the deck, and then without warning, one of them launched itself at me, and I felt its sharp little teeth sink into my arm.

But it was the sight of a man hauling human bones out of the boat that made me scream.

12.13pm

I could tell as the doctor stuck the needle into my arm that he enjoyed inflicting pain. I winced, which caused a faint smile to break the straight countenance of his narrow lips. He had a face like granite rock, weather-beaten, upon which the smile seemed ill at ease.

"That antibiotic should help ward off any infection," he said.

My mother sat at my side, shaking her head. "What the hell were you doing there anyway?" she asked for the umpteenth time.

I sighed, tired of explaining myself. The pulsing throb of a headache didn't help.

People always commented that I acquired my good looks from my mother. At the moment, her blue eyes looked close to tears, although I didn't know whether through anger or concern. Her hair was as blond as mine, but shorter. We also shared the same little button nose, and I think my bosom will be as plentiful too. The t-shirt she bought during our stop in Jamaica made her look cheap. Two sizes too small, it bared her midriff and the pierced belly button she had done last year. It's time she grew up.

My father sat behind her with his back against the wall. He seemed distracted; his thoughts probably on the state of his car components business back home. I don't think he wanted to come on this holiday; I probably inherited my mother's stubborn streak, too.

13.20pm

By now I felt awful. A headache thumped away inside my skull like a demonic parasite and a fever made me feel delirious. Mother sent for the doctor, but it appeared that I was not the only one to have been bitten by the rats, and he was busy elsewhere.

Although I couldn't be sure, I think my mother's more worried than she's letting on. I heard her whispering to my father (which is never a good sign), and they won't let Jake in to see me.

17.30pm

Time felt as though it had stopped. The last few hours seemed to have dragged on for days. I think I've been sleeping, but I'm not sure.

"But she's only sixteen; she can't be dead," my mother said.

I wondered briefly who my mother was referring to, and I tried to turn my head to ask, but I couldn't move.

Panicked, I tried to open my mouth to speak, to cry out, but I couldn't. I couldn't do anything.

A shadow moved into my field of view, and the doctor's face appeared above me like the angel of death. He shook his head and then closed my eyelids. Dark inside, I felt strangely numb.

"I'm sorry, Mrs Hoyle."

My mother screamed.

I wanted to open my eyes; wanted to scream back that I wasn't dead, but I couldn't. My mouth and eyes remained glued shut.

In the background, I heard the captain's voice come over the Tannoy.

"Ladies and gentlemen, as you know, a few hours after leaving Haiti, we picked up a vessel that was floating adrift. Unfortunately, the vessel was harbouring a quantity of rats that have now entered the ship. These rats have bitten a number of people, and it has been found that the rats are carrying an unidentified virus. You are advised not to leave your cabins until further notice. But rest assured that we are doing everything in our power to contain the situation."

Virus. The word made me think back to a recent biology class. Virus: any of a group of sub microscopic entities capable of replication only within the cells of animals and plants.

That didn't sound too good. As I contemplated my predicament, I heard more voices in the room, strange voices, and although I couldn't move, I felt them lift my body and carry me through the ship.

I heard people talking in the background; some cried. Far away, I heard a scream.

19.02pm

When I opened my eyes, the darkness didn't fade; it took me a moment to realise that something rested lightly on my face. I instinctively reached up, glad that my ability to move had returned, and tugged off what turned out to be a white, linen sheet. Light from a bare bulb above cast a veil of luminescence, revealing the room to be some sort of storage facility piled high with boxes.

Before I fell into what I can only assume was a coma, I had felt someone touching me up. I had wanted to scream at them to stop, but of course I couldn't. To all intents and purposes I was dead. That's what made it so sickening. I don't know how far the person would have gone if they weren't interrupted by someone entering the room and announcing another dead body needed collecting – I couldn't help but think that it had been doctor death copping a quick feel.

I now felt hungry. Ravenous. It not only manifested itself as a burning sensation in my stomach, but as an overpowering urge to feast.

I sat up. My body felt different, my muscle fibres tighter, as if they had contracted, and my skin felt leathery. Red blotches marred my arms; where the blood had pooled my body looked bruised. I probably looked as bad as I felt.

15

Swinging my legs over the side of the trolley, I stood up and then almost collapsed. At first, walking proved difficult; I felt reborn, having to learn all over.

There were other bodies in the room, but I sensed that they too weren't dead, that we had been pricked like Sleeping Beauty and had fallen asleep. But no Prince came to awaken us.

19.21pm

Upon leaving the room, my family came to mind. It took a while to get my bearings, but once I did, I made my way back to the cabin we shared.

The ship seemed unnaturally quiet. In the distance, I heard the slap of waves against the bow, and felt the steady throb of the engines vibrating through the floor. My whole body felt attuned.

20.01pm

When I reached the cabin, I opened the door without hesitating.

My mother sat with her head in her hands; she looked up when I entered. Mascara marred her face in tearful lines.

Her expression transformed through surprise, pleasure and finally, shock.

Then she screamed.

It's hard to say what I felt at that moment. Any other time I would have been saddened to have seen her so upset. Now ...

With no sign of Father and Jake, I guessed they were out somewhere. Perhaps Father was trying to explain the concept of death to my brother, but he would be ill-informed.

I opened my mouth and tried to speak, but no words would come – at least nothing that sounded intelligible.

Impelled to move, I staggered forward and grabbed my mother. Apparently too shocked to stir, she gurgled something as incoherent as my own effort at communication, but I wasn't really listening. I needed to quench the burning in my stomach.

I sank my teeth into Mother's neck and clamped them together and ripped out a chunk of flesh as sweet as any prime

16

steak. She gurgled something and for a brief moment, she struggled. But it was futile. Death had empowered me.

It felt almost karmic – seemed only right that Mother nurtured me in death as she had in life.

20.34pm

Sated for now, I sat in the darkness, cradling my mother's severed arm. I didn't feel any guilt. I didn't feel anything.

I sensed the others like me, rising from their dead sleep – felt it through a primal connection that united us in death.

Footsteps echoed outside the door and then stopped; the handle started to turn. I heard voices: my father and brother. I would never make Jake laugh again.

Soon, everyone would be dark inside …

THE END

SQUAWK
By
Remy Porter

I could taste dirt and blood in my mouth, sprawled out and face down. Always the clumsy boy. Back on my feet I picked up the sound of my brother Daz's bellow ahead somewhere, 'Where the fuck are you, Conrad?'

I ran for the centre of the field, brushing the high grass away from my face. It was dark; the only light, a quarter moon, lost in a cloudy sky. Stumbling, I found the silhouette of Daz's broad back. There he was, driving a wheelbarrow forward in wild, weaving steps. Heaped in it was a stolen generator and some copper pipe; metal clanking on metal. 'I'm here,' I hissed and took hold of one handle.

I shot a glance back at the farmhouse. A cacophony of voices, farmer and farmer's sons I guessed. Blinding spot lights shot over the field like lasers, illuminating the woodlands, the fields and fences. Our transit van was suddenly no longer in the shadows, but stuck out like a white blinding beacon.

The throaty roar of a tractor engine started behind us. 'Let's leave it here, Daz.' Moonlight caught my brother's incredulous look – like I was the crazy one. We pushed forward, the balls of our trainers slipping and churning in the mud. Miscellaneous metals fell out either side of the barrow. 'Come on will you!' pleaded Daz.

'Trying.'

Forty feet from the van the back doors sprang open. There he was, the stick thin nicotine-stained midget that was our Dad beckoning to us. He was in his favourite Magic Johnson athletic top that was a good size too big for him. A lifetime of grime, from his wig, all the way down to his Doc Martin boots. He was green blood Irish gypsy stock, and he once chewed a man's ear off. He was proud of that. A yellowing scar bisected his nose, a keeper from a 70's knife fight. A family dispute settled the old way.

'You two eejits ne'er learn. Not a clever bone in either one of yous.'

The tractor ripped across the field for us, people shouting over the din, 'We're coming, you fucking gypos.' Inbred pig farmers for sure.

Me, Dad and Daz had our hands on the heavy gennie, sliding it into the back of the van. Something like this was pure gold dust to us. Transient folk had one hundred and one uses for these units. It would be a big fist of cash, no questions asked.

Something sharp brushed over my hair, a black shape zooming past my peripheral vision. 'What the hell was that?' Daz said, looking up with me.

'Lads, we don't have the time for star gazing,' Dad shouted and scuttled back into the driver's cab.

A new noise, a raw 'SQUAWK'. A crow hit the metal roof of the transit with enough force to leave a dent. It stood up proud and stared down at me and Daz like some pagan god. There was enough light around to see black marble eyes. Intelligent. Watching. What the fuck?

'Fucking have your wings in a satay sauce,' Daz shouted, jumping in the van. I could tell he was spooked; the tell-tale tremor in his voice gave it away.

I looked back to the field. The farmers in their tractor were still a hundred metres away. It seemed every light in the farmhouse was on now. Women and children were stood in the yard watching and throwing half-heard abuse our way. Trust Dad to go and find us the bloody Waltons to go and rob.

As I went to jump in the passenger door, the crow reached its black head down from on top of the roof. It was no more than an inch from my face when it clacked its beak together, a sharp metallic sound. Another ear-piercing screech. I couldn't get past. I threw my hand up to brush it away and its talons raked over my forearm; an angry bloodied line through my rose tattoo. 'You bastard.' The crow retreated two steps. It seemed to be laughing at me.

'Have you got a clean shot?' I clearly heard one of the farmers say.

I looked at Daz and Dad, 'Floor it, floor it now!' The transit wheels spun in the clay mud and I was hanging half in, half out of the passenger door. The van found purchase and shot forward over a cattle grid. Daz grimaced as he held me by both armpits, his grip tearing at my skin. A shot rang out and shotgun pellets clanged into the van's metal side panels.

'They can't do that to us,' our Dad shouted over wild engine revs. 'That's god damn criminal!'

I finally got my feet inside and closed the door. I nodded at him and watched the black woods blur by. Two posts marked the end of the farmer's drive and we lurched back onto tarmac and open country road.

'Are you shot, Conrad?' Daz asked me, holding my arm up for inspection under the cab light.

'The crow got me good,' I told him. I looked up at the quarter moon and clouds and wondered if that fucker was up there watching. Next time it'd get a noose around its oily neck.

The steady tappeting engine had sent me to sleep on the motorway somewhere north of Bradford. I woke to see us back on the small roads between Kendal and Penrith. Daz's heavy head was leaning on my shoulder, squeaking-snores coming from his nose like a congested door mouse. I gave him a nudge and he awoke with a start.

To most people who didn't know my brother he was basically a bruiser. In a certain light you could see Dad's pinched, ferreting face, but instead of skin and bone Daz was all meat. He had big veined, sausage-fingered hands. His build was pure bulk, muscle all the way apart from a protruding pot belly. He would have made the perfect gypsy bare fisted brawler if he hadn't been a bit of a coward when it came to risking his own neck.

Dad had tried his best to push him into fighting in the early days, but Daz quickly learned the art of playing dead. Put him in a ring, with even a boy half his size, and if his first punch missed he could curl up in a ball quicker than a hedgehog on a croquet lawn. In the end Dad let him be. He knew when he was onto a loser.

I looked away from Daz and over at the neat pine tree forest lining one side of the road. The orange glow of sunrise was peeping into view. The road was straight and undulating, and almost empty. No more than a metre from the front bumper sat a small silver sedan. This was one of Dad's favourite games. I'd seen him play it many times. 'Look at those two fuckers. Can you see them, Conrad?'

Dad used the overtaking lane and pulled alongside. I looked down into the slightly worried faces of a bearded middle-aged man in the driver's seat and his presumed wife next to him. To Dad this was like a red rag to a bull. It made no sense of course, and there was no explanation. They were there to be toyed with, like a cat and a canary. The bearded man threw another scared glance up. I could see his white knuckles on the steering wheel. My face was stony – it gave nothing away to him.

Daz was getting excited, leaning over me. 'Pull over, pull over,' he shouted down to the driver. Already he was reaching for his iron bar. 'You are a sick puppy,' I said. I couldn't help but smile, just a little. My brother was mental and I loved him for it. He never knew any better.

Dad kept pace with the sedan driver, constantly making the transit do little swerves their way. He wasn't trying to hit them, that would be far too messy. Finally, the sedan did as expected and came to a complete stop. It always seemed the safest thing to do given the circumstances – who wouldn't stop when three crazy men in a van were trying to run you off the road?

I could see the wife fumbling for her phone, no doubt ringing the police. The bearded man was shouting to her. I couldn't make it out. We felt quite safe; the number plates on our van were stolen. The van itself belonged to a very distant relative. It would be a quagmire for any officer of the law to plough through. Anyway, we weren't going to hang around to get caught that was for sure.

Daz couldn't help himself. He leaned over me and out of the passenger window holding out his iron bar. With a quick swipe he sent the sedan's wing mirror fifteen metres into the trees. He followed up on the windscreen, sending a spider web of cracks shooting across it. 'Good shot there Daz, my son,' Dad said. 'Can't let those beards get away with anything.'

Our wheels span and we left the couple behind. Dad soon had us off the main drag and onto a dizzying set of single lanes. A half hour later I spotted the sign for Appleby. This would be our holiday; the biggest gypsy horse fair in Europe.

'Are you sure you're a proper gypsy?' Daz said to Dad, tipping me the wink. This was another of our little games – see how wound up we could get Dad.

'Are you taking the fucking piss, Daz? I have pure Romany in these veins.' He slapped his chest with a fist, getting slightly red-faced now. 'My olds rode a horse and tented cart all through Romania and those Carpathians. Purest gypsy through and through, no word of a lie.'

'I thought our great grandparents were Irish potato farmers. Perhaps they just went to the Carpathians on holidays?' I said.

'Are you reaching for a slap?' Dad's head was a beetroot. 'Your great grandparents were wrong 'uns in a fine line of gypsy stock. They fell in love with growing those stupid, boring vegetables. Lived in a house; bricks and mortar. They sold out. Thank God my ma and da saw the light and took to the road again.'

'But we own a house, Dad,' I said, hiding a smile. 'Doesn't that make us just as bad as potato farmers?'

'Yes I have one. Yes I may even like it. But I have this too. We are out on the road; we are keeping the travellers' trades alive. Stealing, robbing and selling; we are living the life.'

'Fair dues,' I said. 'But isn't it time you bought your own caravan. Why do we always have to borrow Uncle Fester's old one. It leaks and it's full of rabbit shit. It smells worse than Daz's wank towel.'

'That caravan is a bargain. And don't be so rude about your uncle. He was just born fat and bald ...' Dad stopped speaking. There was a policeman in the road ahead, waving us to stop. Behind him was a patrol car, its blue light flashing. No siren. 'You do the talking, Conrad,' Dad said, giving Daz a stern look.

The police officer made a motion with his hand to roll the window down. The copper wasn't exactly in the spring of youth. He had a grey face and eyes that looked wrinkled and baggy from too many late shifts. I guessed this fella wasn't far from a retirement of model train building and gardening, or whatever the fuck these country folk did in their spare time.

22

Close up I could make out individual stains on his fluorescent jacket; blood on the collar, oil on the sleeves. 'And where might three fine folk such as yourselves be heading now?' he asked, looking past us and into the van. Too dark back there to see and the stolen generator was covered in a blanket.

'How are you doing there, officer?' I said. 'Is there anything we can help you with?' Never give a straightforward answer to a copper; that was the rule.

The policeman sighed. A faint dabble of voices could be heard from his ear piece. He pressed the button on the radio clipped to his jacket. 'Roger; received that.' I thought the game was up.

'You know after twenty five years in this job I know you lads have something back there you don't want me to see. You in the middle look more nervous than a nun at a Hells Angels' Christmas party,' he said, looking at Daz. Daz squirmed in his seat next to me. 'But you know what, I don't care. I'm an hour past the time I should be at home with my feet up and having a beer. Finding something on you guys just doesn't do it for me, I'm afraid. Now listen, round the next corner is a wreck. A caravan went over on its side, quite the mess. One of your pals, I think.' He waved us on.

'Thank you sir,' my Dad chirped in, crunching his way into first gear. Driving forward, Dad looked at us, a wide grin on his face. 'Dodged a bullet there. Nearly lost our holiday stuck down the cop shop. We'll shift the gennie in Appleby fast like.'

'Why do you reckon he didn't know about the car we smashed?' Daz asked.

'Maybe he did. Maybe he just doesn't care anymore. Bored of the game,' Dad said.

Around the corner sure enough there was a caravan on its side. It was coned off and blocked one lane of the road. Debris ranging from smashed crockery to stripy socks covered the tarmac. Two young men stood at the side of the road with an older man and woman. They all seemed to be gesticulating and angry with each other; the blame game. Alongside them was a red Range Rover with its front end folded around a thick oak tree.

The Maldoon family saw us and stopped their bickering, staring at us idling past. Dad hit his horn and waved at them. 'Spot of bother, I see,' he shouted out of the window. Jimmy Maldoon, a wiry red-head and the youngest there, picked up a handful of gravel off the road surface and launched it at the van. 'Touchy,' Dad said and picked up speed again.

For as long as I can remember, the Maldoons and the Beeches hated each other. They hated my Dad, Frankie Beech most of all, ever since he'd bitten the ear off the now deceased Arthur 'Tiny' Maldoon during a particularly dirty bare fist fight back in 1978. It also didn't help that Dad was prone to loudly retelling the story in public when drunk, adding little embellishments such as how he kept Tiny's ear in a pickle jar on his mantel-piece at home. This is, of course, a complete lie as we don't even have a fireplace. Ever since we were kids Daz and I have had nightmares of being pinned down and having our ears chewed off. I wondered if the Maldoon children ever had the same dreams? I'd never dared ask them.

Dad steadily drove the last few miles to Appleby, through the winding country roads, woods and fields that surrounded the area. I knew we were getting close when the road snaked across a barren hill side, with nothing but nonchalant sheep watching us as we rumbled past. A signpost read, 'One Mile to the Historic Town of Appleby-in-Westmorland.'

Traffic began getting heavier, and we found ourselves behind a long line of expensive campervans and caravans being pulled by glossy 4x4 vehicles. 'Look at those show-offs,' Dad mumbled. 'You're just renting them. You're not fooling anyone there.' It was fair to say that Dad didn't buy into the general gypsy consensus of trying to appear ten times more affluent than you actually were. That is why we rattled around in an old Ford transit van, and borrowed Uncle Fester's caravan year after year.

'Isn't it about time you upgraded, Dad? I mean you can't keep repairing the engine with nylon tights and bribing Dodgy Dave at Auto Hot Bodies with a bottle of whisky every time it needs an MOT certificate,' Daz said.

'You are not exactly renowned for making a good point, but you might have something there. Maybe we do a swap with something in your uncle's fleet,' Dad said.

Daz and I just groaned. Uncle Fester's fleet amounted to a frightening range of chopped and shopped vehicles, mostly stolen, and all dubiously incapable of ending any journey without evacuation of fuel, oil or water, or sometimes all three.

'You should've kept your mouth shut, brainiac,' I hissed to Daz.

The first thing you notice about Appleby is it's really quite small. There's just not much to it when it comes to buildings. Just a criss-cross of roads lined with Victorian terraced houses, small and a little bit poky. A wide, shallow river runs through the heart of the place, giving the town a little more dynamism than it deserves.

We snailed our way past the first of a number of tin-pot pubs that littered the centre. Small places, not big enough to swing a cat in. It was midday and already our fellow travelling folk were outside, spilling through the pub tables and filling the curb-side. A group of forty plus men played and bet on the coin game – a simple but addictive gamble where you would bet on a head or tail throw of a coin. Daley, a gypsy with the gift of the gab orchestrated the game from the middle of the crush. I saw him taking wads of cash from gypsies prepared to throw hundreds of pounds on the flip of a coin. 'We should get down here,' Daz said. He loved the game, seemed to have a gift for it.

'Later,' Dad said, driving on. 'Let's find your uncle. Get settled.' Daz pulled a disapproving face and sulked in silence.

Driving over the bridge we looked down and saw horses being washed in the river. Great, gleaming stallions being readied for barter and sale. Other travellers waited patiently on the banks with their mounts, waiting for a turn in the level, crystal waters. On the left was the community centre, out of bounds for the likes of us. It was the feeding point for the dozens of police in their black riot gear under their fluorescent jackets, and the dreaded animal squad, the RSPCA who would look for the slightest infringement to justify confiscating an animal from its owner. If you walked a bleeding animal down into the town it was as good as gone.

More police lined the long dragging hill up to the campsites and show grounds. Dad pushed the van into first gear as we followed a restless horse and its bare-back rider. I saw three kids no more than ten years old clinging to the back of a motor home driving down the hill with the driver oblivious. Two police officers on a junction reacted and started shouting at them. Deftly, the three boys scattered and vanished back into the crowds of people walking up and down the road.

'Look at the talent,' Dad said. 'Some pretty lasses for you boys to chase the tails of this year.' He meant the teenagers in the bright oranges and greens, luminescent colours on their tiny skirts and crop tops, which were meant to signify they were available. Ready for courtship and marriage and all those things that came with it. Our women came colour coded, and whereas Daz looked forward mainly to the gambling and the boozing, my own desire was always to become acquainted with the prettiest 'day-glo girl' I could find.

At the top of the hill, more jaded looking policemen beckoned us under the bridge leading to the huge gypsy fields. We followed the horse all the way, the stupid nag. I'd never bought into all the horse stuff, the riding and trotting endlessly up and down the Appleby hill, and the carriage racing up here on the heights. I just found it nice that we were all here with our people, proud of our heritage.

Dad took the van right through the gate and paid the toll – fifty notes straight off the bat to old gypsy Cyrus in his hunting jacket. He owned the field, and was rich they said, but still liked to take the money personal-like; feel the fresh notes in his hand.

'You got a field full this year, Cyrus,' Dad said, making the small talk out of the van window. The vans, cars, jeeps, caravans, campers, tractors, horses and horse boxes stretched as far as the eye could see. Here and there the fence line divided them, subdividing the expanse of grass into separate enclosures. On each field there was a man to take the coin. Cyrus wasn't the only one getting rich up here.

'Have you seen my brother around? Not answering his phone as usual,' Dad said.

'Aye, he's up here, vehicles everywhere. That caravan you like is looking on the weary side this year, Frankie,' Cyrus said. Daz and I groaned and smiled; another trip living in that heap on two wheels. I swore I'd find a woman with something better.

Dad drove on and navigated the grass roads. To either side, the traveller camp was in full swing. Stalls lined the track, containing everything from reconditioned microwaves to horse shoeing services. Further inside the hubbub there were food vans selling suspect burgers and homemade donuts that would lay heavy on your stomach and then give you the shits all the next day. The queue was long; I guess people here just weren't that fussy.

Uncle Fester was never that hard to find. A portly man in his fifties with a foot long grey ponytail tied back. Typically he was wearing a blue boiler suit and had his head down in the engine of one of his heap of junk vehicles. 'Now there's your problem right there,' I caught Fester saying to the unhappy man next to him. 'With this model you need to check the oil every day. These old army seals are tricky, but you'll get the hang. She's running sweet again now.'

I could see a lot of blue smoke coming out of the green Land Rover's exhaust pipe. There was severe denting and paint scrapes over one side of it, like it had rolled at some point in its life. I wondered if Fester had perhaps found it in a scrap yard or a ditch. 'Anymore problems and you know where to find me,' Fester went on. The man didn't look any happier, and with a crunch of gears and a cloud of smoke drove away. 'Poor sod has bit the lemon with that one,' Fester sighed to us. *You don't fracking say*, I thought to myself.

Fester walked us over to our digs, a Viscount caravan that was probably somewhere near the bottom of the range back when it was built in the 1970's. It was spacious for one, cosy for two and for three felt something akin to being forcefully squashed into a sardine can with the odour of rotting vegetables and lime green mould.

'I'm sleeping in the transit,' Daz muttered.

27

'Now don't be like that,' Fester said. 'Just needs a quick once over and it will be as good as new.'

'Yeah, don't be such a soft lad,' Dad added.

Daz and I dumped what stuff we had with us in the caravan. Dad said something about going to talk to a geezer about off loading the hot generator. It freed us up to go and have an explore around the camp. Finally we were going to have some fun.

'Do you think Angel Taylor will be around?' said Daz.

'That bull dyke will be probably munching some carpet somewhere round-a-bouts,' I said, mystified as usual at my brother's appalling taste in crushes. 'Maybe you should try somebody else this year, Daz. She knocked a tooth out when you finally got the courage to talk to her last time.'

'Aye, but I'd had a beer that time. I'll do it sober this time around. I've matured you know.'

'Yeah and she's matured too. She must be at least thirty pounds heavier by now. A big fat lezzer!'

Daz started to chase me then, a big shit-eating smile on his face. He wanted to play fight, and that would hurt. I jumped over a roped off area and dashed between two static caravans, less than a metre apart. I knew it would slow Daz down with his big shoulders and stomach. Jumping out the far side I cut left and then left again. I got a full view of the fields. There must have been thousands of us up here now and hundreds of vehicles, travellers from everywhere in England, Scotland, Wales and Ireland. I loved it. It was epic.

I was about to dart off on another tangent when I felt a hand grab my shoulder. Puzzled, I didn't think Daz could be that quick. I wondered if he had found a cut-through somewhere. Getting smarter. I turned and stared into the freckled face of Jimmy Maldoon. I could smell beer on his breath. This was going to hurt.

'Jimmy you ginger ...' I said, and then saw black as the bastard cold cocked me square in the mouth. I opened my eyes and saw pooling blood on the blades of grass in front of me. My mouth was like a dripping red tap. 'No need for violence, Jimmy,' I said and got a sharp kick in the ribs that really stung.

'Leave him the fuck alone,' Daz was shouting. Jimmy was pushed back and my brother helped me to my feet. I felt dizzy, but I'd had worse plenty of times. I looked around us – the Maldoon count was multiplying by the second. I could see there were six of them around us now. Daz was going to get a kicking too.

'You know my Dad doesn't really have Tiny's ear on his mantel-piece, don't you? We don't even have one, lads,' I said to them.

'Yeah, Dad fed the ear to his dog Barney. Ate it up like it was bacon or something,' Daz blurted. Oh Jesus, here we go.

'You ready to do some knuckle fighting, Daz?' Jimmy said, taking a step forward. 'Can't see you getting out of it this time, you little coward.'

Daz looked scared as the Maldoons made a circle around us. Jimmy was about to throw the first punch when some old man stumbled in and fell to the ground right in front of us. I didn't recognise him, but he looked pale and sick. He started coughing, a horrible dry retching sound coming from his throat. Black vomit – a fine treacle of gruel – streamed out of his mouth and covered Jimmy's Nike trainers.

'You filthy fucking gash!' Jimmy started screeching. 'They cost me fifty quid.'

The old man was on his back now, and I could see his eyes rolling back in their sockets. One of the other Maldoons was leaning over him, having a good riffle through his pockets.

'Get out of it, you thieving twat,' I shouted at him and kicked his arse. 'Is somebody going to call an ambulance?' Just then one of the Gypsy Lee fortune tellers came out of her caravan with a grey blanket and laid it over the old man up to his chin. In the background I could see two coppers sprinting over with their tit hats in their hands.

'Come on, Daz,' I said. 'I think they've got this under control. Let's get out of here.' We left them to it and headed back to Uncle Fester's caravan.

Things change when the sun goes down at Appleby horse fair. While the day time has the relatively safe and tame equestrian showing off, the horse trading, the races, the stalls and the endless parades of female teens in ridiculous bright mating colours – the night is all about the beer, the gambling, the fighting and the scores to settle. Last year, I remember seeing a man in a deck chair, a burger in one hand and a beer in the other. Someone hit him on the back of the head with a lump hammer, made him twitch and spasm on the grass like a freshly caught flounder. When the police got there nobody breathed a word. I don't think the man died, but I don't think he was ever the same either. Half brain dead.

When I saw the fire I thought it was more of the same. At the far end of the camp, a campervan was alight, sending red raw flames into the night sky. The flashing blue lights of the fire brigade and police swarmed all over it.

'Want to go and watch?' Daz said, his face lit up.

'Okay,' I said and we left Dad and Fester getting toasted off cider next to the caravan.

We hadn't gone more than twenty yards when we heard a woman screaming. High pitched and in pain, it could have passed for a cat if there wasn't words mixed in there. The sound stopped abruptly, cut off. It was hard to know which direction it came from.

'Come on let's get to the fire,' Daz said. He looked as unnerved as I felt inside. There was a strange atmosphere in the air. People seemed to be standing around, worried looks instead of the usual party mood. It was getting very dark. Some vans had flood lights outside, no doubt powered by generators every bit as hot as the one Dad had unloaded today. I flicked on my torch and Daz and I picked our way through the maze of vehicles towards the blaze.

Somebody bumped into me and spun away. 'Watch it, pal,' I said. I couldn't see his face, but the guy looked drunk or drugged. He staggered away from me.

'This place sucks this year,' Daz said.

As we got closer, acrid smoke clung in the air like a heavy fog and made us cough. The torchlight caught twisting pearls of thick grey smoke, stunting our vision to five or ten metres. The heat of the fire felt like an open oven door, and I guessed more than one vehicle must have gone up in flames. 'Come and look at this,' Daz shouted and I realised he'd drifted off to my right.

I fumbled my way towards him and found him next to a police patrol car, its blue lights flashing weakly on the roof. 'You can't steal it, Daz,' I told him.

'No, look at it,' Daz said. I leaned down and saw the doors open. I flashed my light around the interior and saw papers and equipment thrown haphazardly over the seats. Black marks, hand prints were on the dash – I looked closer, reached and touched it. It could only be blood. I looked up at Daz and saw indistinct figures moving in the smoky fog beyond where he stood. What the hell was going on around here?

A fuel tank exploded in the heart of the fire. A bulbous orange fireball turned on the lights for a second, allowing us to see what we'd really walked into here. In amongst the smoke there was a rigid lorry on fire, next to it a van and a horse box all but gone. There were large, smouldering bodies next to the vehicles that could only be horses. One seemed to be twitching, flames still rampant across its back. Two men were on fire, flames engulfed their hair and faces. There were no screams, they just walked, bumping into the other people who ambled and shuffled around the glow.

The light burned down and we were back in darkness. 'Let's get the fuck out of here,' I shouted to Daz. Something bumped me from behind. I looked round, expecting perhaps a policeman, or somebody to take charge or tell me what the hell was going on here. Instead, I shone my torch into the eyes of the old man from the fight earlier. Blood shot and jaundiced yellow, they looked wrong, like they didn't belong in his head. I saw his mouth then – what teeth were left were jagged stumps. His lips were torn and bloody. The old man reached forward and leaned his mouth into my chest, toppling me off-balance. I banged the back of my head on the open police car door on the way down. 'DAZ!' I shouted.

Daz pulled the old man away, tossed him aside like a sack of potatoes. We were on our feet and running. We ran flat out and blind, back towards where Fester's caravan was, tripping over ropes, pushing past caravans and cars, knocking over people that got in our way. Some shouted and cursed, others seemed like the old man and reached at us and tried to grab at us. It was too dark to see who was who. What drugs were they using this year?

Cut, bruised and breathless we found Fester's camp again. My torch shone wildly around, glancing off my dad's Land Rover and the caravan we were supposed to be calling home. I saw the tell tale glimpse of white hair, Fester's back to us near the bins across from his camp. 'Jesus Christ, Fester, where the hell is Dad?' I shouted at him as he turned around. His face looked bloodless and drained, and I couldn't make out his eyes. They looked sunken, like dry craters in his face.

'Fester!' I shouted and nearly tripped, like some horror movie cliché. I felt a hand on my shoulder and thought it must be another of those things, but it was my brother pulling me back into the safety of the caravan. I scrambled inside and slammed the plastic door shut, panicking in the confined space until I found the light switch.

Daz and I looked at each other; he was wild eyed, sweating and his favourite Motörhead tour t-shirt was torn open at the front. There were scratches on his belly. 'Are you okay?' I said, as somebody slammed into the side of the caravan. I imagined it was Fester, but I wasn't in any mood to look.

'What the fuck are we going to do now, man?' Daz shouted and clumsily knocked several pans off the stove. 'Where the hell is Dad? DAD!'

'He'll be fine,' I said moving past him. Already I could see something was wrong inside the van. Things didn't look the same as I remembered. And then I saw it – blood on the cheap plastic handles of the tiny en-suite toilet door. Tentatively, I tried to push it open, but it was locked. 'Dad, you in there?' A blur and Daz's foot appeared at chest level, kicking the toilet door open and off its hinges.

If this had been the aftermath of a bare-knuckle brawl, it had been one that Frankie Beech had lost badly. Face down, with a pool of blackened blood around him in the catchment of the shower, our dad had lost a foot somewhere along the line. His left leg now ended in a raw, chewed mass of hollow bone and flapping tendon. Dad's cheeks kept blowing out like he was trying to impersonate a fish. He looked pale and ill like the things outside. 'I can't get through. It's engaged. We need a doctor! Now!' Daz said, holding up his mobile phone.

'Dad, can you hear me?' I said leaning forward, trying to tie my leather belt around his bleeding leg. Dad wouldn't hold still and started clawing his way forward towards Daz on his hands. Daz backed into the kitchen, terrified. Dad was leaving a snail trail of red behind on the cheap plastic floor, and making a growling, guttural noise like an animal. Then he bit his teeth into the treads of Daz's trainers, and my brother kicked him in the head, trying to shake him off. I grabbed Dad's stump and dragged him back a few feet, then sat on his back. 'Get some rope, Daz!'

My favourite show when I was ten years old was Stig of the Dump. A kid finds a dirty caveman in the local waste pit and they become best friends. I guess you had to be there. Staring out of the dirty window of Fester's caravan, that old show came to mind. Maybe it was all the people covered in mud, or the fact a lot had managed to shed or shred their clothes during the long, monsoon raining night.

The first light of dawn was over the camp now. Usually around this stage of the Appleby Horse Fair the worst thing you'd see on the fields was a layer of litter. This was something else. This was a whole different ball game in some alternative, parallel universe. I watched a man I knew as Rex, who for every fair I'd ever visited shoed horses from the back of his van. He used to transport something like a tonne of iron in horse shoes, every size, every type. The man was a genius at the job.

Rex had been using his hands for the last half hour opposite where we were parked, digging at the earth to get under a low lying campervan. There must have been something he really wanted under there. He was desperate enough to turn his fingers into bloodied, ripped twigs doing it. Finally, he made enough space to wriggle under. A muffled screech followed, human or animal, I couldn't tell. I didn't want to know.

'We need to get ourselves out of here,' Daz said from behind me. His voice set off Dad, in what remained of the caravan toilet. We'd bound him up with every scrap of tie we could find and bundled him back where we'd found him. Every time we spoke he thrashed around and tore more skin around his wrists and ankles. To look at him he had the same glassy, doll-like complexion from the funeral parlours Daz and I used to dare each other to sneak inside as kids. But Dad wasn't dead – he wanted to bite our faces off.

The sound brought more of the zombies over to our caravan. I closed the curtains and backed up as they started to pound on the sides, pressing in on the walls, the door, the windows – they didn't seem to care where they put their dirty hands. Fester's old, cheap caravan started to flex again, the cracks in the plastic widening. 'Okay, we're going to need to get a vehicle,' I said.

In a second there was a crack in the side of the caravan wall big enough for a grimy, bleeding arm to squirm its way inside. I threw back the curtains and counted twenty of those things outside, waiting for us. The wall split from cheap floor to rotten ceiling, and there was a topless woman knocking our dinner plates off the fold-away table. Her hands reached for me, and she would have had me if the flesh of her thighs hadn't snagged on the jagged plastic, hooking into her skin like a fish hook. God love him, Daz wasn't hanging around. He kicked the front door open and shoulder barged two walking dead out of the way. I followed him, going straight into an all-out sprint. I chased Daz's broad back as he dodged into the maze of vehicles again. I hoped to fuck he knew where he was going.

Running down the hill, dodging killer things like a slalom skier, I got another panoramic view of the traveller fields – hundreds of people shambling, aimless. In some places they seemed to mass, crowding around individual caravans and in one case, a port-a-loo. Whatever poor bastard had picked that as a safe hiding place must be cursing his dumb luck. There must have been forty bodies around the blue, plastic cubicle, and as I glanced again I saw it had tipped over on its side. Pure nastiness!

'Daz, slow down will you?' My brother was too fast, and I'd lost sight of him. I was going to die alone. An engine started up behind a line of vans. I pushed an old woman away from me, my hand touching the wet, gaping wound in her neck that must have killed her before she came back. I wanted to hit one in the head with a bat or a brick and see if it killed them like in the movies, but I was too scared to stop. These things were everywhere.

Around the corner I could see Daz sat in the driver's seat of an estate car, hammering on the horn and attracting more attention.

I pushed my way to the passenger door in sheer panic. From every conceivable angle zombies staggered towards the car. Rolling, falling, crawling, trying to get me and my brother. We were going to be overrun.

'Drive, will you!' I screamed at Daz, thumping down on the central locking button as the pale, dead face of a ten year old child slapped against my door window. Drooling mucus and bodily fluids smeared black lines across the window as she tried to bite into the glass.

'We're leaving. Right. Fucking. Now!' Daz screamed, sending the car lurching down the exit track. The dead people were flocking towards the noise of the engine in waves. The whole camping field was alive with movement – a chain reaction all directed at us. Daz, a bad driver even when the world didn't want to eat us, locked the brakes as we approached the open stone wall gate that led back on to the main road. All four wheels skidded on the wet grass and slowly the car turned sideways. I could see us crashed and stranded against the dry stone wall, besieged by hundreds of dead people.

The tyres bit down and the car went straight again, grazing my side of the car on the rusting metal gate. 'Slow down a little, for Christ's sake,' I shouted as my brother accelerated under the underpass and headed down the hill towards Appleby. I could see the speedo creeping up over fifty MPH.

At first Daz managed to swerve round the bodies walking over the road, but the combination of stupid speed and an ever increasing density of dead, meant we started to clip and hit them. One of the gypsy girls in bright day-glo green smashed over the bonnet and exploded the windscreen into a spider web of brain and broken glass. Daz wasn't trying to avoid anyone now, he just drove straight at them. Both airbags went off like gunshots as impact after impact rocked the car. 'We're not going to make this,' I shouted at Daz, my ears ringing. The car's suspension bounced up and down wildly as we mounted and rode over the dead like they were sleeping policemen.

I could see the river, filled now with corpses of people, and what looked like half-devoured horses. If we could just get to the country roads we'd have a chance. It seemed the moment I thought this, the wheels of the car locked and we ground to a halt. 'I can't get it moving, the wheels are jammed up,' Daz said, revving the engine into a high pitched squeal that abruptly died as it stalled. Looking into the wing mirrors it was obvious what had killed the car – the wheel arches looked rammed with the limbs and torsos of dead people. The bones and flesh had been churned up from below like the mud in a field and packed around the wheels and axle until it locked solid. We had to run now.

'Don't bother,' I said to Daz as he tried to drive forward.

'It feels like all the brakes are on at once.'

'Daz we haven't got time. We have to go. Run for the pub.'

Reaching hands came for us as we ran for the pub on the corner, The Royal Oak. I was so scared, I managed to outrun Daz in the twenty five metre sprint to the beer garden wall. The crowds of dead were slow, but I expected to see one of them turn into Carl Lewis at any moment. There seemed to be hundreds of them drifting towards us from Appleby's town centre, a slow moving tsunami of vacant faces and hungry mouths. The whole front row was gingery-haired Maldoons. This was fucked!

I vaulted the wall and tumbled into plastic chairs and a table. I was relieved to have any barrier against the dead, even if this one was only three foot high. Daz appeared beside me with a more elegant hurdle jump.

'Don't do it, Daz,' I shouted as he was about to pull open the front double doors of the pub. I was alongside the side bay window; behind the orange poster for a local pub band, the expansive bar was in darkness. But the darkness was liquid, a jumbled, jostling, moaning and moving room. In that instant I saw the pub for what it was: a pressure cooker packed to the rafters with dead, hungry people.

'Don't open the door; they're rammed in there.'

'What, then?' Daz said, his eyes wild as the dead closed in from every side and beginning to spill over the low wall. We were backed against the pub's front wall, as good as dead.

'We can get up,' I said. My genius idea.

I followed Daz as he started shinning his way up the old iron drainpipe. Hands were grabbing at my calves, trainers and shoelaces as I gained height. I pulled my feet away, feeling the bolts holding the drainpipe into the limestone bricks give a little. Above me, Daz's feet dangled precariously as he pulled himself over the lip of an overhang, and on to a section of roof covering one wing of the building. He made it, but sent a heavy grey slate bouncing off my shoulder. It hurt like a motherfucker and I nearly fell.

'Ssssorry!' Daz shouted down from somewhere above me.

I followed Daz's route, the freezing wind this high up only adding to my vertigo. Trying to drag my body over the lip I could feel my arms weakening. Daz grabbed my left arm. It hurt like hell, but he saved my life.

So there we were, sat on the roof of a public house, freezing our asses off. This was nothing like the Simon Pegg film. What a rip! I would've laughed but figured I'd lose it if I did and start bawling my eyes out. I chanced a look down and couldn't believe they were still coming. The dead drawn to us like a magnet, hundreds, maybe a thousand or more crushing themselves outside the pub, patiently waiting for their dinner. Were there no other living people they could bother? Another chill ripped through me at the thought.

I leaned back on the chimney, closed my eyes to rest for a minute when a new sound jerked my eyes open. I thought for a second one of the bodies had climbed up to join us.

'SQUAWK!' There it was again. The crow had found me. How could that be? The small, rational part of my brain knew it couldn't be the same one from the field —that was impossible. But it was an impossible kind of day. The bird made the same noise again, shrill and awful.

'Look at its eyes,' said Daz. 'The fucker is one of them.'

I looked more closely, as the bird started hopping aggressively down the ridge tiles towards the chimney pots where we sat. Its eyes gave it away, shrivelled and dry, like two raisins in its head. The crow was as dead as the crowds of people below us. It flew at my face, a mass of feathers and talons. I tried to grab it, to throw it away, but the constant flapping left me grasping thin air. I felt the flesh on my hands and forearms tearing open. White pain. My balance was shot, and I felt myself start to slip down the slates towards the edge. With one hand I tried to fend the crow off, and with the other I grabbed at anything to stop myself, trying to halt my slow slide into oblivion.

The bird made its scream again, snapping its beak onto my ear lobe and tearing it in half. Hot blood ran down my neck. 'DAZ!' I shouted out. I couldn't see him for the blur of coal black feathers in front of me. Everything went black, and I braced myself for the fall. Would the drop break my neck before the hungry mouths got to me? Would it hurt?

A crash to my right and there were blue skies above me again. I was still alive, still on the roof. Daz had dived over the top of me and was rolling around with the crow in his hands. One of my brother's eyes was a bloody, red hole. No more than ten centimetres from the roof edge, he held it by the neck. The noise was immense – then cut off instantly when Daz bit the head off the damn bird. Alice Cooper, eat your heart out! He threw the thing away with the contempt it deserved.

'We'll be okay,' I said, shuffling my way across the roof to help him. His eye was a gory mess, and his cheeks had been torn so deep I could see his teeth. 'We'll get you to a doctor.'

'What doctors? There's nobody left, just those dead people,' Daz said. He sounded slurred, sleepy. He looked very pale.

Something caught my eye above us. I wanted it to be a helicopter, a daring rescue with a winch, and medics, medicine and machine guns, but it wasn't. A black ball of movement separated into individual dots. I knew what it was, a flock of death. They didn't fly like normal birds, there was something stuttering and uneven in their wings. A little rigor perhaps? They arched over the distant tree tops, swooping a little and following the river. Below me the heads of the massed dead turned a little I thought. Somehow they knew what was coming – reinforcements from the air. I watched the flock, willed them to pass me by. Their noise was a battle cry. They turned.

'SQUAWK.'

THE END

JENNIFER
By
Iain McKinnon

It was quiet in the flat but there were still screams and the occasional gunshot from outside. He pulled his only weapon, an old pocket knife, out from the corpse's head and wiped it on the dead man's shirt. The blood was dark and stodgy but it wiped off easily enough. Bill flipped the knife shut, slipped it back into its sheath and clipped it to his belt.

He picked up his coat from where he'd left it over the back of a dining room chair and slipped it back on. The fabric rippled as he pushed his arms into the sleeves making a faint hissing sound. He walked into the hallway and faltered by the door. The summer sun cut a warm golden slash across the door from the dining room windows.

With a composing sigh Bill turned round. He didn't want to leave the flat. It wasn't the security that drew him back. He wasn't scared to walk into the turmoil outside.

The moment he left this place it would be consigned to a memory. Bill didn't want this place to be just a memory but already the joy he'd felt here had faded away. He should have savoured the time. In a pitiable act to recapture some of the memories he walked back into the bedroom to see her one last time.

She lay on the bed. Her soft blond hair was tussled and lay slightly across her face.

Bill knelt down and brushed the hair aside with the back of his hand. Her skin felt cold now and slightly hard. It was shocking. The palpable contrast between her warm soft living skin and this bitter empty husk. He knew she was dead but she still held a look of sweet innocence.

Bill drew in a breath through his nostrils catching a faint whiff of the shampoo in her hair and fabric softener in her clothes.

This little girl had been so full of life so boisterous and energetic. And that life had flicked off like a switch never to be turned back on.

A tear started to well up in Bills eye.

Her death was a tragedy, to die so soon, Bill felt angry with himself for allowing it to happen.

He looked up to see the unused school uniform hanging from the wardrobe door.

The tiny white blouse, price tag dangling from the sleeve, and the grey pleated skirt still in its protective wrap of cellophane. All ready for the start of a school term that would never come.

More screams and the screeching of car tyres drifted in from the street. The noise distracted him for a moment.

Ultimately it was a hollow act looking in on her, all he'd succeeded in doing was polluting his happy memories.

Outside, Bill thought, there were a million more tragedies unfolding. What was this one when weighed against the suffering and turmoil of the world outside?

Still this little girl was special to Bill and he didn't think he would ever forget her.

He bent over and kissed the little girl a tender peck on the forehead like he was wishing her sweet dreams.

Bill stood up and left. He marched out of the bedroom and out of the flat, he didn't even bother to close the door.

Why should he? What was the point?

He bounded down the stairs to the ground floor and opened the shared access door. A wave of heat hit him. The car parked on the road opposite the flat was on fire.

Bill took a step back in surprise. He put an arm over his face to shield himself from the blaze and quickly edged passed the crackling wreck.

This was a new world Bill thought as he looked around. This was a normal street in a normal town only normality had evaporated.

Broken glass, loose bricks even a dead body lying on the pavement. These were all normal now. This was a new normality, a new world – a world where Bill could write the rules.

No more household bills, no more tax, no more did he have to pretend to fit into the normal world. No longer did he have to feel suppressed or repressed.

He found he had lost all sense of fear.

Bill's pace quickened like a weight had been lifted from him and a smile rose on his lips. Now he could relax and be himself. He held his head up proudly. He no longer felt oppressed, or meek or insignificant. For the first time in his life he could do exactly what he wanted. There was nothing left to tie him down.

The pivotal moment, when Bill knew the world had changed, had come when he'd seen a policeman and a bystander clubbing a youth to death outside his home.

The garbled news items he'd been listening to hadn't made sense but what he could tell was this was happening everywhere.

A middle-aged woman, legs bent under herself, lay sprawled across his path. She wasn't moving. Her hand still grasped a suitcase by its handle. The locks were popped and the suitcase had fallen open or been prised open. A few garments still clung to the sides of the case the remainder, Bill guessed, stolen or caught by the wind.

With a skip Bill jumped over the corpse and continued walking down the rubble-strewn road.

Sirens wailed and screeching round a corner hurtled a police car its lights flashing. Bill was proud of his composure. He didn't jump, he didn't panic he wasn't startled by it. He'd been nervous at first. He'd been unsure of the freedoms the new normality afforded. But if Bill had been nervous, so had the police and everyone else in this city.

A man came running straight at him. He was young in his early twenties with a colourful blue logo top and a light fashionable jacket. His skin was flushed and as he ran he looked over his shoulder.

Bill tried to sidestep the man but in his terror fuelled flight he clipped Bill's shoulder as he ran past.

"The train station! They're at the train station!" he called back at Bill as he ran on.

Bill quickened this pace and headed for the train station.

The young man was the first of many. Not far behind him came a stream of people. The younger, fitter ones. People on their own, with no one to worry about, or the ones who didn't care enough to worry. They were the ones at the vanguard of the rout.

A business woman, or at least that's what Bill took her for, wearing a matching pinstriped skirt and jacket with a red blouse stopped a few feet away.

She bent over and vomited. Was it the run, or the horror or a combination of both, Bill didn't know.

He stepped up to the woman and placed a comforting hand on her back.

"Are you OK love?" Bill asked with a tone of sympathy.

The woman gasped and nodded.

"What's going on? Were you with anyone?" Bill pressed.

"The train pulled in," the woman panted, "the doors opened and ..."

She bent down again and dry retched.

Bill rubbed her back. "Take your time love."

"I was going to work. I know stupid of me," she said seeing Bills frown. "The doors opened and the passengers, God the passengers they were all ..."

The woman paused, the fear still fresh in her eyes, "They were all covered in blood. Someone must have been infected at the last stop and they couldn't get out."

The woman looked back down the road. Dozens of people were streaming passed them running for who knew where.

"You couldn't tell who was alive and who was dead," she shook her head. "They started pushing onto the platform. It was packed. You couldn't tell who was who. There were people ... whole families getting ripped apart, women and children and grown men screaming as they got attacked or crushed or trampled. It was awful, utterly awful."

Bill stopped rubbing the woman's back and started walking towards the station.

"You can't go back there," the woman called, "it's carnage."

Bill ignored her and continued to walk.

"You'll be killed!" the woman shouted in dismay.

When Bill ignored her she added, "It's your fucking funeral."

The crowd was thicker now. A car belched smoke where it had come to grief at the car park entrance. The car behind had tried, unsuccessfully to shunt it out of the way. It was now wedged firmly between the toll barrier and the crashed car. With the doors jammed shut the occupant scrambled to get out of the window.

More and more people streamed passed him trying to escape the small station and flee to the surrounding streets. Now Bill saw the first injured. Blood streaked faces the red standing out against the ashen grey looks of terror.

One of the injured people spotted the struggling driver and limped over to assist. Or that's what Bill had assumed until the screams made him look again.

"Mummy?" a frightened voice called out from nearby.

Bill looked round to catch a glimpse of a girl between the fleeing figures.

The street was awash with lunatics, some running and screaming, some hobbling and groaning.

"Mummy?" the child was in tears desperate and lost.

Bill pushed through the mob.

"I've got you dear," Bill called out as he whisked the child up and out of the turmoil.

The girl couldn't be any more than five or six. She wore a pink dress with bare legs, white socks trimmed with pink and her matching shoes were held in place with Velcro straps. It was a miracle such a tiny child hadn't been crushed in the stampede.

"It's all right you're with Bill," he said holding her tiny frame in his arms.

He swept some of the child's long dark hair through his fingers careful not to dislodge the ladybird hairgrips.

"That's a pretty dress," Bill smiled. "You on your summer holidays?"

"Mummy!" the girl cried triumphantly.

A young woman, her eyes wide with relief, was swept into Bill by the crowd.

"You're safe," the woman cried. "You had us so worried."

Bill looked at the woman with narrowed eyes. She was a scrawny looking thing. Thin and weak looking. It was a surprise that the crowd hadn't trampled her to death Bill thought.

He slipped his hand down to his belt.

"David!" the woman shouted into the crowd. "She's over here David!"

A man turned round and barrelled his way towards them.

The well-muscled man had no trouble wading through the throng and up to Bill.

"You had us so worried petal," the burly father announced in a sweet voice that belied his appearance.

"Thank you," he said as he plucked the child from Bill's arms.

In an instant they were gone.

A man lunged at Bill his arms out stretched. Bill sidestepped and the drunken attack missed him. His face covered in blood, the man turned and groaned.

The blood gurgled in his throat and droplets sprayed out as he lunged again.

"Get off me, you!" Bill ordered the disdain dripping from his voice.

Bill pivoted away from the assailant at the same time as pushing his shoulder and arm. Knocked off balance, the man stumbled and fell to the ground.

A loud shriek issued from right next to him and Bill looked round to see a fat teenage girl getting bitten on the neck. Blood sprayed out as the assailant chomped on her abundant flesh.

The girl screamed and held her hand out to Bill.

Bill stood for a moment looking at the squat girl, her thick fingers sheathed in cheap rings. One hand was out-stretched begging for help, the other was engaged in a futile attempt to slap her attacker away.

Bill ignored her and walked on. He didn't walk deeper into the chaos, instead, he skirted the edges, working around, dodging his way through. All the time, his neck craned, trying to get a better view, trying to spot what he was here for.

Then he saw them. The woman was stumbling through. She was battling to get away from the station and, on her hip, clutched close to her, was a child.

Bill eagerly kept his gaze on them as he pushed on. He slipped his hand down to his belt and pulled out his knife.

Someone made a dive for him and he jabbed the blade deep into their eye. There was no squeal of pain only a wet slurp as he withdrew the blade and they slumped to the ground. Another person ran into him and Bill lashed out. This time they did scream. Bill pulled the knife out and let the injured man fall. He was still crying out in pain as Bill pressed on.

Up on his toes Bill swept people from his path desperate to spot the woman and child.

The worst of the crush was behind him now but he had lost track of them.

Bill clenched his fist in frustration gripping the knife handle until his knuckles turned white. He had to find them.

Ahead there was a bridge over the railway track that took traffic away from the station. He fought his way up to the vantage point and looked around.

The slick bullet-shaped engine sat adjacent to the platform. The driver's door was open but there was no sign of any staff. Bill looked over the railings at the station below. It was awash with blood and half out of carriage doors or crumpled in unnatural heaps lay the dead and dying. Old and young, male and female; people of every race and standing. Slaughtered. And around those fallen unfortunates, devouring the warm flesh, were dozens of cannibals.

Bill gasped as he watched gore soaked people chewing down on the dead and injured. He'd seen people being bitten plenty of times before. When drunken brawls got messy, or as the last resort of an overpowered victim. But on the platform they were being devoured, skin from muscle, muscle from bone.

There were still occasional screams and sobs from the unfortunates; some were even still trying to crawl away.

It was a scene of horrendous carnage.

"The world's gone to shit," Bill hissed.

A moan sounded from beside him. Bill turned round to see a man drenched in blood shuffling towards him. His arms were outstretched and his hand was missing a good few fingers.

"Fuck off," Bill cursed, infuriated by the intrusion.

This foul creature was nothing more than a distraction. He ducked under the man's grasp and brought him up over his shoulder in a fireman's lift. He then tipped the man over the railing of the bridge.

He didn't scream or call out as he fell. Silently he tumbled down and bounced off a carriage roof before slumping to the track below. His legs and arms were twisted at unnatural angles. But in spite of the horrific fall he didn't lie still. The man on the tracks stretched his neck out in a motion reminiscent of a snake tasting the air. He looked up as if to get his bearings then heaving himself forward on his shattered bones he started to drag himself away as best he could.

"Freak," Bill spat out.

He looked around trying to spot the woman and the child again.

"There," Bill smiled as he spotted the little girl.

A few dozen yards away on a path just off the main road she was alone and looking distracted. She walked a few paces forward then stopped and looked back at a house.

She turned round again and took a few faltering steps. Her cherub face was swathed with a deep frown and even from here Bill could tell she was crying. Her little hands clutched on tightly to the brown and white fluffy rabbit she carried.

"What's the matter honey?" Bill called after her in his sweetest tone.

"Damn," Bill berated himself.

The noise of the chaos had drowned out his shout. He looked around worried that he'd drawn attention to himself with his impatience.

The girl was oblivious to him wrapped up in her own world. She pulled the sleeve of her dress across her face soaking up the tears. Then she turned round and letting the stuffed rabbit drop to the ground she ran to the open doorway of the house.

47

"Wait," Bill called after her.

Slipping his knife back in its sheath he jogged across the bridge down to the house the girl had entered.

The moment he walked through the door he could hear her. The girl was sobbing.

"Mummy," she wept. "Mummy wake up,"

Bill entered the hallway to see the little girl rocking the woman's arm. She lay sprawled on the floor her eyes open, motionless. A pool of blood had drained from the wound on her wrist. It was a messy lesion, all ragged and chewed up.

"It's all right Bill's here to take good care of you," Bill offered.

"She told ..." the girl gulped in air. "She told me to go away."

Tears were streaming down the child's face.

"I didn't mean to do anything wrong," she looked at her dead mother. "I'm sorry mummy, I'm sorry."

"It's OK; just you come with Uncle Bill,"

"Daddy's not coming," the girl looked up at Bill. "We waited but he didn't come. Then the people screamed and hurt my ears. Mummy told me to give her a big hug and squeeze her tight."

The little girl let go of her mother's arm.

"Even when the lady bit her and biting's naughty 'go in time out'," the little girl wagged her finger as if she were telling someone off.

"That's OK; come here to Uncle Bill," Bill offered his hand out.

"I've not to go with strangers," the little girl said.

Losing his patience, Bill snapped, "Come here!"

He grabbed the little girl. She screamed and kicked out.

Bill could feel the small muscles struggling against his hold but for all her energy she couldn't break his grip.

Bill wrapped his arms around the girl holding her close to his chest.

A hand got free and lashed out at his face but Bill quickly parried the attack and had her in his grasp again.

"Oh you're feisty," Bill sneered as he walked to the door.

The child was wriggling furiously and Bill had to change his grip to keep hold of her.

"I'm going to enjoy you," Bill grinned feeling the child's small body grind against him.

"I won't make the same mistake I made last time," Bill promised. "I won't be quite as rough with you my dear."

"Mummy!" the girl cried out.

"Sorry darling Mummy's not around to help you …" Bill froze.

He sensed something moving behind him.

The girl in his arms stopped squirming.

"Mummy?"

Bill turned round.

Mummy was on her feet her skin drawn, her mouth gaping wide.

She cast an expressionless gaze around the hall before setting her lifeless eyes on Bill.

With a reptilian hiss the mother lunged at them. Bill dropped the girl. The child squealed as she hit the ground.

He grabbed his knife and flipped it open.

The child's mother grabbed at him.

With a primal grunt Bill lashed out. The knife slashed across the woman's face splitting her cheek and nose wide open. The pallid skin peeled open but no blood poured out.

Unfazed by the slash, the mother grabbed Bill by the shoulders and pulled herself in.

Her mouth stretched open as she prepared for the bite.

Too close to swing the knife Bill rammed the blade up into the bottom of her jaw. The knife ripped through the muscle and tendons and erupted from her tongue.

The dead mother clamped her mouth shut ripping into the flesh in Bill's neck.

Bill screamed and pushed her away but as he did a chunk of his skin was left hanging from the mother's mouth.

A spurt of blood came gushing from the wound. Bill clamped his hand around the gash instinctively trying to stem the flow. The blood was pouring out through his fingers cascading down his arm and slopping onto the floor.

49

Bill's eyes widened in panic.

"You crazy bitch," Bill spluttered.

The woman endeavoured to chew and swallow the flesh between her teeth but the knife lodged in her palate made that impossible. Instead the mouthful of minced flesh dropped onto the floor with a wet slap.

Her mouth empty she leant back in for another bite.

Bill grunted as he struggled to fend her off. One hand pressed against his neck, the other punching out. But as the warm blood pumped from his neck the room started to spin and Bill's blows weakened.

A third bite found Bill's flesh, then a forth.

Bill screamed, the flashes of pain hurling back the encroaching blackness. He tussled with the mother trying to prise her off, trying to get away from her gnashing teeth. Thick sheets of blood poured from his wounds. He struggled for breath. Faint and exhausted Bill slipped and tumbled to the floor. He landed with a splash in the pool of fresh blood, his vision fading.

As the black edges closed in he could see a pretty little girl framed by the summer sun outside.

She slammed the door shut blocking out the light.

Bill reached out a hand silently pleading for the girl and as he did the dead mother fell upon him snarling and biting and clawing.

The little girl ran screaming from the house. She ran as fast as she could.

Blinded by the panic and the tears she ran and ran just like her mummy had told her.

Suddenly from nowhere an arm grabbed her from behind.

"Calm down," a gentle voice said. "Calm down."

The little girl looked up into the face of a young lady. Her hair was almost the same colour as hers and she wore a sparkly silver piercing in her lip.

"Are you OK?" The lady asked kneeling down to meet the child's eye level.

The little girl sobbed, "My mummy ..."

The tears robbed her of the rest of her words.

"Shhh," the lady comforted. "It's OK, it's OK."

50

The little girl swallowed hard and slowly the sobbing subsided.

The lady smiled. "My name's Sarah, what's yours?"

THE END

CHERRY
By
Tony Wright

When the apocalypse came, Cherry Davis awoke from pleasant dreams of the holiday to come. A romantic getaway with Dave to Alicante was only a day away and her bags were all packed.

Excited, she sprang lightly out of bed and padded into the bathroom. Flicking on the light with the pull switch brought back remnant images of sunning herself on the beach, sipping long, cool drinks and holding hands with her man on moonlit walks through the surf. She could almost feel her skin glow with happiness as the usual morning ablutions washed the last shreds of sleep away.

It was only on returning to the bedroom, a towel wrapped loosely around her head, that she felt something wasn't right.

It was too quiet.

Looking through the window, she saw no traffic. No buses, no cars.

At this time of the morning, there would normally be a long line of people waiting at the bus stop across the road, reading papers, discussing the previous night's TV shows or nodding along to iPods, but today there was no-one.

A puzzled expression furrowed her brow as she saw thick trails of smoke pointing accusingly at the overcast sky in several places on the horizon.

She wandered over to the small TV on the dresser and flicked it on.

No breakfast news sprang to life on the screen, just a static message, white wording on a harsh blue background, which read:

EMERGENCY BROADCAST MESSAGE.
STAY AT HOME, AWAIT FURTHER INSTRUCTIONS.

Cherry pondered this for a moment. There had been scattered reports of rioting in several cities on the news over the previous few days. Sudden instances of violent crime had broken out. This had been explained, by the authorities, as unrest due to unpopular government cuts after the financial crisis that had gripped the world over the last couple of years. Had these incidents escalated into chaos overnight?

Cherry picked up her mobile phone and retrieved Dave's number from the contacts list.

No tone, no ringing. The phone appeared to be dead.

Dropping the phone, Cherry hurriedly dried and dressed in jeans and a t-shirt. Pulling on pink Converse and her leather bomber jacket, she opened the front door to her flat and stepped out into the cool air.

Cherry wrinkled her nose as a smell of burning stung her nostrils. There was also something sickly sweet that she didn't recognise. The rioters must have really gone to town, she thought.

She decided, without a better plan, that she would first try to find Dave. He was a security guard at Mad Joe's Carpets on the industrial estate. It wasn't far and maybe he'd know what to do.

As Cherry stepped onto the pavement, she started as a black cat appeared in front of her. There was something clearly wrong with the animal. It was dragging a bloodied leg behind it.

'Here, puss,' Cherry said, holding out a hand. She hated to see any creature in distress.

The cat stared at her warily and mewed pitifully. As Cherry approached it, she could see that the injured leg had marks on it. Teeth marks! She was no expert, but she could swear that they were human!

Who would do such a thing? She wondered and whistled softly at the cat. As she approached it, it hissed loudly and scratched her outstretched hand.

She cried out in pain and withdrew her hand. Small beads of blood appeared in the scratches.

The cat jerkily away as a cursing Cherry wrapped a handkerchief around the bleeding hand.

The sound of a wildly revving engine broke the unearthly silence.

As Cherry looked up, a police car careered madly around the corner and came up the street towards her.

The driver was clearly not in control. The car scraped along a garden wall, sparks flying into the air as brick hit metal. One tyre was deflated and the wheel rim gouged deep into the tarmac.

As the car flew past, Cherry saw that the driver, a young uniformed constable, was fighting with someone in the passenger seat.

Her mind showed her a last look at the terrified man as his attacker tore into his exposed throat with his bared teeth. The front windscreen splattered with blood as the car mounted the kerb and smashed squarely into a house. It stopped instantly as the bonnet folded in on itself. The occupants were thrown through the smashed windscreen straight into the house's bay window.

'What the fuck is going on?' Cherry breathed, eyes wide and staggering backwards in dismay.

She turned and hurried along the road, not daring to look back.

South Gosforth Metro station was quiet as the grave. Cherry hesitantly stepped onto the platform to find not a soul in sight.

Sighing heavily, she was just about to leave the platform when she heard a train approaching.

"Thank God!" she exclaimed with obvious relief. Perhaps there was some semblance of normality left.

The train came around the corner into her field of view. It was going too fast, she realised and instinctively jumped back from the platform's edge.

A great whoosh of wind flowed through the station as the train, without slowing, passed at high speed.

Another grotesque tableau was played out before her as she pressed herself against the station wall. Flames and smoke billowed from several of the carriage windows and dark, burning shapes were beating frantically at them. Then she heard the screams. The desperate cries of many people trapped, dying and doomed. She could not imagine hearing anything so disturbing ever again.

The train creaked and lurched alarmingly as it rounded the bend out of sight and Cherry was left in stunned silence, alone once more.

Choking back a sob, she gathered herself together and left the station, making her way through South Gosforth and down the bank, towards the Haddricks Mill roundabouts. The eerie quiet was punctuated by distant shouts, explosions and screams.

Despite these disturbing sounds, she didn't see another soul until she drew close to the Brandling Villa pub. Cherry saw a small group of men standing outside the pub. They watched her carefully as she drew near.

One of them stood up and approached her.

'Stay back!' he said roughly. 'Are you one of those things?'

Cautiously, Cherry said, 'What things? You're the first people I've seen all morning. Well apart from the policeman and …'

'We've got a live one,' the man said to his companions, grinning now.

'Not a bad one either, Bobba,' a small weasely man in the group said.

'Yeah,' said Bobba, leering. 'Okay boys, grab 'er!'

Cherry's confusion turned to fear. The world had gone to shit and now these people wanted to abduct her?

As two of Bobba's men grabbed an arm each, Cherry screamed.

The men dragged Cherry into a garage behind the pub. They had clearly been busy. Boxes and tins had been stacked in one corner and a grimy mattress lay in the middle of the damp concrete floor.

Weapons of various descriptions were stacked in another corner; pick axes, clubs, knives, even a couple of shotguns.

'Strip her,' Bobba said with a lurid wink at Cherry.

'No!' the terrified woman cried.

Bobba, a bulky man with a shaved head and an almost visible aura of body odour, went first, informing his compadres in no uncertain terms that he was not one for sloppy seconds. Nobody argued with Bobba.

As darkness fell, Cherry was left alone, locked in the musty-smelling garage, with her torn clothes barely covering her shivering body. The hand that the cat scratched earlier throbbed awfully. She removed the now filthy handkerchief to reveal skin that was tinged green/black. She managed a pitiful whimper then passed out.

The next morning, the garage door swung open and a shaft of light pierced the dark, dusty interior.

Bobba stepped into the garage and began unzipping his pants.

Cherry covered her eyes with one hand then let it drop, blinking.

'Come on, girly. Fun time! Be good and I won't hit you anymore.' He stepped forward, his erect member swayed in front of him.

Cowering, Cherry moved forward on her knees until Bobba's groin was in front of her face.

'Good girl,' Bobba breathed. 'I might let you survive all this crap if you play ball. How'd you like to be my girl full time?"

Bobba knew something was wrong the moment he felt her mouth envelop him. In the half light, her skin appeared dark and bruised and a sickly sweet smell caught in his nose. And her mouth was icy cold.

'Oh, FU–' he screamed as her teeth sunk into his engorged flesh. The teeth clamped hard and a guttural moan escaped Cherry's throat. With a wrench, she ripped the now limp member free.

As Bobba wheeled away, agonised, Cherry sat on her haunches, like something feral and watched him, chewing hungrily.

'Fuckin' bitch!' Bobba managed through gritted teeth as he writhed on the cold floor, holding his bloodied crotch with both hands.

Cherry rose up and clumsily moved toward him, blood oozing from her mouth and dribbling down her chin.

Dave Marchant sat in the security office of Mad Joe's Carpets, watching the CCTV monitors. So far, power was still available, but he was sure it was only a matter of time before that went, leaving darkness in its wake.

He had discarded his clip on tie and his shirt collar was open as he slouched in the comfortable leather chair.

Since all Hell had broken loose, he had just sat in the relative security of his office, unsure what to do.

He had tried to contact his girlfriend, Cherry, but the phones were out. He had also considered leaving his post and going to find her, but, if he was honest with himself, he was shit scared, so had stayed put.

Self-preservation instincts had won over the concerns for his girlfriend. He would just wait and see what happened.

Wearily, he wiped a hand across his brow and allowed sleep to take him.

A banging on the main doors across the hall awoke Dave with a start from his slumber. Who the hell could that be? He wondered, blearily.

He glanced at the monitor that covered the main door. It was dark, but he could just make out a shape. Small, petite and female. Dark trousers. Black jacket, a shock of blonde hair.

The image was fuzzy, but he recognised her …

Cherry, Jesus!

Dave ran to the doors and fumbled the key from the chain at his belt.

'Cherry! I'm coming!' he shouted. The banging abruptly stopped.

The key, after a few fumbled attempts, slipped into the lock, turned and the door swung open. It was Cherry all right. She fell forward into his arms.

'Oh, Cherry, baby!' Dave said, sobbing. 'You came here on your own? I'm sorry I left you alone! I didn't know what to do.'

Cherry pushed him back, gently, and her bloody mouth grinned at him with something that, in life, might have been a joyful smile. In death, it was terrifying.

Dave saw her then as she really was. Not his Cherry, but a shambling, gradually rotting, facsimile. Yet, somehow, here she was; she had come to find him.

As Cherry suddenly lunged forward, tearing into his throat and feasting on his flesh, he knew that he and Cherry would be together forever. Until death and beyond.

Two shambling figures walked along the Quayside together the next day, decomposing fingers entwined.

Were it not for the gore that dripped from their mouths, the jerky, unnatural walk, and the smell of death and decay that hung around them, they could have been any loving couple enjoying a relaxing walk in the fresh air.

It wasn't quite Alicante, but the sun was shining as if it shone only for them.

True love never dies. At least, not in the case of Cherry and Dave.

THE END

A SIDE OF CRANBERRY SAUCE
By
Clyde Wolfe

With a trembling hand he lifted the shot glass. Brimming two-hundred year old scotch threatened to cascade with every tremor. It took supreme effort to bring the glass to his lips, nearly half the contents spilling over the rim in tiny amber rivers. He threw it back in a rush; smoky, liquid fire burning and sliding down the throat, vapours opening long clogged sinus passages.

The glass clinked to the table, fallen from numb fingers. His head dropping into his hands. Sobs wracking the body. The scotch traversing his veins, mollifying anxieties and warming flesh.

"Madness," he whispered. "Complete madness."

Warren sat, head bowed over tear-stained hands. Before him lay a well-thumbed journal filled with scrawling handwritings and crude diagrams.

Steel cages rattled again. Warren didn't bother to look up, knowing the horrible wailing was about to begin anew. He would have covered his ears had he not become immune to the sound over the last week.

Warren reached for the bottle, the need for more drink controlling his actions. The bottle was heavy in his hand yet freed from the tremors he was able to guide it to his lips without waste. He took a long pull, nearly sputtering on the single malt as it flooded his gullet. He sucked like a greedy infant at its mother's teat, trying to drown himself free of the weight of ever-present anguish.

Half-shed tears shimmered on his eyelashes when at last he pulled the bottle away. He took several hyperventilating breaths until he was able to regain control.

Metal bars shook and rattled. Disturbing moans underscored the clank of steel.

"Such madness."

The solution – salvation – was right in front of him. Was Warren Valinson strong enough to accept it?

Autumn was in full bloom. The trees were sporting a miraculous range of vibrant golds and yellows, deep reds and oranges. Few of the leaves were fallen; admirers given this one last chance to witness the splendour of nature before the cascade of colours morphed into nuisances to pile and bag for garbage collections.

Warren could summon no joy at the sight. As a man of science, a mid-level chemist of Valinson Pharmaceuticals, he was patently aware of the reason for the change. The trees were literally starving their extremities, blocking essential Chlorophylls and choking their leaves to death in a creeping, ghastly manner. Nature was a merciless bitch-mother.

The phenomena mirrored the state of Warren's soul so keenly it stripped the glory of the spectacle. He too was suffocating. Mental asphyxiation was stealing him away by inches, sanity dispersing to the winds.

The world mocked his pain.

For many years Warren carried the burden in silence. The progression of ghoulish excitement to heavy, burdensome guilt had been an insidious worm gradually boring through heart and soul.

It had been nothing like imagined, Warren's hopes and desires polluted by a shouting conscience he had not known he possessed. Finding his uncle's papers and plumbing the depth of their import had trebled the acuity of his sorrows.

Warren had come out for a stroll this Sunday morning to clear his head. It helped, marginally. The underlying problem was not one capable of being undone. Rectified after a fashion, perhaps, but truly effaced? Never. Too many nights lost inside the depths of a bottle. Too many nights lost to sleepless hauntings of terrifying fancy and visitations of condemnation.

It had to end. Madness was steps away from dominance. Oh, he was guilty, no doubt of that. Warren bore no contrary illusions. Yet could it be done? Would some measure of reparation assuage the glut of his sin?

There was a way laid out for him, just a few mental leaps and a bridge or two and it became clear as polished crystal. Darkly veiled possibility delivered by the providence of serendipity. Had he really found those notes and charts by accident? Was it mere twist of Chance or the offered means by which to soothe his torment and right the wrong? Did he dare?

Church bells chimed in the distance announcing the end to a service of the faithful. Warren had not been inside a church in six years, not since Uncle Gerald's funeral. Such an unholy deception that had been. Crocodile tears and affected sorrows. Warren listened to their tolling until the bells reverberated into silence. Heralds of endings and new beginnings.

Warren felt the tolling deep within and gave the world a last glance. The season was changing, the air full of vibrant death. Beautiful decay. Thanksgiving was mere weeks away and Warren found himself bereft of anything to be thankful for. Unless ...

No, he decided. It couldn't just be a quirk of fate.

Some higher force, divine or otherwise, must be showing him the means to rectify his errors so that he *would* act. This was the chance for redemption he had pined for. How could he fail to act now, when it was all unfolding for this very purpose?

Warren pulled the coat tight around his body as a chill thrilled his bones. The unkindness of years and faulty genes had little to do with the cold. He changed direction so fast he nearly trampled a woman walking several steps behind him. She freely spoke out her indignation, but Warren had no ears for it. Feet ate up ground as he hurried home. He had a phone call to make.

Lungs protested the race homeward. Warren barely had the breath to climb the steps to the mansion's door. He used the railing as a crutch while recovering. Once inside he nearly ran down his maid-servant like the woman on the street, muttering a hasty, garbled apology before disappearing into his study.

A bottle of whiskey called and he answered by pouring two fingers into a tumbler and throwing it back neat. Alcohol set about calming nerves as he reached for the phone.

Warren's older sister picked up after the fourth ring. "C-Cynthia? Hi, it's Warren."

A decidedly feminine voice carried over the line, full of confusion and surprise, "Warren?"

61

After brief moments of the usual pleasantries exchanged between estranged family, Warren steered the conversation toward his goal. The holidays were nearing, what better time for a family gathering.

Cynthia's voice, while not unfriendly, barely resembled the girl Warren had looked up to as a child. There was a disaffectedness where once reigned laughter and smiles. "I doubt Harold and Paul would want to get together just because of the time of year. Let alone Ophelia, you know how she is, Warren."

"Right. T-that's why I wanted to pass it by you first. I-if anyone can get us all in the same r-room it's you, Cynthia."

"You know that's next to impossible a feat."

"Yeah, I know. It's just, well," Warren allowed his voice to drop an octave. "I f-found something in Uncle Gerald's papers we should discuss. What better time than over Thanksgiving d-dinner?"

There was silence on the other end of the line. Warren held his breath; bowels clenching and spasming, the taste of bile rising to the back of his throat. A tremor started in his left hand. He shoved the offending limb between his knees to still it.

Warren was just about to ask if Cynthia was still on the line when she came back.

"I'll see what I can do."

"Great, Cynthia. Thanks, I—"

The connection cut off with a click.

"Thank you, Gloria. That will be all." Better if she wasn't around. "Take the rest of the day ... no, take the weekend."

Dismissed, Warren's servant left with a nod and plastic smile. Perhaps later, once everything was settled and the lawyers finished picking over estates, Gloria would come to remember him fondly. After all, he was leaving everything to her. Years of faithful and diligent service and all that.

One by one they had arrived. First Paul, clean and pressed as always. Then Cynthia drove up minutes later. Ophelia and Jerry arrived together, their marriage seemingly still intact when pundits gave the union no more than forty-eight hours to dissolution way back when. It amazed Warren that of all the Valinson children, it was the youngest and most impulsive whom managed to keep her marriage intact. Paul was a twice divorced bachelor and even mild-tempered Cynthia had one failed attempt under her belt. Warren himself never found the time nor the inclination to seek out a mate.

Meagre conversations took place while they waited for everyone to arrive, mostly concerning the weather. If Warren had not grown up in the same household as the rest of them, he could have sworn they were a gathering of strangers. It wasn't long until silence reigned. No one was happy to be here.

Ice clinked as glasses were emptied and refilled. Then the doorbell rang. The final guest had arrived.

"Warren," Harry said by way of greeting.

Though it had been near to eight months since last seeing his brother Harold Valinson made no move to embrace Warren, not even a handshake. It was just as well. Harry, once a collegiate linebacker, had lost only a fraction of his youthful strength. The days of pink-bellies and wedgies were not so distant a memory to Warren despite the divide of years. Harry was no more than a bully delighting in the torment of others; as likely to attempt to crush the fingers of a proffered hand than not.

Everything was coming together. All living members of the Valinson bloodline were accounted for, the hardest part accomplished. Cynthia had done her part, unwittingly, to be sure, but she had succeeded in proxy fashion nonetheless.

Warren herded his siblings from the guest parlour into the dining room, downing three fingers of whiskey on the way to steady himself.

Deep, staggering breaths calmed juddering spasms of the heart and lessened the outpouring of moisture beneath his armpits, along his spine, and at his crotch. He pulled out a silken handkerchief and wiped away the layer of grime that had formed along the back of his neck and the edges of his receding hairline.

He hoped no one noticed, but knew they were scrutinizing his every move.

Warren was the first to enter the dining room, leading a group of people whom had never deigned visit or call in spite of the so-called familial allegiance. They could contemplate and commit murder together, sure, but a friendly "hello-how's-things-going" was out of the question. He immediately moved to the head of the table on the far end.

The table itself was almost as large as the room and laden down with so much food it could feed a starving nation for a day. Warren had not skimped on the selection, at least seven dishes for each guest in attendance. And more of the same just waiting to replace emptied bowls. Mostly the staples of the holiday, but with a few of the more expensive cuisines sprinkled in to appease more refined palates.

Six place settings were prepared including Warren's own. To Warren's right was a seventh seat, the furniture and place setting covered by a voluminous white sheet. There was an empty, eighth chair between this enigma and the next setting.

The guests milled around the doorway, unsure what to make of the scene. Wary, hostile glances washed over the white sheet. Warren realized he would need to placate them in order to further the evening's plans, the aroma of fine victuals not enough to override and entice. Another moment of truth to hurdle. "The reason I wanted us all t-together is under this sheet," he offered in the same mousy tone and stuttering cadence Warren always unconsciously affected around his kin.

"Funny," Ophelia sneered. "Cyn said this all had something to do with old Uncle Gerald. Not your laundry."

Jerry, ever the sycophant, was nodding enthusiastically at his wife's side. He even set his lips in a snarl in time to Ophelia's own expression. Warren could never tell if Jerry was loyal to his marriage out of a real desire to be with his shrew sister or out of financial dependency. Most likely the latter; Ophelia was only obsequious or courteous to those above her station. Why she chose to shack up with a rat from the low end of society in spite of lofty ambitions and tastes was a puzzle best left unfathomed.

"P-please," Warren said, indicating for them to enter and find a chair. Trickles of icy sweat were running down his spine. He hoped none of the anxiety he felt gnawing at his bowels was

64

showing on his face. "If you'll just take a seat and s-start eating ... there's a lot to c-cover." He tried to finish with a smile but his lips faltered.

Cynthia was the first to seat herself. Just the catalyst Warren needed.

Jerry followed suit, remarking how much a waste it would be to let dinner grow cold as he noticed the many bottles of vintage wines and spirits lying in the open liquor cabinet and the piles of fruit-filled pies and sweets laden on the dessert cart.

They stepped into the dining room until they were all finding a place at Warren's table. In the six years since their mutual, ill-gotten windfall this cosy scene had never once come to pass.

The door swung shut with a barely audible click. A second later there was a louder *thrum* and several heads turned to regard the door. It was the only way in or out.

Warren could see suspicion written in Paul's gaze through his thick glasses as their eyes locked across the landscape of delectable delights.

"Uh, that door has a h-habit of sticking. I h-had stronger h-hinges installed to ensure that it closes flush," Warren lied. "Dig in. No need to stand on any formalities. We're all f-family." The words were meant to diffuse the growing tension yet produced the opposite effect.

Again it was Cynthia who came to Warren's rescue. She reached out, poured herself a generous glass of sherry, and began to daintily stack green beans and baby carrots on her plate. It wasn't long before all hands were reaching for bits of the proffered banquet. Decorum was loosely observed, fingers snatching a portion for their owners before another could steal desired morsels away.

Jerry sat closest to the mini-bar and desserts, of course. Ever the greedy lush, that one. Next to him Ophelia wanted to turn up her nose at the food. The selection was too ... quaint for her tastes. Without complaint she joined the feasting, but only after realizing no one else was going to remark or refuse. Harry, sitting next to her, stacked his plate with both turkey legs and one of the wings and trying to heap half the mashed potatoes and cobs of corn onto an ever crowding plate. Just for good measure he added a rack of lamb to the towering foodstuffs before withdrawing his plate to consume its weight. Cynthia, her place directly opposite Warren, patiently waited out the initial feeding frenzy before finding the rest of her share. That left Paul, hoarding shrimp cocktails, to fill the remaining chair between Cynthia and the gap.

They're eating, Warren sighed in relief. His own plate remained bare; no appetite to cater to. The delightful scents did naught but cause his stomach to roil. The next phase was about to begin.

Warren had to swallow a few times to work moisture back onto his tongue. This was happening. Pricks of nervous sweat beaded on his skin as his body flushed cold. He wiped them away surreptitiously. *Keep it together for just a bit longer.*

Beneath the table, out of view of prying eyes, Warren uncapped a syringe and manoeuvred it beneath the white sheet. Once in place Warren's thumb depressed the plunger.

Seconds ticked by.

"Salt."

At Ophelia's demand Jerry sprung into action. His rat-like head twitching back and forth in search of a shaker, at last spying one right in front of the place setting covered by the white sheet. He reached across.

The sheet jumped.

With a cry of astonishment Jerry fell back into his seat. Around the room silverware clattered against china.

Ophelia blurted a string of obscenities as a fleck of freshly baked dinner roll touched her silk blouse. Flying hands followed, the smack of flesh on flesh mingled with the tinkle of gold bracelets as Ophelia's palm connected repeatedly with the nape of Jerry's neck. No one came to Jerry's rescue.

The white sheet continued to rustle and twitch.

"What is this?" Paul asked with more than a trace of annoyance as he pushed his glasses back into place with a manicured thumb. Harry was frozen in mid-motion, a cracker full of beluga hovering outside his mouth.

Warren took a deep, calming breath and slid out of his seat. "It's time," he grabbed a corner of the sheet and flourished it off its hidden occupant.

No turning back.

The stench of medicinal disinfectants and old, desiccated flesh escaped into the air. Even accustomed to the odours of the laboratory, Warren cringed away from the initial smell. The wrongness pervaded the dining room, smothering the delectable scents of feast meats and vegetables.

The revelation brought gasps of horror from Warren's guests.

It bore the shape of a man, features hairless and shrivelled. Skin was parchment dry and rough, pale as a terminal cancer patient's. There were no eyes in the cavernous holes that were once eye sockets. Its mouth was full of black and yellowed teeth, several of which were missing. Straps crisscrossed the naked body, a spindly collection of emaciated limbs once belonging to a healthy male specimen, holding the occupant in place.

The mouth opened, exposing a gray tongue that flopped against teeth like a fish out of water. The head lolled and rolled back and forth on a neck of loose, hanging flesh. No sound ushered forth and that mute silence was more perturbing than the most bloodcurdling shriek. The Thing attempted to buck and twist, the straps stymieing movement.

Jerry jumped out of his seat, the heavy oak chair hitting the wall and gouging an ugly scar in the wall's cherry-wood panelling.

"W-what is it?"

Warren clapped his hands together as he faced the Thing. A twinkle flashed in his eye and a childlike grin spread across his face. It was all about to come out. Weight sloughed off Warren's shoulders in a quickening avalanche. The end, near.

"Warren, what the fuck is going on?"

Ah, Ophelia, Warren thought. *Ever the eloquent one.* She was on her feet in an instant, hands clapped around her mouth and nose in effort to ward off the smell. Her voice pitched high, strands of coifed hair escaping their intended places. "You little shit, what is this?" Ophelia gagged on lungfuls of the detestable air.

67

Harry slammed his fist on the table. A ladle fell out of the mashed potatoes with a gooey plop. "Enough of this! Warren, whatever the hell that is you better get rid of it. 'Phelia, Jerry, sit down. Now!" Just like Harry, always able to bellow loudest.

"Oh, I don't think we'll be taking orders from you anymore, Harold. No one is going to do-as-you-say-or-else," Warren said and laid his hands on the shoulders of the Thing in the chair. The wizened skull swivelled toward his left hand, thin-lipped mouth gaping wide, rotten teeth glistening with thick slime. Warren quickly removed his hand, patting the creature on the head before stepping away.

"Listen here you dumb—"

"No, *you* listen. All of you," Warren jabbed finger at them like an accusing judge. "We're filth. Scum. Evil. We crossed the line of simple human decency. And for what? For money that we could have had freely with just a modicum more patience and respect. We murdered out of pure greed and avarice and for that we shall pay."

That set them back on their heels. It would ruin them if just one of their number decided to blab. They couldn't believe it was Warren – nerdy, geeky little Warren – whom would betray their secret. Uncle Gerald's death was not the result of a long-standing battle against an intractable and incurable disease like the world outside this room believed. The dining room was filled with murderers.

"Warren, we all agreed. We *all* agreed. Even you," Cynthia said, hands calmly folded atop the table. He turned to his sister and felt his thunderous expression soften. Cynthia was the one person whom Warren might have spared this fate, at least she had not been frivolous with her share of the blood spoils. She was known in the upper echelons for her work as a charity organizer and sponsor, but it was not enough. Not nearly enough. He had never heard a word of shame or regret pass her lips, as content as the rest of them to revel and cavort on another's dime.

Harry, Cynthia, Ophelia, Jerry, Paul. Each guilty in equal measure; Warren did not exempt himself from the list. He had gathered them to receive their apportionment of the retribution.

68

"That's it," Paul, silent until now, rose from his chair. He tossed his napkin onto the table and smoothing his Armani suit as he turned to leave. "I'll have none of this farce. You can bet I'll have my lawyers come down on you like the Wrath of God. Whatever it takes I'll have you locked away so deep they'll forget they ever saw you, Warren." Paul grabbed the doorknob.

It turned. The door, however, remained firm.

"What the hell is this?" Paul glared back at Warren, pushing his slipping spectacles into place. He struggled to get the door to open to no avail. "You're in deep enough, you little shit," Paul whirled around, cool mask fallen away. "You want to add unlawful imprisonment to your list of idiot moves today? You can't keep us here. Open this goddamned door!"

"No one is leaving. I had hydraulic pistons installed in the doorframe. Once closed, the door won't reopen. Not from this side."

Ophelia was spouting a colourful string of obscenities as Paul started for Warren, coming up short an arm's length away from the Thing in the chair. The Thing tracked Paul's movements even bereft of eyes.

It was Cynthia who had the most level head, retrieving her cell phone and dialling out. The vexatious chiming of a busy signal greeted her ear. Cynthia checked her signal, "Does anyone's phone work?"

Ophelia grabbed her own phone, checked the bars and threw it down in disgust. Plastic casing shattered, splinters finding their way into the strained carrots and creamed corn. "You bastard. What did you do to the phones?"

Paul reached into his jacket to check his device, "Dead," he confirmed. "Warren, you're going to pay through the nose for this. Guaranteed."

The Thing strapped into the chair was swivelling its head back and forth like an infant unable to focus its attentions. Every outburst was a new source of interest. When Paul again attempted to slide around, the Thing strained mightily against its bonds, mouth questing to reach him. Paul jumped back. "Son of a ..."

69

Harry was glaring death at Warren from across the table. Luckily the combination of dessert cart and liquor cabinet was enough to block the path from the other end. Warren had no illusions about how long he would last in that behemoth's grip; concern for a five-thousand dollar suit the only thing keeping Harry from jumping across the table and inflicting violence upon Warren's person. The proximity of the Thing in the chair was a concern second to Harry's vanity. Even so, Warren positioned himself behind the hideous Thing in the chair as a precaution. All he needed was for Harry to start reliving his old football days and attempt a flying tackle.

"What the hell did you do to our phones?" Harry roared. The man practically trembled with unvented rage.

"Nothing," Warren replied affecting nonchalance despite the fluttering of tiny wings in his stomach. A calm was descending and Warren embraced it; tranquillity of the soul he could never find no matter how many bottles consumed. "This room is constructed to block outside signals."

"Oh, you're dead. Dead." Paul was busy tapping buttons on his PDA. Soon he was holding the device up and panning the room with the tiny camera lens embedded in the back. "Keep talking. Every word will be a nail in your coffin."

Let him record, Warren thought. It might help to illuminate their sordid tale for whoever managed to find the remains of the approaching tableau of the macabre.

Threats continued to hurl across the table. Harry and Paul each continued to triumph with their own brand of intimidation. Ophelia, surprising everyone, offered Warren more money if he'd let them out. Jerry protested and received a smack across the jaw for his trouble.

Such a wonderful family gathering.

Warren reflected on the rotten core within his siblings. There was no saving grace amongst them.

Nothing would alter Warren's course. The miraculous calm had cleared his head and stilled his nerves, and no need to guzzle a bottle! Warren was in control. It was a totally new experience, so long bullied and overlooked by his family. With such freedom, such clarity, Warren was assured his path was true.

70

He laid a hand on the evening's Guest of Honour. The Thing twisted and lurched but could not swing its emaciated head enough to reach Warren's flesh.

"Don't you recognize him? Our Uncle Gerald?"

Shock and incredulity greeted the pronouncement.

Jerry, unable to fathom the scope of things taking place around him, sank back into a chair that was no longer beneath him. He dropped to the floor with a *thud*. Ophelia's face turned as red as the beets on the table, cheeks puffing in apoplexy. A scathing diatribe bursting forth in a torrent of incoherent rage from her glistening lips. The others embraced the news with better self-control. Cynthia flushing a pale, alabaster white, pale even for her naturally pasty complexion. Paul took another step back, hand straying to his chest while he blinked repeatedly; PDA forgotten. Harry continued huffing and fuming, fingers flexing into fists.

"Let's all say our most heartfelt thanks to Uncle Gerald for giving us everything we have. Today is Thanksgiving after all."

Harry took action. "Fuck this." The former football star shoved his youngest sister aside and trampled her useless husband on the way to the door. Harry pounded the wood with a meaty fist, the thumps echoing down the empty hallway. "Let us out of here!" Hammer hands became straight rights that splintered wood but did little to force the door.

After the third punch Harry howled in agony and fell away. Warren impassively watched his oldest brother cradle a broken wrist and stagger away.

"While all of you were frittering away your share of our ill-gotten inheritance, I was wracked by guilt over our crime. Our sin," Warren said returning to his seat at the head of the table. For the first time in years he felt a total quietude of the soul. It felt … good.

"We are all equal in culpability," Warren continued. "I waited for so long for our judge to appear, for heavenly retribution to descend and smite us. Anything offering forgiveness or punishment. But no, it was not to be. As a man of science it was hard to beg a higher power for absolution, you

71

can imagine. But I tried. And then, one day it finally materialized. Providence showing the way. You can imagine how equally difficult it was to accept, a *deus ex machina* solution, but the evidence I gathered bore out. Conclusive testing. There is but one way we can hope to erase the stains and balance the scales of our misdeeds. It found me. All the better because our uncle's was the innovative mind that made this possible.

"Do any of you know how many compounds Valinson Pharmaceuticals has stockpiled, waiting for federal approvals and testing to complete? Or how many so-called failures we house in the clean vaults?"

From across the table Cynthia, head bowed, whispered, "Please. Don't do this, Warren."

Warren felt the slightest twinge of mortification rush through him. He was about to murder the remnants of his family. Just like they all murdered Uncle Gerald. For money, wealth and power.

Warren crushed the feeling and sat up straighter.

"No," he said firmly. This was not about material things; this was about justice long overdue. Murder could be redeemed by death and death alone.

Uncle Gerald's attentions swung his way. Warren let himself imagine the bobbing of that skull-like visage to be supportive confirmation. He nodded back.

"Did we give Uncle Gerald a choice? We tinkered with his meds, causing a fatal reaction because we had grown weary of the cycle of deathly illness and miraculous recovery. We wanted the old curmudgeon to just die already, fork over the empire to a bunch of ungrateful brats. We rationalized, saying it was justice for the years Aunt Linda suffered under Uncle Gerald's domineering. Everyone blamed him for Cousin Stefanie's suicide when he disowned her over the issue of her sexual preference. Our father – his own brother! – cursed his name on his deathbed for a lifetime of petty evils. We all hated him for various personal incidents and cruelties.

"And for that we labelled him worthy of execution. But was that really why? No! Sheer greed the cause."

Warren ticked off the list of their crimes.

Paul had wanted the money for his real estate company. Shady dealings that saw more people fall into homelessness than domiciled. Not to forget the prostitutes or cocaine.

Ophelia needed the wealth and notoriety of being an heir to the Valinson Pharmaceuticals name for parties and socializing, hobnobbing with the blue-bloods and affairs with rich and powerful men.

Jerry, the penultimate used-car salesman, for the crumbs Ophelia would throw his way.

Harry had to cover up the feelings of inadequacy and failure at not making it into the pros, "And hide your secret of diddling little boys. Oh yes, Harry. We all know about your tastes," Warren said.

Harry's eyes shot wide. He looked around, ready to violently deny the accusations before seeing the looks of revulsive acknowledgement.

"My own damnable research and experimentations required financing. At least Cynthia did something worthwhile with her spoils. Yet not one of us was willing to stand on our own merits, make our own way through life and amass our own fortunes. Impatient and too lazy to earn it." Fury was flowing freely, years of repressed anger and shame tumbling out with such vitriol.

"What right did we have? What right?"

Dumbfounded silence was the reply. No one met his gaze. He had finally done it. Warren had shamed them. Every crime uttered was stark truth.

Whose idea it had been originally was moot, time effacing that particular detail. They all played a part. It just sort of, happened.

Warren bolted from his chair, towering from the head of the table. "Absolutely none. And here lies fitting punishment. All I had to do was steal the right compounds. Once the initial tests proved conclusive I simply smuggled Uncle Gerald's body from cold storage, not that any of you would ever notice its absence. Unlike all of you I still put in a day's work instead of frittering away my time and money. At our departed uncle's company, no less. It was easy."

Warren motioned to the struggling form strapped in the chair to his right. "And there he is. The bastard himself. Not quite alive, but no longer our victim."

Warren lifted a small remote control detonator he had kept hidden beneath his napkin and pressed a button. There was a brief flash from the back of the chair and the smell of cordite fused the air.

"Life returns to dead tissue at a cellular level, with some interesting side-effects," Warren said and settled back into his chair.

"Good thing it's Thanksgiving. Plenty of food to go around."

Uncle Gerald's bonds loosened and fell away. The shrivelled Thing was free, the knot keeping the straps in place having burned through by the controlled explosion. In a moment the freed corpse jerked to its feet and lurched forward.

At the other end of the table four co-conspirators jostled each other to be the furthest from the advancing revenant. The shouting drew Uncle Gerald toward them. Only Cynthia remained in her seat; a flood of tears raining from her eyes, the deluge staining the tablecloth with mascara and sorrow.

Warren tried not to watch. He'd seen enough during his initial testing.

The rats were the worst, far too dreadful to be used as a punishment even for this lot. The dead hobo hadn't been as voracious as those beasts. Yet every result was the same. They felt no pain. Age of a corpse was irrelevant unless decomposition had destroyed motor function entirely. Uncle Gerald was relatively limber once defrosted.

Warren reached for a clean plate and began to pile on strips of succulent turkey breast and heaps of creamy mashed sweet potatoes.

As he spooned peas onto his plate he heard the high-pitched, unmanly yelping of Jerry as the others shoved him to the forefront. Uncle Gerald lay cold, clammy hands around the living sacrifice's throat, pulling. A second later choked screams took on a new level of anguish as a rancid maw latched onto Jerry's cheek and rotten teeth sawed through soft pink flesh.

Uncle Gerald's head reared, rent flesh glistening redly as it was chewed with emotionless contentment. The scent of fresh blood mingled with the air.

"Oh my god!"

Harry started pounding on the door again, Paul knocking Ophelia aside and joining his brother in trying to break down the portal. Warren took a sip of water and considered the gravy; sure they would fail to break through the sheet of steel embedded between planks of wood. He had planned well.

Ophelia was on her knees blubbering and crying as she regained her senses from Paul's bludgeoning. Only she was close enough to hear the sounds of chewing meat ushering from the spectacle of her dead uncle mauling her living husband. No matter how cold Ophelia had been throughout her life, the grisly scene was enough to break her façade. Her throat tore as she screamed in terror. Jerry's cries subsided to a gurgling hiss as fleshy morsels were gouged from his gut.

"None of us are leaving here," Warren said. He stuffed a piece of turkey in his mouth. It was tasteless, like masticating paper.

Jerry's death-rattle went unheard beneath the din.

Carnage was mounting.

Uncle Gerald rose up from the cooling body and lurched towards Ophelia. This was another phenomena Warren had observed during his testing – the reanimated lost interest in feeding once life had faded from a meal. New, fresh meat would be sought. Warren's youngest sister constituted the nearest living flesh.

Ophelia tried to crawl away, but Uncle Gerald's fumbling hands found her ankle and began to tug. Lacquered nails left furrows in the carpet as Ophelia desperately tried to hold on. Her once immaculate make-up was smeared and runny. Bubbles of snot burst in her nostrils as she was yanked back into the cold clutches of Uncle Gerald. Her silken blouse offered no protection from unfeeling fingers and teeth.

Warren glanced at his watch and began counting along with the ticks of the second hand. Right on cue, one minute later, Jerry's ravaged corpse rose up with vacant eyes and slack

75

jaw. The holes in his torso were leaking red messes. One eyeball drooped out of its socket, held on by a glistening pink thread. Crimson ooze dripped from Jerry's lips. A quivering, low moan followed the bloody flood.

Warren nodded to himself and continued his flavourless repast. He ignored Ophelia's pleas and the futile pounding of his brothers, spooning more sweet-potatoes onto his empty plate. Flesh ripped and tore. Anguish and terror filled the room. Warren himself was ravenous.

When was the last time he ate? Days? Too bad everything tasted like ashes in his mouth.

Even as Uncle Gerald and Jerry bore down on Harry and Paul, Ophelia was rising from the dead and joining ranks. Warren decided to look up and watched his younger sister reach out for their brothers – entrails swinging freely from her once toned abs like a blood-slick pendulum – as they fought against Gerald and Jerry. The carpet soaked up rubies of life.

Warren dipped a dinner roll into the gravy boat. He brought the dripping bread to his mouth and sampled it. Still tasteless.

The outcome of the life and death struggle was never in doubt for Warren. Uncle Gerald and his newfound allies were as inexorable as the tides. They would not tire, they would not flag or yield to thoughts of mercy. Harry, Paul, and Cynthia had nowhere to run.

Drawn out moans joined the cries of fright at the other side of the room. A glass shattered.

Warren spotted the cranberry sauce and wondered if that would prove to titillate. *Only one way to find out*, he mused. He reached. *And the last chance*, he added a bit later.

Even with the Damoclesian blade about to befall, it wasn't a depressing thought, more freeing than anything. He scooped a thick spoonful and transferred it to his plate.

At the other end of the table Warren noticed Cynthia's head lying at a weird angle against the back of her chair, a dearth of foam gushing from her gaping mouth and rolling down the front of her chiffon dress. An open bottle of pills lay next to her half-eaten dinner. Warren never would have thought Cynthia capable of resorting to suicide, but he supposed, had the roles been reversed, he might have done more than consider the option himself. Either way the guilty were punished. Perhaps her humanitarian works did allow for mitigation of her suffering. It was now out of Warren's hands.

Harry's and Paul's cries transmuted from frightened horror to torturous howls. The struggle was nearly over. The doom of the Valinsons' had come.

Warren used his fork to skewer the quivering red gelatine and bring it to his mouth. The tart substance burst to life on his tongue. At last, something with some flavour. *Delicious!*

He closed his eyes and savoured the texture and the taste. Somewhere in the background Harry and Paul were gutted and gnawed. The walls dripped gore. A Thanksgiving charnel house was born.

Warren scooped up another lump of cranberry sauce and sat back, eyes closed and serene. He plopped the spoonful into his mouth and held it on the tongue, savouring. Waiting.

Guilt was dissipated. Blown away on an autumnal night's breeze like the leaves from a tree.

THE END

DIG
By
Lee Kelly

"Are we there yet?"

Steven knew fine well that they weren't. They'd only been in the car for twenty minutes and he knew that it was at least another hour before his parents would be arguing about who forgot to pack the deckchairs.

His dad didn't answer, so Steven decided to ask again.

Through a gap in the headrest Steven could see his dad's neck turn the fiery red of repressed rage. "No. I'll tell you when we're there," he muttered through clenched teeth. Steven giggled at his father's reaction and plucked his 'Combat Dan' action figure from the open rucksack at his feet.

"No. I'll tell you when we're there," the toy echoed in Steven's best Dad voice. Combat Dan was bouncing along the back of his mum's seat, parroting the phrase over and over. "No. I'll tell you when we're there. No. I'll tell you when we're there. No. I'll ..."

Steven's mum reached around and snatched the toy from his grasp, throwing it onto the dashboard. "For Christ's sake, Steven! Give it a rest!" she barked

He watched his mum in the rear-view mirror, her eyes narrowed as though daring him to say something else. He knew better than to argue back when she had that expression on her face so he hunched down in his seat, drew the hood of his jumper up over his head and sulked in silence.

The peace in the car was suddenly shattered by a string of expletives aimed at the vehicle in front as it slowed to a halt yet again. Dad gripped the steering wheel tightly as though choking the life out of the driver of the Volvo. "If we'd have set off when I wanted to we'd have avoided all of this traffic."

"I thought this would end up being my fault," sniped Mum.

"What're you talking about?"

"You know fine well what I mean. You just can't help yourself, can you?"

78

"Well it wasn't me fannying around in the bathroom, was it?" Dad's voice was rising in volume, even managing to drown out the honking horns of the grid-locked traffic.

"For fu …" Steven's mum caught herself in time, glancing at her son in the rear-view mirror. She lowered her voice to a quiet hiss. "Ten minutes makes no fucking difference, John. Stop being a dickhead and let's try and enjoy ourselves for once, shall we?"

The bickering continued, but Steven didn't hear a word. He was far too busy daydreaming about pirates, ice-cream and burying Dad alive.

There were no pirates, the solitary seafront café was closed for refurbishment and Steven had been threatened with a good hiding if he kept on getting sand on his dad's trousers. Things were not as much fun as he had imagined.

The beach was deserted; in no part due to the icy winds and black skies. The family were wrapped up tightly, and Steven's mum had even huddled up beneath a tartan rug that they kept in the boot of the car. No-one was speaking after the deckchair argument and out of bloody-minded stubbornness neither adult would break the silence and suggest that they head home.

Mum projected an aura of fury from beneath her tartan hummock, slurping angrily at her lukewarm thermos coffee whilst reading her latest Mills & Boon bodice ripper. Dad flicked through a gardening magazine, turning each page as though it caused a personal affront.

Steven was largely oblivious to the mood, so intent was he on The Project. With Combat Dan supervising, he had decided that he was going to see how far down he could dig before the tide came in. He had high hopes for reaching Australia, or at the very least finding some lugworms that he could use as bait in a seagull trap. He'd only been working for thirty minutes and already the red plastic of his spade vanished completely into the hole with each scoop. The dribbly yellow dry sand had long-since been replaced with the wet, brown stuff that was much heavier for him to lift but did make a wonderful sloppy sound.

Action Dan lay on his stomach, peering at Steven through the gun slit of a bunker made of sand and seashells Steven too was lying on his stomach, affording him an extra inch or two of reach when digging. He was struggling to reach the bottom of his hole and the difficulty was beginning to chip away at his enthusiasm for the task. He was close to giving up and going to chase some gulls when the spade hit something hard. Surprised, he slapped the flat head of the spade into the hole and was rewarded with a solid thump, not the harsh crack of rock against plastic. Perhaps it was buried treasure? Buried pirate treasure!? Steven gave a high-pitched squeal of excitement, that roused a "Ssssssh" from both his mother and father in unison.

With great care, like he had seen in films, he let the corner of the spade rest against the edge of the object and began to slowly follow the outline to determine its size. It was big; and ovoid. Steven knew that treasure chests were boxes, not egg-shaped, so what could it be? He scraped the flat edge of the spade over the top of the object, dragging the sand away to reveal a lump the colour of spoiled milk. Several long, straggly hairs were plastered wetly against its surface.

Steven was non-plussed. No matter how he tilted his head, or from which side of the hole he looked in from, it was still just a hairy lump that reminded him a little of his granddad's head when the wind worried at his combed-over hair. He needed to know whether it was worth digging out or if he should go and eat his packet of Wotsits. He puzzled over his options for several moments before taking action. He hit the lump. Hard, with the edge of the spade. There was a percussive thump, heavy and wet. A split opened slowly in the object releasing a cloud of foul air and a viscous red substance that began to slowly ooze from the tear, blackening as it trickled down into the sand.

The lump moved. Only slightly, but with enough force to create cracks in the wet sand around it. Steven scuffled back from the hole in surprise and hid his face behind Action Dan's bunker. Several tense seconds passed before he felt brave enough to venture back, even then moving only in a slow shuffle and with his neck craned high so that he could peer into the hole

80

from a safe distance. Nothing had changed. The lump was still, the cracks were no wider and the red sludge still stained the sand black. Steven picked up Action Dan in one hand, clutching him close to his chest for comfort. The other hand reached out beside him and closed around the red plastic handle of his spade. He advanced.

Steven's face contorted in pain. Sweat beaded his brow and tiny veins stood proud at his temples. Wiry little arms shook uncontrollably as though in spasm. The pile of sand on his spade was far too large for him to comfortably lift, but he was eager to continue unearthing his discovery.

Steven paused to wipe his forehead, leaving behind dirty streaks of sand where it clung to the sweaty skin. Eyes closed, he let the chilly, rain-specked breeze soothe his reddened face. It was a rare moment of tranquillity for a six year old, and one that was interrupted by an incessant clacking. Opening his eyes with the weariness of an old man, Steven looked down in the hole. Yet again the nameless head was gnashing its jaws, trying desperately to bite into haft of the spade.

"No!" Steven admonished the head with a slap from the flat of his spade against its forehead. As he pulled the blade away a long, translucent strip of flesh was torn free, dangling momentarily from the red plastic before dropping down into the water-logged sand. A thin, watery liquid dribbled from the wound and trickled down over a lidless eye, staining the dead, clouded orb pink.

"You know you're not meant to do that. Stop being naughty!" The head tilted upwards, gazing silently towards Steven. The mouth opened and closed several times as though the creature were trying to speak but the only sound that passed its lipless mouth was a watery gurgle.

Satisfied that the creature would behave for at least a little while, Steven recommenced the excavation.

"Dad, do you want to come and see what I've dug?"

"Yes, yes, that's lovely. Why don't you show your mum?" Dad hadn't even bothered to look up from his book. The

81

gusting coastal wind had long since claimed his magazine and he had resorted to one of Mum's romance novels out of boredom.

Steven looked over to his mum, cocooned beneath the rug and snoring soundly. He didn't bother to wake her and walked back over to the hole alone. By now the whole of the creature's head had been uncovered, along with its shoulders and the top of its chest. Everything else was still trapped beneath the crushing weight of the sand. Steven wondered how long it would take for him to fully uncover the thing.

He got back to work

With tireless effort Steven had been able to dig away enough sand for the creature to free an arm. Scraps of clothing hung to a skeletal limb that shed folds of water-pruned skin with each movement. Steven had thought it looked rather sad waving around in the air with nothing to do, so the thing now held Action Dan in its putrescent grip and was dashing the toy's head repeatedly against the wall of its prison.

The head of the spade sliced sibilantly into the sand again and again. The sound was given the rhythmic counterpoint of Action Dan's head slapping against the higher, drying sand. Steven was having fun and it seemed that the creature was too.

Steven looked over to his parents, wondering if they'd like to join in with the fun. Mum was still fast asleep and Dad was engrossed in the tawdry paperback whilst eating a packet of Wotsits. Steven's packet of Wotsits! He slammed the spade down petulantly and opened his mouth to shout out in protest, but the creature beat him to the punch. A loud, ululating cry filled the air, sending the seagulls into a frenzy and causing Steven to jump in fright.

"Steven! I won't tell you again! Play quietly!" snapped Dad without as much as a glance up from the book, even the animalistic nature of the howl failing to rouse his attention.

Steven looked back into the hole and was shocked to see the creature's second arm was now free but that the hand was missing all four fingers. A bloody ichor seeped from the stumps, coating rotted flesh and tattered clothing. The fingers themselves were trapped beneath the edge of the spade where they continued to twitch of their own accord.

The howl ceased and was replaced by a low, mournful moan that made Steven's skin crawl. The creature scrabbled ineffectually for its missing fingers with a hand bereft of digits. With its remaining hand it began to claw ineffectually at the sand; fingernails cracked then peeled noisily away from the fingers, its hand tearing into a red ruin as it fought to gain purchase and drag itself free.

The jerky marionette movements frightened Steven and he decided that he didn't want to play this game anymore. In fact, he wanted to go home. He was cold, wet, hungry and he didn't think that he wanted to be friends with the thing in the hole after all. It smelled funny and it hadn't played with Action Dan properly.

Action Dan! He couldn't go home without his toy! He looked around in the hole and spotted Dan lying half buried in the sand near the thrashing thing. He wouldn't be able to reach it with his hand from up high and the creature's movement would prevent him from scooping Dan up in his blood-slicked spade. He glanced over to where his parents sat wondering whether to ask for their help, but he knew that they were in a bad mood and that he'd get in trouble for not looking after his toys.

Despite its efforts the creature remained stuck fast and gave a growl of frustration. The sound very nearly made Steven turn around and run back to his parents, leaving his toy behind to remain stuck in the hole with the thing. But Action Dan was his favourite, his walls at home were covered in Action Dan wallpaper and his duvet even had Action Dan covers. He'd never be able to forget what he had done. No, he had to be brave and get Dan back.

The creature had grown very quiet. It was watching Steven intently as he sat perched on the edge of the hole. The bloody tatters of its fingers wiggled in the air, grasping at nothingness though it made no attempt to reach out to him. Dry sand began to billow over the lip of the hole as Steven edged himself forward. Seeing his movement the thing began to slowly open and close its mouth, teeth clacking together with a snap. Still it made no sound.

Steven's feet touched the floor and he paused expecting the thing to lurch forward, but it remained still, save for the awful writhing fingers and piston motion of its jaw. Pressing tightly to the wall and with his eyes scrunched fearfully shut, Steven began to squat down to bring himself in reach of Dan. His hand swept across the sand, searching blindly for his toy without looking at the nightmare vision buried in front of him.

His fingers brushed against something. It felt like Action Dan's leg so Steven made to snatch it away quickly. The object moved and a watery moan began to grow slowly in volume. Steven opened his eyes.

"Can that kid not keep quiet for one minute?" snapped Dad.

The piercing shriek woke Mum with a start but was snatched away by the wind before her eyes had even opened. She looked over to where Steven had been playing and watched with sleep-fogged eyes as a body hauled itself slowly from the hole.

Casting the rug from her shoulders, she allowed herself a long, luxurious stretch, face aimed skywards as she rubbed the sleep from her eyes with balled fists. She could hear the susurration of weary feet dragging through sand and allowed herself a small smile. The poor thing had obviously tired himself out. Perhaps now they'd all get some peace?

THE END

APOCALYPSE NOO
By
Vallon Jackson

Getting away from it all was an idea that Josh Linaker prescribed to. Now in his mid-thirties, the haunts of Ibiza and Benidorm and the other party spots he'd once graced had lost their appeal. In fact, some of the lads from work had asked him to go on a booze cruise with them around the Balearics; to him that sounded as appealing as having a six inch nail hammered through his nut sack. No, he'd done the drinking and wenching thing, the staying up all night, and sleeping through the hottest hours of the day, and he was sick to the back teeth of it. He'd been working hard, sometimes fourteen hours a day, and all he wanted now was rest.

When he was a kid, his dad used to take him fly fishing on the Tyne, out Hexham way, not on the muddy flats that ran through the Toon. He recalled hazy, lazy days on the riverbank, a sense of peace and tranquillity invading his usually overactive child's mind. Going fishing sounded like a great plan. He always remembered his dad extolling the virtues of the rivers and lochs of Scotland, and when he was younger, they had planned on taking a trip and hiring a cottage somewhere, and wasting a full week or two dangling their rods in the water. Josh had sniggered at the innuendo, and laughed hard when Dad didn't get the joke. Of course, those plans never bore fruition. Josh grew up, became a man with his own ideas of a good time, and took his holidays with the other piss-heads from 'the job'. He wished now that he'd taken up his dad's offer. Unfortunately, his dad was dead and gone, almost ten years to the day.

This was a trip of reconciliation. Things had grown fractious with his dad towards the end. His dad didn't approve of his career choice, couldn't understand why his lad had chosen to join the coppers, an enemy he'd fought tooth and nail when Maggie closed the pits. Dad didn't understand that the police service was different than during the miner's riots, that PACE had changed everything and these day's coppers were decent blokes. Dad couldn't get past the "bad old times", though, and

85

had never fully recovered from the beating he'd taken in the back of a Black Maria. The fact that Dad had been snatched while kicking the shit out of some poor bloke who had chosen to feed his kids instead of the Unions was beside the point. When he first saw Josh in his uniform, his son could tell that his dad was thinking only of the ruptured spleen and broken hip that had made him an invalid. They had turned away from each other and didn't speak again. Josh regretted it now, wished that he'd gone to his dad's funeral; made his peace. That's all he wanted now, peace. Maybe if he was sitting on the shores of a loch, his dad's spirit would be close to him and he'd be able to tell his dad he loved him, always did, despite their differences.

On the drive up from Newcastle he'd had the radio on, and it must have been fate or something because the *Mike and the Mechanics* lament about the living years had come on; maybe his dad had joined him for the ride after all. He had to pull over at a Little Chef while he got a grip of his emotions. A cup of tea and a fruit scone that cost him nearly eight quid had put him in another state of mind and he'd continued his journey north without stopping. It was a long run, up the A1 and over the Forth Road Bridge. The traffic was horrendous. Part of him wished that he'd taken the A69 over to Carlisle and up the west side instead, because it would have cut his journey by an hour or two. Things got a little easier once he approached Perth and he followed the Inverness road towards Pitlochry. His sat-nav told him to take a left, but he'd a mind to see the famous salmon ladder at Pitlochry and continued on. The trail to the ladder was closed, the local council re-laying the cinder path, and he made do with stretching his legs in the town. A sausage and bean melt from the local Greggs made up for his over-expensive breakfast, but not for his disappointment at missing the first landmark on his trip. Back in his car he headed off for the remote Loch Tay and the cottage he'd hired.

He cut through Aberfeldy, and along a winding road. Bolfracks Garden, four acres of woodland and flowers planted by the Menzies clan during the eighteenth century, held no interest for him, other than the name was decidedly odd to his Geordie ear. Another two or three miles on and he couldn't remember its actual name, having transformed to Bollocks Garden in his mind.

Loch Tay was a wide gouge in the terrain, really a widening of the river of the same name. At its western end was a tiny town called Killin, but coming from the east, Josh arrived in Kenmore, a village that time forgot. There was a hotel, a church, a row of white cottages and a tiny post office that looked exactly like they would have two hundred years ago – if not for the cars and 4x4s parked in every available spot. A bridge spanned the river and on the far side were a walled holiday complex, a mini-shopping mall and a caravan park. Josh had no intention of going that side of the bridge. He wanted to get away from it all, so he took the narrow trail that ran along the southern banks of the loch. He noted a reconstructed Neolithic 'round house' built on the water, and pinpointed it for a visit later in the week.

His landlord lived in an ultra-modern split-level house with views over the loch to die for. Josh had booked over the Internet, exchanged emails, and arranged to pick up the keys. The guy made an impression of his credit card, got Josh to sign the slip; no such a thing as chip and pin out here.

'You know where you're going?' the bloke had asked.

Josh shrugged, said, 'I've got my sat-nav, but it seems to be on the blink.'

'You won't get any reception on your mobile either,' the landlord chuckled.

'Suits me fine,' Josh said. 'A week without hassle, that's what I'm here for.'

'Then you've come to the right place. Keep going that way for three miles, look for a white gate on your right; it'll be open. If you see a phone box, you've gone a wee bit too far.'

Christ, Josh thought, if you saw a phone box in Newcastle you'd have gone back in time!

Back in the car he'd followed the road, noting that the further it progressed the less maintained it became. Before he found the phone box and had to perform a hairy three point turn, the road was primarily loose gravel and potholes. Backtracking, he found the white gate and pulled into a steeply descending drive, and at the end of it the small cottage he'd been seeking.

Beautiful, he thought.

The cottage was sandstone, with a slate roof and wooden conservatory, all of it practically hidden beneath a blanket of ivy and flowers he couldn't identify. Bethany would have loved the place, would have thought it idyllic and charming. She'd have loved to have walked hand in hand with him over the brook – or *burn* here in Scotland – and down to the waterside. Maybe they'd have even made love out on the pebble-strewn shore, the sound of the chuckling water a romantic backdrop. The thing was, his relationship with his wife had turned as frosty as had the one with his dad. His own fault; he shouldn't have shagged that blond probationer in the back of his police van. It had been a slow night, but that was no excuse. Beth found out about his dabble from a well-meaning colleague, and that was it. She left him, went home to her mum, and the divorce was through within eight months. It seemed like the back of a police van was anathema to all Josh's family relationships.

More than a hundred years old, he half expected the cottage to be old fashioned, but it had been done out with all mod cons. Nevertheless he could feel the history in the house, could almost imagine the hustle and bustle of the many generations that must have dwelled here over the years. The landlord had stocked up on the necessities; bread, milk, bacon, tea and coffee, even a few home baked scones. A fire was already burning in the stove in the living room and a small bucket of coal and a basket of logs were set out for him. He fed the fire, and settled down with a mug of tea and bacon buttie. Tomorrow he'd get his fishing rod out and go down to the loch, but now it was getting dark, and, anyway, he was at peace with himself. And that's what the trip was all about. Peace and getting away from it all.

There was one problem he hadn't considered: how did anyone get away from the end of the world?

Josh was wakened in the night by something strange.

He had fancifully entertained the notion that his father's spirit would join him on this trip, but it had been an abstract thought at most. Josh didn't believe in ghosts. Not really.

The sound was a series of knocks, a rhythmical cadence that speeded up towards the end. *Bump ... bump ... bump ... bumpbumpbump.*

Ever the brave copper, this time something held him tight in the fireside chair. The fire had burned down to cinders, where only a red glow of smouldering coals gave any light to the room. He'd fallen asleep without putting on any of the lamps, and on the floor at his feet were his empty sandwich plate and his cup with a film of cold dregs in the bottom. He was fatigued from the long drive up here, but hadn't realised just how tired he was. He couldn't recall placing down the cup or plate, and must have done so in a semi-dream state. Now he was wide-awake and his heart was jumping in his chest.

He peered behind him, checking out the unfamiliar room, craning to inspect the narrow flight of stairs to the bedrooms and bathroom. He half-expected to see someone standing on the stairs, having chased the ball that had bounced down them. There was no one there.

He heard the sound repeated.

Bump ... bump ... bump ... bumpbumpbump.

A smile of embarrassment flickered for a moment. Josh leaned over and tapped on the stove. Again the sound repeated itself, but this time it was followed by a gurgle of water through the pipes. The stove was cooling, and so was the water in the central heating; the bumping was the contracting of the pipes as they settled.

'Ghost, my arse!'

The eerie feeling persisted in him though, and his pulse was still up. He thought that there was no way he would get back to sleep. Not for a short while at least. He stood up, flicked on a lamp, and grabbed logs from the basket and fed them into the stove. When that was done, he went through to the kitchen and boiled the kettle. He used a different cup, left the dirty dishes for tomorrow, a habit born of bachelordom. Then he went outside for a smoke.

89

A small garden ran down the side of the cottage, with a high hedge, but at the end it dropped off sharply to the brook. He could hear the water rushing by, but couldn't see it in the darkness. Out beyond the brook were the floodplains that gently descended towards the loch, but he had no impression of the immensity of water, or the hills on the far side. The clouds had built through the evening, obscuring the moon and stars, and it was as if he stood at the edge of a black void. He stepped back, taking solace in the soft glow of light from the living room window and in the red pinprick glow of his cigarette tip.

He heard a scream.

At least he thought it was a scream.

Could have been an animal – a fox, or one of them huge grouse things the size of a turkey he'd heard roamed hereabout – but he wasn't sure.

Jesus, he thought, I hear enough screaming in the Toon of a weekend. I could do without it here as well.

He retreated back to the cottage, and this time took the steps up to bed.

It would be the last time he ever slept soundly again.

'I love the smell of haggis in the morning!'

The young waitress didn't get the movie reference, and Josh wondered if they were so out of touch here in the remote outback that they hadn't got satellite TV or DVDs or any of the other things a big city lad took for granted. Then again, it was a pretty lame play on the famous Apocalypse Now line. Except the breakfast she plonked down before him looked like it was familiar with napalm. The bacon was nigh on black, the eggs crispy, the sausages torched and even the toast was sliced carbon lathered with butter. The haggis looked good, though, and Josh was looking forward to tasting the local delicacy.

He'd discovered that the monstrous grouse thing was called a capercaillie, and he was sitting beneath one that had been stuffed and mounted on a cross beam in the café. He thought the huge dog reclining just inside the front door was stuffed as well, but the old thing was just sleeping. It was a docile beast for all its size, and he'd stepped over it without it stirring and entered the café. There were two girls waiting on, but they outnumbered the clientele this morning. Josh was the only one who had turned up for a fried Scottish breakfast.

'Is it always as quiet round here?' he asked.

The girl, a pretty thing with pale, almost translucent skin, and fair hair pulled back in a ponytail, looked back at her friend who was watching from the till. The teller looked almost identical to the waitress now that he thought about it, perhaps a sister rather than a friend. The girls exchanged a shrug.

'I thought you might have got a few visitors from along at that time share spot at Kenmore.' Josh looked at them both, hopeful for some interaction at least.

'It's the flu,' his waitress said, her accent a pleasant singsong. 'Naebody's oot and aboot at the minute.'

Josh thought of the news reports, the panic over the recent rebirth of the swine flu, a more virulent strain than the one that had raged throughout the world last year, and thought it was just another of the bad news stories he'd have left behind in the 'real world'. Shit, there'd been all these calamities lately, with unprecedented snowfalls, floods, earthquakes and recently – like a Biblical prophecy of doom – in America an entire flock of birds had reputedly fallen out of the sky stone dead: anyone would think that the end of the world was nigh or something.

'Is it bad here? I'd have thought it wouldn't've spread here, being so … uh, remote.'

'We get loads of tourists through,' the girl said defensively. She sniffed, wiped at her nose surreptitiously with her sleeve. She gave him a look that told him he might be a virus-infested sack of pestilence and moved away from him. 'They bring it here with them. But you needn't worry aboot catching it; we've had oor jabs here. Enjoy your breakfast.'

'Uh, thanks,' Josh said, but he'd lost his appetite.

Ten minutes later he'd finished pushing the burnt offerings around his plate – although the haggis had been good – and he took a walk over the bridge and onto the waterfalls that made Killin a stop off on the tourist trail. There were signs to an ancient clan burial ground on an island in the centre of the river, but the path across to it was gated, the gate padlocked. So much for seeing that landmark, too. He watched the rush of white water over the rocks, wondering if the fish were biting. That turned his mind to his real reason for being here and he returned to his car and took the narrow south road back to his digs. On the way, he flicked on the car radio. The reception was hit and miss, and – coincidentally – the news report was about the flu epidemic sweeping the country. Not to worry, though, the NHS was on the case and had already implemented a nationwide vaccination programme, despite fears of side effects from the rushed and untested vaccine. Some doctor or other guested on the show, offering advice and calming the listeners over the unsubstantiated rumours of … the radio cut out.

Josh turned it off. The road demanded all of his attention. Jesus, it was even worse at this end of the loch. Up and down it went, twisting and turning, following the contours of the land. He could see where recent rain had washed miniature landslides over the road, and from the lack of disturbance to the dirt and twigs it didn't look as if many vehicles chanced this route that often. He passed a hotel set on the hillside. When he'd researched Loch Tay, seeking his ideal getaway, he'd learned that the hotel was a popular eatery, with top grub on the menu. He thought that anyone risking this road of an evening must have a strong constitution to eat a meal afterwards. There were vehicles in the car park. He saw a woman, her hair under a woolly hat, wearing a North Face ski-jacket, but for all of that she still looked cold. Her features were ruddy, her nose streaming with mucus, and she was shivering wildly as she watched him drive slowly by. It looked like some five star grub would do her good, because the lingering stare she followed him with was one of intense hunger. He thought that she even took a couple of steps after him, but then she was lost to sight by a bend in the road.

Coming this way, the ancient telephone box was on his right. It had been there so long, at the mercy of the elements, that it had required many coats of paint over the years. The latest paintjob was beginning to look a little worse for wear, and the box had sunk at one corner so that it now leaned awkwardly towards the water. He followed its lead and looked across the loch, watching the sunlight sparkle on the crests of waves kicked up by the breeze. He couldn't recall it being that cold when he'd been at the falls at Killin, but maybe here where the valley broadened out, the wind was chilly as it raced through. That might explain the state of the woman he'd passed a couple miles back. Or she had the frigging flu.

He turned into the lane that led down to the cottage.

There was no time like the present, he decided. He'd paid for a license to fish on the loch, and the cottage came with a private strip of beachfront. He collected his rod and tackle, his bait box, and headed off down by the water.

Out of the fly fishing season, he elected instead to bait his hook with maggots he'd purchased before leaving Newcastle and carried here sealed in a Tupperware container. It was a long time since he'd been out on the Tyne with his dad, and back then he hadn't taken much interest in the technicalities of fishing. He had been more interested in sitting in companionable silence with his dad, feeling the closeness, the connection without the need for conversation or instruction, and catching fish was secondary. He felt out of practice now and wasn't fully sure he was using the correct method for a loch. He believed that most lochs had gently sloping shallows that then dropped off to great depths. For such places his dad used to employ a method called ledgering, where a baited hook was supported by a float that 'dangled the bait over the ledge', attracting the fish that gathered there. Because he wasn't necessarily interested in catching fish here, as much as he was attempting to rediscover that feeling of peace he'd once known at his father's side, Josh made do with baiting a hook and adding a couple of lead weights. He cast the line out into the water, and then sat down, supporting his rod across his knee as he waited for the almost imperceptible tug that a fish was biting. For him, the waiting game of fishing was meditative, Zen-like.

Usually.

Now he felt agitated.

'Well, Dad, I'm here. I made it.'

He felt foolish talking out loud like this. He took a squint over his shoulder, back across the floodplains to where the cottage was lost amid its screen of vegetation. There was no one around. From here he could see across the loch and high up on the opposite hills could make out the pale shapes of buildings, but he could imagine that he was the only man left alive in the world and that this lake, serene in its beauty, was all his. But he couldn't be sure of that.

Lowering his voice a tad, he asked, 'Dad? Are you there? Can you hear me?'

There was a plop somewhere from across the water; a fish breaking the surface. Josh laughed to himself. It would be ironic if there was such a thing as reincarnation and his dad had come back as a trout. Typically, Josh would hook him and piss him off even more. He laughed at his stupidity, and realised that laughter was a great healer. He felt more at ease.

'I wish you were here with me Dad. I wish things were like they used to be between us. I'm ... I'm sorry.'

He wasn't sure what he was apologizing for. Nothing he'd done to upset his dad could be called a fault. Not joining the police force at any rate. It was a good career move, an honourable and noble calling. He understood that his dad would have a disliking for the uniform, after the violence he'd been subjected to, but that was a thing of the past, not indicative of the modern police service. Yet he felt he must say sorry, because his dad had always been too stubborn to do so. Jesus, before he'd died, the old man had given express instructions that Josh should not attend his funeral, and having a stubborn streak of his own, Josh had said he had no intentions of going anyway. He had stayed away, too, even though it had broken his heart.

'Dad. I know you didn't mean it. I didn't either. I hope now that you can see that. Please, I want things to be good between us again.' Josh checked around, making sure no one was in earshot. 'Can you do something ... give me some sort of sign that you have forgiven me? I don't expect miracles, but a tug on the fishing line would do. If it's not you,' – he coughed out a laugh – 'at least I'll maybe catch a fish.'

The line didn't tug, and he didn't catch a fish, but he did get a sign of sorts.

He heard a scream.

Bloody capercaillies, he thought, noisy buggers are going to scare away the fish.

Josh wondered about taking supper along at Kenmore village. The hotel there had a bar, and a couple of pints wouldn't go amiss either. Except a couple of pints would probably end up as four or five and there'd be no way he could drive the car back along that narrow road if he was three sheets to the wind. He wasn't being holier than thou, not concerned about a copper being caught drink driving, but it was a certainty that he'd end up driving off the road and into the cold water of the loch. There were still a couple of eggs and some rashers of bacon left over from the landlord's supplies, so he opted for a fry up instead. His second of the day, but what the hell, he was on holiday!

Once he'd eaten his fill he was at a loss at what to do. He thought about turning on the TV, but he'd promised himself that he wouldn't. He wasn't here to vegetate in front of a bloody television, he could do that at home. He decided to take a walk, maybe even try and catch sight of one of the super-grouse he'd heard calling earlier. When he went out he was surprised at the density of the night. Someone who spent most of their time in a city had no real comprehension of darkness, not until they were somewhere as remote as this and it fell on them like an executioner's hood. Josh had *appropriated* a Maglite torch from the storeroom back at his nick, and he went to fetch it from his car. He flicked on the beam and followed it back along the driveway to where it met the main road. He had two choices, left or right, because he couldn't bring himself to enter the forest directly ahead. He took a right, thinking about checking out the telephone booth, and seeing if it really did have all its glass intact, a working receiver and if the coin box hadn't been jimmied. He made himself a bet that – even out here – somebody would still have taken a piss in it.

In the car the booth had seemed practically adjacent to the cottage's driveway, but it was much further on foot, in the dark. Josh wasn't too bothered, he'd stocked up on calories and was dressed warmly, and actually enjoyed the feel of gravel crunching underfoot. Plus, he had another cigarette as he strolled, feeling liberated. Back home in Newcastle, he often felt like a leper when he sparked up, and couldn't abide the disapproving glances from the café culture set who'd taken over the city centre. Jesus, once the Toon was the domain of the rough and ready working class, now it was so far up its own arse that it'd be better off down the poncy south.

Coming to the phone booth he took a squint inside. All – as he'd guessed – appeared to be in order. Yet, the nagging doubt that criminals were everywhere these days won out and he lifted the receiver and held it to his ear. He smiled in self-satisfaction. There was no dial tone, no nothing in fact because the line was dead. There was a card for a local taxi firm shoved into the doorframe. Back home in the Toon it would have been flyers for "escort" services. He glanced round, feeling rebellious, thinking of christening the telephone box with his own mark, but decided against it. He loved the remoteness of this landscape, the beauty and tranquillity, and he wouldn't despoil it by taking a leak in the living antique of the phone box. He turned slowly from the box and looked up a short track to a couple of cottages set back on the hillside. Both were in darkness. He couldn't recall seeing anyone in or around the houses earlier in the day and decided that they were probably holiday homes, vacated much of the year by owners working in the City. His rebellious streak was still nagging at him for action and he made do with flicking his cigarette end in the direction of the empty homes. The sparkling ember shot through the dark like a miniature comet, struck the drive and dissolved into a shower of sparks.

He sent the beam of the Maglite up into the forest. The stark light was in contrast with the night, casting dense shadows from the tree limbs, and he fancied that things were moving just beyond the arc of the torchlight. He steadied the beam, probing the dark. Nothing. Not a super-sized grouse in sight. He grunted, what were the chances of seeing one of the illusive creatures anyway? As far as he'd been able to glean from his brief discourse with the twins at the café earlier, capercaillies were as rare as Geordies around here.

So what the fuck was making all that noise?

Twice now he'd heard faint squawks from some distance.

Now he heard one much closer, and again he couldn't help but think that it sounded chilling, more a scream of pain than a birdcall.

He turned full circle, running the beam over the forest, the road, down towards the loch and then back to the forest again. He was no coward, and it wasn't the first time he'd heard screams, but something about these sent an uncanny feeling squirming into the pit of his gut. He began to slowly back-pedal, before turning and walking back towards his rental cottage. Before he knew it his steps had grown more rapid and the torch was jiggling in his fist with the jarring contact of his boots on tarmac. Feeling stupid, he made an effort at slowing down, but he couldn't shake the feeling. He was creeped out and the feeling didn't sit well with a tough copper from the Toon. To calm himself, he stopped and pulled out his packet of cigarettes. He thumbed one to his lips, and set a flame to it from his chuckaway. It took a couple of attempts; each time he placed flame to ciggie his rapid exhalations doused it. He swore softly to himself. Down by the loch he had been hoping for the spectre of his dead father to come stand alongside him, but now that he was imagining all kinds of supernatural beasties out in the woods he was trying to convince himself that he didn't believe in ghosts. He practically jammed the lighter to his cigarette and drew the flame to it with an angry intake. The smoke invaded his senses, giving him more of a rush than the first fag he'd had. He shuddered out his breath and blue wisps veiled his face, swam across the torch beam. The smoke stung his eyes, bringing forth tears. He flapped his left hand to clear the smoke from his vision.

'Fuck me!'

He stepped back, at the same time lifting the torchlight to illuminate the figure that had suddenly appeared from out of the gloom. He bit down on any further expletives.

The last thing he had expected to meet out here in the remoteness was a small girl.

'Hello … uh, what are you doing out here at this time of night?' The girl wasn't dressed for the cold, in pyjamas and bare feet. 'You must be freezing. Where's your parents?'

The little girl stood as she had since she'd appeared on the road. Her hands were tight by her sides, her chin tucked on her narrow chest, her hair hanging lank over her face.

'Little girl,' he tried again. "I'm a policeman, OK? There's nothing to be afraid of. Where's your mum and dad?'

He took a step closer, conscious of making any quick movements that might frighten the child. The last thing he wanted was to spook her and have her race off into the woods. Shit, for all he knew the kids out here were tough little buggers and often roamed around in their PJ's, but he doubted it. No way did he want to be responsible if she ran screaming from him and got lost in the forest to perish from exposure.

He used the torch to illuminate himself, just briefly before returning it to the child. 'Are you lost? Do you need help?'

The girl didn't answer, but she did turn her head slightly as if listening.

Or had she looked towards the seemingly empty holiday homes?

'Do you live up there?' He pointed back the way he'd come.

Again he got no reply. Hedging his bets, he took another slow step forward. He expected the girl to flee at any moment, but she didn't. The opposite was true, she matched him with a step of her own. He glanced down at where her feet were pale blurs against the road surface. They looked blue with the cold and were smudged with dirt. Now that he was closer he could make out a motif on her pyjamas – some cartoon character he was unfamiliar with – but also that her PJ top was smeared with dirt and something that glistened as the torchlight played over it. Christ, if she didn't look like one of the latchkey waifs from the estates ...

The girl lifted her head.

Where the beam struck her features it was reflected wetly and he saw that thick globs of stringy mucus hung from both nostrils. The streams of snot ran down her top lip, over her chin and hung like ribbons of gel all the way down her front. Poor kid, that was one hell of a head cold she had. No, not a cold, he realised. The poor sod had got the flu that was raging throughout

98

the country. He had to wonder now if she was suffering from the illness and she'd wandered away from her home in a delirium. As much as he wanted to avoid catching the flu he couldn't allow the kid to be out like this.

'Hey,' he called again, 'we have to get you inside, little 'un. Will you let me take you home?'

'Noo,' the girl said.

His instant thought was that she'd said no, but that wasn't right. The sound wasn't as much a word as it was a groan that came deep from her chest.

'It's OK. I'm a policeman. I'll make sure that you get home to bed. You're parents are waiting for you ...'

'Noooooo.'

The little girl's head had come up further, and though he didn't want to temporarily blind her, he stroked the light across her features. The beam sparkled on the goo on her lower face, but it was as if the dark pits of her eyes sucked the light into them. Despite himself, he felt his anus twitch a couple of times as he stared into their endless depths; they were lifeless voids, the eyes of a corpse.

'Jesus,' he said under his breath.

'Noooooooooo ...'

He took a step back now. Her voice had risen in pitch and volume, and he watched as her mouth stretched to a wide oval as she reared back and continued the weird call.

Noo, he thought, what the fuck is that? It took him all of a split second to realise. He was in the depths of Scotland: she wasn't saying "no" she was saying "*now*". Actually, she wasn't saying it; she was screaming it at the top of her lungs. And there was only one reason why she'd be calling "Now". It was a command, a direction, a fucking signal for someone else to act.

In the next split-second he understood. The girl was a decoy. She had held his attention allowing someone to creep up on him.

He spun round, bringing up the heavy torch as if it was a Neanderthal's club.

For the second time in as many minutes he was stunned by what he saw.

Another child was behind him; a boy this time, a little older than the girl, but still slight and waifish. His mouth and chin were smeared with mucus and his eyes were as dead as the girl's.

If that was all he faced then he wouldn't have been too concerned, but there was movement at the periphery of his vision and figures began to shamble out from the tree line above and from down by the loch side. He took a step back, realised that the girl was too close behind him and spun round to see what had become of her. More figures were stepping out of the darkness, and some of them were chanting the same word over and over. 'Noo. Noo. Noo.'

Then he heard that same high-pitched screech that had punctuated the night already. It wasn't the mating call of a bloody capercaillie after all! It was a sound of hunger and longing that some of the shambling figures emitted. Like the girl's single word, the shriek too was a signal, and he didn't have to be a genius to understand what it meant.

Attack!

His mind flashed back to during the earlier drive back from Killin, and the look of hunger that the woman in the hotel car park had sent after him. The radio had been a distraction that he hadn't really been paying attention to but its message must have sunk in subconsciously. The radio signal had been breaking up, crackling, stuttering, but he recalled the stories of the flu plague and the attempts at vaccinating the sufferers. He recalled the unsubstantiated rumours that the "expert" so flippantly dismissed. But it was true, it wasn't a story conjured by the panicking populace, a flight of fantasy borne of fear, of loathing, of mistrust of a despised government. The vaccine – untested and rushed – had dire side effects. It was killing people in their droves. But worse than that … it was then bringing them back. And they were hungry!

The boy grabbed at him.

In terror he kicked out and sent the boy tumbling across the road.

A fat farmer type, a flat cap perched over a once flaccid face, grabbed at him and he had to dodge aside to gain space.

He snapped his gaze around, watching as the figures shambled towards him. Dozens of them, blank eyed, mouths open and drooling. Some of them already carried signs that they had already fed because there was blood on many chins. Some even showed that they had been previous victims, but that they had risen to join the ranks of the undead puppets of the vaccine. Some missed parts of their faces, or their limbs; one even tripped over his own entrails that were pooled around his feet like links of sausage in a butcher's window.

He caught a waft of hot air, a charnel house stench that made him gag, as the nearer figures lurched towards him. Their hands were coming up, reaching and grasping.

He sought a way past them, but he was surrounded.

He was in the wilds for God's sake! How could there be so many people here to fall victim to the plague?

Of course nowhere in the mainland is that remote anymore. Even in an outback, out of the way place, like this loch valley, there'd be dozens, no hundreds of people. He remembered that a few miles away at Kenmore there was a large holiday complex, a hotel, a village. The same could be said for Killin, and all of the hamlets and farms dotted in between. Christ! He had come here to get away from it all, but that wasn't possible. There was nowhere on earth safe from the Apocalypse that was coming, he now understood.

He wouldn't give up, though. Not while there was a chance. Even the slimmest opportunity for survival had to be grabbed at.

He ran.

There was no clear way through, for the shambling things were encircling him, but there was a narrow gap just ahead of him filled only by the small girl. Those around him were primarily adults, some of them slighter, but most bulkier than him. The girl therefore was the easiest target for his torch as he ran headlong for her.

He swung the Maglite up and back over his shoulder, then at a full gallop swiped the heavy torch down like an axe. It smashed the child's head, and the rest of her down to the floor and he vaulted over her collapsing figure. Hands snatched at him,

101

but he jerked free and continued running. A chorus of screams followed him, but he broke free and fled, his heart in his throat, for the safety of his rental cottage, and the car that waited for him there.

The phone box was broken; his damned mobile phone had no signal out here. His only hope of escape and assistance was if he made it to his car, locked the doors and got the fuck out of there as fast as he could.

He found the white gate standing open as he had left it, and pounded down the gravel drive. Ahead of him was the flower-covered cottage, and the light he'd left on in the kitchen was like a beacon to him. But he'd no intention of going in to the cottage. He swerved for his car and grabbed at the door. Locked. He had fetched the Maglite from the car, locked it out of old city-bred habit. He grabbed at his pockets, searching for his keys. All the while he snatched glances back the way he'd come. His movements became more frantic as he saw the first figures shambling through the darkness towards him.

Josh dropped the torch so that he had both hands to help in the search. Jesus–fucking-Christ, where are they? He couldn't find his keys.

Dread struck him.

When he'd pulled out his cigarettes earlier, when he'd been spooked and required calming, he must have also snagged his keys alongside the packet, and dropped them back there on the road.

Holy shit!

He snatched up the torch. Not for its light but that it was a handy weapon and then fled towards the cottage.

He banged through the door and into a mudroom, then into the kitchen beyond. He looked for a knife, anything. Then his stupidity struck him and he ran back to lock the outer door. Figures swarmed through the small garden outside. Faces peered back at him, eyes like black pinholes amid faces glowing with starvation and need.

The door would hold them, but not the windows.

Josh retreated into the kitchen and through that door shut, slamming home the bolts. There were windows in the kitchen, but these were double-glazed and sturdy and would thwart most attempts to get in. No, that wasn't true. He had to shake his first impression of the walking dead. He'd grown up on schlock horror movies, the more recent video games where zombies were mindless and stupid eating machines. By setting the little girl as a decoy, these things retained some semblance of intelligence and it wouldn't take them long to find something with which they could smash a way inside. He fled through the kitchen and into the living room. He slammed shut the door and then wrestled a sideboard over to keep the door shut. There was a window at each end of the room – small, original features – and he upturned the settee and jammed it in front of one of them. At the other end of the room was a small study area, and he made use of the desk by upending it and jamming it solidly in the window frame.

He stood there in the centre of the living room, gaze switching from window to door to opposite window. He could hear them outside; their shrieking calls to feed were growing louder in pitch and frustration. Perspiration pooled out of him. It was nothing to do with the fire still smouldering in the stove, because this was the cold sweat of terror.

Bump.

He heard the thud from the stairs.

Bump … bump … bump … bumpbumpbump.

Josh exhaled.

Just the bloody water in the pipes, like the last time.

Jesus, he thought, and there was me worrying that the fucking cottage was haunted!

Bump.

He glanced at the door that led to the stairs.

Even here in the living room was no safe haven. If they were as intelligent – not to mention as hungry – as he credited them, they'd be in here in no time.

Upstairs was the best place to be.

He could stand at the top of the flight of steps. They were narrow between two solid walls, and quite steep. Only one of the damned things could come at him at a time. If he had a more telling weapon than the Maglite he could defend the stair head. Sooner or later the numbers would dwindle and he could make his escape from the cottage, maybe get down into the water of the loch and swim to someplace further along where he could raise help.

He looked towards the stove and the long metal poker resting on the hearth beneath it. The poker was a foot and a half long, steel, with a spike and prong for raking the embers. He switched the torch to his left hand and grabbed for the poker.

Bump ... bump ... bump ... bumpbumpbump.

Fucking pipes!

He lurched towards the door to the stairs just as the kitchen windows shattered with a deafening bang and clatter.

They were starving indeed and going straight for the main course.

A body rebounded off the living room door, moving the sideboard wedged against it a half inch.

Josh shoved the sideboard back again. Threw a coffee table on top of it, then dragged over the easy chair he'd napped in and jammed that against them both. His barricade wouldn't stop the undead, but it would slow them while he gained a defensive position.

He had to drop the torch in order to haul open the door.

It swung inwards towards him and he had to twist his body to give it clearance.

He twisted back and took a step up for the first stair.

'Noooooo ...'

The woman was waiting for him. The one he'd seen staring at him from the hotel car park. She'd seen him, targeted him, fucking followed him back here. She had waited for him to leave and sneaked inside while her friends corralled him back here. The bitch had laid her trap.

Bump ... bump ... bump ... bumpbumpbump.

Her heels skidded down the stairs, and she came at Josh open mouthed, her teeth glistening in the wan light. Snot was all over her, drool pooling in the corners of her lips, her eyes deep, hollow pits.

She shrieked.

Not a call to feed this time but because he'd rammed the sharp end of the poker into her stomach.

The length of steel held her for only a second. She didn't fight to get away, only came forward, remorseless, throwing her weight along the metal rod as she grabbed his face in her hands.

Josh tried to wrench loose, but her grip was rictus-like, fuelled by a strength that had nothing in common with the world he knew or understood. She continued to push along the poker and the tip burst from between her shoulder blades. He let go of the poker, but it didn't help. Her grip on him was unflinching. He pulled and wrenched but her fingers were digging into the flesh of his face.

Josh howled in agony.

Her fingertips were digging directly into his flesh, the nails grating along the bones of his skull. One of her thumbs found the corner of his right eye and began to squirm deep into the socket.

'Noooooooooo!' he screamed.

Half-blinded, half-insane with agony, nothing came near the terror that welled up in him as the woman snapped her teeth into his throat. He felt her grind her jaws together, felt the cartilage of his windpipe collapse under the horrific pressure. Then she tore back and blood filled the air between them.

Finally she loosed her grip and he crumpled down. The weight of his upper body caused his knees to fold, torque sideways and Josh flopped over backwards to lie on his back at the foot of the stairs.

He moaned, but nothing issued from his ruined throat but bubbling froth.

Over him the woman stood, munching in satisfaction on the chunk of flesh she had torn out of him.

Absurd if it wasn't so real.

His good eye rolled up, his lids flickering rapidly and Josh saw the living room door forced slowly open. The furniture toppled, crashing down close by his head. He didn't have the strength or the will to flinch. Figures stumbled into the room, all of them hungry and grinning in anticipation. He hoped they were as hungry as they looked and didn't leave a morsel behind, because he sure didn't fancy joining their ranks.

If this was the Apocalypse then he wanted to go now.

Or, noo, as it happened.

Well, Dad, he thought, if there is an afterlife I'm going to see you soon. Hopefully you'll let me make my peace with you then?

THE END

THANKSGIVING FEAST
By
A.M. Boyle

Emil H. Larson eagerly licked his craggy lips and smiled. The hunting knife was a beauty, for sure. Not like the cheap crap they sold at the big chain stores these days. This was a handcrafted gem, and with only a little bit more work, it would surely be up for the task that lay ahead. He pressed the edge of the blade lightly against the motorized grinding wheel. The sparks danced merrily in the air, like miniature fireworks, and the high-pitched squeal prickled his ears. After a moment or two, Emil withdrew the knife and examined the blade. It glinted in the shallow light of the workshop, showing the grandeur of its former self.

He'd meticulously removed every spec of dried blood from the ornate wooden handle, paying special attention to the carved initials. *EHL II.* They were his great grandfather's initials. Hell, his great grandfather's initials were just about everywhere in this old homestead; carved into the fireplace mantle, engraved over the door frames, etched into the side post by the slaughter barn, even scratched into the beams in the old attic where he'd found this hidden treasure of a knife just a few days ago. It was as if the founder of this farm had tried to carve himself into the very fabric of the place, permanently marking it as his. And why shouldn't he? Back in the day, he'd supported his family from the turkeys he'd raised. It had been quite an operation, supplying not only the small town of Shakers Point with their Thanksgiving feast but three other adjacent towns as well. Back then it had been a much bigger business. Maybe that had been the problem; it had been too big.

The old man had worked himself to death trying to keep up. Rumour was that his great grandfather had lost his mind from being around too many turkeys for too long. He'd tried to attack a customer and had gotten shot by his own rifle. No one in the family ever talked about it, so who knew what the truth really was? Either way, with each new generation of Larsons the operation had gotten smaller, and each successor had lived just a little longer. The business was so small now that Emil could handle the whole operation by himself, which was a good thing, since he had no successors to hand it down to. Hell, he might just have to live forever to keep the old farm going. Otherwise, how would the hundred or so folks who still bought their turkeys from Larson's Farm ever get their Thanksgiving meals on the table?

Emil chuckled. He might not live forever, but at seventy five, he still had a lot of life left in him, just like the old hunting knife he held in his hands. He was sure his great grandfather had held this knife and admired it, just the way he was doing, right before the slaughter. Why would someone stash such an heirloom up in the attic, stuffed in an old shoe box, disrespectfully wrapped in a ratty dish towel? He probably wouldn't have found it if he hadn't been up there looking for those old photographs for his daughter. He'd promised to mail her some in time for Christmas – something about a scrapbook of some sort. He'd thought it best to get them to her before the holiday rush. Mail to Germany took long enough as it was. The old shoebox had been stashed behind a trunk filled with his dead wife's clothes, and he was sure it contained the photos his daughter had asked about. But when he'd unwrapped the dish rag bundle, the knife plopped into his lap. There had been a note with it, too, wrinkled and yellowed with time.

Although he could no more read what it said than read the entire works of William Shakespeare, he'd smoothed it out and had laid it safely under the lamp next to the sofa. His great grandfather, by all accounts, had been a frugal man of word and deed – much like himself – so if he had taken the time to write a note, it had been because he had something to say. Day after tomorrow, he'd ask Sheriff to read it to him. Sheriff was always early to pick up his bird, and he always sat for a short spell to sip on some coffee. But, in the meantime, he'd honour his great grandfather, and hopefully make amends for this disrespectful way the heirloom had been treated, by using it for the slaughter.

Emil sighed at the thought of the night's work that lay ahead. Slaughtering one hundred turkeys, then cleaning and dressing them was tiring work. Often he wondered how his father had done twice that many at his age, and his grandfather three times as many before that. 'Course, he'd always been around to help. Well, maybe not always. When he was real young, maybe six or so, the sight of all that blood had turned his stomach, and he'd hide in the root cellar until it was over. His father used to laugh at his reaction and joke that, in the Larson household, the first turkey slaughter was a thing of beauty since it brought the colours of Christmas – the red blood meant green money.

But as he'd gotten older, he'd begun to appreciate his father's trade, and had learned how to do it efficiently and economically. Everything was still done the old fashioned way. No fancy equipment or automated nonsense. Shakers Point had remained a small town, and many of the younger residents got their birds from the market, frozen like a brick and as tasteless as one, too. The older folks who knew how much better a fresh turkey tasted trusted him to supply their feast. It was time consuming, but with only a hundred birds for Thanksgiving and about seventy-five for Christmas, it was manageable. Besides, it was more of a hobby than as a means to make a living. At forty bucks a pop, though, it wasn't too bad.

Emil gingerly placed the edge of the blade against the spinning wheel one last time. He winced at the shrill wail, then pulled it away and slid the knife back into its leather sheath. Stretching and yawning, he glanced at the clock above the work bench.

Almost 10:00pm

Time to get started.

If he waited too long, he'd run out of steam before the job was done. These birds were heavy buggers – ornery, too – and every year it was getting harder and harder to hoist them into the shackles. Tomorrow was Tuesday and he'd spend most of the day cleaning, dressing, and wrapping the birds for pick-up on Wednesday. Starting at 7:00am on Wednesday, one hundred lucky townsfolk would be coming one by one to pick up the grain fed, all natural star of their Thanksgiving celebration. And the birds had better be clean as a baby's bottom by then. Heaven forbid there should be any gory reminders that their delicious meal had been alive and kicking only a short time before.

It would be a long night tonight, and an even longer day tomorrow.

Emil took his killing jacket from the hook in the workshop and shrugged it on. It carried the pungent odour of dried blood and turkey piss, but it was just too much trouble to get it to the dry cleaners. He didn't leave the house much anymore, since the arthritis had settled into his hips. Frank down at the Mid Town Market sent his orders once a week, and his prescriptions came by mail. He had the occasional doctor's appointment, but otherwise, he was pretty much a home-body. Gas cost too much and the old pick-up was on its last legs anyway, so what was the point of going anywhere?

He took the sheath from the workbench, clipped it onto the belt of jeans, and stepped into the brisk night. Breathing deeply, he filled up on the fresh air he wouldn't smell again for hours, and admired the view. The farm wasn't that big, but it always seemed more expansive at night. The hen barn was set off in the back, furthest away from the house. In there, he kept his hens and the toms used for mating. That's where he raised the poults for next year. His father used to call it the "Happy Barn." The slaughter barn was closest to the house, but at enough of a distance so that the odour and clamour of the turkeys didn't drive him too crazy. His great grandfather had built both barns and, aside from a few modifications necessary to keep out predators in search of an easy meal, it was the same as it had been on the day he built it.

Sturdy and strong, tried and true.

Proof again that the old fashioned ways of doing things were still the best ways of doing things.

The light breeze was heavy with the scent of pine needles and the promise of rain—maybe even snow, depending upon how cold it got. It wasn't that unusual to have snow on Thanksgiving in this part of Pennsylvania. Hell, it wasn't unusual to have snow on Easter either. The cold made the birds sluggish, so it certainly wasn't a bad thing, but the dampness made his hips ache, which slowed him down almost as much as it did the birds.

110

This time of night, the turkeys were half asleep anyway, which made the whole process easier as well. Another trick he'd learned from his father. Still, despite the late hour, when he unlatched the door brace, tugged open the heavy barn door, and turned on the overhead light, the turkeys immediately began their incessant gobbling, as if sensing that there was something different about tonight.

Over the years, he'd grown accustomed to the racket they made, but as the holidays drew closer, and the flock was more mature, their voices were loud enough to grate the nerves. It was always a relief on Thanksgiving morning, and even more so on Christmas, when raucous gobbling of these birds was silenced.

"Good evening, you poor bastards."

At the sound of his croaky voice, the flock quietened a bit. They knew his voice. He'd raised each and every one of them. They trusted him, as much as a turkey could trust anybody.

Emil patted the knife at his side. "Tonight's your night boys. More than half of you are going to that great turkey pen in the sky."

A row of twenty leg shackles hung against the side wall over several blood basins. The wall was indelibly stained with dried gore. Four rows of twenty inverted draining cones were lined up alongside the wall, each cone tucked securely, narrow side down, inside the wooden rack that his great grandfather father had built. The rack was on wheels, and resembled an oversized checkerboard, with plastic cones in place of red and black checkers. The cones had been replaced a few times over the years, but the wooden rack was as stable as ever. Good workmanship; another testament to doing things the old fashioned way.

The toms were bunched together in a large pen opposite the shackles and wooden checkerboard, a bobbling sea of white feathers. Tonight one hundred birds would be slaughtered for Thanksgiving, and the remaining seventy five would stay in the pen until Christmas week. Emil went to the pen and opened the gate, careful to block the exit so that he didn't waste energy chasing any birds around the barn. The turkeys gobbled louder

111

as they surrounded him, expecting a handout of grain or some other goody. He grabbed the nearest turkey, a nice plump tom that squawked in protest. Emil tucked the bird under his arm, holding the wings tightly. The wing muscles flexed as the bird struggled against his grip, and knew that by the end of the night, his arms would surely be aching. Hopefully, there'd be enough hot water for a nice bath to soothe his sore bones.

He carried the bird to the shackles and, with an ease that comes with years of practice, hoisted the bird upside down, clamping each leg firmly into the first set of shackles. The bird squawked and screeched, wings flailing, feathers flying. The other birds looked on, warbling softly, seemingly unaffected by the plight of their fellow pen-mate, oblivious to the fact that they would soon be in the same precarious position.

"Settle down, you damn stupid turkey. You're only hurting yourself."

Emil shook his head. These dumb birds didn't even realize that the more they struggled the more painful the shackles would be. They were so heavy that the repeated struggling usually dislocated their hips and wings. And people wondered why it was so easy to get the leg sections off some turkeys but not others.

One by one, Emil grabbed a bird and hoisted it into the same position as the first, shackled firmly by its feet, hanging upside down. Each bird in turn squawked and complained until their wings tired from flailing and their tiny brains were about to burst from the blood rush. When each of the shackles held a plump turkey, Emil proceeded to the second step. He slipped his great grandfather's knife out of its sheath. Starting with the first bird, with one quick swipe, he slit its throat.

The knife sliced through the thick skin efficiently and smoothly, and Emil could swear a pleasant tingle emanated from the handle as it slid effortlessly across the turkey's gullet. It was as if the knife itself were expressing its gratitude for being used again after having laid dormant for so long. The noisy squawking of the bird abruptly ceased, while its beak opened and closed futilely. Its head waggled obscenely, still attached to the neck by a thick flap of skin and muscle, as blood poured into the basin. The turkey flapped its wings with renewed vigour, but couldn't escape the inevitability of death.

Emil twisted the knife in his hand, admiring once again the way the blade caught the light on its edge, and then continued down the line, slitting the throat of each bird so that the blood could run out, marvelling all the while at the proficiency of his great grandfather's knife. How fluently it cut through the necks of the birds, and with each use, the pleasant tingle became more electrifying, until the knife itself seemed to glow with invigorating energy, humming with the thrill of being valuable once again.

When Emil reached the end of the row, he slipped the knife back into its sheath for the time being and returned to the first bird, now limp and flaccid. He unshackled it and placed it head down inside the first cone, so that the rest of the blood could run out. He did the same with the other nineteen shackled birds, until twenty birds were arranged securely in the cones, head down, tail feathers up, feet still twitching. Satisfied with the first group, he returned to the pen, and one by one, started loading the shackles again. He'd have to repeat the process four more times, so that when he was done, he'd have eighty birds draining in the cones, and the remaining twenty draining in the shackles. Then he'd take a short break – maybe catch a twenty minute nap – allowing some time for all the blood to drain out, before carting them off to the cooler and dumping the blood in the stream out back. In the morning, he'd finish the job – gutting, plucking, trimming the wings and legs – so when his customers picked up their birds, they'd be perfect, no blood, no gore, not even a feather.

Emil's arms burned more fitfully with each bird he hauled into and out of the shackles. Slitting their throats was actually the easiest part as it gave his aching muscles a rest. The strange, electric feel of the knife made it even better – enjoyable, even. When Emil finally sliced the gullet of the last turkey, he heaved a sigh of relief and squinted at his watch. 2:03am Not bad. Years ago, he'd been able to do this part of the job in three hours, tops. But age carried a price.

His bones throbbed and his arthritic hips were on fire. Still, the wonderful knife had made the job easier. He idly watched as the flailing of the last bird slowed and gradually stopped.

That was it. Break time.

He wiped the blade of his great grandfather's knife on his slaughter jacket, placed it back in the sheath, and washed up in the basin. The rest of the birds watched him warily, their jabber quieting as the night's excitement ebbed away. They'd been spared until the Christmas kill.

"Sleep tight, you lucky birds. You got a few weeks to go before it's your turn."

Emil glanced around the barn one more time, turned off the light, and latched the door. He'd be back in less than an hour, but it didn't take long for predators in these mountains to catch the scent of fresh blood, and he'd worked too hard for some fox or bear to come along and enjoy the free fruit of his labours. He stopped at the tool shed, shrugged off the blood stained jacket, placed it back on the hook, and laid the knife next to the grinder. The chilly night air nipped at his flannel shirt as he dug his hands into the pockets of his jeans. He relished the silence as he made his way back to the house. The hens and mating toms were fast asleep in the back barn, and more than half the kill birds were done. For a while, the incessant racket the birds made would be dimmed considerably – a welcome respite. Without even turning on the lights, Emil sunk into the comfort of the well-worn arm chair across from the sofa and sighed. His great grandfather's note was still tucked securely under the lamp, and he wondered what words of wisdom it might impart.

"Whatever you got to say in that note, Great Grandpop, I sure do appreciate your gift. It's a superb knife. Real quality. Thank you." His voice sounded groggy even to his own ears. Normally, he'd grab a snack in the kitchen, but tonight food took second seat to exhaustion. He shut his eyes and hoped a twenty minute nap would give him enough energy to lug the turkeys out to the cooler and empty the blood basins. Maybe he was just getting too old to keep this up anymore.

At 4:23am Emil's eyes popped open.

Even before he saw the display on the cable box, he knew he had overslept.

Dread churned in his stomach. The birds had been left hanging in the barn too long. They should have been in the cooler by now. Not only would the stench attract unwelcome visitors, but one time his father had left a batch out too long, and a good number of folks got sick. Poultry was a fickle meat.

"Damn it! Don't need no spoiled birds after all that work!" He pushed himself out of the armchair as quickly as his tight muscles would allow, and tried to stretch the soreness out of his back and hips.

That's when he noticed the sound.

Something he had been so used to hearing, but was completely out of place.

Turkeys warbling, loud and boisterous in the stillness of the pre-dawn air.

He stuck his index finger in his ear and wiggled it around. Was he hearing things? He'd been around these birds all his life, and knew every nuance, every intricacy of the noises they made. This was not the sound of seventy-five tired turkeys waking up at an unnatural hour. This sound was louder, more raucous, and more distressed.

Was there a predator in the barn?

He scurried to the door as quickly as his hips would allow and headed outside. The noise was definitely coming from the slaughter barn, where about $4,000 worth of fresh meat hung. The sun had not yet broken over the horizon and darkness still shrouded everything in heavy shadows. Emil didn't have time to hunt for a flashlight. If there was an animal in the barn, time was crucial. His heart pounded loudly in his ears, not only from the effort of hustling outside, but from the thought that some crafty beast was helping himself to a free meal at his expense. His great grandfather used to keep a shotgun perched outside the barn door, but ever since the unfortunate shooting, the shotgun had been banned. His father had secured the barn doors and windows so well that they'd never had a problem with animals getting in – not even a squirrel. The shotgun had been replaced

115

by a baseball bat, more of a security blanket than as a functional weapon. Nonetheless, Emil grabbed hold of the bat.

He eyed the barn warily. The latch on the door was still securely in place, but the darkness prevented him from seeing the windows clearly. It was possible that some ravenous beast had chewed through the mesh, although he didn't think it probable. But as he stood outside the door, the gobbling from within reached a frenzied pitch – a sure sign that something was wrong.

With a shaky hand, he unlatched the door. He gripped the bat securely, holding it at the ready over his shoulder, and edged the door open with his foot.

The gobbling stopped suddenly, leaving an eerie silence.

Thick velvety blackness swallowed up the inside of the barn, stunting his vision. He listened intently for the sound of movement, the scuffling of a wild animal caught red handed.

Nothing.

Something wasn't right. Not right at all.

He hesitated at the edge of the door, his forehead slick with sweat despite the chilly air. He licked his dry lips, and, while keeping hold of the bat with one hand, slowly snaked his free hand around the corner of the door, groping for the light switch. Heart thudding loudly, he flicked the switch, and the overhead fluorescents sputtered to life.

Nothing jumped, nothing moved, nothing uttered a sound. From where he stood, in the glare of the bluish light, the checkerboard cones were in clear view.

They were empty.

Eighty dead turkeys had been propped in those cones, feet sticking up awkwardly. Now they were empty.

As his mind grappled with the implications, a caustic bubble of angst rose in his chest.

They'd been stolen. Eighty of his best turkeys stolen right from under his nose.

And the perpetrator had to still be in the barn.

Rejuvenated by a sudden surge of anger, he brandished the baseball bat with both hands and kicked the door open the rest of the way.

A sea of one hundred and seventy five mutilated turkeys stared back at him, silent and menacing.

At least half of the turkeys had their heads hanging, dangling from severed throats, waddles red not from anxiety, but from the stain of their own blood. Their white feathers were mottled with brownish-red gore, and many of them listed to one side or the other, standing awkwardly on legs that had been broken or dislocated. Others, with heads still intact, had bloody tufts of flesh and feathers hanging from them where they had been gouged and scratched by their counterparts. The beak of one hung down from its face; the eyes of another had been plucked out, leaving nothing but gaping dark holes, empty yet filled with malice; and still another had entrails spilling from a gaping hole in its side.

Emil blinked hard, unable to fathom what he saw.

The floor swayed under his feet and he almost lost his balance. For a moment it was as if he was floating outside of himself, watching what was happening, but not really part of it. He was barely aware of the bat falling from his grip as he stared, mesmerized, at the implausible sight.

It was impossible.

He must have lost his mind, like his great grandfather before him.

Vaguely, it registered that twenty birds still hung in the shackles, clamouring noisily, heads waggling violently from severed necks. The pen was empty, the bedding stained with blood and gore. The birds that had been in the pen, now mangled and disfigured, stood with the birds that had been in the cones, the lifeless birds he had left upside down to insure all the blood had been drained from their carcasses.

But here they were. Dead, but alive.

His insides roiled and their fetid odour filled his nostrils, nearly overwhelming him. A wave of dizziness challenged his balance, and he almost toppled into the silent horde. One of the grotesque birds stepped forward, its head hanging by a thin strand of bloody sinew, and gazed at him sideways through a bulging, glassy eyes. Its beak hung open at an unnatural angle and a string of mottled drool slid from its mouth. With sudden

117

clarity, Emil realized that, whether he had lost his mind or not, each repulsive creature now stared at him with greedy hunger.

His stomach sunk through the floor as one thought finally burst through his shock:

Run. Get the hell out of there.

Still, he didn't dare make any sudden moves, and he didn't dare turn his back on the maimed flock. Slowly, legs trembling, he stepped back from the putrid mass, hoping to back through the door, retreat to the safety and sanity of his little house.

As soon as he moved, the grotesque horde raised its collective voice in a deafening roar of guttural, unnatural garble. The sound pierced his head like a javelin and he threw his hands over his ears.

As if the movement was some sort of sign, the turkeys lurched forward.

Some crawled along on distended bellies, legs dragging from dislocated hip sockets, others tripped and stumbled over their own heads which swayed precariously from severed necks. Others, though, with legs intact, were swift and determined. They charged him, some with wings outstretched, all with malevolence reflected in their black eyes.

Emil stumbled backward and tripped on the baseball bat he had dropped. He landed with a sickening crack and screamed as incredible pain shot though his left hip. In a flurry of disjointed feathers and twisted gore the turkeys descended upon him. It was all too much and Emil could no longer suppress the gorge rising in his throat. The meagre meal of soup and crackers that he had had for dinner came surging up, burning his throat and nose. As he gasped to catch his breath, the zombie turkeys took full advantage of his vulnerability. Heavy wings beat against him and sharp claws dug into his skin as they drilled their beaks into his limbs and torso. The pain was excruciating, yet he was overpowered by their numbers and their frenzied hunger. He could not get away.

"No! Please no! Leave me be!"

His desperate pleas only increased their fervour and his cries were muffled by the fetid horde that covered his face, his nose, his mouth; suffocating him as they tore into his flesh. Agony burned through him and tears of anguish filled his eyes. As if attracted to the saltiness of those tears, several of the birds clawed and pecked at his face and eyes. Completely at their mercy, Emil surrendered to the anguish as his body twitched and spasmed and his life seeped from him. At last, he gave into his tormentors, melding with them, feeling their greedy lust for flesh as if it were his own, letting his pain melt into their satisfaction, feeling nothing more – nothing but desire, nothing but a thirst, nothing but an insatiable, driving hunger for more ...

Sheriff Gary Turnbull was always the first to arrive at Emil's place on Wednesday morning. His shift started at 6:00am and even though Emil didn't start handing out the birds until 7:00, the old man had always made a special exception for him. After all, he would say, if you can't bend the rules a little for the law, who can you bend them for?

He always got his pick of the turkeys; one of the few fringe benefits of his position in this dull little town. He swung his cruiser into the long drive and rolled up the gravel to the front lawn.

No lights were on.

Strange. Usually by this time, Emil had a big pot of strong coffee brewing. Maybe the old guy had overslept. He parked the cruiser, wandered up to the door and knocked hard. The door creaked open. He frowned. It wasn't like Emil to leave his door unlocked, let alone open. He pushed the door a little further with his foot, unlatched the strap on his gun, and laid his hand on the weapon. His pulse quickened at the possibility the he might have to use it. Not much call for that in Shakers Point.

He inched his way in.

"Hello?"

No answer.

"Emil?"

Nothing. He wandered into the front room, then into the kitchen. The aroma of freshly brewed coffee was conspicuously missing. Emil was nowhere to be seen. Gary

crept to the stairs and called loudly. "Emil? You here?"
Nothing.

Maybe the poor old guy had kicked it. That would suck, croaking the day before Thanksgiving. It would suck even more to have to buy a frozen turkey every year from now on, instead of enjoying one of Emil's rare gems. He should check the bedroom just in case.

Gary plodded up the steps, hand still on his weapon. He peeked into the bedroom.

"Emil?"

The room was empty. The bed didn't look like it had been slept in.

Gary checked the bathroom, and the spare room at the end of the hall before making his way back downstairs. He rubbed the back of his neck and went into the front room. A note was tucked under the lamp. He hadn't noticed it before.

Maybe Emil had written a note explaining his absence. But then again, the poor old guy couldn't read a lick, so how could he write a note?

He gently lifted the lamp and took the note. It looked old, tattered and discoloured. The scratchy handwriting was faded, but legible.

To whoever finds this here Nife. You need to leave it be. There's something real bad about this Nife. Evil. Don't do nothing with it. Don't use it. Don't try to destroy it, or it will destroy you. Don't use it on nothing, or the evil will spread. Just leave it be. LEAVE IT BE-or else. EHL II

Strange note. Gary scratched his head and looked around. There was no knife.

Could Emil have written this after all? Probably not. Either way, the note didn't make much sense.

An unusually loud garbling disrupted the eerie silence. Gary reached back, pulled the curtain aside, and peered out the window toward the side of the house. The light in the barn was on. That's where Emil kept the holiday turkeys for slaughter. Most of those turkeys should've be cleaned and dressed by now, wrapped and sitting in the cooler, but from the sound of it, it sure didn't seem that way.

Emil must be behind a few steps this year. It'd be a sin if the turkeys weren't ready yet. People sure wouldn't like that. Folks in this town didn't like their routines disrupted. He'd better go out to the barn and see what was up with the poor old guy.

He placed the note back on the table, clipped the safety strap back in place on his weapon and headed out to the slaughter barn.

THE END

OATMEAL COOKIES
By
Eric Dimbleby

"Don't let her in," Tyler whispered in his sister's ear. She was a good foot taller than him, which she never failed to mention alongside her being three years his senior. And so Tyler had to stand on his tiptoes. He leaned against her backside, and the sticky residue around his mouth temporarily glued to the back of Susan's grimy shirt.

Susan nudged him back with her shoulder, huffing in annoyance. "I'll do what I want, y'little brat." Susan tossed her golden pigtails aside and peered through the peephole again. "She doesn't look so bad."

"She's sick. Just like Mommy and Daddy," Tyler whined, trying hard to bite back the tears of the realizations that were coursing through his brain. He was only six years old, goddammit. This wasn't how things were supposed to be. His only defence was his sister, who couldn't care less about what happened to him. Why couldn't he have been born earlier? If so, then *he* would be in charge. Susan would have no say. Fate was a cruel bitch, and so was Susie.

The oldest always has all the power, thus goes the kingdom of children. "But she's our grandmother, chump. Back up," Susan threatened, showing her teeth. A couple of her formerly white fangs were missing, but the Tooth Fairy had not come. In fact, the Tooth Fairy was *nowhere* to be found these days, which troubled them both. Tyler had not started losing teeth yet, and so the prospect that the Tooth Fairy had also *turned* made him angry.

"Please, Susie. Please!" Tyler shouted, not wanting to see his Gram ever again. She was a monster, an undead beast like all the rest of them *out there*. A zombie, as Susie had once explained.

"When you broke your leg, who brought you oatmeal cookies?"

"Gram did," Tyler whimpered, suckling on his thumb in an attempt to make all the bad things go away. It didn't always work.

"That's right. And who brought you to church every Sunday?" Susie asked next.

"Gram," Tyler replied in the same tone as before, though he despised going to church. Everybody smelled of cabbage there, wet and steamy cabbage. "But ..."

Susie snapped, "Then shut your hole! All the grownups are dead, and our Gram is here to save us, you dummy. Don't make me bite you." Her threat was not idle, for she had bitten him on dozens of occasions, each time worse than the last. Based on her progress towards more violent chomps, Tyler estimated that she would fully bite an entire appendage off by the time he was ten years old.

Pulling open the door to their fifth floor luxury apartment in New York City, Susan smiled at her grandmother, reaching out her arms in a hazy embrace. "Gram!" she called out, a delusional void filling the logical side of her brain. This was not her Gram, though. No matter how well Susan had talked herself into the opposing truth.

Grandma was a zombie.

In a nursing home on the other side of the city, she had succumbed to the gray-skinned attackers (*roamers*- that's what the news guy called them before the televisions had shut off for good, *roamers*) while in her sleep. She had been bed-ridden for the past year, crippled by a debilitating disease in her nervous system, but now had come across a new invigoration. *Undeath* was kinder to her than life had been, and she had returned to capture the brains of her two favourite grandchildren. Most roamers were known to do just that, to roam. But Gram was different. Something innate at the base of her brain had called her to action. Brains always tasted better when you were acquainted with the brain.

Their visiting Gram was somehow different than the rest of the brain chompers. She was disconnected from their chaotic wiring, a spoiled bit of zombie. Perhaps that differentiation was the driving force behind Susan's quick acceptance of her own delusion.

"We've missed you so much, Gram!" Susan said with tears edging her eyes. She tumbled forward, wrapping her arms

123

around her grandmother. Tyler could only look on, shaking his head from side to side, worried for his sister's unflinching ease, for this was *not* his Gram. No way, no how. "You came back for us," Susan mumbled in a dreamy voice. "Finally."

Was she so naïve to believe that her disease had been cured?

Tyler braced himself.

When Gram bit into her granddaughter's scalp, blood jettisoned from the open wound as though Susie's head was a liquid piñata. It coated Tyler's face and chest, forever marring his Captain America pyjamas, which he had been wearing for more than a week now. Susan crumpled to the ground, weeping as she gave in to the pervading darkness behind her eyelids. "Susie!" Tyler cried out, backing away from his grandmother's malice while she lorded over his sister's twitching body. The last sight she ever saw was her grandmother's pink bunny slippers. Gram gnawed on a torn piece of skin and hair while she glared at Tyler, groaning low and wishing for more, more, *more.*

By the time his Gram was knee deep in her granddaughter's demise, Tyler was locked away in his bedroom, thankful that his father had installed a lock before he died. Tyler prayed to the God he had forever questioned ("It's like a movie, Gram," he had once purported) during those Sunday morning church visits.

Though it was a feat of immeasurable uncertainty, Tyler was able to slide his big-boy bed a few inches to the left, blocking the door. Between the lock and the roadblock, it would not hold Gram back, not if she was determined to gain entry, but it was enough to hold her at bay, if killing him was her intention. The brutal strength that she had employed upon his sister was what made his nerves cringe.

Within only a few moments of slurping at her granddaughter's body, Gram was banging at his door with her liver-spotted fists, moaning in a guttural language native to the earthly Dead. Tyler would forbid himself from being as gullible as his sister had been. His grandmother had always baked blissful oatmeal cookies, but they weren't quite good enough to make him forget how ravenous she had become, with that new desire for human flesh and brains.

Tyler, for the first time in his short life, was all alone.

While his grandmother released her death rattles from outside his door, insisting in her undead language permission to enter, Tyler did what he had always done when he was nervous; doing in fact what all children only knew how to do. With only one universal stress reliever at his disposal, he played with his toys, tears soaking his eyes and cheeks, but still maintaining a smile the best he could. Just like his Gram had often told him, "If you can't smile by yourself, you'll never smile at all."

Tyler had a personal bathroom off his bedroom. He was thankful, like the lock on the door, for that perk. The running water still worked, for the time being, as did the toilet. He imaged having to pee in the corner, and the smell that would come from that. Such thoughts felt overly adult to him, but the days of thinking as a child were over. When an animal is backed into a corner, it survives by any means necessary.

Hours passed in gruelling tedium. Tyler's stomach began to seize in ripples of pang. Gram had quit her incessant thudding upon his door for several minutes, but had returned again. This continued on through the night. Tyler could not be certain where she had gone off to during those absent moments, but it seemed that she was not easily forgetting that he was within her potential reach. She had retained enough of her living memory to walk halfway through the city, to remember the exact address, floor, and apartment number. Most of her had died, but part of her being seemed to troop on, undeterred by her decreasing state of living and breathing.

Tyler could barely remember the last time he had eaten. It had been breakfast, the previous day, but he wasn't sure how many hours that was. He wasn't all that crafty with time calculations, though he could recognize the significance of certain numeric representations on digital and traditional clocks. If it was near the six, and it was getting dark out, then it was dinner time. If it was near the twelve, and it was light outside, then it was lunch. When he woke up (usually around seven), it was time for breakfast. He, like his dead sister in the next room, had always depended on his mother for scheduling and management of his activities, feeding, and life.

Since their parents had turned to undead beasts, Susan had been steadfast and effective in the care of her younger brother, though begrudgingly so. It was her duty, and she understood that from the outset. But she had acted like a *doofus*. Her misguided hope had trumped her reason. Tyler could not let himself mourn for her, like they had when their parents had turned away from the human condition. They had run away from home for several days, hiding in the basement of their apartment complex, nestled behind the garbage shoot with the rats. When they thought it was safe to come out, they had returned to their apartment, to find it empty. Their zombie Mommy and Daddy had abandoned them, and Susie had informed him that it was for the best. They had cried for days on end, but soon found a new sense of bravery, that which they had never known existed inside of them.

Now he was alone. He had once watched a movie about a little blonde kid who had been left alone by his parents. Two robbers tried, throughout the moronic (even at the age of six, Tyler understood the concept of *moronic*) movie, to gain entry to the boy's home. In a series of booby traps, he defeated the robbers. Real life was nothing like that movie, Tyler had discovered. He *wished* that he only had to deal with bumbling burglars. He wondered to himself what the blonde kid may have done if under the duress of a zombie attack. Tyler assured himself that the boy from that movie knew nothing about zombies, and probably didn't even know what a zombie *was*.

"A zombie's like a vampire, but they don't drink blood. They try n' eat your brain," Susie had informed him during one of the days that they were cowering in the basement, hiding behind the trash chute as they wondered what had happened to their doting parents. Tyler had replied to Susie that he didn't believe in *things like that*, and that she was just trying to scare him. In fact, he had originally believed this to be some sort of prank. His Daddy had always tried to startle him, jumping out from behind doors or out of closets. Tyler could only laugh at such antics, though. This felt altogether different. "You better start believing in them, Ty," Susie had responded with unblinking eyes, the smell of garbage making her nose twinge. "Because they're everywhere. We're all alone now."

All alone.

Tyler dropped his Mega Monsters on to the carpet. He was bored, but also frightened. Taking his mind off things with make-believe Mega Monster scenarios would only work for so long. Tyler was denying the truth, and prolonging his entrapment. Gram was out there somewhere, plodding around the living room, wanting to eat his brains, and it was inevitable that he would have to exit his room. Eventually.

He put his ear to the door, listening for her. Not a peep. She was either gone, or waiting for him in the shadows, ready to jump out and terrorize his delicate senses, like his father had often done. "Gram?" he whispered against the door, wondering if she would respond to him with a grunt, because that is what the undead did. They grunted. Horrible, ugly grunts that were not of this world.

Unlocking the deadbolt, Tyler pulled his race car bed back from the wall, just an inch, enough to open a crack in the door and look through. He climbed up on to the bed, on his knees, and lined up his eyeball with small fissure. No Gram, at least not in his direct line of his sight.

Maybe the human part of her brain had shut down for good. Maybe Gram was gone, fully sucked into the zombie world. Tyler sighed in relief, pulling the bed back a little further. He walked from his room, scanning the hallway and the living area. No sign of his sweet old Gram, she of the Oatmeal Cookie Baking tribe.

She, like his parents, had moved on.

Tyler pulled on the curtain in the den, looking out into the streets below. Zombies roamed, bumping into each other and groaning. They looked confused to him. As though they had lost their puppies, but hadn't the first inkling as to where they should start their search. Some of the gray and green roamers would start off in one direction, careening off a parked car or even a brick wall, turning back in the other direction and wandering until they hit another roadblock. He observed them for several minutes, taking a certain delight in one particular undead beast who was ricocheting off of two aligned parking meters. It would walk into one, turn around, and then walk into the next meter down the line, over and over again. Tyler wondered how long this had gone on for.

They were brain dead. But not like his Gram. Not like … Susie?

Tyler's heart skipped a crucial beat in his chest. He hadn't thought to check Susie's body.

Had she turned as well, and wandered off into the night?

As if she could have read his thoughts, Susie snatched the collar of his pyjamas, turning him around to face her. She was in a horrific condition, ever more maligned than Gram had been. The damage that Gram had done to Susie's face and neck region made her almost unrecognizable. One of her eyes dangled from the socket by a thin tendril of pink flesh. Her scalp had been half pulled back, presumably for easy access for Gram's hungry teeth. Her hair now descended all the way to the back of her knees, following behind her like a hairy shadow of what she had once been.

She growled, sniffing the air as she manhandled Tyler. "Susie, no!" he cried out, trying to pull away from her but finding her grip to be too strong. He reached behind him for leverage, gripping his hand around a flower pot (the flower itself, withered from a lack of care). Susie looked upon her younger brother with one good eye, craning her head as a curious puppy would, some niblet of her consciousness telling her that Tyler had once meant something to her. She had, once upon a lifetime, bossed him around, the unofficial leader of the children of their brood. And now, he was different than she. Or was *she* merely different than *he*?

Tyler let out a sob as he swung the orange pot at Susie's forehead, bursting into a million pieces. She fell to her knees, groaning in anger, then looked up at him, fury pulsating through her. "I'm sorry!" he called out, skirting past her, ready to return to his room. He couldn't hurt Susie again. Not like this. He could pull her hair (although now it may have tore the rest of her scalp off), but never anything more. Deep inside, aside from their squabbles, he loved his sister more than anything. He loved his parents, wherever they went. And his Gram.

As he scuttled to his room, Susie rising from the ground behind him, Tyler considered his food situation. He was starving and would be holed up in his room again. He glanced to the kitchen, and then at Susie, who was touching her forehead with curiosity, unsure of how she had been bested by the strange young boy who seemed quite familiar to her ineffective brain matter.

There were cupcakes, individually wrapped, in the cupboard. In the days and weeks following their parents' turn for the worst, Susie and Tyler had eaten with wise consideration, first consuming the food that would spoil (vegetables, breads, and dairy products), then moving on to the frozen items, then to the canned goods. When Susie had finally turned down that non-retractable path, they had been down to the last of their reserves. Susie had warned him, "We're gonna need more food by next week. We'll have to go out. *Out there.*" They had looked out the window together, holding hands, wondering if there were any other survivors, and where those people were obtaining their food.

Tyler sighed and ran into the kitchen. Before he could pull open the cupboards and fish for sustenance, he came upon Gram. She was staring at the oven, moaning beneath her breath, touching the smooth white surface and the burner coils with puzzled fingertips. She hesitated when Tyler entered the room. He froze where he stood, only three feet away from his mother's decomposing mother. She stood between him and the pantry, which was to the left of the stove. "Gram?" he asked. He sensed defeat in her eyes as she looked upon him. She groaned again, trying to say something that was not there. Looking back to the stove, realization snapped back into play in her head, jerking her head to the side and looking at Tyler again, this time with hunger. She reached out for him, but he gave her no opportunity.

He was back in his bedroom in a dizzy frenzy that he could not label or recall. He had passed Susie, but she was too slow. They were both so docile, but deadly once they had you in

129

their grips. Their strength was unbelievable, though their mobility was hindered by the misfiring synapses in their damaged minds.

Tyler pushed his bed back into place, locking the bolt again, placing his butt on the floor, his back flush against his brightly painted walls. He looked down at his stomach. It started to grumble and protest. Why had he not at least *tried* to get around Gram, to retrieve the cupcakes in the cupboard? He regretted his snap decision.

Why couldn't they just leave him be?

His stomach turned and flipped and screamed bloody murder.

Tyler couldn't keep his eyes focused. He expended as little energy as possible, using his bevy of toys to keep his mind sharp. The hunger that had possessed his whole being was taking its toll. When he napped, he dreamed of roast beef sandwiches and Gram's oatmeal cookies. He dreamed of his parents, as well. And Susie, the way they had once been, and not the monsters they had all become. He dreamed of ice cream and even foods that he would have normally thought to be deplorable, tofu and green beans included. How he would ravage a big wet block of squishy tofu right now. It would have made his mother proud, just to see him eating the stuff.

His Mega Monster toys had started to talk to him. Frankie Deadbolt, a cartoon character loosely based upon Frankenstein's monster, was more vocal than the rest, though he said nothing. He only groaned, and this reminded Tyler of the zombies, and so he avoided Frankie Deadbolt at all costs. "Shut up, Frankie," he would warn, holding the toy up to his face, watching as Frankie's plasticized expression would contort into one of shame.

Vlad the Mad (a modern day Dracula character, dressed in jeans and a t-shirt) would pipe up, "Don't think nothing of that bubble brain. He's only trying to scare you. You can trust us, even with all his pissing and moaning."

"What should I do?" Tyler asked Vlad, bouts of tears trickling down his cheek.

"You're starving, Ty. I can see you withering away to nothing. You need to get those cupcakes. You need to leave this damn building. You need to go shopping, but you also need to be careful," Vlad suggested, all of his advice falling on Tyler's deaf ears. He knew this, all of it. Vlad was no help.

Fish Fingers chuckled at Vlad and Tyler. He was a bulbous eyed, grinning version of the Creature From The Black Lagoon, adapted for children into the whacky goofball of the Mega Monster troupe. "He needs to chop their heads off with a butter knife. That's what he needs to do. Gram and Susie, they're nothing but bad news, and they're not going anywhere. You need to poop on their dead bodies, Tyler! Do it for us! Do it for your friends!" Fish Fingers shouted, cackling in delight as he rubbed his tiny webbed hands together.

"But I can't hurt them. And I can't poop on them. That's gross and it makes my tummy hurt," Tyler reasoned, slumping his head and rolling on the floor, his toys surrounding him like Japanese in a Godzilla movie.

Frankie groaned, a slight grin seeping into his face now.

Vlad shook his head from side to side. "You're starving, kid. You don't eat soon, you're gonna be talking to more than just your toys. You're gonna be talking to God himself. You don't want to die, do you?" Vlad asked.

"No," Tyler replied with a tremble in his voice. It was true. He didn't want to die, even though everybody he loved had already gone that way. There were still joys to be had, though he could not think of them yet. Once he found other survivors, things would start looking up, or so he hoped. If there were other survivors out there.

"Kill them. Kill them all, you bozo," Fish Fingers suggested, his comedic wit turning more sinister.

"I can't. I can't do it."

Fish Fingers threw his green plastic arms in the air, protesting Tyler's obtuse disagreement, "Kill them all, you little shit!"

The grumbling intensified on what felt to Tyler like the millionth (though he knew the word, he could not count that high yet) day of his exile. His mother had never sent him to his room while she was still alive- and not trying to eat people's brain matter- but his father had done so on one occasion. Tyler had accidentally destroyed one of Susie's favourite toys, a doll named Gabby. She had taken an epic ride down the garbage shoot. His father had gone into the basement, in that same place that his children would one day hide in fear of him, and retrieved the doll, but her head had broken off, forevermore. Her doll resembled what Susie now looked like, a mangled dirty mess of inhuman flesh. And for that treachery against her favourite plaything, his father had sent him to his room for an entire Saturday night. To rub salt in the boy's wounds, Susie and his parents had rented a stack of movies from the video store, and had consumed massive amounts of popcorn and peanut butter candy, his fondest sugar fix.

That had felt horrible, but not nearly as bad as this. How Tyler yearned for having his family with him again, if only through the door, in the next room, enjoying themselves while he wallowed in misery. Just to know that they were there for him, ready to step in and defend him from the harsh realities of the world. *Six years old!* He wanted to scream this, and then made that inkling of blurry thought a reality, biting his lip and screaming at his Mega Monsters, "I'm six years old!" They looked up at him, shrugging as if age did not matter, which it did not, when faced with the apocalypse.

He had not heard Susie or Gram stirring outside for several hours, but Tyler could not build up his nerve again. He could not face them, not even for the danger that they presented to him, but for their ghastly appearances. The smell of their disintegrating flesh. They were not the people he knew and loved, and that troubled him deeply.

Tyler put on his last set of clean pyjamas, scanning himself in the mirror. He was as thin as a rail. Tyler, like his undead family, was unrecognizable from his former self. "You don't eat soon," Fish Fingers announced, with Vlad nodding in agreement, "And you're going to die. Do you know that, Tyler? Do you even know what death is yet?"

The boy nodded. He knew the word, but could not quite grasp what he saw in his parents' face when a family member – like his Aunt Ginny when he was four – perished. Their pain, where did it come from? He was starting to realize it. "A devastating event like a zombie infestation tends to do that to you, no matter how old you are," Vlad said. Frankie grunted, nodding his head. "My boy, you're about to grow up really fast," Vlad added.

Fish Fingers readied his next campaign of persuasion, but decided against it. The child was so emaciated that he could barely understand them anymore. They were screaming for notice, but his attention span was dwindling with every quake of his belly. He needed food, and soon.

Tyler awoke with a start.

That smell. He knew that smell.

Sunday mornings during the summer. Tradition, wafting back through the air. While his mother and father ate breakfast, during their vacation at the beach house, his Gram had other plans. "Who needs eggs and toast on a beautiful day like today?" she had once asked Tyler. Her smile had warmed him, and the magnificent odour had pounded that joyous nail home. Susie and he had looked back and forth at each other, wiping away the sleepy disbelief from their eyes.

"I disapprove of this," they had heard their father say to their mother from the dining room.

"We're on vacation. Don't sweat it," their mother had replied, and though they could not see her, they could detect that glowing smile upon her face. She knew exactly what Gram was up to, because she had often done the same thing with her when she was a child.

"Cookies for breakfast?" Susie had asked of her Gram, studying the woman with a face that could not reconcile the absurdity of her suggestion.

Tyler whiffed the air. "Oatmeal!"

"That's right, Ty. Your mom used to eat them when they first came out, when they were still hot. And then she'd start stuffing them into her pockets, for safe keeping she would say. Oh, I tell you. That made her brothers awful mad," Gram explained, a casual glance out the window, as if she could still see that particular day, in her mind, and it was just as pleasant as she remembered it. And now, she was revisiting those rituals with a new generation. "Oatmeal cookies for breakfast. The excuse is in the oatmeal!" she said then, patting their heads and giggling. Their father would not approve, which he had already expressed, but all rules were out the window when Gram was on the scene.

"*They* make us eat bran flakes," Susie noted with disgust, thumbing her nose towards the dining room, where their parents were having a silent argument about their intrusive grandmother. *The crazy old bat!*

"I would never do such a horrible thing to you, my sweet," Gram said to Susie, winking and offering a loose hug.

Tyler inhaled again, and drifted back to reality, to the here and now.

The smell was identical. The same hints of cinnamon and touch of nutmeg. The ground walnuts, sugared and crunchy. The plump raisins, so big that it made you wonder how fat the original grape may have been. Likewise, Gram had been a grape at one time. But now she was a raisin ... a raisin with strong hands and violent hunger.

Tyler could hardly control himself.

"Don't do it!" Vlad blasted.

Fish Fingers piped up next, "Cut their heads off!"

With a sickly feeling pervading his empty stomach, Tyler pulled his bed away from the door and exited his room. The first thing he saw was Susie, standing in the corner of their den, groaning and biting at the drywall. She had clawed away huge chunks of the wall, and was now trying to eat the dusty material. Dust and chips of paint covered her mouth and lips. She stopped, looking to Tyler, the realization drifting into her head that *he* was that boy who had cracked her in the head with the flower pot.

Tyler did not linger.

He could only think of that smell. Of oatmeal cookies.

Tyler drifted into the kitchen, his eyes growing heavy at the sight of his grandmother. The oven was wide open and the heat emanated the entire kitchen. Tyler started to sweat.

Sitting himself at the table, he stared at Gram. The cookies weren't quite done yet, but it was time, all the same.

Reaching into the open oven, Gram grasped at the black

tray of cookies. Half of the cookies were almost finished, but the other half were raw due to a burned out coil. Her hand sizzled as she gripped the pan, turning and trying to smile at her grandson. She wasn't sure what a smile was anymore, but she knew that she simply had to do it, that you could not serve oatmeal cookies without smiling.

Sliding the pan across the table, Gram grunted.

Tyler plucked an almost finished cookie from the wax paper. He shoved the first cookie into his mouth while Gram trundled to the refrigerator, where a spoiled carton of milk awaited. You couldn't have cookies without milk.

With a voracious series of chomps and grunts, Tyler worked his way through half the pan, groaning in delight. They tasted simply magical. Though it was not the best batch his Gram had ever made, it was something special, all the same. He had never felt so gratified in all his life. He smiled at Gram.

Gram dumped a splash of curdled, thickened milk on to the table next to Tyler and he slurped at it.

Silly Gram.

She put her hands on his shoulders, studying the back of his dirty scalp.

He ate his oatmeal cookies.

THE END

IN THE END
By
R. M. Cochran

Independence Day never meant as much as it did over a year later, after the plague had reduced humanity to near nothingness. Only a few ragtag groups were left to defend what was left of civilization, forced to live out their days in compounds haphazardly built, thrown together in the last ditch effort to save what was left of mankind.

Held together by any means possible, the fencing around Donovan's Wake was a series of patchwork, composed of debris left behind by the onslaught of the dead. Doors, refrigerators, trash bins; anything that could be welded or strung together was used to defend the compound. A few cargo containers were upended, used as watchtowers, manned by the few who were skilled enough, or lucky enough to have survived. The loud, idling trucks did little to distract the marksmen, poised on the cargo containers and rooftop, firing into the crowd of creatures who fell, one after the other as their skulls splintered, exploding from the barrage of bullets.

Bolted to two massive pillars that remained from the original fence, the main gate stood constructed out of rod iron, sealed on the outside by sheets of plywood. The monstrosity slid easily on a set of wheels that were salvaged from a compact car, just outside of the compound. Atop the pillars, a set of concrete gargoyles sat poised like watch dogs, looking out at the undead who were gathering in number, waiting for an easy meal.

Having pre-planned a 4th of July celebration for later that night, they coupled the idea with the need for supplies. If there was any time left after the group returned, the party would ensue. They were running painfully low on everything, and the necessity to restock outweighed the much needed reprieve from the seriousness of their situation. In an existence amongst the undead, survival always came first.

Brae looks over the compound wall, his dreadlocks sway in the breeze like the tattered American flag above his head. He stares out at the ocean of bodies spread out in every direction.

They all seem to be following him, eyes locked on his every move. No matter how many of the undead were eradicated, there were always more over the horizon to take their place.

The few survivors that were left at Donovan's Wake were barely holding on, and the growing numbers of the undead only made their hopes fade like the civilization they were trying to hold on to.

Brae didn't know who Donovan was, or why this place was his namesake, and it really didn't matter. All that he cared about now was helping the others so they could get a convoy out, past the gates and into the city to search for supplies.

The engines of the trucks rev in unison as the front gate is opened unleashing the city plough out into the mounds of the undead that litter the streets. Bodies deflect from the thick steel blades on the front of the truck, pushed to the side like so much waste. Popping body parts fill the air with a stench both vile and unrelenting as the trucks flatten flesh and bone on their way out of the compound.

Brae climbs down from the wall and jumps into the passenger seat of one of the big rigs, rifle in tow.

"Took ya long enough," Mitch smiles at Brae through the heavy moustache that covers most of his upper lip.

"Yeah, yeah … just drive," Brae raises an eyebrow, returning the smile in his own way.

Mitch hits the throttle, catching up to the other two trucks as they jerk wildly, bouncing over fallen bodies, slowly crushing them beneath the tread of their tires.

"Now that's music to my ears," Mitch laughs as if he's finally getting to enjoy himself.

"You know man, you're a little sick in the head," Brae comments.

"I know," Mitch laughs again, lighting a cigar with the lighter from the dash.

The engine whines as Mitch floats the gears of the old Kenworth, gaining speed as the tires send bloody gore out of the fender wells, misting the windows with a light film.

"Damn, these bastards sure are messy," Mitch pulls deeply on the cigar, filling the air with smoke from his methodical exhale.

The convoy takes a tight, right hand turn into the warehouse district, speeding up once the corner is made.

A gravelly voice comes through the radio, "It's going to be three stop signs on the right, don't bother with the gate, just run it through."

Brae replies, "Were right behind you, Mark."

Most of the lettering has fallen off the face of the building, revealing W** *art **per S*ore in between scorch marks.

The walkie-talkie squawks to life, "Brae and Mitch back into bay 4, Ed, back into bay 2. We'll get in and open the doors. Make sure the trailers are tight against the building, we don't want any repeats of last time."

"Roger," Brae replies.

"And stop calling me Roger," comes the response, causing Mitch to cough out a cloud of smoke, unable to hold back his laughter.

The snow plough stops in front of one of the side entrances to the warehouse and Mark jumps out, shotgun raised, salt and pepper hair reflecting in the sun. Taking aim at the door, he pulls the trigger, blasting a hole the size of a fist through the metal surface. From behind him, the parking brake of the plough is engaged, sending out a rush of air behind the cab, accompanied by a puff of dust.

Ed has already made contact with the loading bay as Mitch begins backing the truck into position. The trailer slams hard against the bumpers fastened to the wall, startling Brae with the sound of twisting steel and screeching rubber.

Brae is out of the truck and on top of the hood as soon as he feels the impact. Rifle poised, he fires into a small crowd of the undead. With a loud crack, the bullet hits home. The creature stops mid-stride, thrown to the ground in a heap. Its head hits the pavement like a silent prayer in the middle of a battle field. Levelling the rifle again, Brae puts a bead on another pus bag. As he exhales, he pulls the trigger. What used to be a nurse is now but a fragmented face, falling prone to the asphalt, tripping one of the other meat sacks behind her. Like a chain reaction, the other brainless wonders fall suit until all five are on the ground, wallowing in the remains of the first two.

"We're good," Brae yells before Mitch even has a chance to get the door of the rig open.

"Damn, boy. You sure can shoot!" Mitch yells, heading to the door, right behind Ed.

Brae falls to his ass and scoots off the hood, landing firmly on his feet. Like a madman, he sprints to the door, cut off by a pus bag, dressed in a dishevelled suit and tie. Before he can raise his rifle the creature's head explodes, sending a torrent of brain and bone across the pavement next to it.

As the body falls, it reveals a bent moustache smiling back at him.

"We're all going to die in the end, I guess it's just not your time, kid," Mitch states, lowering the smoking revolver to his side.

Brae shakes off the shock, high-tailing it into the warehouse, followed by Mitch who pulls the door closed, locking it with a pin attached to the bottom, firmly kicking it into place.

A series of slams hit the outside of the door like hail on a tin roof. Brae recoils as he lifts his rifle to eye level, panicked by the sudden sound.

"Unless they learn how to pull, they're not getting in," patting Brae on the shoulder as he walks by, Mitch heads over to the rest of the group.

A week's worth of beard growth moves as Mark's jaw drops, saying, "Looks like we've hit the mother load." He stares at the stacks of pallets positioned floor to ceiling in nearly 10,000 square feet of warehouse. "OK, Jesse, you and Ed go grab one of those pallet jacks and start loading the trucks. Mitch, come with me, we're going to find out if this place has a pharmacy."

Brae, still somewhat in shock, "Boss, what should I do?"

"Well, I suppose you can keep staring at the door, or help load the trucks." Mark nods his head before turning, passing through the far door, vanishing into the sales floor beyond.

Tossing his rifle over his shoulder, Brae walks over to Ed, who is inspecting one of the pallets.

"Canned meat. Thank God I lost my taste buds months ago," Ed states shaking his head.

Jesse walks over to the far end of the warehouse in search of a pallet jack while Brae and Ed sort through the rows of boxes. A crash breaks their concentration and they run off after Jesse who is on the ground, struggling with one of the undead who has tackled him to the floor, pinning him to the spot.

Ed is the first to react, pulling his pistol, as a large piece of flesh is pulled free from Jesse's neck. His scream is terrible, only drowned out by the report of the gun. The creature's head snaps back so it's looking straight up like it's asking for a final reprieve from some higher power. Its body falls limp to the side, head bouncing off the cement floor like a deflated ball.

Brae pushes the creature's legs off Jesse to get a better look at the wound. Muscle tissue is exposed beyond a small scrap of skin, torn and twisted with teeth marks around the edges. Ed rips a piece from his shirt and applies pressure to the wound as Mark and Mitch run up from behind.

"Christ, wasn't anyone watching his back?" Mark exclaims, kneeling down beside Jesse who has a blood bubble gurgling up at the edge of his mouth.

Jesse tries to talk, but only air escapes as his eyes roll to the back of his head, prompting Mark to pull his side arm and shoot him between the eyes.

"Damn it, you have to watch out for each other! No more fuck ups. Brae, watch Ed's ass and go get the damn pallet jack. Let's get this shit done and get the fuck out of here," he yells, clearly unnerved.

"Boss, I'm sorry about your ..." Mitch is cut off before he can continue.

"Let's just get the supplies and go."

Mitch and Mark head back into the sales floor to retrieve supplies and as much first aid as they can fit in a couple of packs that they heist from a display on their way through the store.

Brae and Ed load up as much food as they can pack into the trailers, leaving the doors open to escape through the small hatches at the top while waiting for the others to return.

"I should have been watching out for Jesse," Brae exclaims, holding his head in his hands as he sits on the floor, cross legged.

Ed stares down at him. "We both fucked up, you can't

blame yourself for a mistake that it took two of us to make," he shakes his head. "You can't take back what has already happened."

Mark and Mitch return with several packs, loaded to bursting, and throw them into the trailer.

Turning back to Brae, Mark can see the torment in his face. "Listen, kid, it could have happened to any one of us, you're not the only one to blame. We're all in this together, and hell, I could have probably been watching out too."

"I'm sorry, Mark," Brae adds, rising to his feet and taking a deep breath.

"It's OK, kid. Let's get his body and get the fuck out of here."

They wrap Jesse's body in a plastic tarp and place it in the trailer, at the very back, away from the supplies.

Looking through the hole left by the shotgun blast, Mark peers through the door, "Fuck, there's too many of them out there, I'm not going to be able to get to the plough." Looking back at Ed, he continues, "I guess I'll be catching a ride with you."

From inside the trailers, each group of men, stationed at the opposing trucks, close the doors, leaving the warehouse bays open to the elements.

Escaping through the roof hatch, using the crates as a ladder, Brae peers out at the sea of the undead that have gathered around the trucks. There are hundreds of them, shoulder to shoulder, packed in tightly against the vehicles, leaving little room for escape.

"Shit," Mitch's voice is shaky, "I left the driver's side window open, you'll have to go first."

"Fuck you! You go first!" He yells back at Mitch.

"I'll take the rifle and cover you. It'll be alright, trust me," Mitch reassures him.

Brae blows out a breath of panic from his lungs, trying to calm himself. It looks like he is testing the temperature of a pool as he reluctantly steps down onto the mirror frame, sliding his other foot onto the edge of the door.

He hears screaming, followed by a series of shots, just

141

above his head. Sliding into the cab backwards, he can see Mitch firing towards the other truck as he feels something tug at his hair. He pulls hard, and one of his dreads is yanked free, clutched tightly in the hand of one of the creatures. Its nudity takes Brae back a bit as he scans the waste between its legs, realizing the thing had once been a man, but now resembles a butchers experiment gone wrong. He steadies himself, sliding fully into the cab, and looks past the monstrosity to see Ed slip from the roof of the other truck, landing, back first into the crowd of hungry hands.

Mark fires madly into the crowd. Emptying the shotgun, he pulls his side arm, levelling it at the newly formed horde that fills in the space where the others had stood.

Brae can't see what's happening on the other side of the truck where Ed landed, but the screams are more than enough to assault his imagination. What he does see is Mark empty his pistol and jump into the crowd after Ed, madness overtaking him.

He sees Mitch's leg on the door, followed by the other, gracefully sliding into the cab like he's done it a million times before.

The big rig roars to life as Mitch hits the ignition and slips it into gear. Releasing the clutch, he floats it into second gear, making the rig gain speed.

"Wait, what about Mark?" Brae's alarm is obvious.

Mitch points toward the other truck as they pass the gore, saying nothing. Brae opens his window, throwing up along the truck, spewing bile and chunks out against a few of the straggling undead.

"God, why did he do it?" Brae asks, wiping his mouth on the sleeve of his sweatshirt.

"Kid, not everyone is cut out to accept fate. He just lost it."

Solemn, Brae eases back into his seat, staring at the ceiling of the cab with his hand over his mouth. He had befriended Mark the first day he waded through the spent bodies of the dead and made his way into the compound. It was hard to think of him as gone, hard to face the fact that he would never see him again.

142

If he could count how many people he had lost along the way, he would probably curl up in a tight little ball on his bed at the compound and never move again. He does his best to push those memories out of his head, to never think of the shitty hand life had dealt him. It was always better to forget. It was always better to repress those memories and get on with the fight for survival, but it didn't make it any less painful.

With a deep exhale, Brae looks out at the road ahead, watching the random undead as they pass by. It's hard to believe those things were ever human. That they, just like him, had lost loved ones, had endured the sorrow of the fallen.

"Look at them," Mitch points out at a random corpse, walking in circles at the edge of the street.

"What about them?"

"They're so fucking pointless. That's how it ends, no matter who you are, that's how we all end up. But you can never think for a moment that they are people, you hear me?"

"Mitch, they are people . . . or were, at least."

"Who they were doesn't matter, it's what they are now, and what they are now would sooner chew off your face than let you pass by."

The truck tilts dangerously as Mitch makes the next turn, holding tightly to the wheel, he pulls the vehicle through, glancing off of a wrecked passenger car that is half way out into the street.

"Alright, we don't have the plough, so it's going to get bumpy when we start getting close," Mitch breaks the silence. Pointing out the inevitable, "You might want to hold on."

With that, the rig begins to bounce, losing traction on the gore, and sending up chunks of pulp once the tires grab asphalt. Brae gains flight several times as the air ride seat overcompensates against the unnatural road conditions, jogging him back and forth along the cushion.

Terror falls over Brae's eyes as he sees the compound coming into view, "What the fuck?"

"Son of a bitch!" Mitch exclaims as he peers through the partially open gate. The undead are flooding in and out through the opening with scraps of fat and flesh hanging out of their wretched maws.

He slams the brakes, nearly jack-knifing the rig and suddenly begins tapping them repeatedly to slow the truck down rather than twist it up into a heap. He slows the truck considerably, and begins to inch it forward through the pulpy mess from earlier in the day. The tires slip ever so slightly upon the remains, tendon and bone letting loose against the mud flaps. As his jaw drops wide from the scene laid out before him, "They're gone . . . every one of them."

"It was a massacre," Brae exclaims, putting his hand over his mouth like someone trying to keep their soul from escaping.

Bodies crawl over one another, tripping and sliding through the spilled entrails, all trying to work their way into the compound. A triumphant moan escapes from a corpse that has become androgynous through decay, indescribable in its putrification.

"What do we do?" asks Brae, at the edge of a full on break down.

"We get the fuck out of here!" Mitch replies, turning the rig down the next street, the eight wheels of the tractor slipping slightly on the soup beneath them.

"But what about everyone?" Brae cries, looking at what is left of the compound as the truck passes.

"Listen, kid. Everyone is gone. No one could survive that, no one."

"But Mitch, we can't just leave them there. There has to be somebody alive!" he pleads.

"God damn it, kid! There's nothing we can do. There are only the two of us. I don't know about you, but I'm down to only a few rounds. You need to get a grip, it's fucking hopeless."

Silence falls over them. Mitch knows that there might be a slim possibility that someone could still be trapped in there, but common sense, the very thing that has kept him alive for so long, says to keep moving.

Brae, still in shock, leans into his hands, weeping, "Fuck Mitch, everyone?"

"You saw as clearly as I did. If anyone did survive, chances are that they're smart enough to get out of there," Mitch squints his eyes, and then opens them wide like he suddenly remembered something. "We'll head to the compound in Chicago like everyone planned if something went wrong. If anyone survived, that's where they'll go."

Mitch's response did little to reassure Brae, he had seen this happen before and the outcome was never positive. He couldn't even believe there would be anything left of Chicago either. It was hard to find hope in a world controlled by the undead.

All he could do was stare out the window, watching the abandoned cars go by, caught up in the sorrow he felt for everyone who was lost that day.

This was truly Independence Day, independent from life, liberty and the pursuit of happiness. For where the undead roam free, you have a snowball's chance in hell of seeing tomorrow.

Mitch pulls the big rig off the two lane highway, slowly cruising the lot before engaging the brakes, parking in the front of an abandoned gas station.

He is worried about Brae. The kid hadn't said a word for nearly eighty miles, and it was beginning to become unnerving. He had never known the kid to be so quiet. Brae was never much of a talker, but he would occasionally drop a joke or two for good measure.

"Brae, what I meant when I said that everyone dies in the end is that no one gets out alive, no matter what you do, everyone eventually fades away into whatever oblivion it is that exists on the other side of life.

You'll never know when it's going to happen, and there's no way to prepare for it. People die. That's the end goal. It's what you do up to that point that really matters.

You just have to take it on the chin and do your best to keep on fighting. We live in a world full of nightmares, and until that nightmare is over, we have no other choice than to fight. Do you understand what I'm saying?"

"Yeah, Mitch. I understand," Brae replies.

Mitch grabs Brae by the arm, forcing him to look into his eyes, "Damn it, Brae. There was nothing we could do!"

"I know Mitch," Brae's voice is detached and distant.

145

"OK, kid. I need to get some sleep. We'll leave first thing in the morning. Chicago is only a hundred and twenty miles away, so we should be able to make it by tomorrow night," Mitch says, moving the clipboard from between the seats, and negotiating over the rope and supplies that are laying in the way of the sleeper.

"I'll pull out the bottom bunk for you. You should probably get some sleep too," Mitch states, situating himself.

"Yeah, I will. I'm just going to stay up for a little while longer," Brae replies, still staring out the window.

Mitch settles down into the sleeper, wrestling with himself to go to sleep. In his mind, all he sees is death. Wave after wave of images, warped and twisted; faces of those who were lost, transforming into the undead, frame by frame.

He wakes up in the middle of the night, checking on Brae who is passed out in the passenger seat. He turns over bunching the pillow up beneath his head, surrendering to a few more hours of unconsciousness.

Brae nestles his rifle closely, hardly finding sleep between moments of sorrow and uncertainty. The day plays over and over in his mind. He sees Jesse, Mark's younger brother laying on the cold concrete, blood seeping through his shirt, puddling up below him. He recalls Ed slipping from the cab of the other truck, the look on his face as he goes down. He can see Mark jumping in to save him. The snarl of an animal spreads across his face, the sorrow of losing someone close, battering him deep inside.

"I'm sorry, Mark. I'm sorry, Mark. I'm sorry ..."

Startled, Mitch awakens, sitting up fully in the sleeper. He can't see Brae and immediately senses that something is wrong. It wasn't like him to just up and leave.

He crosses over into the driver's seat and stretches out his arm to open the door when something catches his eye. The clipboard that he had been left between the seats last night, now laying on the passenger seat.

Across the driver's log sheet, left by the previous owner, a note is scribbled in dark black ink ...

He flies out of the truck running with everything he has.

There, swinging from the canopy, just above the gas pumps, hangs Brae's undead body, his neck red where the rope burnt his skin from the friction of his movements.

Brae's arms reach out in a futile attempts to reach Mitch, kicking at the air, trying to get closer, bent on the promise of warm flesh.

"Ah hell, kid ..." he says, pulling the revolver from his side, turning back and forth in frustration.

Using the barrel of the gun, he tilts back his baseball cap, shaking his head in disbelief. He pulls back the hammer of the pistol, taking careful aim, lining up the sight, dead centre on Brae's forehead.

"God damn it, kid. It didn't have to be this way," he says to himself, pulling the trigger, landing one clean shot between Brae's eyes.

Firing once more, the rope snaps, dropping the body to the ground in a heap. Mitch ties the rope to Brae's feet, dragging him away, towards the rig.

After a few minutes of sorting through the sleeper, he comes out holding a small, military shovel and begins to dig. Sweat beads up on his face, he wipes it away with his shirt sleeve, glancing back at Brae's body.

He drops Brae into the earth and covers him with a blanket he retrieved from the truck. Checking over his shoulder every few minutes to make sure he's still alone, he fills the hole, losing the boy with every scoop he adds.

He has never been one for long good-byes, and he doesn't know how to start now. He tilts his hat over his brow, mutters a few words under his breath and walks back to the truck.

From inside the cab, he looks out through the windshield, holding back an emotion he hasn't felt in a very long time. His eyes are glazed over as he wipes his face, ending at the grizzly brush upon his face.

Turning to the seat next to him, he reads the note, one last time:

We all die in the end.

THE END

NAKED FEAR
By
Tonia Brown

Howard kept his eyes downcast, watching as the sun-warmed sand crunched under his timid steps, tumbling over his toes and dusting his bare feet in a layer of soft, gentle white. It wasn't that the sand was particularly interesting. It was the view that awaited him — should he lift his eyes — that had his vision glued to the ground. He clutched his complimentary robe tighter about himself and shuffled along, step by nervous step, wondering if he could really do this, knowing he couldn't.

"Come on now, Howard," Martin whispered. "It's going to be okay. Trust me."

"Trust you?" Howard asked Martin's liver-spotted feet, because he was unable to bear raising his head enough to talk to Martin's liver-spotted face. Or the other liver-spotted bits of the old man. "I trusted you for five years, and look where it's gotten me."

"I'm only trying to help you."

"I'm starting to doubt that."

"I'm your friend."

"You're a crazy man."

"Now, now. That's my line." Martin was smiling.

Howard didn't have to look to see it. He could feel it in the man's words.

Martin cleared his throat before he added, "And besides, hands-on therapy is good for the psyche."

"Hands on!" Howard's heart raced at the thought of someone actually touching him. It was bad enough being seen like this. "You said it was all look and no touch!"

"Calm down. You know what I mean."

Howard supposed he did. But still … "None of that changes the fact that you're a crazy man."

"That's as it may be; I'm also your therapist. Now lift your head and look around."

"No."

"Come on. At least take off that robe. You look silly with it on."

"I can't." Howard's lip quivered. And where there was lip quivering, tears were bound to follow. Which was par for the course, he supposed. Only he would end up in tears on a gorgeous beach in the middle of summer on such a beautiful day.

And all because he was afraid to be nude.

No. It was more complicated than that.

Howard Straw wasn't just afraid of his own nudity, he was terrified of it. His was a commonly misunderstood condition, often misclassified as someone ashamed of his naked self, but nothing could be farther from the truth. Physically, he knew he was normal for his age, with nothing to be ashamed of: normal weight, height, build and, from what he had been told, he was blessed in certain anatomical areas. Yet he couldn't bring himself to expose this normality to others, or himself. Even alone, in the shower, in the bed, he always wore something, anything, to keep from being naked. He wasn't exactly comfortable with others being naked, but just the mere thought of someone seeing him in the buff sent him into a cold, sweaty panic.

"Howard," Martin begged.

"I can't do it," he said.

"Of course you can. Here. I'll make it easy for you. I'll go first."

Howard's eyes widened to saucer proportions when he heard the telltale slither of the old man's dressing gown slip open. He watched in horror as Martin's robe – the only thing that kept the doctor's wrinkled rear from facing the rest of the world – slid down his calves and pooled at his bare feet like the shed skin of some terry-clothed animal.

"Ah," Martin sighed. "Very liberating. I should have done this years ago. Your turn."

"I can't."

"Look, son, we agreed before we left that you would see this to the end."

"But I just can't."

"You signed a contract with me. Remember? You're not going to welsh on your word are you? That would violate our therapist-patient bond. I mean, how can I trust you if you're just a liar?"

Howard bristled. That was a low tactic, calling a man a liar. "I'm not a liar."

"Then prove it. Drop your robe."

"No."

"Young man, I will not tolerate this kind of nonsense. We have come too far for you to start regressing on me. Now, raise your eyes and look at the people around you. The naked people."

Howard hated when Martin said that word aloud. The old coot always stressed it like it was a disease of some sort. But the old coot was right. Five years and thousands of dollars worth of therapy had left him brave enough to agree to this lunacy. He couldn't back out now. He was under doctor's orders; a brief visit to an all-nude resort was surely the cure for his weary soul.

"Raise your eyes," Martin commanded.

Just to silence the badgering old coot, Howard took a deep breath and did as he was asked. To his surprise, everyone looked normal. Nude, but normal. Folks were playing volleyball or swimming or sunbathing, all in the natural. A handful of people were pleasant to look at – shapely bodies with well-proportioned assets. The majority were, well, not as pleasant to look at. But, more importantly, no one was pointing or laughing or running or screaming. They were just … living.

It was peaceful. Nude, naked, exposed peace.

It bolstered Howard's courage. He stood a little taller. Breathed a little easier.

"That a boy," Martin said, patting Howard's back.

Howard looked to his now-nude therapist, and winced. Somehow the effect wasn't as peaceful when he knew the dressed person beforehand. His glance darted south for a moment, below the other man's waist, before he quickly looked back up to greet Martin's smiling eyes.

"Not bad for an old man, eh?" Martin asked, waggling his furry eyebrows.

Howard refused to answer those eyebrows.

"Take off that robe," Martin said.

"I don't know if I'm ready," Howard whined.

"As your doctor, and your friend, I declare that you have never been readier."

Howard was pretty sure that was Martin's afternoon Martini talking, but he also knew that it was indeed now or never. The doctor was right about at least one thing: Howard did look silly in the robe among a sea of nude bodies. He was the odd man out in this situation. For once, by not being nude, he was the outsider. And perhaps that was the whole point of this exercise. Howard Straw closed his eyes, drew a deep breath, undid the tie of his robe, and let it fall to the sand.

To his delight, the world did not explode.

The warm sun caressed his bare bottom.

A salt-laden breeze stirred the hair across his bare legs and arms and other places.

A woman screamed.

Howard opened his eyes. That didn't sound right. The brochure said nothing about screaming. The brochure said he would find acceptance among the other nudists, no matter his body type. Was his greatest fear true? Was he really that odd looking? Did he truly have something to be ashamed of? Could he ever be naked again?

The woman screamed once more, and Howard scrambled for his robe.

"What's going on over there?" Martin asked. He snatched Howard by the shoulder and jerked him toward the commotion. "Come on. They might need help."

Howard didn't have time to grab the terrycloth covering.

After a short nude sprint, or rather a short nude drag behind the overexcited therapist, Howard found himself standing at the waterline, very close to a woman sprawled on her back across the wet sand. She was quite beautiful, with wide hips and blond hair and full breasts – or breasts that would have been full if it weren't for the fist-sized chunk taken out of the left one. The woman writhed on the ground, screaming blue murder and bleeding all over the place.

The beach frothed with a pink lather; crimson blood and white sand mixed into foam by her ever-kicking heels.

"Get away from my wife," said a hefty man, who stood over the woman in a protective stance.

"I'm a doctor," Martin said. "I can help."

The hefty man relaxed at that and moved to one side, giving Martin access to his injured wife. In a gathering crowd of exposed breasts and free-swinging genitalia and plump rumps, all Howard could focus on was the woman's mauled body. The sight nauseated him. Nudity was one thing, but this was something else. This wasn't therapy. It was the opposite of therapy. It was … nightmare-apy.

"What happened?" Martin asked.

"Something attacked her," the hefty man said.

"What?"

The man shrugged. "Shark maybe?"

"He bit me!" the woman screamed as she clutched her mangled breast. "He just came out of nowhere in the water and bit me!"

"Who?" Martin asked.

But the woman never got a chance to answer. She just closed her eyes, gave a single violent shudder from head to toe, and then fell still. No one spoke for several seconds, which felt like an eternity to Howard. The circling crowd stood in silence and stared at the bleeding body, unsure what to do next.

At length, her husband asked, "Is she okay?"

Martin took on a grim look as he passed his hand over the woman's eyes, closing them and answering the husband's question without speaking.

"What attacked her?" Howard asked.

As if on cue, another woman screamed. Then another. Men joined in the hollering, and all at once, the beach was pandemonium, parting in a scramble away from the water's edge. That's when Howard saw them: a group of men, five in all, staggering onto the sand from the surf. They looked ill, sickly green and bloated about the neck and face. But odder than that was the fact that they were clothed. Each man sported a ragged set of combat fatigues that had seen better days. They weren't part of the resort, neither staff nor visitors.

At first Howard wasn't sure what the big deal was, why folks were running away and screaming, until one of the men lunged at a nearby old lady and sank his teeth into her neck. Howard stared, wide-eyed and open-mouthed, as the woman's crimson life squirted in an arc against a sparkling background of oceanic blue.

In seconds, the beach went from pandemonium to full-scale chaos.

The nudists scattered, copious amounts of flesh bouncing and bobbing, this way and that, all in an effort to escape the mauling maniacs and their rabid attacks. Howard's senses were overwhelmed in an instant. He could barely handle seeing other naked people, but to bear witness as they ran amuck, crawling and ducking and rolling, all in the altogether ... It was just too much for him. His psyche shut down. He closed his eyes, locked his knees and seared himself to the spot. He couldn't move. He wouldn't move.

Under the shrieking, he heard the widowed husband ask, "Honey?"

A low growl met Howard's ears.

"You're still alive!" the husband shouted.

The growls grew louder, and the husband's shouts warped into pain-filled screams.

"Come on, Howard!" Martin yelled.

Howard could hear Martin calling his name, could feel the aged therapist yanking on his arm. But Howard wasn't on the beach anymore. He was in his happy place. In his mind, he was at home, wrapped in his warm blanket, under which he had several layers of clothing on. He was not on a nude beach. He was not surrounded by excited, running, naked people.

"Howard!" Martin yelled. Then he shrieked in surprise, perhaps even pain, "Get off of me, you harpy!" The next sound the therapist made was a strangled, wet choke and cough and gurgle. After this, he made no noise at all.

Wet warmth splattered across Howard's torso.

Howard decided to risk a peep to see what this fresh hell was, and immediately wished he hadn't. A sheet of crimson painted Howard's chest and tummy, but it wasn't his own blood.

153

It belonged to Martin, who now lay at Howard's feet, split groin to gullet, like a human watermelon dropped on the sidewalk from very high up. Over the yawing cavity that once was Dr. Martin Jones, stooped the dead blonde. Only she wasn't quite as dead as she had been just moments before. She stared up at Howard through cloudy eyes as she gnawed upon the loose, wet loops of Martin's innards. Just a few feet behind them lay the twitching body of her husband, his blood-soaked groin missing a few vital organs.

Gagging, Howard turned his head from the gory scene just in time to see a certain blood-covered little old woman get to her feet, ragged throat and all. The octogenarian ran with a speed that belied her age, and then launched herself at a portly man who was doing his best to waddle to safety. The pair of them tumbled to the sand, arms and legs and naked parts entangled, gore flying fast and furious.

Another growl arose, and with it, Howard found his feet, running full tilt toward the bathhouse in the distance, sprinting away from the blonde and her now-rising husband. All around him, people were screaming and fighting and dying. He'd lost track of the five soldiers, but that no longer mattered. It didn't take a genius to realize what was happening here. Perhaps not the why, but Howard had a handle on the what. The original five were just the beginning; for each following victim that struck the ground, there came a new threat.

Make that a nude threat.

Howard skidded into the bathhouse, and whipped about to close the door behind him. Handle in hand, he paused – for a millisecond, a breath, a single heartbeat – to stare at the carnage. The beach was alive with the unclothed dead, some walking, some running, some slithering along on their blood-slicked bellies, all seeking fresh flesh to rend. The panicked crowd ebbed and flowed in all directions, a naked throng manic for shelter. Most fell under the mauling hands and gnawing teeth of their crazed nudist brethren before they could find safety.

Howard slammed and locked the door behind him, praying the thin barrier would hold. Within seconds of his securing the door, a flurry of pounding arose from it. Whether it was hapless victims seeking help, or the maniacs hot on his trail, he didn't stick around to find out. Howard set off again, running the length of the narrow bathhouse until he emerged from the opposite end. He had to get the hell out of this nightmare resort.

The gravel walkway that led from the bathhouse to the main entrance cut his bare feet as he ran along, but Howard ignored the little bites and pushed forward, seeking a safe haven from this insanity. He was in good shape, though not an athlete by any stretch of the imagination. But he supposed that with the right motivation – such as fear for life and limb – he could and would run for a very long time. The walkway ended in a parking lot, which Howard forwent, seeing as how he'd left his keys in his pants. And his pants were in his room at the hotel. And the hotel was back there, with those things.

Howard slowed at the end of the lot, near the road, stopping for a moment to catch his breath. As he stood, stooped, with his hands on his knees, heaving for precious air, he heard the roar of an engine behind him. A bright red Mustang zipped past him, but before it reached the road, it came to a screeching halt. At first Howard thought the driver was stopping to offer him a ride. The driver's side door swung open, and out popped a screaming brunette woman, heading for the bushes along the drive.

"It got in my car!" she yelled as she ran past Howard in a wobbling limp.

No sooner had she spoken than a blood-soaked man leapt from the confines of the car and set off after the limping woman. The man was missing his right arm, but his injuries didn't seem to slow him one bit. Howard never got a chance to react, and neither did the woman. Like a rabid beast, the one-armed man snarled and lunged for the limping gal, dragging her to the ground with his single hand, and spilling her blood across the asphalt with nothing but his gnashing teeth.

The sight of this once again encouraged Howard to flee. He leapt over the struggling couple and ducked into the still-running car. Slamming it into gear, Howard put his pedal to the metal, burned rubber, and left a smoking trail behind him as he fled the scene. He had to find help. And fast.

The village that bordered the nudist resort was a mere five miles away. With the help of the sports car, Howard was able to reach the town in record time. Along the way, he found a towel draped across the passenger headrest, and used it to clean the blood from his body, trying his best to stay on the road as he retched and wiped. He pulled onto Main Street doing an easy eighty, and came to a screeching halt just outside the first building he found, a place called Mother's Diner. The diner was bound to have a phone, as well as other folks he could warn. Others had to know what was happening. The world needed to be warned of the dangers on the beach. Howard sprang from the car, hustled up the sidewalk and burst into the busy diner.

"Help!" he cried. "Please help me!"

All movement and sound in the diner ceased, as every patron stopped what they were doing – some in mid-bite, some mid-drink, some mid-conversation – and stared at Howard. A woman shrieked, not very loud but enough to set Howard's already frayed nerves on edge. He spun in place and pressed his face against the glass doors of the diner, seeking the source of the woman's concern, certain something or someone had followed him here.

There was nothing. No one.

Howard turned again to face the occupants of the diner. "Please. Call nine-one-one. There's been an accident on the beach." Taking a few steps forward, he raised his hands, entreating them for help.

Another woman screamed. Mothers and fathers throughout the room covered their children's eyes. The diner seemed to shrink away from him, as a whole, shying from his oncoming form. Howard was bewildered. Why would they reel from him? He wasn't one of those things. He was alive! He was trying to warn them!

"Sir?" a man to his right asked.

Howard swivelled his head to the question, narrowing his eyes in utter confusion.

The man smirked and pointed at Howard. "You can't come in here like that."

A little girl giggled, and inside her tittering laughter, Howard realized his mistake.

In all of his struggle to survive, in his race for his very life, he didn't have time to stop and dress. He hadn't even thought about it. So there he was, standing bare-ass naked in a diner filled with fully dressed folks. And he also realized that he just didn't care. All at once, his fear of being nude, of seeing others nude, of nudity itself, seemed silly. Meaningless. Stupid. In the face of this real threat, this terrible ungodly happening, being naked ranked very low on his list of concerns.

At the top of that list was getting out of this alive.

As for everything else, as far as he was concerned, clothing was optional.

THE END

UNDEAD SIDE OF THE MOON
By
Lyle Perez-Tinics

To Whom It May Concern:

My name is Elroy Collins and I am sitting in a prison cell awaiting punishment for a crime I did not commit. The trial is over and I have been convicted of the murder of my team and every resident at the Moonlit Resort. The only thing left for me to do is to write down my side of the story, so I am writing this as a true and honest account of those events. Perhaps someday, this letter will help prove that the Zilith Corporation covered up the truth.

We needed to learn to take care of planet Earth before we headed off into outer space. I was against opening the Moonlit Resort for business so soon, but the Zilith Corporation wouldn't listen. Why would they listen to a roughneck like me? I was just head of their covert search and rescue team; no one important.

In 2036, the Zilith Corporation was responsible for the Apophis asteroid impact. By this time, NASA had lost all funding due to the rise of privately funded space exploration. After it disbanded, the Zilith Corporation released suspect evidence, stating that NASA had made a catastrophic error and that the asteroid *was* on a collision course with Earth. The United States Government authorised Zilith to shift the asteroid's orbit in order to ensure that the near Earth object struck the Moon, instead of Earth. The mission was a success and the entire world watched as Apophis collided with the Moon.

I had been only fifteen years old, but I remember it as clear as if it were yesterday. In fact, watching that event changed my life. It was then that I fell in love with space travel and dreamt of becoming a Space Marshal. The impact threw a great cloud into the atmosphere that gave the viewing billions on Earth a glimpse of a stunning light show.

The Zilith Corporation was hailed for saving the world and the people rejoiced. Then, as is the way, the people went back to

158

their lives. Like the Moon landings in 1969 and the Space Race between the United States and the Soviet Union, the people lost interest.

Five years after the Apophis collision, the Zilith Corporation revealed their plan to build a multi-trillion dollar resort on the surface of the Moon. The dust storms had still not settled from the impact, but advances in nano-technology and an abundance of raw materials made the audacious plan more viable than ever. A sustainable air supply was still a major issue, Zilith's bioengineering labs were working on an artificial lung mechanism, and they were just a step away from surgically implanting their invention into a handful of human test subjects. I'm no scientist, so I can't go into any detail. To this day, I am still unaware of any successes.

Despite the atmospheric problems the Apophis collision had caused, Zilith Corporation managed to fully erect the first lunar hotel in only seven years. A team of international scientists chose the site, and, by 2048, the hotel was completed. As with the Apophis collision, the world was glued to their E-vision sets as Zilith streamed live video and photos during the final stages of construction.

I had been working security for Zilith for two years by the time construction was completed. Zilith was not the kind of company that advertised openly for recruits; if they were impressed with your achievements, they would find you. I was stunned when a recruiter visited me at my graduation. I finished first in my Space Marshal training class and went straight to work for Zilith, with my own team to oversee.

Officially, they claimed that no lives had been lost in the construction, but I know the truth. Zilith has a PR machine second to none, with politicians, media magnets and officials in its pockets. I personally lost two friends to the project. Their excavator hit a gas pocket and they were blown into space. Their supervisor told me the truth before he died from a heart attack.

The Moonlit Resort remained closed for the next five years, while it underwent stringent safety and stress testing. When the doors finally opened in 2053, the rooms were fully booked for the first four years. A one night stay was a flat rate of one-million per head, plus an additional fifty-grand for the lunar shuttle ride each way. Needless to say, the only people able to afford the trip were the extremely wealthy.

Everything ran like clockwork, until we suddenly lost communication with them only a few weeks ago. What follows is my firsthand account ...

We lost communication with the Moonlit Resort on December 28, 2059. The next departing shuttle was put on hold until we could regain contact and work out what the problem was.

For a week, engineers tried to restore the link, but without success. The Zilith Corporation maintained a total media blackout throughout. With communications still down, my team was despatched to find out what had happened. I didn't understand at the time. What reason could there be to send an armed response team? There was already a significant security presence at the hotel and no distress call had been sent. I was certain that it would just be an antenna malfunction, so surely it was just an engineering issue. We expected a simple antenna failure, but our training insisted that we planned for the worst.

"Space Marshal Collins," I heard someone say as I packed my kit bag. I turned to Sam Wallace. He was my direct line manager to the big wigs at Zilith Corp.

"Sir?" I looked into his dark eyes. His white hair was unkempt and he looked like he hadn't slept for several days.

"I have a message for you from upstairs." He retrieved a digitally sealed memo and handed it to me, saying, "Good luck."

"Thanks, Sam," I said as we shook hands.

He walked out of the room without another word.

Frowning, I opened the note, which read,

Space Marshal Collins

This investigation is highly confidential. Neither you nor your team may not have any contact with family or friends until fully debriefed at the end of the mission. You will be in direct violation of your contract if you disobey this directive and will be subject to severe penalties. We expect you to

160

report in within four days. Thank you for your loyalty to the company. Be Safe.

Zilith Corporation

I could understand their need for secrecy, given the circumstances, so I thought nothing more of it and stowed the note in my back pocket. After finishing packing, I flung the sack over my shoulder and headed towards the staging room.

"Space Marshal. Ten-hut!" Mick barked. The four other men in the room instantly stood to attention.

"At ease," I replied. I had never quite gotten used to men snapping to attention like that in my presence. Besides, these men were not just my team, they were my trusted friends. "Are you guys ready?" I asked, looking around the room.

Patrick Swan, our pilot, stood wringing his hands together. Next to him, was Mick Greenwell, my second in command and the deadliest sharpshooter I had ever seen with an S-801 rifle. He was a big man with long black hair tied in a ponytail.

John Megs was our communications specialist. I was expecting John to have the hardest job of the lot of us. He had tagged along with us on several previous missions to Moonlit Resort and he had gradually become part of the team, even though, officially, he was only a technical liaison.

Still packing, were the two brothers, Orlando and Austin Flint. Their job was straightforward firepower.

Staring at the brothers, I said, "We're on the move in five mikes. John, start your final checks and get us ready for flight."

The men nodded and began filing out of the room.

Space flight had moved on pre-2020. Shuttles resembled inflated airliners and our jump ship was not much larger than an F-16 fighter jet. It took the Apollo missions three days to reach the Moon. Our ship would reach it in approximately twenty two hours.

Orlando, Austin and I walked into the spacecraft. John and Mick were already strapped in. Patrick was at the control console, prepping for takeoff. I took a seat next to him, while Orlando

161

and Austin stowed our packs and weapons in the storage containers.

Our weapons weren't that different to the ones used on Earth. Bullets must be exploded out of their casing, but in order for it to fire, there needs to be oxygen present, which is a major issue in space. The casings we use are slightly bigger in order to entrap more oxidizer to propel the bullet. One noticeable difference is that rate of fire and accuracy are both considerably increased in space due to reduced atmospheric pressure.

"Control, this is Shadow Three, copy?" Patrick was saying. "We are go for launch. Please confirm for Runway Alpha. Over."

After a pause, the response was, "Copy, Shadow Three, I have you as an unscheduled departure, but I have no record of authorisation. Please confirm. Over."

Patrick looked questioningly at me. Switching to external comms, I said, "Control, this is Shadow One, copy? This is black ops authorised. Contact Wallace for confirmation. Over."

After another lengthy pause, Control replied, "Shadow One, you're clear for takeoff in t-minus five for Runway Alpha. Over."

"Thank you, Control. Shadow One over and out." I said then returned external comms to Patrick.

I glanced back at my team, who were holding on to their seats. Take off and landing was always a tense time. They were outwardly relaxed, but I knew their muscles would be like coiled springs, awaiting that final lurch into outer space.

Patrick began the countdown. "Powering up in three, two, one," he said as he turned on the first thruster. The aircraft began to move forward slowly. "Firing thruster two in three, two, one." He flipped the switch for thruster two. The ship jolted forward and rushed along the runway at over a hundred miles an hour.

"Ah shit, here we go!" someone in the back yelled.

I gripped my seat as Patrick said, "Firing thruster three in, three, two, one … Hold on to your hats!" He pushed the third thruster.

The ship surged up to three hundred miles an hour. Patrick pulled back on the steering column and the ship lurched into the air.

As the ship gradually increased altitude, Patrick said, "Turbo in three, two, one." He pushed the red button. The spacecraft rocketed towards the upper atmosphere at over 25,000 miles an hour.

"I love this shit!" Patrick yelled.

"Knock it off," I managed to say.

Patrick levelled out and punched the destination into the nav-com. When the target location was locked, Patrick released the controls and sat back. The ship blasted through Earth's atmosphere in seconds and the shuddering began to subside.

The rest of the team were already applying the masks. Patrick was quick to follow suit. I was the only one who would rather wait twenty-two hours than be knocked out. As they drifted off, I stared out of the portal into the blackness of space.

I had travelled into space more than a dozen times before, but I never tired of the view.

I awoke with a start from a natural, not induced sleep. Twenty-one hours had passed. As the others slowly began to stir, I began preparations for the arrival.

As Patrick regained control from the nav-com, the rest of the team did an equipment and weapons check.

"You know the drill," I said. "We check the communications array first. If we get green lights, we move on to the Moonlit Resort. We proceed with caution every step of the way." The thrusters shut down and we began descending.

I caught a glimpse of the communications tower. Outwardly, the structure appeared undamaged. "Set us down as near to the tower as you can. We'll head to the hotel complex on foot from there."

The ship dropped vertically and landed with a jolt. The craft groaned as it settled onto the lunar soil. A clear liquid released from several vents underneath the ship and sprayed the landing zone. The Moon's dust was prone to clogging thrusters and filters, so the purge prevented that from happening.

"Grab your gear," I said as everyone unbuckled.

Our respirators resembled ski masks with a small canister strapped to our belts no larger than a can of hairspray. The oxygen in those containers would last twenty-four hours. The respirators were also equipped with com-sets.

"Let's move out," I said.

The door hissed and dropped open, exposing the rocky surface of the moon. John, jumped out first, followed by the rest of the team. After forming up, we half-walked, half-jumped toward the towering steel communications array.

The service hatch was unlocked, so we cautiously entered. I located the light switch and vanquished the gloom. With the airlock resealed, John took off his mask and began examining the gauges. The room was cylindrical with a computer console in the centre. At the far end was a stairwell that led to the top of the tower.

"Marshal," John called out to me. "There's something here you should see."

I walked over to John as he pointed toward the wall. A dark smear ran along it at shoulder level, heading towards the stairwell.

"Two line formation," I ordered. Orlando and Austin took point as Mick and Patrick fell in behind them. They slowly began to ascend the stairs when we heard it. A loud and sluggish moan drifted down from above us.

"What the fuck was that?" Mick said, craning his neck.

"Sounds like someone in distress," Orlando suggested.

We heard steps beginning to descend down the staircase. Gradually, the figure shuffled into view. The image of that man still haunts me to this day. His skin was pale with a greenish hue. Part of its right cheek was missing, revealing teeth and jaw. The man's nose had been caved into his face, leaving a piece of smeared bone jutting through its parchment skin. Most of its hair had been ripped out of its scalp, leaving gory scabs. The monster continued shuffling down towards us as we gaped in shock.

Breaking the spell, I snapped, "Fall back!"

The creature tripped over its feet and tumbled down the remaining steps. It landed face first on the ground with a sickening thud, only a foot away from Orlando. We stared at it for a moment, weapons trained on it, as it remained motionless. One of its arms appeared eaten away, bone clearly visible beneath rotting flesh.

"What ... is it?" Patrick uttered.

"I ... don't know," I answered. Nothing could walk around with all those wounds.

As I spoke, the creature suddenly spasmed and wrapped its hands around Orlando's shin. It yanked the man's leg towards itself and sank its teeth into his calf, ripping a chunk of cloth and flesh off. He screamed out as Austin rushed to his aid.

Austin dragged the creature from his brother and shoved him away, kicking it across the face. Orlando fell back as blood gushed out of his wound, splashing onto the concrete floor.

Its sudden speed had shocked us all, but now I yelled, "Patrick, take Orlando to the entrance and dress the wound. Everyone else fall back. Nobody get anywhere near that thing."

The creature began to rise to its feet. It chewed on the hunk of flesh from Orlando. Blood spilled out of its mouth and dribbled down his overalls as it chewed.

As Patrick dragged Orlando to the door, and the rest of us backed up, the creature shambled toward us, emitting that same haunting moan.

I raised my rifle and pulled the trigger. A three round burst tore open the creature's chest and splattered black gore against the stairwell. Despite intestines spilling onto the floor, it continued walking toward us.

"Fire at will!" I gasped, blinking in disbelief. Nobody needed telling twice. Bullets ripped into the creature's body. Flesh and black bile splattered in all directions. It fell backwards and thrashed on the ground.

"The bastard's still alive!" Austin said as it struggled back to its feet.

Mick took careful aim and fired a round through its forehead, blowing brain matter out the back of its head and spraying it across the wall. The creature dropped to the ground, still.

Austin turned to assist Patrick with his older brother while the rest of us stood staring at what was left of the creature.

Pulling myself together, I walked over to Orlando. He was deathly pale, but Patrick had managed to stem the bleeding with a field dressing.

"That's about as much as I can do," Patrick said. "He's lost a lot of blood. He needs a medical team."

Orlando suddenly contorted and burst into a rattling cough that brought up the same black liquid from the monster that bit into him. He curled over onto his side and repeatedly vomited. The black bile was spewing out of his mouth, nose and even his eyes.

"We need to get him back to the ship," I said.

Mick walked up behind me and said, "No, we can't. It looks like that creature was infected with something. It looks like Orlando has it too now. He needs to be quarantined immediately."

Austin had been cradling Orlando's head, but now he jumped up. "We're not leaving my brother like this! He needs help!"

As much as it pained me, I knew that Mick was right. The creature was clearly infected and so too was Orlando. I looked over to John who had quickly put his mask back on. As the others followed suit, Orlando began to convulse on the ground. His skin was turning grey-green and black spittle was spraying from his contorted mouth.

"Jesus, look at him," Mick muttered, stepping back. "We need to get out of here."

"I'm not leaving him!" Austin yelled.

I look from Mick and Austin back down at Orlando. He abruptly stopped moving and then his eyes turned black. He rose to his feet as I opened my mouth to shout a warning.

Mick saw him first and quickly stepped back, raising his rifle.

Austin spun around, saying, "Orlando?" It was on him in a split second and, in one swift movement, ripped Austin's mask off and bit into his face above his right eye. He sucked the eye out of its socket and chewed down.

Austin shrieked in agony and pushed his brother back, covering the gushing wound. Orlando lunged at him again. Mick

166

opened fire. The bullet burst through Austin's head and buried into Orlando's temple. Both brothers crashed to the ground on top of each other as blood and black bile mingled on the ground.

"Sorry ..." Mick uttered, staring at his two dead colleagues splayed at his feet.

He acted on instinct and his reasoning was sound, but it was still something to have to kill your own team members ... your friends.

"No need to be sorry," I said finally. "You did what you had to do. You had no choice." Tearing my eyes away from my two dead teammates, I said, "Listen up, we need to fall back to the ship. We take our Austin and Orlando with us. We don't leave anyone behind. The comms clearly aren't the problem here – I'm guessing that they had to isolate that thing in here. We'll drop Orlando and Austin off at the ship and then head for the resort to get some answers."

After retrieving body bags from the ship, we moved our dead teammates to the ship's cargo hold.

"Shouldn't we call this in?" John asked as we gathered outside the ship.

"No," I replied. "We need to get some answers first. We have to check out the main complex first."

From the landing zone, we could just make out the hotel structures about a mile away. We headed at a fast pace, concern etched into all our faces.

"I can't believe Austin and Orlando are dead," John muttered, breaking the silence. "What the hell was that thing?"

"I don't know," I admitted. "It certainly looks like he was infected with something – something I've never seen before." As an afterthought, I added, "Have you ever read *The War of the Worlds?* The Martians thought they could come and take Earth away from us. Despite everything humanity threw at them, it was a simple infection that ultimately killed off the alien invaders ..."

"So we're the invaders here and the Moon wants us to leave?" Patrick asked.

I managed a shrug and the group fell silent.

We finally reached the main structure. The grey steel and glass building was three-stories high and curved like a giant

167

dome. A sign that flashed the words *MOONLIT RESORT* was positioned just above main entrance.

I took point and opened the first set of doors. As we entered the airlock, at the rear, Patrick closed the doors behind him. The soothing tones of a well-spoken woman welcomed us and instructed us to wait as oxygen began to fill the room.

We readied our weapons as the automatic doors opened.

What had been an exquisitely furnished lobby was now utterly decimated. Sofas were overturned, tables smashed and broken glass and pools of blood littered the once expensive carpet. Amongst the debris were severed limbs and torn chunks of flesh.

Mouth agape, I slowly crept into the room.

"This is crazy, man," John whispered. "Everyone's dead. Let's get the hell out of here."

"Stow it," I hissed. The front desk was to my right. Straight ahead was a large dining room and to the left were stairs and elevators. "Hello?" I called out as the lights flickered overhead.

Only our soft footfalls broke the silence.

"This is Space Marshal Collins."

Nothing.

We walked in a square shape formation, everyone covering their sectors. We checked the dining room first. The lights were off, but the gloom did not hide the destruction. Tables and chairs were overturned and dishes and rancid food was spread across the floor.

"Hello?" I called. This time a reply came. Several collected moans echoed in the room. Figures began standing up from amongst the wreckage. Before we could react, the room was filled with dozens of infected creatures, shambling quickly towards the open doors. They stared with vacant, hungry expressions. There were men, women and even children. Some seemed to move quicker than others, but the children were quickest.

"Fall back," I ordered. As we backed back into the lobby, we saw more creatures pouring in from the stairs.

Mick raised his rifle, saying, "Marshal?"

I didn't hesitate to yell, "Open fire!"

Mick fired targeted headshots into the crowd emerging from the stairs to bring down the monsters closest to us. John and Patrick opened fire, spraying snapshots into the creatures pouring out of the dining room. They managed to drop a few, but most shots struck limbs and torsos and barely managed to slow them down.

Mike and I tried to clear a path to the exit, but sheer numbers made it impossible. A sea of black glaring eyes descended upon us in all directions.

We fell back to the front desk, firing and reloading constantly.

"I'm running low," Mick yelled. "We need an alternative exit!"

As I opened my mouth to respond, music began to play from the PA. It was some kind of jazz. The creatures stopped moving and stared at the ceiling that had been painted like a summer sky. They stood still, with an expression not unlike confusion. Some sounded like they were humming along with the music.

We resumed firing, dropping as many near the door as we could.

"We'll have to make a run through them," I said, reloading once more.

We ran for it, cutting down those nearest. The music suddenly stopped when we were only half way to the exit. As one, the creatures turned to stare at us.

I was in the lead, with the others close behind. The creatures came at us from all directions. Spindly hands grasped Patrick's suit. As he disappeared into the masses of outstretched arms, I caught glimpse of him pulling a grenade from his webbing. I heard him scream as they started tearing him apart and then a loud beep. We were pushing forward when the grenade exploded. Bodies and torn limbs flew in all directions and the floor beneath our feet shook. The blast threw me against the door.

The doors swept opened and I fell inside. My rifle was empty, so I held it up like a club as I spun to around. I couldn't see any of the others. All I saw were dozens of creatures spilling

169

towards me, slipping and stumbling over the gore-splattered floor. I hesitated, shouting out, but the creatures pressed in and the doors shot back into place.

Everything else was a blur. I do remember crawling all the way back to the ship. Patrick had prepped the ship ready for a quick departure, so all I had to do was set the autopilot and the ship would do the rest.

When I made it back to Earth, I was instantly quarantined and put into the cell I'm in now. I was interrogated and eventually diagnosed as clinically insane and responsible for the murders of everyone in Moonlit Resort and my own team members. I have been sentenced to be hanged until I am dead. They refused to listen when I told them what happened at the resort, about the strange lunar infection that killed everyone and turned them into mindless walking corpses. Deep down, I have a feeling that the Zilith Corporation knew what was happening on the Moon and they needed someone to blame. That someone was me.

There was one thing I didn't tell them. When I got back to the ship and took my suit off, I had scratches on my right shoulder that quickly healed before I landed on Earth. Maybe while I was making my escape, one of them scratched me. I'll never know what kind of an effect it'll have on me when I'm dead.

Space Marshal Elroy Collins
January 3rd 2060

THE END

A CHANGE IS AS GOOD AS A REST
By
Tom Johnstone

Kevin got to see all sorts in his line of work.

People would come up to him and tell him how lucky he was to work as a municipal gardener. Perhaps they imagined that he spent his days hovering around floral displays like an over-sized, green-clad bumble bee, or manicuring lawns with a pair of nail scissors.

The things he would find in the park of a morning!

Condoms (used and unused).

Hypodermic needles (used and unused).

Wine and beer bottles (broken and unbroken).

Discarded boxer shorts smeared in the former owners' faeces.

It wasn't all bad. From time to time he would find a five or ten pound note lying under a hedge or rose bush, discarded as casually as a sweet wrapper; on one or two occasions, he had happened upon a large bag of high quality skunk nestling innocently in the morning dew, its crumpled, grey-green fronds clasped around golden buds, with their sweet heady fragrance. Such finds made the job more rewarding.

One rainy day saw him fishing a discarded snake from the pond, its scaly skin baggy like a punctured bicycle inner tube.

One hazily sunny morning, he had to remove a bright red bicycle that some joker had seen fit to suspend from a lamp post in the rose walk. It hung there, wrapped around the black, cast iron post, like some demented Christmas decoration.

But that was nothing compared to what he found hanging from a lamp post one Tuesday morning after the May bank holiday.

He had expected an unholy mess that day – especially as the fun fair had come and dumped itself unceremoniously on the Green. But there was very little green about the large, flat expanse of worn, yellowing grass, criss-crossed by tarmac paths, in the town centre. On and around the benches surveying that area, planted on raised grassy banks behind cast iron railings, the winos would gather to watch and laugh and jeer at the spectacle.

They had been getting rowdier and lairier, since their new tipple had hit the off licences. It was called Ultrabrew, and questions had been asked in parliament about its combination of a lethally high alcohol content (75%) and the rumoured presence of opiates and psychogenic substances within the beverage. Its toxic chemical fizz had very little to do with fermented hops and barley grains; about as much as the new white cider LHC had to do with the bucolic wassailing of rosy pippins.

Kevin often saw the drunks huddled around their bench in the mid-afternoon, and he would think himself lucky that he had a secure job with the council, or about as secure as a job could be in the present climate. He often wondered how long it might be before the axe fell, and then he might be joining them around the bench.

But lately he had been giving them a wide berth. There was a distinct atmosphere of menace about the way they lurched and swayed around their bench, this last week leading up to the bank holiday. *And with a funfair and a children's playground nearby!* Kevin decided there was no way he would bring his kids to play here.

He felt even more certain in this opinion when he came into work on the Tuesday after the bank holiday. It wasn't so much the mess – he was used to that. It was more the nature of the thing he found on the lamp post.

And what it was doing.

It was a breezy morning, and the sun was still low in the sky, and when later questioned on the subject, Kevin put the phenomenon he witnessed down to the action of the wind and the play of the bright light dazzling his eyes, though he didn't mention the effect of the contents of the bag he had found under a bench giving the incident a certain hazy, dream-like quality.

At first he took it for an old-fashioned, upright vacuum cleaner bag, still attached to its hose pipe, which appeared to be waving like an elephant's trunk in the breeze. Approaching closer, Kevin realized that there were in fact not one but two bags, and that they were wet; pinky-grey and organic in texture.

The thing swaying and pulsating on the lamp post was a pair of human lungs, complete with wind pipe, though lacking the rest of the human body.

Kevin noticed sooty black striations visible through the organ's mucous membranes, reminding him of pictures of lungs displayed on packets of cigarettes and rolling tobacco.

"I would say these lungs belonged to a heavy smoker."

"Great Heavens, Holmes! How did you—"

"Simple deduction, Watson. These blackened, tarry deposits here point to a ..."

Kevin snapped out of his detective day dream, registering the thing that his mind had been trying to shut out: the lungs appeared to be breathing, expanding and contracting like a pair of spongy bellows.

Kevin's gorge was rising, and he felt a sudden urge to dash to the gardeners' mess hut, vomit in the toilet and enlist the help of one of his colleagues. After all, he couldn't just leave it up there on display for all the children and pensioners and other decent citizens who would soon be descending on the park on this bright May morning. It was an eyesore! Not to mention a health hazard. But as he strode rapidly in the direction of the mess hut, his stomach churning with each step, he remembered that he was alone in the park. His colleagues were nowhere to be found, probably off attending to other garbage-infested recreational facilities (either that or skiving off), and the council had not hired any seasonal staff due to cutbacks.

However, he didn't have to worry about the lungs hanging about up there. It turned out that they were able to extricate themselves from the lamp post without his help. Fortunately for his sanity, he wasn't there to see the wind pipe winding its way down the post like a snake, the wheezing lungs flopping about like balloons full of water. After he had sat down in the hut for a few minutes to regain his composure, he returned to find that the thing had crawled under a privet hedge. At least, that was all he could gather from the agitation of its lower leaves and branches.

That way, he was able to put the whole dreadful experience down to the wind, the sun in his eyes, etc.

He carried on insisting on this explanation for a few days, before it became impossible for anyone to deceive themselves about what was happening around them. He might have found it harder to rationalize it in this way had he been in the park the day before.

"The medical profession called it Death Immunity Syndrome – shortened to the acronym DIS. The red-top papers had a field day, bemoaning the new phenomenon of the "undeserving living": the way that the "beneficiaries" of "infinite life expectancy" (another media buzz word) seemed to be alcoholics and drug addicts. *Why should drugged-up scroungers and criminals live forever, while decent law abiding tax payers die?* was the kind of headline that was to become typical in the months to come."

–Professor Charles Marcuse, *We Belong Undead: 'The Change' and Social Change, Oxford University Press*, 2013.

WPCSO Jane Harvey was not without misgivings as she approached the group of shabby figures gathered around the bench on the edge of the park. Her colleague, PCSO Simon Craven was calling to her from a few yards behind her, where he was hanging back, his face tense and apprehensive, *like a ferret*, she thought.

She glanced back. She couldn't hear what he was saying over the cacophony of fifty seven different varieties of adolescent pop, R'n'B and dubstep pounding from the whirligig frenzy of the funfair. But she got the gist of it from the way his arms were gesturing her to *come back, come back*!

"We can handle it!" she called back impatiently. "Are you coming with me or not?"

Not far away, parked on the corner of the road adjoining the park, was a squad car containing two uniformed officers from the police proper. She knew that they were watching, eager to see the "hobby cops" fail. PCSO Craven's attitude was: *They're the professionals; they've got the equipment and training, let them deal with it!* Jane could see where he was coming from, but she didn't want to give them the satisfaction of seeing her bottle it.

174

Anyway, it wasn't as though she was going to confront an armed robber or something, she was just going to chat to a few drunks getting bladdered on the May bank holiday. In Iraq or Afghanistan, they'd call it the battle for hearts and minds. Not that this was a battle. It was just that it was going to get dark soon, and someone needed to ask them nicely to move on, before there was any trouble between them and the teens and casuals who frequented the fair.

Better to approach them now, while there were just a handful of them scattered around the plinth where the bench stood. It was difficult to see exactly how many of them there were in the shadow of the elm that spread its darkening leaves over that corner. Was it the dying sunlight that made them appear so menacing, as they swayed to and fro lifting their cans in what looked like a mock salute to her?

Jane noticed that the lurid labels on the cans: Ultrabrew, LHC. *The new legal highs in a can*, she had heard her colleagues mutter. How had the brewery got away with it? They still hadn't disclosed all the ingredients. *They've obviously got the government by the balls*, she thought.

A man stumbled out from the shadow of the elm, grinning at her with teeth like corroded tomb stones from beneath a leather cowboy hat.

"Simon!" she called, glancing behind him. As she thought, the weasel-faced PCSO had vanished. She stood her ground, and within a few lurching strides, the ridges of the man's battered face were within inches of her own. She heaved slightly at the sour, hoppy reek of booze on his breath, and then breathed out with relief, as she glanced down at the brown bottle in swinging from his hand. He wasn't drinking Ultrabrew.

"'S aright, swee'heart," the man slurred. Then he flung a long arm back towards the group she had been about to approach. "I'm no with them. Ye should stay awa' fae them! Wha's a nice wee lass like ye doin' on duty on Mayday Monday anyway? Ye a for'ner, or summin?"

He pressed his splintered face closer to hers in support of his interrogative, and grunted, "Hmm?"

"No, I'm not a foreigner," she replied. "I was born in this town," she added. "Lived here my whole life."

"Prob'ly goin' tae die in this town …" he muttered, and drifted off for a moment, then came back to himself abruptly. "Listen, hen, take ma advice …" He clapped his hand down on her shoulder in a rough but good-natured way. "Go home. Now! Choose life. Choose a sickie. 'S Mayday Monday for fuck's sake, a friggin' holiday–a *holy day*! Might be the last one an' all …"

"Ah well," she replied evenly, wishing he'd go away, "a change is as good as a rest."

"A change is good as arrest! You gonna arrest me?" he demanded.

"No, I–"

"Well, listen tae this then! Back in the day, the workers never work't Mondays. Follow Saint Monday, like me!" And he began to croon softly, "Saint Monday brings more ills aboot, for when the money's spent! The children's' clothes go up the spoot, which causes discontent! For when at last he staggers hame, he knows not what tae say! A fool is mair a man than he, upon a fuddlin' day! Tha's what I'm sayin' … It's no' healthy for a young lassie stayin' around here, not with *them* aboot. It's that muck they drink – sends 'em fuckin' loopy … That and them solar flares we've been havin'! Did ye see the northern lights? I did. Point is, it's messin' with oor radar – human race's, that is. Me, I drink decent muck! Gets me mortal, but no' like yon muck they're chuckin' doon their throats."

He broke off again, lifting the dark bottle to his cracked lips, then tossing it aside with disgust when he realized that it was empty. It smashed on the path beside them, and the noise seemed to jolt the drunk into sudden sobriety.

He gripped her shoulder.

"Let go of me," she said slowly, injecting steel into her voice.

"Keep away fae them," he hissed, nearly forcing her off balance as he let go of her, and lurched away with a sudden, frightened urgency.

She shot a defiant glance at the squad car. *Thanks for the backup guys.* She headed for the shadow of the elm.

As she moved closer to the dark figures under the tree, the first thing she noticed was how quiet it was. This came as something of a relief after the previous encounter. Though she wouldn't have liked to admit it to her "superiors" in the squad car, the drunken Scotsman's ramblings and unpredictable behaviour had left her just a little shaken. There was something almost soothing about the way the elm's leafy, over-hanging branches seemed to muffle the shrieking hubbub of the funfair.

Less soothing were the things wriggling in the dark leaf mould near the bench. *Worms,* Jane told herself, *five of them.*

"Excuse me," she began. She tried to catch the eye of a young, shaven-headed man in a black, hooded tracksuit top and shapeless, grey jogging bottoms, but it's difficult to make eye contact with someone whose eyes appear to have shrunken inside his head, and whose pupils have been reduced to sub-atomic particles. She felt excruciatingly self-conscious in her high-viz jacket. She stood out like a sore thumb. A sore, fluorescent yellow thumb.

"There's been a complaint," she continued, "about some anti-social behaviour."

She heard suppressed, asthmatic mirth from the bench.

It appeared to come from another man sat sideways, facing away from Jane, bending over a woman whose head was thrown back over the top of the bench, jaw slack, mouth wide. Something about the attitude of the two figures unnerved her deeply, and she began to wish that she had not tried to approach the group alone. Still, there were only three of them, and she could always radio for back-up from the squad car.

The woman on the bench let out what Jane thought was a faint whimper.

Jane didn't want to get any closer.

"You alright, love?" she asked in a tentative murmur.

The shorn, salt-and-pepper stubbled head of the man on the bench turned slowly towards her; eyes grey shadows, mouth smiling dimly.

"She's aright, officer," he said. His voice was a rumbling growl, punctured by rusty barbed wire. "She's had an overdose, that's all. We all 'ave. Smack on top of alcopop's smacked my bitch up!"

Faint, smirking laughter played around her from the shadows.

"Wanna join the party, officer?" he offered in his cracked, dusty tones..

She saw that one of his hands was stroking the woman's matted hair with a retracted Stanley knife; the other held what was left of her hand, which finished just before the knuckles like a sick joke without a punch line.

"Look, she needs medical attention," said the WPCSO, fighting to keep the steel in her voice. "It's alright. I'm a trained first-aider."

"No need," said the voice like a dry well, a bottomless pitch. "She won't die. She can't die. None of us can. That's the thing we found with them new alcopops, see? None of us can die. Not one little bit of us."

He snarled the last thing with a terrified vehemence, perhaps realizing the implications at last.

Then she glanced back at the five worms knuckling their way through the leaf mould that blackened the stubby fingernails, and her own hand groped for her radio.

"Lady fingers, anyone?" continued the builder's rubble voice, and sniggering, qualified the offer: "but you'll 'ave to catch 'em first!"

The woman suddenly giggled stupidly. "You're welcome to 'em, love—I didn't need 'em anyway!"

Then Jane realized two things First that another three or four had joined the group, circling her to cut off her exit, with more lurking in the shadows of the elm, Stanley knives, machetes and screw drivers in hand; second that the dense, over-hanging foliage that muffled the fairground noise would also muffle her screams.

"'Right, bruv!" the stubble-headed man grinned at one of the new arrivals. "Good to see you've skinned up – pass the joint around, will yer?"

Jane's head jerked around involuntarily at the mention of illicit substances. But it wasn't that sort of joint, or that kind of skinning up. The new comer, the stubble-headed man had been addressing, was hopping on one leg, offering his other around for the others to gnaw.

"There was also a great deal of scare-mongering about murderous cannibal ghouls. There was some truth in this. The chemicals that gave rise to the phenomenon did release latent homicidal, even anthropophagous tendencies in some DIS patients. But on the whole, these were people hell-bent on *self* destruction in their previous lives. In their new earthbound after-life, they carried on in the same vein."
–Professor Charles Marcuse, *We Belong Undead: 'The Change' and Social Change*, Oxford University Press, 2013.

PC Graham Bradley let out a loud belch as he wiped his hands on his empty kebab packet, then stuffed the ketchup crimson paper into the squad car's globe compartment. At first, he thought his partner PC Harry Lowther had answered in kind, but it was a growl of static morphing into a woman babbling something that could have been "bath tub" in a tremulous voice, followed by less intelligible noises distorted by screeches, then a ripping, then a gurgling.

Lowther snapped the radio off irritably.

"Amateurs!" he remarked, rather smugly, Bradley thought. "Might have known they'd go to pieces if there was any problems ..."

Bradley tried to switch the radio back on, and regain the signal, but could only hear some sort of howling.

"Damned radios," he complained. "Been playing up for the last two months!"

"Sarge thinks it's something to do with them flare things," remarked Lowther.

"Flares?"

"Solar flares. Radiation or something. Anyway, best kill it for now."

Lowther switched the radio off again, and pulled his cap down over his eyes. Time to catch forty winks before the fair got out of hand.

"Hang on though," said Bradley. "Did she say 'back up'?"

Lowther, the older of the two, lifted the peak of his cap above his eyes to glare at the other policeman.

"Nah!" he said.

Then he pulled the peak back down again.

So he didn't notice the lump of jelly thing crawling sluggishly towards the road nearby, a liver playing chicken with the traffic.

"Scientists have been unable to agree on the exact trigger for 'The Change'. While the nation's self-appointed moral guardians were quick to blame the marketing of super-strong alcoholic beverages like Ultrabrew and LHC (named after the Large Hadron Collider, also named as a possible contributory factor to DIS), others have drawn a link between DIS and a recent intensification in solar activity, also associated with a notable more dramatic manifestation of the *Aurora Borealis.*"

–Professor Charles Marcuse, *We Belong Undead: 'The Change' and Social Change,* Oxford University Press, 2013.

PCSO Craven told himself it was the wind blowing the leaves that gave the impression of sudden, frenetic activity in the shadow of the over-grown oak tree behind the cast iron railings. It wasn't as if he had agreed to go with Jane to talk to the drunks. She didn't need him to hold her hand. She had already made that perfectly clear. He still felt a gnawing resentment at her for failing to reciprocate his romantic approaches.

That wasn't the reason why he had refused to accompany her on her fool's errand. He just thought that patrolling the funfair would be a much better use of his time. That was where most of the trouble would usually start; hormonal teenage boys trying to act hard in front of the girls they were competing over amidst the heady cocktail of flashing coloured lights, deep frying oil, candyfloss and darkness.

A group of skinny-jeaned youths sniggered at him as they swaggered past him, their chunky belts glinting in the lights from the fair, their feathered haircuts fluttering in the breeze. A cage full of pinioned bodies rose high into the night sky, then plunged metres to the ground. While other rides had garish paint jobs, this one was a brutalistic, industrial steam press, with squealing human passengers. It was called "LHC". He felt a heavy thump on his lower back then the sensation of something dripping down the back of his police community support officer's trousers.

A can of beer. He looked at the half empty can rolling away from him like a fleeing criminal, and it flashed its neon name as it spun, a kind of half-hearted advertising jingle: "Ultrabrew".

He glanced around, looking for the culprits, but they had melted into the darkness. Four girls stared at him, wet lips parted, representations of desirability crudely daubed in shocking pink and electric blue on the side of the Waltzer. Just ahead the Horror Tower loomed, and PCSO Craven saw a young man and woman secured into one of its cars, their pale hands brandishing Ultrabrew cans with distinctive neon logos. The leering, scarred, lobster face of Freddie Krueger and the fanged pout of Ingrid Pitt welcomed them into its portals.

The man in the kiosk was too busy to notice that the couple didn't come out, and couldn't understand when subsequent customers complained of rats skittering around in the purple-strobed darkness.

"You wanna get it checked out, mate," one young woman said, tossing aside her diagonal fringe. "Must have been some kind of mutant. Five legs, it had, and no head!"

Others complimented him on the new additions to his display. That eyeball that swivelled at you as you hurtled by in your car, from the skewer it was impaled on, was very realistic, although the pupil was a bit small. Some thought the exhibits were a bit too gross: the entrails that writhed, the slithering intestines. One man asked why that effigy of a half-dismembered cadaver sprawled in the rocking chair was wearing a high-viz jacket and community support police woman's hat, though he did admire the attention to detail: there were even bite marks on what was left of the ragged borders of the dummy's contorted limbs!

The man in the kiosk simply shrugged: he didn't set up the displays, he just took the money.

You have to remember that it was dark, and many of the customers were half cut, so they didn't notice the odd stains on their clothes until the morning after.

As many people were to find out in the days to come, they weren't the only ones who were half-cut.

"If anything, the loss of their deaths, the prospect of endless lives of self disgust and despair increased their desire for oblivion. The super opiates associated with 'The Change' made them resistant to pain. So the Death Immune just went around trying to chop each other ever smaller, still living and sentient pieces. It was like slicing up a tape worm: you just end up with more of them. It was one, big, messy, futile suicide pact, distressing and a minor public order problem, but largely non-threatening to the mortal public, so safe to ignore."

–Professor Charles Marcuse, *We Belong Undead: 'The Change' and Social Change, Oxford University Press*, 2013.

Later the following morning, Kevin Williams sat in the back seat of the works van, listening to Paul and Barry as they spied on the acting senior gardener, Matt. Paul and Barry weren't their real names, but Kevin had adopted the Chuckle Brothers' first names as his own private nicknames for them.

"Look, the Ranger's still there."

"I knew it. He ain't even left the yard! He's been in the mess room the whole time."

"Bet you anything when we go in there it'll be spotless."

Kevin imagined himself a fly on the wall to this exchange, during which the two brothers neither invited his complicity, nor even acknowledged his presence as a witness or possible dissenter. Their father, the senior gardener proper, would have done exactly the same as Matt had he been there. The fact was they just didn't like taking orders from Matt – especially Paul, the younger and cockier of the two, who saw himself as the natural heir to his father's petty fiefdom.

"Pikies have gone then," said Paul.

"Yeah," his brother confirmed. "Left a right bloody mess though! Found a load of offal lying about in the grass."

"What *is* this? A fun fair or a butcher's?"

"Funny thing was, I went back to the van to get a bag to put it in, and it had gone."

"Seagulls must have eaten it."

"Didn't see none. Still it can't have just crawled away by itself!"

Kevin didn't mention the animated lungs. They already thought he was a bit weird as it was!

"Told you he wouldn't do no work while Dad's away," muttered Paul.

Kevin thought of the six billion pound bonus paid by some high street bank to its chief executive.

No wonder they're getting away with it, he thought. *They've got us gnawing scraps off each other rather than tearing strips off the fat cats.*

Then he thought of those corny zombie movies that were always on, where the dead feed on the living. If the zombie apocalypse happened in real life, he reckoned, the dead wouldn't unite against the living; they'd just rip each other to shreds!

He didn't know back then how close he was to the truth.

What Kevin had seen that morning, after the funfair had been and gone, was an early by-product of this process; a pair of lungs, trying to hang themselves from a lamp post, and then crawling under a hedge to die.

And failing.

Some say a change is as good as a rest, but they just wanted a rest. And the Change wouldn't let them.

"Perhaps the last hope for the Death Immune lies in the new project set up by a working group of particle physicists and molecular biologists. They are seeking volunteers among the DIS community for an experiment, in which they would be fired through a particle accelerator. The scientists would then test the resulting sub-atomic particles for signs of life. In this way, they hope to discover if they can finally cure Death Immunity Syndrome."

183

–Professor Charles Marcuse, *We Belong Undead: 'The Change' and Social Change*, Oxford University Press, 2013.

THE END

STORM COMING DOWN
By
Iain S Paton

The white-haired black man sat in the elegant parlour, seeking refuge from the sweltering summer. His unseeing eyes stared at the distant wall as the maid poured him a cup of chicory-scented coffee.

The mistress of the house sat opposite. 'That'll be all, honey.' A massive fat arm waved lazily, and the young white maid was dismissed.

The man turned his face towards the woman, whose weight must have been over three hundred pounds, bulging out of her sweat-stained white dress. He couldn't see her, but he sensed her bulk, and her presence. She was black, with a mass of frizzed grey hair, and she sat in front of a deck of Tarot cards.

'Tower struck by lightning.' She turned over one of the skull-backed card. 'There's a storm coming down.'

The man sipped his tea.

The woman turned over another card. 'The second in the trinity. The Moon. The storm will come from the tides, bringing night without end.'

She turned over a third card. The man's cup clattered on the saucer.

'Death.'

Michael was annoyed. The flight to New Orleans had been delayed, and he was tired enough as it was. The lengthy queue at arrival control did little to improve his mood, a line of sullen-looking passengers who were supposed to be in holiday spirits in anticipation of Labour Day and the never-ending parade of festivals hosted by the city.

'Name,' the official demanded, as he handed over his passport and disembarkation card. She was squat and very round, bulging out of her uniform.

'Michael Greenwood.'

'Purpose of visit?'

He agonised for a moment, pondering the inevitable question. Business or pleasure? He felt he was owed a holiday, after all those weekends darting around Europe. But the book came first. 'Business, I suppose. I'm writing a book.'

The mask of officialdom slipped and she smiled. 'Really? What's it about?'

'It's a collection of ghost stories, about cemeteries and graveyards which are meant to be haunted. I've already been around Europe, up in Scotland, then London and down to Paris. But they say there's nowhere like New Orleans for cemeteries.'

She smiled. 'Got that right, Sir. Nowhere does death like Noo Awleans.' She stamped his passport. 'You have a good trip then, Sir. Maybe make a bit of a vacation of it, check out Bourbon Street an' all. There's no place like it for partying.'

He caught a yellow cab outside the Louis Armstrong International Airport. A skinny black man with greying hair grinned at him from the driver's seat. 'How are you, Sir?'

'Fine, thanks, well a bit tired to be honest.'

'Where to?'

'Downtown, please. The Sheraton on Canal Street'.

'You from England?'

'That's right'

'What brings you to the Big Easy?'

'A working holiday, I suppose. I'm writing a book, on haunted cemeteries.'

The man crossed himself, and whistled. 'Well you'll be wanting a guide around the St Louis graveyards then. Don't be goin' there alone. You'll either lose your wallet, or your soul – or maybe even both.'

Michael noticed the chicken leg bone and feathers dangling from the rear-view mirror.

'Do you know any good guides?'

'Depends what you want to know. You look like a serious fellow.'

They sat in silence, until Michael found a $20 bill in his wallet.

'Well, there's two sides to Noo Awleans. There's the nice tourist side, which has its thrills, but is never too dangerous. And there's the true face of this ol' lady.'

The driver held the wheel with one hand while he rummaged in his pocket. 'Mind if I smoke?'

'Not at all. Please go ahead.'

'This city has deep roots, even in soft ground. The French, the Spanish, refugees from Haiti.' He drew on the cigar. 'And Africa, it all goes back to deepest darkest Africa. This city was the heart of the slavery trade, but it had the biggest number of free black men and women anywhere. A city of contrasts you might say, white and black, light and dark, but never far apart. As close as sides of the same coin.'

Michael was sweating in the clammy heat. 'Do you have any air conditioning?'

'Sure I do, if you don't mind the cigar smoke.' He rolled up his window. 'Getting towards hurricane season, so it is. You can feel it in the air. Energy, like electricity.'

The driver crushed out his cigar. 'Anyhows, I was going to tell you about a fellow who might know a cemetery guide. Talk to Blind Willie. No-one knows the Big Easy like him. He doesn't see with his eyes, but he sees damn well more than others with 20-20 vision. Sees beneath the surface of it all. You'll find him in the Rising Sun, just off Bourbon Street before … I think it's Dumaine Street. Tell him that Slim sent you.'

It was three o'clock by the time Michael checked into his hotel. He slumped on his bed, shattered by the long journey and the feeling he should be fast asleep despite the daylight outside. At least the hotel room was air conditioned. He drew the curtains and tried to doze, but sleep would not come.

He shrugged on a lightweight shirt and trousers and headed out. It was a short walk to Bourbon Street and its pastel-coloured French buildings, ornate Spanish balconies, and of course the sweltering heat. Most of the bars were shuttered, but there were a few strip clubs open. As he walked, he noticed the rainbow flags of gay bars increasing in number.

He found the Rising Sun. It was on a litter-strewn offshoot of Bourbon Street which stank of urine and vomit.

New Orleans' Oldest Coffee and Liquor House, proclaimed the faded sign. A tall black man in a porkpie hat lounged next to the door, chewing a toothpick and glaring at him through sunglasses.

'You comin' in here, boy?' asked the man. He put his arm up, blocking the doorway, which seemed to indicate otherwise.

'I think so.'

'You English?' The man spoke with a friendlier tone, but still blocked the way.

'Yup. Slim said I should come here.'

'Okays then,' he nodded. 'In you go.'

The bar was empty of customers. A lone bartender was polishing glasses behind a chipped and stained worktop. The floor was wood, varnished with age and decades of spilled alcohol.

'Excuse me,' said Michael. 'Do you know where I can find Blind Willie?'

'Who the fuck are you?'

'Slim sent me.' He took another twenty from his wallet.

The barman pocketed the bill. 'Drink'll be extra. You need to wait awhile. Willie does his drinkin' after sunset. Darkness means nothin' to him.'

'Any bands playing?'

'Not until after dark.' The barman was a man of few words.

'A beer then, please.'

Although the bar stank of stale liquor, it was cool and dark, a welcome relief from the heat of the street. Michael felt the tiredness drain from him as he sipped the ice-cold bottle. He lifted up his bag and took out his small laptop.

'Wouldn't be flashin' that around here, man,' warned the barman.

Michael took out his notebook instead. He scribbled down his impressions of the city, from the airport to the hotel and the famous Bourbon Street.

'Another beer, please.'

He read through a guidebook he had bought at home, intending to read on the aircraft, but which had been mistakenly packed in his suitcase. The city had been founded by the French

Mississippi Company in the early 18th Century, named for the Duke of Orleans. It had passed from French to Spanish control, then back to the French before being sold to the United States in 1803. The cosmopolitan environment of the city was partly the result of the slave trade, and the migration from Haiti following their revolution of 1804, bringing a rich fusion of French and African cultures, also Catholicism and African Voodoo beliefs.

He finished his beer. It was getting dark outside, so he checked his watch. 7.30pm.

He signalled the barman, who pulled out another beer from the fridge. The barman was about to pop the cap, when he put the bottle down unopened. He pulled a dusty bottle from a high shelf and poured some clear green liquid into a shot-glass. He balanced a spoon over the glass and gently placed a sugar cube on top of the spoon, pouring water from an ice-jug over the sugar cube. The liquid turned cloudy.

The barman popped the beer cap and thumped the bottle down beside Michael. 'Man'll be in shortly.'

A few minutes later, a blind man walked in. He was dressed in a white suit, waistcoat, shirt and hat and black glasses obscured the milk-white eyes which were occasionally visible from the side. He was black and very old, with fissured ebony skin and a clipped white beard.

He sat on the stool next to Michael, leaning his silver-topped walking-stick against the bar.

'Slim said you should go lookin' for me.'

'How did you know that?'

Blind Willie laughed. 'Easy. Slim drove me here, in his taxi-cab. Now, what you be wantin' to know?'

'Well, I'm writing a book, you see,' said Michael. 'It's about haunted graveyards and cemeteries. And nowhere's as famous as New Orleans for graveyards.'

'You got that one right,' said Willie. He sipped his absinthe. 'We got the Saint Louis graveyards just uptown from here. You'll have heard of Marie Laveau, the Voodoo Queen?'

'Yes, I have,' said Michael eagerly. 'What do you know about her?'

'Nuthin',' laughed Willie. 'That story is voodoo bullshit! They say you need to knock the tomb three times and put three crosses on the tomb, but that ain't no more than a tale to scare children. That lady ran a cathouse and was a hairdresser to rich white folks. She peddled voodoo charms on the side, to the poor and stupid. Plenty say she's not even buried there.' He spat, onto the ground.

'Nope, that is just horse-shit. But there are plenty spirits in there. The dead are restless. And not just in Saint Louis. But all over Louisiana.'

Willie sipped his drink again. 'Git yersef a beer, my man. And listen good. Only one phantom around here that'll freeze your blood and kill you where you stand. And that's Monsieur Fouet, or Mister Whip.'

'I heard this story from my grandma. She told me stories a lot, seeing as I couldn't read them. I was blind from when I was born, but she always said I had the Sight. I can walk down Bourbon Street outside there, and know when trouble is a'comin. Then I mostly get out of the way. And whenever I can't get out of the way, I use the stick. I can hear them as they move and breathe, and the head of that cane is solid steel. Broken quite a few heads. There are other ways, of course, to protect yourself, but that's another story.

Monsieur Fouet. Mister Whip. No-one could remember his real name. He came across from Haiti at the start of the century before last. Some said that he was a revolutionary, and others said he worked for the slave-owners. But he was fleeing something all right. Because he was a free man, he was able to hire himself out. And it wasn't long before a plantation owner's agent took him on as an overseer. For that man was good with a whip. Very good.

Didn't matter that he was a black man. Some said he was a delicate featured mulatto, other that he was as black as darkest Africa but as beautiful as a Nubian. But he only cared for the red flesh under people's hides. The cotton was planted and gathered in record times, because of that whip. Didn't matter that people died under it, there was always plenty more and Fouet always knew which slaves were prized and which were not. He took to wearing a white coat, a bit like mine, but he needed to change it every day because of the blood. And he put on airs and graces, no matter that he was a nigger at the heart of it. Mister Whip. Monsieur Fouet.

His employer loved it, a man called Louvière. That was one sick motherfucker, both of them in fact. He was French, had all the decadences of the salons of Paris and then some. He had fled the Revolution and the guillotine. Rumours that he drank the blood of the slaves and even sacrificed their babes in black masses. Plenty of Society back then wouldn't go near him, only bought his cotton because it was cheap. So he kept to his own devices. Took to listening to some of the wise men and women, the voodoo priests and such like, and learned even more devilry, visiting rituals in disguise, in a cloak and hood like a ghost. Some say that is where the Ku Klux Klan took their sheets idea from. Anyways, Mister Whip and his employer got on just fine and dandy.

Until Louvière came back from some midnight soirée, and found Fouet on top of his lady wife. What he was doing to her was never said, but that man was dragged out into the courtyard in burning torchlight. Plenty of slaves were willing to hold him down while the boss sliced off his lips and tongue and made him swallow them whole. Fouet knew he was lucky to escape with his life, as well as his balls, and didn't seem to care much for his disfigurement. He went around with those grinning teeth and started painting his face like a skull, taking the lash to more and more of them, to the point of death.

One night, not long after, he whipped the hide right off one poor soul, laid his back open. When the fellow was still dying, Fouet took that knife from Louvière and cut the spine right out of his back and ribs. He hollowed those bones out in front of the poor man, carved them with voodoo symbols and threaded them onto his whip. When he cracked it, the bones would rattle. Plenty of things changed that night. It was a full moon, evil in the air, spirits in the bayous and swamps. Some said that Papa Legba had opened the gates to the Loa, and Baron Samedi himself walked that night. Anyhows, Louvière dragged

191

his lady wife out and cut her heart out, in the light of the moon. They feasted on it there and then, Louvière and his overseer. Then they killed every last one of those slaves; men women and boys.

But they didn't die.

Fouet lashed them with his voodoo whip, every one. And they bled and fell as the flesh was torn off them. But then they rose. And they were put to work in the fields, far cheaper than living slaves, the corpses that they were. But only at night time. The sun was no good for them, and no good for the Louvière either, who had taken to blood-drinking every day. Those fields sat unworked during the day, and no one would dare venture near them at night. Louvière sent his agents to get more slaves, who were bled and whipped to death, and who then rose again. And his cotton got cheaper and cheaper, and folks held their nose and bought from him. He used the money to buy more and more fields and to extend his plantation even further across Louisiana. He might have bought the whole God-damned State if things had carried on that way.

But it could never last, even if only because of economics and not morality. No morality among slavers anyway. Plenty of people with money saw plainly what was happening. They knew they could not compete with the undead slave-fields, and that they would end up ruined, their own fields trodden under decaying feet. So, one night, they formed a small army. Worthy men and city fathers amongst their numbers, so they said, but they were afraid of voodoo vengeance. So they put on white hoods and cloaks out of fear, like Louvière had done out of deceit, and as their descendents would later do out of hate.

They killed Louvière. He did not die easy, until someone hammered a length of wood through his heart. The slaves did not put up much of a fight, and were burned. But Fouet would just not die. They hung him from a tree and burned him, but still he twitched and jerked. Not knowing what to do, they wrapped him in that twisted whip, which seemed to still him. Then they nailed him in a hardwood casket and placed him in a vault, in the Saint Louis Cemetery, where he lies until this very day, unable to move. But, even if he could move and shrug off the whip's cold

192

embrace, he would be damned to scratch on the inside of that casket until Judgement Day. And, even if he managed to claw his way out, he would be damned to drag his bony fingers down the brick walls of the vault until Judgement Day. And let us pray that he never manages to wriggle loose, scrabble free, and pull down those walls, otherwise we will all be doomed. For he will bathe in blood and will raise all the dead around him.'

'Where can I find his vault,' asked Michael, draining his fifth beer.

'Dunno,' shrugged Willie. 'Some say it is unmarked. Others say he is buried in the Louvière vault. That's a common name here though.' He sipped his absinthe, the third drink that had been prepared for him.

The wail of an amplified guitar cut through their conversation.

'Anyhows, mister,' said Willie. 'Leave me be. I want to listen to the music in peace. Come around tomorrow at the same time and I'll tell you more.'

Michael felt too tired to enjoy the bustling bars on Bourbon Street, which had burst into life in a river of noise and colour. So he had an overpriced sixth beer in the hotel bar, watching the silent newsreader on the TV screen as the subtitled headlines crept by.

Tropical storm has passed over Florida, but now diminishing …

Then, he went to bed.

Next morning, Michael woke early. Partly because of jet-lag, but mainly because of the noise outside. He looked out of the window. Canal Street was blocked with stationary traffic, engines idling and the occasional blast of a horn.

He switched on the TV. The newsreader sat in front of a satellite image of the south-eastern United States, with a cloud mass over the Gulf of Mexico. Michael recognised the significance of the telltale hollow centre before the newsreader mentioned the word 'hurricane'. Named Katrina, it was heading towards landfall on Louisiana and was gaining strength after apparently dying down over the Florida panhandle.

'Many citizens have taken it upon themselves to evacuate or stormproof their homes,' said the newsreader, a glossy blonde woman. 'At this stage no evacuation has been ordered, although the surge from Lake Pontchartrain threatens to overwhelm the levees.'

Michael looked out of the window again, overwhelmed with indecision. He packed his suitcase as the newswoman talked on in her breathy over-enunciated voice. Then he emptied the suitcase on the bed and pulled out a rucksack. He stuffed it with a change of clothes including a waterproof jacket and trousers, and wrapped his laptop in thick plastic duty-free carrier bags, placing it at the back of the rucksack. He had a meeting planned that evening, and somehow he thought that the doors of the Rising Sun would not be closed by a hurricane and that Blind Willie would be sitting at the bar again that night.

He put his passport and money in a pouch, slung around his neck inside his shirt. As an afterthought, he tore a street map page from the guide book and shoved it in his pocket. He packed the rest of the clothes back in the suitcase and locked it in the wardrobe. Then he went downstairs to the lobby. The lift doors bore a hand-lettered sign reading 'lifts shut down as precaution.' Other guests were gathered in the lobby, some with bags packed, trying to arrange taxis. Michael approached a harassed looking manager.

'No sir,' the man said, 'we're not closing the hotel yet, unless there is a general evacuation order. I think they'll use the Superdome as a refugee shelter. But we've lost some staff members already and we may not be able to offer anything beyond a room and bed.'

Michael grabbed a coffee from the self-service machine in the hotel bar and sat down with a few dozen others to watch the unfolding news. He felt jittery after downing the coffee and ordered a gin and tonic at the bar. The barman, unmistakably gay with cropped blond hair and a diamond earring, grinned. 'Don't worry, I'm not going anywhere, at least not until after Decadence next week' he said. 'And who wants to give up a ringside seat at a show like this?' He passed over a couple of half-litre bottles of water to Michael. 'On the house. You might want to put these in your backpack.'

The breakfast buffet was overwhelmed by hungry patrons, but Michael managed to grab a plate of cold meat, boiled eggs and bread. Fortified by his gin and tonic, he decided to venture outside. He took plenty of digital photographs of the queuing traffic, the people dragging suitcases and the residents and owners sandbagging their properties.

The Rising Sun was open for business. The door had been half-sandbagged, reinforced by sheets of plywood and two small stepladders were propped up on either side. The same tall man stood outside as the previous day.

'Man, you ain't gettin' in here this time,' he growled. 'Regulars only.'

Michael turned away. But a gravelly voice called out from inside the bar.

'Let the boy in. He stood me two drinks, so he's a regular.' It was Blind Willie.

'Okay,' said the door-guard. 'But if you come in and goes away, you ain't gettin' in a second time.'

Blind Willie was sitting on the same stool as the previous evening. 'I don't normally take a drink durin' the day,' he growled, 'but this is a special occasion. Storm comin' down.'

The barman popped the cap off a beer and passed it to Michael. 'On the house. One less for the looters to take.' He placed an oil-shined pump shotgun on the bar. 'If they want to try, that is.' He dragged a TV on top of the bar and fiddled with the cable at the back. 'Might as well see what's comin' down.'

They followed the path of the storm on the TV, drinking all afternoon. The number of patrons grew in number as the storm progressed and rain battered down outside. Michael was the only white man in the bar, but he didn't feel particularly conscious of the fact, as he seemed to be accepted as a friend of Willie's.

'Man's declared an evacuation,' shouted one of the drinkers as he watched the mayor speak at a podium.

'Too fuckin' late for us,' roared another man. 'Not that they gives a shit anyway.'

Not long afterwards, the power went off. 'Shut that door, Marvin,' yelled the barman, who Michael had found out was in fact the owner, named Louis.

The door was closed and bolted. It was solid with no windows and little enough light penetrated the small windows on the street front. Marvin dragged sandbags to the other side of the door.

'Now listen up,' called Louis. 'This bar is all I have. No insurance or nuthin'. Drinks are on the house as long as you boys stay here to keep it safe. Don't think that Bourbon Street will flood much, but it's people that worry me. Half the cops will have run away and none of them ever gave a shit anyway. Got food and water in the storeroom and four solid walls, all that we need.'

One of the patrons wandered around with candles stuck into bottles, placing them on tables where they cast flickering light. A man sat on the stage and plucked a guitar, strumming blues chords. 'Woke up this mornin' ... storm was a-comin' ...' Some others began to clap and stamp their feet, and a short fat man pulled a harmonica from his pocket.

Michael smiled through a hazy beer glow. This was New Orleans proper. And he'd completely forgotten about cemeteries or graveyards.

He was woken by noise. He had no idea of how long he'd slept, and had a pounding hangover headache. He had fallen asleep on the floor, using his rucksack as a pillow. Others were sprawled around and some were still drinking.

Louis was listening to a portable radio. Some of the noise was from the radio; the rest was from screaming and shouting from outside. Firelight flickered outside, glinting in the windows. Some water had trickled in through the sandbags, forming a pool near the door.

'Situation's bad, fellers,' he called out to a hushed bar-room. 'Plenty flooding and the roof's nearly off the sports dome. It's full of people and they're all fighting and stealing. Mayor's declared a state of emergency. We need to wait on the National Guard comin' in, to clear away the looters.'

'Most of the Guard are in Iraq,' yelled one man. 'My brother's with them. How the fuck they going to get them back from there?'

'Let me take a look outside,' said Marvin, picking up a baseball bat from next to the door.

'Okay,' said Louis, grabbing the shotgun. 'But I'm right behind you.'

Marvin threw back the bolts on the door. Bat in one hand, he kicked the sandbags away and pulled open the door. He clambered onto the sandbag revetment and looked around the corner.

Then, he vanished, torn from sight by unseen hands. And the screaming started, shrill agony beyond hope of saving or healing.

'Holy shit,' yelled Louis. He jumped onto the sandbags, looking over the shotgun barrel. He pulled the trigger and worked the slide, but he was dragged outside as well, and joined in the chorus of screams.

Then they came through the doorway. Shambling corpses, stinking of the grave and the floodwater, with ravenous hunger in their hollow eyes.

Although the hurricane had passed the city by, the storm surge from Lake Pontchartrain had overwhelmed the inadequate levees, causing enormous flooding. Some areas were completely under water and, at that moment, householders were trapped in attics and resorting to hacking their way through roofs with axes and hammers. If they had known what was on the outside, they would have preferred to risk drowning.

The floodwater had reached the French Quarter, including the cemeteries of St Louis. The waters had flooded through the stone and brick tombs, loosening masonry and slabs, floating corpses and coffins. Unseen by living eyes, a skeletal form had crawled from an unmarked tomb, loosened from its rope-like bindings, clawing through soaking rotted wood, pushing through brickwork aged by time and soaked by water. It had slithered through water, mud and the fetid remains of other corpses. As it touched them, they too began to writhe. Possessed by blood hunger, they staggered onto their rotting limbs, and shambled off in search of sustenance.

The walking dead fell upon the living with ravenous hunger, tearing throats and jaw-bones, closing vicelike on fleshy arms and legs, gulping down blood. They grew in numbers as the slain found themselves dragged back to the realm of the living, driven by agonising hunger.

Michael watched Blind Willie as he slumped on his bar stool. 'He's out.'

'What can we do?' yelled Michael. Behind him, patrons were fighting with the undead. The occasional crack of a gunshot drowned out the meaty smacks of cleavers, knives and pool cues, as well as the throaty gurgle of fallen victims.

'Nuthin' much we can do.' Willie pulled out a silver derringer and raised it to his head.

'Wait!' Michael grabbed his arm, jerking it. The pistol shot echoed around the bar-room but no-one looked up. 'There must be something we can do!'

'That was my only bullet, shit-head.' Willie threw down the gun. 'I've no goddamned choice now.'

Michael looked behind him. The living patrons were in a deadlock with the shambling corpses in the doorway.

'We've got to get out of this place! Grab onto me!'

Michael grabbed a bar-stool as a battering-ram and entered the fray, Willie clutching the back of his belt. He pushed with all his effort, forcing the corpses back. One of them, a slough-faced skull with empty eye-sockets, swung at him with its crab-clawed talons, but he dodged easily and the blow passed by his face, leaving only the fetid stench of decay in its wake. They were slow creatures. He thrust the stool forward, momentum with him, but his feet slipped on the slimy floor. He didn't want to look down and see, or smell, the mess of blood and putrescent slime beneath him. But hands grabbed his back, and forced him forward as others joined in behind him. They pushed the corpses backwards through the door, and spilled out onto the street.

'Get to the cemetery,' hissed Willie, in his ear. 'The whip. The bone whip. It might be there.'

They ducked round the corner, into an alleyway, and Michael pulled out the map he had torn out of the guidebook. The St Louis cemetery wasn't far, just three blocks away. The trouble was that he was knee-deep in floodwater, surrounded by the living dead which were intent on tearing the flesh from every last living person, until they too rose as walking corpses. And he had to escort a blind man, although Willie held the handle of his cane in a menacing grasp.

The walking dead seemed to be intent on attacking the largest groups of the living, including the former patrons of the Rising Sun, who had run into more of the creatures in the main street. Michael slipped past them, leading Willie, ignoring the complaining shouts. 'Chicken-shit motherfucker,' they called in his wake. He glanced back over his shoulder and saw one of the patrons hack the maggot-ridden arm off a corpse with a cleaver, before he was dragged down by two others. The creatures bit into his face and throat, which disappeared in a red spray.

They splashed up Dumaine Street, towards the Louis Armstrong Park. The fetid oil-slicked water soaked their legs, and Michael dodged floating branches, toys, drink cartons, polystyrene boxes and other debris. A scum-covered body floated past, and he gave it a wide berth. It did not move as it glided past serenely, face-up, but something snagged his ankle and he screamed. Another body had slid past behind him, face-down in the water, arms trailing in its wake.

The elegant buildings, arches and trees of the park were all lapped by water, but deserted of living or dead humans. Flames lapped in the distance, reflected on the underside of dark gray clouds. Michael was not sure if it was day or night. Most of the noise and activity seemed to be to the south, near the Superdome and Warehouse District. He checked his map.

The cemetery was next to a deserted red-brick housing project, and south of the raised St Claiborne Avenue Expressway. Bedraggled refugees trudged wearily southwards along this, presumably towards the Superdome, escorted by National Guardsmen. The cemetery gates were wide open and

Michael passed between the white stone pillars, leading Willie into the twisting avenues of the raised memorials and tombs.

'I don't know where to start, Willie,' said Michael. 'It's all under water.'

The blind man sighed. 'It's halfway down Alley Number Two. Name of Louviere. Most of the tombs are brick and stucco.'

'I think we're in Center Alley,' said Michael, squinting at the map. Ahead was a meandering path through the looming monoliths. 'Alley Number Two is one of these offshoots.' Willie splashed after him, and they paused as Michael looked nervously at the dark passage to his left, overshadowed by the tombs, in darkness because of the power cuts. He took a deep breath and turned down the alley.

Michael placed one foot gently after the other, frightened of stumbling and being pounced upon by the undead. Hairs crackled on the back of the neck as he edged past the cracked-open vaults and tombs, which stared menacingly at him like eye-sockets in a row of skulls. He tried not to gag on the sweetly-fetid air which wafted from the abandoned sepulchres. Willie breathed heavily behind him, muttering what sounded like prayers to some distant god.

'Believe we're passing the Glaipon tomb,' mumbled Willie. 'That's the one where the voodoo queen is supposed to be buried.'

Michael squinted at the vault on his left, broken open like the others. It was hard to make anything out in the darkness, but he could sense nothing in the inky-black void.

'Louviere tomb is round this corner,' mumbled Willie. 'I can feel it, as well. In my bones.' He laughed morbidly.

And there it stood, at the end of the dead-end labyrinth, stained stucco mostly fallen away from the structure like scabrous skin peeling from a corpse.

Michael inched forward, shining the light on his mobile phone around the inside of the broken tomb. The blue-white glare picked out scuttling spiders and ancient cobwebs, broken stones and stones jutting through the floodwater like teeth. But there was no whip.

'Do I need to go in and look?' Michael was shaking with fear, close to tears. 'Do I have to? I will if I need to, but I'm fucking terrified!'

The tomb entrance radiated fear, an obscene black hole sucking in all other emotions other than terror.

'Go on and look, son. I'm here behind you.' Willie's flat voice didn't inspire confidence.

Michael edged forward, his body shuddering, hairs up at razor-sharp angles.

'Do I have to put my hand in it?' He was crying now, unashamed of his terror.

'Only if you kick something with your foot.'

Michael swung his leg around, swishing the water into waves, avoiding the stones which stuck out of the water, and leaning back as far as possible.

Clunk.

Something connected with his foot, in a dull thud.

He bent forward, every sinew of his body poised for flight. He plunged his hand into the water and pulled something out.

It was a human backbone, stripped of ribs.

'Got it! I've fucking got it!'

Willie sighed. 'That ain't it. That's some poor other dead soul's backbone.'

Michael slouched out of the tomb, drained of all emotion, filled with numbing despair.

'What do we do now?'

'Only thing I can think of is to see Marie Lavieu.'

'The Voodoo Queen? But we passed by there earlier?' Michael shrugged. 'Why didn't we check there first?'

'You ain't been listening. She ain't there. She lives downtown, a couple of blocks away.'

Michael kept to the shadows, which was most of the side-streets, other than the light cast by flames and distant searchlights. Willie stumbled after him, tired by the effort of carefully placing his feet in the floodwater, and soaked to the bone.

'Think it's next one on the right,' said Willie. 'Difficult to tell, though, shufflin' along like this. She always said it was a light pink colour.'

'Is she really the Voodoo Queen?'

'I don't know, and nobody does, other than her. She was born and grew up like anyone else. I knew her as a babe in arms. But she had power, even then, or so they said. A soul doesn't need to die when the body does, if you know the rituals.'

They passed an intersection and Michael glanced down to fire-lit Bourbon Street. A shape crouched over something, tearing and gnawing. Michael looked away just as he realised what it was, bile flooding his gullet. He bent double, retching into the flooded street.

A hand clasped his shoulder. 'I can hear it,' said Willie. 'We gotta be strong.'

Ahead, on the corner to the right, was a pink-stuccoed mansion, white pillars and facings. Michael stopped. 'Is it a big place, on the corner?'

'I think so,' said Willie.

'We're here then.'

They crunched up the glass covered steps, shards glinting like diamonds in the firelight. The door had been kicked open.

'Doesn't look good,' said Michael.

'I think she's here,' hissed Willie. 'I can feel her.'

The wooden floorboards were strewn with broken and shattered furniture. Ahead, at the top of a grand staircase, was what looked like a barricade assembled from tables and chairs.

Michael crept towards the staircase. He wished he had a weapon of some kind, but knew they would be useless. Ahead, at the top of the stairs, loomed a shadowed bulk, stepping carefully through the obstacles.

'It's her!' Willie grinned in relief.

The shape stumbled and fell, crashing down the steps onto the two men, crushing them with its bulk.

Michael caught a glimpse of burning red eyes in the bloated face, contorted into a hate-consumed mask. He writhed frantically to escape, slithering under the blood-soaked folds of flesh.

Willie moaned weakly for a few seconds, until the teeth found his throat.

Michael wriggled free just as hot fluid splashed his skin from a spurting artery. He stumbled away, glancing back at the hulking shape which tore and gnawed at the dying man on the ground.

At the Superdome, all hell had broken loose. The evacuation plan had been thrown into chaos. Hordes of decaying and more recent corpses were throwing themselves against the fortress-like structure. The National Guard had flown in sharpshooters and machine-gunners, who were setting up on the roof and upper levels. The bullets thudded into the dead, and they fell in great numbers, but still they came on. Even worse, they were at the rear of the living survivors who were struggling to get into the shelter of the Superdome under helicopter floodlights. They tore into the living even as bullets tore into them and, when they fell, fresh corpses clawed themselves upright to take their places.

A sniper team on the roof covered the northeast, along the axis of the expressway. The spotter saw movement through his binoculars, a kilometre distant.

'Target two-o-clock, seven-fifty metres.'

The marksman shuffled on his foam mat and looked through the sight of his fifty-calibre rifle.

'You reckon that's a zombie motherfucker?'

'Can't quite see what it is. It's shuffling along, covered head to toe in filth.'

'I can't see much either, just got a figure in my sight.'

'Put it down. Looks like a corpse to me.'

The rifle cracked, the massive bolt sliding backwards, catching open on an empty chamber. The distant figure crumpled as the gunshot's echo faded.

'Need a fresh magazine.'

'Okay. Here you go.'

The magazine clicked as it slid into place. 'This sucks. Take me back to Baghdad right now.'

'Reckon we'll be out of here in a few hours. This place won't last long. There's too many of the motherfuckers, and they just won't stay dead.'

The command centre was half empty. Only those with 'need to know' clearance were allowed to join the President of the United States as he viewed the real-time video footage.

'Heck of a mess, isn't it Brownie?'

'Yes Sir. Maybe a hundred thousand were holed up in the city, twenty thousand of them in the Superdome. They're all walking corpses now.'

The President turned to his Secretary of Defence. 'What can we do, Donny?'

'Nuke 'em?' The bespectacled man laughed. 'Only joking. We've got thermobaric bombs; that's the best bet. Vaporise those sons of bitches in the streets, and burn anything that's left.'

'It needs to be kept top secret with a cordon around the place and the media kept at bay, at all costs.' The President rubbed his chin. 'We can blame it on Al Qaeda. Or maybe not, gas explosions might be better.'

'We need to get one or two of those waking dead creatures alive though.' The President smiled. 'Oh dear, or whatever they are, alive or dead. Dead or alive, even.' He laughed.

A uniformed man spoke up. 'Mister President, we've sent out recon patrols. They're still out there, searching block by block for any artefacts or isolated corpses. The creatures are throwing themselves at the Superdome for the time being. We've got another twelve hours or so before they overwhelm the place and we have to burn it.'

'Keep 'em at it. There must be something causing this.' The President munched on a pretzel. 'Whatever it is we could really use those in the War on Terror, in Afghanistan, in Iraq.'

He looked at the chaos on the screens, arms thrust in his suit jacket pockets. 'Just think what they could do ...'

THE END

ROCKETS' RED GLARE
By
Bowie V Ibarra

Calavera City, Texas
Reloj Co.

"Little faggots popping fireworks for the Fourth of July tonight?"

Trevor and Todd's sole purpose was to drink beer and make people feel miserable at Calavera City Community College. The five people they rolled up on were some of their favourite targets, both in and out of school.

"Don't you guys have a douchebag meeting tonight or something?"

Geoff was always the first to respond of the five friends. He gave a high-five to his two buddies, Bruce and Lawrence, who were standing next to him when he uttered the response. They immediately began laughing. The laughter was just another way to get under Trevor and Todd's skin.

"You're just jealous because we can afford them, asshole," said Belinda, joining the boys with a barb of her own. Heather, who was standing by Belinda, laughed along with the boys. She knuckle-bumped Belinda.

"You're the only girl I know, Belinda," said Todd, "that would settle for a little queer boyfriend like Bruce who doesn't even have a car."

"I'll take personality over having a car any day, asshole," she said, flipping him the middle finger.

"Why don't we just go inside your house?" said Todd, indicating her home. "You can see how big my personality is."

"Fuck off," she replied as Trevor and Todd chuckled.

Two 5-tonne Army trucks pulled up behind Trevor's Mustang GT. The bright lights of the first vehicle cut through the early evening. The driver honked.

With the arrogance of a true jerk, Trevor took a long and defiant swig of beer, before saying, "When you girls want to hang out with some real men, call us." He revved the engine before peeling out in front of the group of friends. The white smoke of burnt rubber filled the air as the car shrieked like a Detroit-born banshee then sped away. With a grumbling clamour, the trucks drove on.

"I should've tossed a bottle-rocket in their car," said Bruce.

"That would've been hilarious," said Heather.

"Speaking of," said Lawrence, "let's send another salvo." He handed four bottle-rockets to his friends and they immediately placed them in their bottles on the sidewalk.

"Try and delay the lighting," suggested Belinda. "Let's see if we can get them to pop in one-second intervals."

"Hey babe, this isn't the fireworks at the Tower of the Americas in San Antonio, now," chuckled Bruce.

"Just do it. Ready?"

The friends had their punks lit and ready. "Go."

They each waited for the person beside them to light their fuse before they lit theirs. As the last of the five friends lit theirs, the first rocket went off. Then the second, third, fourth, and finally the fifth rocket took flight. Like Belinda had planned, they whistled into the sky in a crude, yet coordinated, salvo. They burst in the sky in intervals, and the friends cheered.

"Respect the soldiers," a voice behind them said. The friends turned around. They knew who it was. It was Mr. Fuentes, who had rolled up on his bike. Or, as students at Calavera City Community College knew him, he was Pete the Nutty Professor. "Respect the soldiers on the Fourth of July. They are with God now. They died so you could live here in freedom."

"Guy's nuttier than squirrel turds," whispered Bruce.

"Leave him alone," said Heather. "He's just old."

"And annoying," said Geoff, lighting a small string of Black Cat fireworks. As the fuse lit, Geoff yelled out, "Hey, Nutty Professor, here's to the soldiers!"

Before his friends could stop him, Geoff tossed the firecrackers at the old man. The old man gasped as the fireworks crackled on the ground around him. Cringing, he got back on his bike and rode away.

"Respect the soldiers, you little bastards. Respect the soldiers," he said as he disappeared down the road.

It wasn't quite like watching a guy in an old western dance around the ground as a villain was shooting at his feet, but it was still pretty funny.

As the others laughed, Heather snapped, "Geoff, that was mean." She hit his arm, but struggled to contain a chuckle of her own.

"You thought it was funny," said Geoff.

"It was funny," said Bruce.

"He's always talking religion," said Bruce. "So, like my mom says, if he was mad at us, he should forgive us."

"I forgive you," said Belinda, walking up to her man. Her hands held in a pantomime of religious fervour, she added, "I forgive you."

The five laughed again and dug out more fireworks to set off.

As the friends laughed, Trevor and Todd were plotting against them.

"Hey, check it out," said Trevor, indicating Deputy Jacobs at the Whataburger. "It's the Sheriff."

"Let's get out of here," Todd said, lowering his beer. "If he sees us drinking, we're done for."

"Don't worry, it's Deputy Jacobs," said Trevor. "He's my brother-in-law remember. He owes me a favour, too." Trevor finished his beer and threw the empty can into the back seat before driving to the restaurant. He pulled into the parking lot and pulled up right beside the deputy's vehicle. "Watch," said Trevor, stepping out of the car and walking to his lawman-in-law.

In the car, Deputy Jacobs was eating a triple-cheeseburger as Trevor knocked on the window. Diced onions and a dribble of sauce had fallen onto his distended belly, and the deputy made no effort to wipe them off as he rolled down the window.

"Trevor," said the deputy, as he chewed. "What are you up to?"

"Well, brother, I just wanted to report some lawbreakers to you."

The deputy stuffed several French fries into his mouth, before saying, "What do you got?" A gruesome blend of bread, melded with ketchup, fries and meat sloshed around his mouth as he spoke. Mustard oozed down his chin.

"There's a group of kids popping fireworks just two blocks down. There's a restriction on using fireworks in the city limits, right?"

"That's right." A small piece of lettuce dangled on his moustache.

As if on cue, a Roman candle lit up the sky, over where Trevor was indicating.

"Well, as you can see," said Trevor, smiling and showing off his crooked teeth, "those kids are clearly flouting the law."

Deputy Jacobs took another big bite of the burger and said, "I'll be right over there, Trev. Thanks for the tip."

"Anything for my brother," said Trevor, giving a thumbs up.

The deputy cocked his eyebrow and added, "Have you been drinking?"

"Brother," said Trevor, slyly. "I don't drink and drive."

Trevor returned to the Mustang and cracked open another Natural Light, toasting his in-law. Todd shrugged and returned the toast as they pulled out of the lot.

Deputy Jacobs finished off his burger and fries. He wasn't in any hurry.

"Man, those were awesome," said Bruce, craning his neck to stare up into the clear evening sky.

"We got the heavy duty Roman Candles," said Heather, rummaging in the bag.

"And we haven't even pulled out the mortars yet," said Belinda, smiling.

"Ya'll got mortars?" asked Geoff. "I want to light one of those suckers."

"We have to finish with the mortars," said Lawrence. "Always go with the big finish last."

"True, true," said Belinda. With a wink, she added, "Right, Bruce? Big finish?"

Bruce smiled. "Oh, yeah. Big finish."

"You guys are so gross," said Heather, laughing.

"Big explosion, right Bruce."

Bruce blushed. "Oh, yeah."

"You guys are nasty," said Lawrence.

They set off another series of fireworks, 'ooh-ing' and 'ahh-ing' at each display.

Another car pulled up at the mouth of the street. At first, they ignored it. But when the overhead red and blue lights flashed, they realised who it was.

"We are just outside the city limits, aren't we?" asked Geoff.

"Err, not quite," said Belinda, cringing. "I think it's the next block over."

The police car was heading right for them.

"Quick," said Belinda. "Into my house."

The five friends grabbed the remaining fireworks and ran into Belinda's house. They slammed the door as the car reached the house.

"My mom's coming back soon, so we can't stay here. Out the back," said Belinda. They quickly followed her out the back door and into the back yard.

"What now?" asked Lawrence.

"Just follow me," she said, walking through the back gate into an adjacent alley. Beside the alley was a crude barrier that they bypassed to head into a dry concrete waterway. They followed Belinda under a nearby bridge.

They waited expectantly, awaiting their pursuer.

"So," said Heather, "what are we doing here?"

"Let's give panzon a little time to lose interest, eh?" said Belinda. "Then let's go to the cemetery and pop more fireworks."

"Oh, no," said Heather, shaking her head vehemently. "I hate that place! What with all those dead people."

"They're dead, Heather," said Lawrence with a sigh. "They died in wars a long time ago."

"In wars?" asked Heather.

"It's the military cemetery, not the public one. They're not going to bother us."

"Dead soldiers tell no tales," said Geoff with a chuckle. "I wonder if they still have their weapons."

"Shut up," said Belinda, rolling her eyes. "They don't bury soldiers with their weapons."

"I suppose a military cemetery would be the perfect place to shoot more fireworks, though," conceded Heather.

"It's outside the city limits, too," said Bruce.

"Just let this marinate," said Belinda. "We'll head in and have some fun in just a few. Tubby shouldn't be too long."

The five friends spent the next few minutes talking about school and gossip, until Belinda decided that it was time to go.

By the time they set off out of the dry waterway, full darkness had set in. A half moon shone high in the night sky.

As they walked, Lawrence said, "Hey, did you guys hear the rumour that there's a secret military base under the cemetery?"

"What?" said Geoff, raising his eyebrows.

"Yeah," Lawrence continued. "The government sponsored renovations on the cemetery in the early '80s. There was loads of tunnelling – they sealed off the whole area. It took like three years before the construction crews left."

"It's true," said Bruce as the five entered the cemetery. "My dad told me about it once."

"I heard there was a UFO base under it," said Belinda.

"It was that they made them, not an actual base," said Lawrence. "And I heard it, too. They might be hiding one."

"Or two," said Belinda.

They took the main road through the five acre cemetery. Hundreds of headstones were interspersed with groomed lawns and mature trees. They decided to head to the rear of the cemetery where they had less chance of being disturbed.

As the kids began setting up their fireworks, Trevor and Todd waited in their car a hundred yards from the entrance to the cemetery. When the coast was clear, snuck up to the iron gates and drew them closed.

"Gimme the chain," said Trevor, snatching it from Todd. It was a simple bike security chain, but it would do the trick.

As Trevor locked it, they both sniggered.

"This is going to be great," said Trevor, heading back to the car.

"Hell yeah," said Todd. "I'm gonna make those little pricks beg."

They returned to the Mustang and cracked open two more beers. They could see the fireworks in the distance, dazzling in the black sky.

The friends might have wildly speculated what was below them, and, although there were not UFOs under the cemetery, there was a government-sponsored biological weapons laboratory. No one knows what caused the explosion, but the consequences were devastating.

A deadly experimental bio-toxin filtered up through the ground, through coffins, and to their decaying inhabitants. There were hundreds of graves in the vicinity of the blast.

The ground had shuddered under the group's feet. They all fell silent, glancing nervously at each other.

"Did you feel that?" asked Heather, hoping that it was just her imagination.

"Yeah," said Geoff. "Like the ground moved, right?"

The others nodded in agreement and strained their ears, listening for anything out of the ordinary. The cemetery was bathed in silence.

"What do you think?" asked Lawrence to no one in particular.

"Earthquake?" Belinda suggested.

Heather laughed nervously. "Yeah, that's it. Just a little tremor."

Shrugging, Geoff said, "Forget it. Let's get some more fireworks."

Glad for the distraction, they continued with their firework display. As they set off another salvo, a new scent filled the air that wasn't sulphurous.

211

"Who farted?" said Geoff, wafting a hand in front of his nose.

"I did," said Bruce, chuckling.

"Cochino," said Belinda, cringing.

Frowning, Heather said, "I smell it, too."

"Whoever smelt it, dealt it," laughed Geoff.

"Forget that," said Belinda, lighting a Bouncing Betty. "Check this out."

As the fuse sparked to life, she tossed it into the air. It blazed in a circle, gliding. The spark of the firecracker spun the firework in the air before gliding down to the ground where it exploded.

As it exploded another underground tremor rocked the cemetery.

Holding onto a tree, Geoff said, "Holy crap! What did you light?"

"Just a Bouncing Betty," said Belinda, holding onto Bruce's arm.

"Check it out, guys," said Heather. "There's, like, fumes coming out of the ground."

As they looked on, delicate plumes of green gas danced into the air, swirling across the grass and between headstones.

"What … is that?" asked Heather.

"Ghosts?" said Geoff and managed a nervous snort.

"Shut up, stupid," snapped Bruce.

"Looks like some kind of gas," said Belinda. "Did the firecracker light it?"

"Light my gas," said Geoff, but he was no longer laughing.

"Hey," said Lawrence. "Someone's over there."

They all turned to look where Lawrence was pointing. Emerging out of the darkness was what appeared to be a US Marine in dress blues. The soldier's stark white hat was unmistakeable.

"Hey, Jarhead!" yelled Geoff.

"Shhh," said Heather. "Don't make him mad."

"C'mon," said Bruce. "It's the Fourth of July, after all. We're supposed to respect our soldiers."

"OK, Nutty Professor," said Belinda. "We're sorry."

212

"Hey," said Heather. "It's another one," she said, pointing.

They all turned to look. It was true. Another figure, but this one resembling a Doughboy from World War I, was ambling towards them.

"OK ..." muttered Belinda. "What's going on here?"

"Relax," said Bruce, rubbing her back. "I'll say something."

"Wait," hissed Geoff. "Can you hear that?"

They fell silent. Muffled voices, scraping and banging noises filled the air.

"This is not cool," said Bruce as Belinda clutched his arm.

"What is going on here, guys?" asked Lawrence, pointing to three more figures, also clad in military regalia of different eras.

As they gawped at the three new figures, the ground under their feet began to shift and move.

"Oh, shit," Geoff spat, staggering backwards.

"They're rising!" yelled Lawrence. "The dead are ... rising!"

"Is this ... for real?" asked Heather, tears brimming in her eyes.

"I think it might be," said Lawrence, backing away.

"These things can't be coming for Saturday morning cartoons," spat Bruce. "This is not good!"

Gathering his senses, Geoff said, "Stay calm, guys. Stick together."

Their mounting terror was almost palpable.

"What do we do?" asked Heather, tears rolling down her cheeks.

"Light something," said Geoff suggested. "Throw it at them!"

Everyone scrambled for fireworks; mortars, Roman candles, bottle-rockets. Anything they could get their hands on.

Trembling, they huddled together.

"Wait," said Lawrence. "Won't these ignite the gas?"

"He's right," agreed Heather. "This place is going to light up."

They looked around again. The Doughboy and the Marine were closest, but at least a dozen more figures were closing in.

"And the Rocket's Red Glare," said Geoff, lighting his Roman Candle.

Everyone else followed suit.

"Here goes nothing," said Bruce and held his breath.

Geoff lobbed his at the Doughboy as the rest tossed their respective fireworks into the approaching crowd.

Clouds of gas ignited in rapid flashing detonations that scorched grass and headstones. Another blast rattled the ground again, signalling fresh explosions beneath them.

Screaming, Bruce and Belinda frantically patted each other as sparks had ignited their clothes. Their friends help, quickly extinguishing the flames. Several of the shambling creatures had also been set alight, but they made no attempt to douse them.

Doughboy reached out for Geoff, moaning softly. Flinching, Geoff jabbed his Super-Deluxe Roman Candle into its open mouth as it began to shoot its fiery load. Flames shot down the creature's throat, making its paper-thin skin appear glowing and translucent. Suddenly, belching flames tore out of its belly and engulfed the whole creature.

Geoff backed away, uttering, "Awesome …"

The rest of the fireworks began exploding and whizzing in all directions, striking the undead and bursting into flames. A bottle-rocket struck a World War II paratrooper in the eye, a tail of sparking flames shooting out of the socket.

They fired off more and more, but their stocks were quickly dwindling and more and more creatures were appearing to replace those who sizzled and crackled on the ground.

Todd and Trevor were standing at the gates, beers in hands, staring at the dazzling light display.

"Damn," said Todd. "Those guys are really setting them off."

"No shit," agreed Trevor, sipping his beer.

"This isn't working!" cried Heather. "There's too many of them!"

214

Dozens of creatures were pressing in from all sides.

"We've got enough for one more, guys, and then we make a break for the front gate," said Geoff.

The five lit another round of fireworks and threw them as grasping hands broke through the grass at their feet. Their shrieks mixed with the explosions from the fireworks.

"Let's go!" said Geoff, leading his friends in the direction of the front gate. The others followed without hesitation. The creatures were moving slowly enough for them to weave through, but their numbers were growing fast.

Standing at the gates, Todd and Trevor stood and gazed across the cemetery.

"Check it out," said Trevor. "Here they come."

"Who are all those other people?" asked Todd, squinting.

"Probably more fags with fireworks."

"Why are they running?" asked Todd.

Concentrating on the five fleeing friends, they failed to notice the shifting ground at graves nearest to them.

The group of friends reached the gate, gasping for air. Todd and Trevor began pointing and laughing.

"What now, faggots?" Trevor managed between sniggers.

"See, Belinda," shouted Todd. "If you were with me, you'd be on this side."

"Let us out!" Belinda yelled.

"Open the gate!" Heather chorused.

The two boys' laughter intensified, Todd clutching his stomach.

"You and the rest of those freaks will just have to wait," said Trevor.

"C'mon, beg," said Todd. "Beg and we *might* let you out."

"Listen, Trevor, you asshole," snapped Geoff. "Those aren't people! They're dead!"

"What have you been smoking?" said Todd, but a troubled frown marred his features as he glanced back at the approaching crowd. "So they're zombies!" He laughed again, but it sounded hollow.

"What would soldiers be …" Trevor stopped in the middle of the sentence.

Shambling towards the five trapped friends, he could see a sailor in a dirty and moth-eaten blue shirt and denim bell-bottoms. Its flesh had almost completely rotted away, leaving bones peaking out here and there. A soldier nearby, in green fatigues, was dragging a foot behind him that was hanging on by slivers of rotting flesh. In the graves nearby, others were rising through the ground, clods of soil falling from their dead grey faces.

"Oh, shit," whispered Trevor, backing away. "Oh … shit."

Todd gaped at the horrific scene, but then managed, "Open the gate, Trevor. You know the combination. Open the goddamn gate!"

Trevor was staggering backwards, muttering 'oh shit' over and over again.

"Trevor, let them out!" yelled Todd. The five friends screamed at him.

Todd grasped at Trevor, but he shoved him back, crying, "No, no!" Trevor bolted for the car. Todd started after him, but a cry for help stopped him short.

"Help us!" the trapped friends were begging. It was Belinda's that Todd concentrated on.

He ran back to the gate as Trevor revved the car and sped away.

A multitude of groans were rising on the wind as the shuffling mass drew ever closer.

"I don't know the combination," said Todd, tugging at the chain.

"Fuck it! Break for it!" yelled Geoff.

Todd watched, helpless, as the five friends scattered. Lawrence and Heather dashed in one direction, Geoff in another and Bruce and Belinda in another.

Todd desperately yanked on the chain then, glancing around, he noticed a large stone. Grabbing it, he started smashing it against the chain.

Belinda screamed. Looking up, Todd saw Bruce stop in his tracks. He dropped to his knees by a hole in the ground, screaming, holding his hands out.

216

Todd watched in horror as one of the creatures fell into the open grave.

"Belinda!" he cried out.

Bruce scrambled into the hole.

Belinda's screams reached new heights. Todd frantically searched for options. The bars to the cemetery were too close together for Todd to slide through, but he had to try.

With stone in his hand, he wriggled against the iron bars. His legs and even his chest cleared them, but his head was too wide, no matter which way he tried.

Several creatures were moving towards him. Ignoring them, he kept trying. He had to help Belinda.

Taking a deep breath, he drove his head through. The bars tore at the sides of his head. He howled in pain, but kept pushing. Cold iron tore at his ears and blood dribbled down his cheeks. With tears in his eyes, he finally sprung free of the bars.

Swiping at the oozing blood, he ran to the hole where Belinda and Bruce had fallen inside. Looking down, he saw Bruce wrestling with the creature. Belinda was behind him, sobbing.

With a scream, Todd jumped into the hole, knocking the creature onto its back. The creature grasped for Todd, but he raised the rock and brought it down on the creature's skull with a sickening crack. He repeatedly brought it smashing down onto the creature's head until the entire skull caved in, spewing brain and gore out into the sodden earth.

Todd stood up to see Bruce cradling Belinda.

"Keep hold of her," said Todd. "I got it."

Another creature dropped into the hole, and Todd leapt at it, smashing it in the face.

"Get out!" yelled Todd.

"We tried," said Bruce, holding a blood and dirt-smeared Belinda. "It's too high!"

Todd gave it a try, but loose dirt gave way in his hands.

A third creature dropped over the edge and Todd struck out at it.

Yet another creature fell into the hole while Todd was struggling with the previous one. It landed right on top of Bruce,

217

pinning him to the ground. It bit into his shoulder and blood sprayed Belinda's horrified face.

Todd leapt at the creature, dragging it clear and then battered its head in.

Geoff appeared at the top of the hole, panting and red-faced. "Can you get out?"

"No," said Todd.

"Oh, shit," he muttered, staring at Bruce and Belinda.

"Just run, dumbass. Get the hell out of here!" yelled Todd.

As Geoff hesitated, two creatures grabbed him and bit into the soft flesh of his neck and arm. He screamed as they stripped flesh away from his body and wrestled him to the ground.

"Fuck!" cried Todd. Geoff's cries quickly turned into feeble gurgles.

Crying, Bruce was shouting, "Belinda!" The creature had managed to bite her on the leg and arm before he had fought it off and blood was pooling around her. "Belinda, please!"

She emitted one last rattling gasp and then her eyes rolled back into her head.

Heather and Lawrence had ran in a wide arch, dodging creatures this way and that, and had managed to work their way back to the gates. A vehicle was pulling up and they cried out in desperation.

Several figures dressed in chemical response suits and respirators approached the gate. Heather and Lawrence huddled together, glancing over their shoulders as one soldier cut the chain with bolt cutters.

The soldiers pushed open the gates as Heather repeated, "Thank you! Thank you!"

Their gratitude was greeted with gunfire as two of the suited soldiers gunned them down.

The soldiers entered, followed by several US Army HMMWVs and trucks. Several soldiers at the rear of the column re-secured the gates and stood guard as dozens of soldiers dismounted from the vehicles.

Systematically, present US military went to work exterminating the ghouls of past soldiers, past patriots, past Americans.

Bruce wept over the body of his dead girlfriend. "My sweet Belinda ..." He was oblivious to the gunfire above them, but Todd wasn't.

"Jesus Christ. What the fuck is going on up there?" asked Todd. Tracers lit up the sky above them.

"The Army? They've come to save us," Bruce muttered between sobs.

"Hopefully. Just wait. If they're getting those things, we don't want them to confuse them with us."

Bruce looked down at Belinda. Her eyes were closed. A tear fell from his cheek onto her already cold, pale face.

Her eyes opened and glared up at the night sky.

"Belinda?" uttered Bruce in shock. "Belinda!"

Like an infant child taking in the world for the first time, she looked into Bruce's eyes. The light that he found in her eyes, the light that once filled his heart with joy, was replaced with a cruel darkness. A milky film rested over her eyes like cataracts. She smiled.

"Oh, Belinda! You're alive!" he cried and bent down to kiss her.

"No!" shouted Todd.

As Bruce kissed his young love, for a moment it felt like their past kissed, but then he felt the chill on her lips and her stiff, searching tongue.

He started to pull away, but Belinda grabbed his head and pulled him to her. This time, Belinda kissed with her teeth, tearing his lips away from his face. He tried to wrestle with her vice-like embrace, but she bit again into his shoulder.

Todd jumped in, kicking her in the head, knocking her away as Bruce screamed. Bruce scrambled away as Todd smashed Belinda's head with the stone. Tears fell from his eyes as his heart broke along with Belinda's skull.

In desperation, Bruce clawed at the loose earth at the lip of the grave.

"I'm so sorry," Todd whispered weakly. Chunks of Belinda's hair and scalp clung to the rock in his hand. Her blood dripped from his fingers.

An explosion rocked the ground nearby, knocking small bits of earth onto their upturned faces.

Blood loss and pain finally started taking its toll on Bruce. Clutching his wounded shoulder, he crouched in the corner, whimpering through his torn mouth.

Todd couldn't bear to look at him. The boy's face was mangled. His whimpering slowly ebbed away.

The gunfire was getting closer, louder. Todd cringed in fear. A sense of impending doom filled his heart.

Todd glanced at Bruce. His trembling was growing weaker. Todd and Trevor used to take great joy in humiliating others, making them cry, making them beg for mercy. The tables had turned and now he was the one terrified and praying for mercy.

"I'm sorry I called you a faggot, Bruce," Todd managed in a hoarse whisper. "I'm so sorry."

Bruce gazed at his former enemy through glazed eyes. Thoughts of his parents, of his faith, filled his mind as it spun towards oblivion.

Seeing Bruce's face grow pale, Todd began to whimper. As tears began to lace his cheeks, two masked figures appeared at the top of the grave. They looked down into the pit swimming with death.

Staring up at them, Todd begged, "Please don't hurt us." He couldn't remember if he had ever begged before. But now, he held his hands up in submission. "Please, help us."

For Bruce, it was as if time all but ground to a halt. As life drained from his body, he glanced up as another explosion rocked the grave. Tracers lit up the sky, and just out of the corner of his eye, Bruce caught sight of it. It was waving in the cold October night. Old Glory. The Stars and Stripes. The American flag. In all the chaos, he hadn't noticed it before. Someone had placed the flag at the graveside, for the soldier whose home it would become.

Bruce managed a rasping laugh as explosions and tracers lit up the night sky. The National Anthem filled his darkening mind:

"… and the rockets' red glare
The bombs bursting in air
Gave proof through the night
That our flag was still there.
O, say, does that Star Spangled Banner yet wave
O'r the land of the free and the home of the brave?"

The masked figures opened fire.

THE END

ZOMBIE WORLD
Death Perception
By
Calvin A. L. Miller II

OK, so the letter read something like this:

Mr. Christian—

We received your request to live among the undead population at our ZOMBIE WORLD Theme Park Reserve. Your desire to journal it for your next book, "Death Perception", is quite intriguing to us. We feel it's a great match and have contacted your publisher to make arrangements.

We look forward to working with you and will be in touch to prepare you for your indoctrination at the end of the month.

Sincerely,

Tom Stevens

Director, Zombie World Parks, Inc.

A "working vacation" living amongst the undead ... I got the idea when I first heard about Zombie World, the new 'Living Dead Theme Park Reserve' that was created out here in the New Mexico desert after people in several parts of the U.S. refused to die. I say this because it's the best way I can think of to put it. People, who by all accounts should have been dead, weren't. They kept walking. Some even kept talking. At first they didn't do much else. They just kind of staggered around harmlessly, going about their business or least trying to. As you can imagine, this caused quite a bit of confusion and fear wherever it took place. There didn't seem to be any real danger, so a full on "Zombie Movie" style war against the dead seemed to be a little cruel and unusual. They were people after all, and like I said, they didn't bother anybody.

At first.

Seems it didn't take long to become that "Zombie Movie" in quite a few areas around the country and the world. Not a huge Apocalypse type deal, we're talking thousands not millions, but the dead did begin to viciously attack and eat the living.

222

They even attacked each other on occasion. Bites, scratches, or any exchange of bodily fluid from the undead would kill the living and turn them into, well, Zombies. Seemed like the longer one of them was around, the angrier and more dangerous he or she would get. So the best way to handle them was early on, as soon as possible after reanimation. They'd comply with being moved or confined fairly easily then. That ease of handling, coupled with the fact that the incidents of infection were few and far between, allowed most of the civilized world to control this whole new way of death to some degree. Sure there continued to be 'incidents', but these were under control for the most part. The U.S. and the entire Western Hemisphere, Western Europe, Eastern China, Japan, and Australia are all safe and controlled. At least for now. But there are no flights in or out of Africa at all anymore. Same with Eastern Europe and most of Asia. The problem is too widespread and dangerous there. At least that's what they tell us.

But how do you answer the big question? What do we do with the undead? Many folks, including yours truly, viewed them as sick, mentally incapacitated victims of whatever man or God-made malady that had befallen them. Couldn't just put them down now could you? That works fine in fiction, but in real life people have rights even if they don't have a true heart beat. And they did need to be studied, because no one had yet figured out why the hell they were still walking. Complete mystery. Theories included a viral infection, religious repercussions, and even mass hysteria. As if people were just imagining the dead walking? Not a chance. It was real and people were scared, amazed, and interested in the undead. And in this world fear, amazement, and interest equals opportunity.

So 'ZOMBIE WORLD, Your Ultimate Vacation Destination' was born.

Some corporation thought up the idea to capture and herd them all into reserves and parks and charge admission so people could see real 'live' Zombies. The money taken in would go to researching the cause and the cure of the outbreak right there in labs at the parks. 'Come and make your vacation something spectacular, something you'll remember, something AMAZING'

223

read the ads for the park. Hell, I was intrigued and thought about it a lot. Several different packages were available, from a short stroll through the park on a raised protected path right up to riding in a fortified bus through the 'middle of the insanity'. I was intrigued and started wondering if there was a way for me to write a story on these undead people and how they 'lived'. But a view from a bus didn't seem to be enough to really understand them and write a proper story. Then one day it just hit me after my girlfriend Carrie went off to work one morning. I would live amongst the undead, you know, like that Monkey Lady. She lived alongside the monkeys and they recognized her as one of their own. I could do that with the ghouls of ZOMBIE WORLD. I could act like them and keep a journal of what went on. Death Perception seemed like a great title so I went with it. I would live with them, see how they reacted with one another, and learn what was going on in their ranks. My publisher, Nick Carroll, and I contacted them and I got the letter of acceptance about a month ago.

So here I am, waiting for my 'ride' to the park to come get me. They had some people come by a few days ago and talk to me about the whole deal and how it would go down. Where I'd be staying, how they'd take me there, and what I would need. Also the steps I needed to take to disinfect and prep myself for the adventure. They don't want any strange smells or infectants on me, for my own safety. Evidently the park residents attack what smells too much like the living, or even the dead at times, so it's best to be completely sterilized. They have an amazing sense of smell. To make sure I did everything correctly, they had a couple of guys come out and get me ready this morning. Real top notch folks they are, and I appreciate all the help. They really make me feel safe.

To prepare to journal my activities once I arrive, I recently started practicing my long hand. Doesn't seem practical to write my journal any other way then by hand, so I'm recording any ideas I have now to get used to writing again. Not as easy a task as I thought it would be. All these years of typing must've really done a number on my penmanship; I mean I hardly write at all anymore. I type everything now, but who doesn't? Not sure when they're going to be here so I just sit here in my chair and wait, writing and catching up on my daytime TV. Not many game shows or talk shows on anymore, but a shit load of celebrity news and court TV. I start thinking about how I watched old sitcoms as a kid when I was home from school and hunt for them now. Nothing. No matter, I'm ready to go and they are probably coming soon. With that there's a knock on the door and my publisher, Nick, walks in before I have a chance to get up and let him in. He rarely waits for me to answer the door. The familiarity is comforting, and a bit annoying, but he's my best friend.

"James it's time to hit the road," he says with his usual energetic voice. "I hear you've done the disinfecting procedures with the gentlemen that came earlier, so are you ready?" I nod and smile.

"Where's Carrie?" I ask. I hadn't seen my girlfriend since I signed up for the story. She thinks it's risky and stupid and hasn't spoken to me in weeks.

"Carrie couldn't make it, James, we talked about that. She sends her love though," Nick answers. It's probably best she didn't come; I hate to see her cry. Besides, I had told her I wanted to do this alone. I have to, or it won't work out right.

"Let's go," I say as the park folks walk me out to the black SUV with Nick. We get in and begin to move.

"Now James," Nick begins. "This is going to be like nothing you've ever done. You need to watch out for yourself, some of these undead bastards are dangerous. You have to blend in and not cause any trouble. That's the best way to survive. Don't do anything to attract attention."

"I know. I have it under control." I assure him.

I look out the window and notice all the cars parked in the lots and think a while about all the people that must vacation here at the park. It wasn't a very long ride to get here since I live fairly close. I love it in the South-western U.S. and I've lived here since I was young. The desert nights are great for writing and pretty much anything else. We get out of the car and walk up the ramp into the facility. Nick and I say our goodbyes and he tells me again to be careful. He's the best friend I've ever had, and I can't control myself. I break the rules and give him a long embrace.

"Separate them before he's contaminated!" One man shouts. "We can't risk contamination!" As they pull us apart I realize I shouldn't have done that. I say goodbye to Nick and I'm escorted in to begin processing. Evidently my contact with Nick contaminated me enough to require me to be disinfected and prepped again. Like I said, too many different smells are bad, and Nick can wear some cologne. My escorts are already in Hazmat suits so they won't contaminate me. I think hard about what I'm going to do, but I was told the dangers and I'm willing to take the chances. The opportunity to write this story is literally the chance of a lifetime.

I'm taken into a room and strip down to shower. A much more thorough cleaning than I had than at home. The water is hot and smells like a hospital at first, but then like nothing. A complete absence of odour. Amazing. I'm then given a few shots in the arm and abdomen, no doubt to protect me as much as possible from the park's inhabitants. I start to feel anxious and excited as I'm walked down the ramp into the park.

"God be with you," one of the escorts says as they close and lock the double doors of the gate behind me.

I'm in.

I have my journal, some food and water, and my iPod in a backpack. Lots of the undead still carry personal possessions so that shouldn't give me away as being alive. I mimic the shuffling walk so common in the Infected, and I seem to blend in well. They did a great job of prepping me. I scan around and see a group of undead milling about what looks to be a mock-up of a convenience store. I decide to approach them slowly to see how they react. Before I can get close they all turn and look at me in unison, about twelve of them. They start toward me, sniffing the air through their nostrils and also breathing it in through their mouths. As if they're smelling and tasting it. But I don't run. If I do, they may give chase and even though they are fairly slow I have to sleep sometime. From what I've heard they don't give up, ever. And I've also heard they have a way of communication that would have other undead on me from all directions in no time. So I remain still, and even stare at them as they stare at me.

They get to within a few yards and break off their advance. As they turn and walk away one or two look back suspiciously. Still they continue to walk away. I guess I'm assimilating! I am passing as one of them! I follow a few into the convenience store to see what's going on. I imagine no living person has been in there since it was constructed, and I'm making mental notes to write later. I don't want to take out the journal and write so soon after being accepted as one of their own, it may give me away. As I enter the store, the smell of rotting flesh is strong, but there is another smell I can't quite place. Strange, it's almost pleasant. They all seem to be sharing a pig that, from the looks of the blood trail, they dragged in here. I heard that they would eat meat other than human at times, but didn't know what to believe. The fact that they eat us just seems so horrifying, even after all the recent movies and documentaries I'd seen on the subject.

The next thought I have is one I had hoped to avoid. ALL the Zombies are feasting on the pig. If I did not, wouldn't I be noticed? Perhaps I'd join in and merely rub some about my face. I had been practicing in my apartment by eating raw meat to prepare myself, and as disgusting as it was I managed to keep it down. I thrust my way into the pack and seem to be recognized as one of them again. I pull some of the flesh from the pig and smear it on my face pretending to eat. It was then I noticed that this is not a pig at all but the remains of two human beings. Tourists perhaps, but that only occupies my brain enough to allow me to vomit all over the kill. Many of the others are doing the same, even the ones who look to have been here a great while. Perhaps it is as disgusting to them as it is to me? I immediately spit out what's left in my mouth, but continue to vomit. I must write about this later. My thoughts move to wonder where these human entrées came from. Were they actually unlucky tourists? Zombies themselves perhaps? Or maybe corpses given to the undead to eat as part of a deal the park may have with a local morgue? The latter seemed very unlikely, but not totally improbable.

I now need to find myself a 'home' for the next few days. The park is set up like a city, so there are plenty of abandoned building replicas, bridges, old cars … Plenty of places to lay claim to. After a short search I find a place by a creek under a foot bridge and sit down for the night. I'm not tired so I decide to log my journal.

Day 1: Assimilated into the park well after lengthy in-processing. I have been accepted as one of the *Zombies* and will continue to take steps to ensure I remain in their graces including group meals, gatherings, and 'acting the *part*'. There seems to be a semblance of a society here and my next step is to investigate the particulars of it. I joined in a feeding on what I thought was a pig, but turned out to be two humans. Although I did get quite sick, I was not discovered. It was a highly unpleasant experience, and I continue to feel extremely ill.

I keep writing as it gets dark. The noises from the undead seem to be amplified in the desert night air. It's quite cold but I'm comfortable and I write through the night. I do get up a few times and walk around in an attempt to make myself tired enough to go to sleep. I shuffle, in true undead style, all over the park and witness its grotesque and pitiful inhabitants going about their routines. Many act as they did when they were alive. I see three men in a circle feebly kicking an old red ball to each other. Some women seemingly admire each other's clothing. Many of them even smile. Most, however, just scream and scratch at walls and the ground completely mad. I look up and see the lit walkways with the park's guests looking down at us. Perhaps thinking that it could just as easily be them down here … Perhaps not …

As the sun rises I'm sitting under my bridge by the creek writing. It makes me feel comfortable to do what I love. I have a strong desire to shut out the world and 'not look up from the page' as it were. My writing and I, forever … It seems more possible every minute I'm here. I begin to hear voices and realize I've picked a spot near where visitors come to view the undead. The voices are garbled at first but soon become quite clear. I can see the people as they approach, and I can smell them as well. I can smell their cologne, their perfume, their sweat ...

I can smell their warm blood.

"Hey I know that dude!" One voice rings out over the rest. "Shit that's James Christian the author! He's a freakin' Zombie? No way!"

"Yeah it says here in the program that he killed and ate his girlfriend, that actress Carrie Cassidy, after he turned! Then he attacked and killed his publisher after he brought him here!" The other onlooker exclaims. "Wait, is he trying to write in that notebook? I gotta get a pic of this! It says here they try and hold onto what they loved in their lives."

I hear them and see their gawking faces. How I wish the bridge and wall between us weren't so high so I could taste their flesh. Fully aware, I look down at my journal. Torn, blood-scratched pages, nearly a hundred, turn in the breeze. Not a legible word to be found on any of them. It was now going to be impossible to fool myself any longer. The mind is a powerful tool, and you can make yourself believe anything really. But this charade may be over. I kept it alive as Nick and those men took me out of my apartment to bring me here. How long have I been dead? I really don't know. The horrified looks from Nick and Carrie began weeks ago, just after I was bitten by the woman I thought was delivering my Chinese food. They tried so hard to keep me hidden in my apartment. Hoping I would stay docile. Hoping a cure would be found. I guess after killing and partially devouring Carrie that morning something had to be done with me. I enjoyed that immensely, but miss her terribly. When it did come time to be moved, Nick even wrote me that letter to make it easier on me. It must have been him; I knew deep down it wasn't from the ZOMBIE WORLD Director. Nick fooled me into believing the story, out of love. And how did I repay him? By taking a large bite out of his neck in the receiving room as he dropped me off and said goodbye. But I truly feel no remorse ... They kept me too long. It's their fault not mine. I'm ill damn it! Sick to death literally! It was THEIR fault!

Yet somehow I managed to push all that out of my mind. To stay sane? Perhaps. Will I be able to do it again? There's no way of knowing, but I hope I can. It's blissful not to know. No matter now, as I'm likely about to continue the descent into uncontrolled madness that all of us eventually seem to succumb to. I'm as dead as any of the other poor souls here in ZOMBIE WORLD. I look up at my two fans taking pictures of me and talking to each other. I smell the air and I can almost taste their sweet flesh. I keep hoping somehow they slip and fall over the bridge and into my cold lifeless arms. The thought of tearing into their soft abdomens causes me to shriek at them long and loud. Loud enough to make them step back in fear, angry enough to make me smile a broad, toothy, smile.

I'm so very hungry, but I must stay on task. I must continue my writing. I'll block them out; I'll block them all out and work on my journal. Yes, I'm a writer after all, and I do have this journal to complete documenting my time here. My writing is all I have when push comes to shove. I'm a writer. A writer of books.

"Look he's tryin' to write again!" The familiar voice shouted. "He's just scratchin' at the paper. I think he believes he is writing. Poor bastard. Poor undead bastard ..."

I hear them and laugh quietly at the fact that they are taken in by my ruse. I'm a writer and an actor it seems. I'm doing a story, a story that needs to be completed. I'll shut them out, I'll shut everything out, and journal it all.

I'll write ...

Day 2: I was viewed by park spectators today and even seemed to fool them into thinking I was a *Zombie*. They took pictures, amazed at how I acted and looked. How much more amazed they'll be when they read this book! I'll walk the grounds today and continue to gather entries. This opportunity is great and I need to stay on point to make the most of it. Once my time is up Nick and Carrie will come back for me and I can finish the book at home. I miss them both so much. Until then I'll be a 'card *carrying*' resident of ZOMBIE WORLD.

THE END

SCHOOL'S OUT
By
Derek Gunn

Richard Doyle leaned out his car window and looked along the line of traffic in front of him. He sighed as he saw an endless line disappear round a corner at least half a mile away. Bloody traffic, he thought, it was getting worse instead of better. He jabbed at the off button on the radio, cutting short some politician's boring tirade about the wonders of the new traffic and road signs that had been unveiled that week in preparation for the tourist season.

"You should come out here and see the chaos your bloody signs have caused and you wouldn't be so smug," he snapped at the now silent radio and then shrugged and looked around sheepishly at the other cars in case they had heard his outburst. No one had. He spent a few minutes looking around at the people in the lane next to him. He shrugged, smiled weakly and raised his eyebrows as he caught a woman's eye in a car stuck in an equally long line going in the opposite direction. She smiled back with a bored expression and Doyle continued to look around. The early morning sun was already high in the sky and the heat through the windshield made him squirm uncomfortably in his seat. He loosened his tie and rolled down the window.

It wasn't much better with the window open; the air was heavy with exhaust fumes and the stench set off a dull throbbing in his head. But the faint cool breeze was welcome regardless. He certainly hadn't expected such good weather after yesterday. The news had been full of stories of the damage from the storm; trees uprooted, house roofs stripped bare and downed electricity lines all across the country. The warnings of the still dangerous cables pumping their power into the ground had filled the airways before that idiot with his road signs had come on.

Doyle only lived three miles from the school but it could still take nearly an hour to get to there. Of course, it didn't help that he had left late either. He had stayed in the pub for a couple of extra pints last night, the unseasonable electric storm had made walking home something to avoid until the very last minute. Unfortunately, his late night had ensured that he just couldn't get out of the bed without setting off explosions of pain in his head. He had been able to feel the heat from the early morning sun through his bedroom window. He had forgotten to close the curtains last night and he had lain in his bed, eyes tightly closed in fear of the searing light that he knew lay in wait, ready to pierce his eyeballs and send daggers of pain through him as soon as he opened his eyes.

It wasn't until Jill had kicked him out on to the ground, where his bladder had decided that it deserved more attention than he was paying it, that he finally stumbled blindly to the bathroom. Once he was up it had been easier to dive under the shower and let the water kick his senses into gear than risk Jill's wrath for disturbing her.

The cars moved another ten feet before stopping and Doyle moved forwards dutifully and pulled at the handbrake with a little more strength than was needed, leaving him struggling with the release when the car in front moved on again. The car behind announced its displeasure by honking loudly, its occupant gesticulating wildly.

"At least it's the last day," he sighed. Although, even one more day teaching those brats about their heritage just didn't have the same appeal as it had a few years ago. He passed the gates of the cemetery on his left and his spirits rose; it was only another hundred yards to the school.

He'd always considered the placement of a school right opposite a cemetery a rather strange decision, but no more strange than putting unintelligible signs up all over the city and unveiling them for the first time on a Bank Holiday weekend. "People are dying to get in there," he quipped as he finally moved past the cemetery and pulled into the car park, locked his battered Volvo and entered the building.

"All right settle down," he said as loud as his throbbing head would allow. He had just managed to grab a strong cup of coffee before collecting his books and rushing to class, making it just in time before the bell rang. The Principal was just looking for an excuse to haul him over hot coals, pompous git that he was.

"Henshaw, sit down," he snapped without even having to look up to see if the boy was indeed out of his seat. Henshaw was always out of his seat and, sure enough, this morning was no exception. Some things in life were gratifyingly constant.

The morning dragged and Doyle found his attention drifting as the boys wrote furiously. He had been delighted when he remembered that he had scheduled an exam for this morning, an extra hour to let his head settle was just what he needed. He glanced out at the sky and frowned. The sky had been blue when he had come in but now a large black mass was spreading over the sky like a cancer, corrupting the pure blue on contact and bringing with it a strong wind that whipped at the tops of the trees around the school.

He heard a noise in the class and snapped his head towards it, grimacing as his head reminded him to be gentle.

"Henshaw, not again. Would you please ..."

Henshaw was looking out the window and his sniggers had already distracted those around him.

"Henshaw, you have ..."

"But, sir," he pleaded, "there's a woman out there with no clothes on." The following rush of thirty five boys in the prime of their adolescence to the windows was unstoppable and Doyle resigned himself to letting them look before he even attempted to regain order. He gave into his own curiosity as he peered over the boys, ignoring their crude guttural grunts and comments as to the size of certain parts of the female anatomy.

Doyle's classroom was on the first floor and at first he couldn't see what the boys were ogling at. He was about to look away when he noticed two figures at the far end of the yard. They were just far enough away to make him squint but close enough to see that one of the figures was indeed female and totally naked.

What the hell? He thought. The woman was too far away to see in detail but he could see that her hair was plastered to her head in a wild tangle that covered most of her face and her breasts drooped badly as if the muscles had been unsupported for years. She stood perfectly still and didn't acknowledge the man standing beside her.

The man, even more surprisingly, didn't cast so much as a glance in her direction. He wore a suit; however, even at this distance Doyle could see that it was dirty and dishevelled. He was about to call the boys back to their seats when he saw John Gatley exit from the side door and approach the two figures, his coat outstretched, ready to wrap around the woman.

It would be Gatley, he thought as he watched the portly Maths teacher approach the woman. Gatley was a nut; frowning on drinking, smoking and any talk of a sexual nature. He condemned these vices and many others, damning any who might partake in any one of them. Doyle was hard pressed to find one of them he didn't regularly partake in so he pretty much stayed away from Gatley. He had gotten used to the severe looks he received when he arrived into school somewhat the worse for wear.

Gatley reached the woman and Doyle could see his lips moving constantly, he was either praying really hard or giving the poor woman a hell of a lecture. The woman and man simply stared at Gatley for a second longer and then lurched towards him.

Doyle felt his heart pound in his chest as he watched the two figures approach the teacher. They moved awkwardly, almost drunkenly, and Doyle realised that they must be either pissed, stoned or both. He exhaled a breath in relief and opened his mouth to call the boys back when he heard the screaming.

The three figures appeared to be dancing in the yard with Gatley in the middle. Doyle squinted his eyes almost closed to try and see more clearly but they were too far away. Gatley screamed again and then fell to the ground where the two figures straddled him and began to tear at him. The woman leaned in close towards his head and seemed to pull hard at something before jerking backwards suddenly with something in her mouth.

"Oh Shit!" he whispered as his brain began to fill in the pieces. "Henshaw, Pierce, you two run down to each of the classrooms on the other side of the corridor and ask the teachers to come in here urgently. Don't panic them but be firm. Higgins,

Blatty, you two take this side. Everyone else back to your seats, now"

"But, sir," a chorus of complaints filled the room.

"Now." The boys recognised the authority in his tone and reluctantly obeyed. Doyle wasn't entirely sure what was going on but Gatley had stopped screaming and his body was ominously still. The two figures continued to tear at the Maths teacher's body. Doyle's heart thumped painfully in his chest. Wild thoughts threatened to pull him in directions he really didn't want to go but he forced himself to breath calmly. He would take this one thing at a time. First things first. He needed to secure the school and then he could allow himself to consider his raging imagination. Doyle scanned the yard just as Teresa Stuart, Geography and PE, came through into his classroom with a frown on her face.

In the yard below he could see that three more figures had just appeared.

"What are they?" Guy Fallon asked as he watched another two figures stumble across to what remained of John Gatley. Five minutes had passed and all seven of the upstairs teachers stood huddled close to the window. Doyle's class shifted uneasily in their seats, their initial high spirits over the interruption of their exam and seeing a naked woman had quickly turned to fear once it became obvious that their Maths teacher was dead. Those sitting by the window could see that all that remained of the man was a bloodied heap and their ashen faces were enough to convince the others that they should sit tight and await instructions.

"I don't know," Doyle replied as his mobile phone continued to blare out the same annoying sound. He lowered the phone in frustration. "I don't know if there's no signal or if the masts are down from the storm." He thrust the phone back in his pocket. "I can't get anybody."

"They can't get in can they?" Theresa Stuart asked as she fidgeted with her hands.

"Oh shit, the doors are still open," Doyle cursed, annoyed with himself that he hadn't thought of it before. "Guy, take three of the boys and head down to the doors by the pool entrance and close them, pile up anything you can around the doors to make sure they can't break in. I'll get the keys from the Principal's office and send one of the boys after you. I'll take care of the other end." The man nodded and went back to his class to pick the boys he could trust.

"Peter," he gripped Peter Matthews, the Physics teacher, by the arm and pulled him to the side. "I need you and two others to go down to the classrooms downstairs and bring the boys up here. Do it quietly if you can, the classes on the far side won't have seen what's happened yet and we can't afford a panic." The man nodded, gathered up his team and left the room.

"Theresa." The woman jumped at the sudden mention of her name and Doyle took her hand gently in his. "I need you and the others to keep the boys calm up here. Keep trying my mobile and see if you can get emergency services." He fished in his pocket and passed over the phone as the woman nodded. "Try to keep them in the rooms over on the other side of the corridor if you can. The less they see of what's out there the better. I'll be back in a few minutes."

He left before anyone had time to argue or wonder at the fact that he had just given orders to staff far more senior than himself or even that they had obeyed without argument.

By the time he was half-way down the stairs there were already a number of teachers and students out in the ground floor corridor nervously swapping stories of what they had seen or heard. Nobody was panicking just yet but there was definitely a charge in the air. He could see Peter Matthews and his chosen team struggling through the mass of bodies as they tried to get to each of the teachers and pass on his instructions. They weren't getting very far. The situation was liable to become uncontrollable soon enough if someone didn't take charge.

"All right, pay attention now." His voice boomed out over the crowd and his elevated position on the stairs gave everyone an easy focus. The clamour reduced and then disappeared after a chorus of 'hush' rang out from the teachers. "We need you all to make your way quietly up to the classrooms upstairs. Johnson," he snapped as a boy pushed open the main doors, his cigarettes and lighter in his hand as he tried to sneak in a quick fag in the confusion. "Close that door right now and get upstairs before I suspend you. Move."

Nobody really knew what was going on yet, thankfully. Some had heard screams but the view of the yard from the ground floor of the school was mostly blocked by hedging so they had been mercifully spared the grisly scenes. Doyle sighed with relief as the students and teachers started to move up the stairs, the teachers looking puzzled and suspicious but were experienced enough to recognise a situation when they saw one and herded their classes up the stairs.

Doyle ran down the length of the corridor. The school housed five hundred pupils and fourteen teaching staff. The building was shaped in an 'E' shape but without the central protrusion. There were two doors at either end of the structure on both sides and a main, central door half way up the long corridor. Classrooms were situated on both sides of the corridor and the Principal's office was at the far end on the main road side. Doyle paused briefly in front of the office to catch his breath. He didn't like Principal Atkins and was pretty sure the feeling was mutual. He sucked in a breath, turned the handle and proceeded inside.

Atkins bolted upright at the unannounced entry and began to rise. "What the hell ..."

"Headmaster, we've got to lock the doors to the school," Doyle interrupted and saw the man go red with anger as he stood up so quickly that a number of reports fell to the floor.

"Doyle, why aren't you in class?" The headmaster stretched to save another pile of files from falling to the floor and then cursed as they fell anyway. "What the hell do you mean we have to lock the doors?" His deep, gruff voice was in total contrast to his wiry frame. "You ..."

"Sir," Doyle interrupted again and tried really hard to remain calm and respectful. He needed the headmaster's co-operation so pissing him off wouldn't help anyone. "There's been a bit of trouble outside and there's a crowd gathering in the yard." Doyle had decided to keep the story simple for now, at least until the doors were safely secured. "I really need the keys."

"A crowd? What the hell is a crowd doing in my school? Really Doyle, must I do everything myself? I'll move them on." Atkins pushed past Doyle who was so startled he merely let the man brush past and head towards the back door.

"Sir," Doyle hurried to catch up on the headmaster but the man had already opened the door and disappeared out into the yard. "Shit, that didn't exactly go as planned," he muttered and hurried through the door after him.

Doyle rounded the corner so quickly that he was unable to avoid the now stationary headmaster and bumped into the man's back. Atkins would normally have snapped a stream of abuse at anyone for being so clumsy but he seemed not even to notice. He stood still and looked out over the yard as if in a trance, his face pale and gaunt. There was a group of around fifteen figures standing only twenty feet away. There was a stench in the air; at one minute strong and cloying as the wind whipped around them.

The figures themselves were totally silent. Some of them shuffled, stiff-legged and awkward as if they had only just learned to walk. Others just stood there with their heads raised slightly as if they were sniffing the air. Now that he was closer, Doyle could see that these people were far from normal. Their skin was pale, almost translucent, and their eyes were dry and lifeless.

The naked woman stood closest to him and he could see red smears around her mouth and jagged red lines down her skin where blood had splattered her and dripped down. The shapeless husk of what remained of John Gatley lay in a wide pool of blood at her feet. The headmaster dug both hands into his pockets and retrieved a large set of keys with one hand, while bringing a handkerchief to his mouth with the other. He handed them mutely to Doyle.

"Sorry, Doyle," he whispered at last. "Quite right. We need to lock the school and protect the boys." Just then the naked woman seemed to notice them. She opened her mouth silently and started to shuffle towards them. The figures around her fell into step behind her. The situation was surreal. Doyle's mind screamed at him to move but he remained rooted to the spot. He could hear the shuffling of feet and the dry rustle of old clothes. His eyes took in the grey, ashen faces before him, the dead eyes. At one level he knew what these people were but his rational mind refused to allow such thoughts and his mind swirled with alternate explanations. It was the smell that finally snapped him out of his stupor. It hit him like a slap as the wind changed direction again. Nausea burned in his stomach and bile rose in his throat. He retched and, suddenly, he could move.

He ran back towards the door, grabbing the headmaster's jacket and pulling him back inside the school where he slammed the door closed. He fumbled with the keys, there were so many, and tried key after key as he divided his attention between the lock and the approaching crowd. He had seen such scenes in the movies over and over again, where the hero fumbled with keys and the bad guys drew closer and closer. The thrill of seeing it on the screen did not translate well to real life.

He was terrified, the keys slipped in his sweaty hands and the lock seemed to grow smaller with each failed attempt. One of the figures stumbled and fell against the door, catching the lever in its jacket as it slipped down and holding the latch open. The door opened inward slightly. Doyle tried to push against the door but the weight of the other figures proved too much and the gap began to widen. Doyle slammed his foot against the door to stop it opening further but the distraction caused him to drop the keys and they fell on the door jam and slipped onto the ground outside.

"Shit!" he muttered and dropped to his knees, while balancing his foot against the door. The sheer weight of the bodies against the door was forcing his foot inwards and hands began to force their way in and tear at him. He tried a number of times to shoot his hand out through the gap but he kept snatching his hand back as one of the attackers made a swipe at him.

The door was open wide enough now to allow the lead figure to squeeze its head through and Doyle knew that he only had one more chance. He sucked in a breath and made a dive for the keys, ignoring the hands that grabbed and raked at him. One

239

hand gripped his wrist and the coldness seemed to suck at his own body, numbing his arm in seconds.

The hand was caked with dirt; its fingernails were long, split and torn but its grip was limp and without force. Doyle pulled his hand away and stretched towards the keys. His finger pulled at the ring as another hand grabbed his hair and pulled. He screamed. The attacker who had fallen against the door was suddenly in front of him, looking straight into his eyes.

The reek of decay hit Doyle as the attacker leaned towards his outstretched hand with its mouth wide open. Doyle steeled himself and forced his hand closer to the gaping mouth, grabbed at the keys and wrenched his hand back. Drool from the thing's mouth smeared his wrist and he spent precious seconds wiping his hand in disgust against his trousers before he could bear to continue.

He pushed hard against the door but one of the things had got its head through and Doyle couldn't force the door closed. Suddenly the head was struck by a wooden plank and the figure was sent sprawling back against its companions, allowing Doyle to slam the door closed. He looked up to see Atkins with a metre long weapon in his hand and nodded mutely. He looked down at the keys again and finally found one that looked right. He rammed it into the lock and slumped in relief as he felt the lock click home.

The naked woman pressed against the glass and Doyle found himself rooted to the spot as he stared into the woman's dead eyes. His mind was still trying to come up with a rational explanation but the theories proposed were getting more and more desperate. These people were dead. Of that he had no doubt. How they could move about he had no idea but that they were dead was certain. The naked woman was fairly recently deceased but some of the figures behind her had been dead for some time. One man had decayed to such an extent that much of the flesh had already peeled away from his skull and one eye had fallen from its socket. Another woman had obviously been involved in an accident of some sort and bore puckered scars across her throat that exposed the bone.

"Here, this might give it better support," Atkins came up behind him with a desk that had one of the wooden supports missing from its main strut. "There are a few more in the store room," Atkins panted as he manoeuvred the desk into place against the door. Doyle was surprised at the headmaster's calm; he had expected the man to be impossible and overbearing, even in a crisis. He nodded at the man and sighed in relief. They just might get through this after all.

There was mayhem upstairs. Students stood around on the stairs or wandered aimlessly along the corridors in small groups, their pale faces attesting to the subject of their hushed conversations. The buzz of their exchanges was like a swarm of bees and Doyle could see teachers moving among the groups, their voices raised in pitch but lacking any real authority as their own fear stripped them of their authority. They were frightfully outnumbered by the students and losing control fast. Doyle was about to shout when Atkins surprised him again. He strode forward into the throng.

"Right, first to third years into rooms twelve and thirteen, open out the partition so you can all fit. Seniors, take room eleven. Move it, boys." His calm, authoritative voice easily cut through the melee and the boys began to filter into the rooms like chastened sheep.

"Impressive," Doyle heard himself mutter.

"Why thank you, Richard," he replied and walked after the boys to ensure they followed his instructions. Doyle was left staring at the man's back with his mouth open.

He saw Theresa come out from the classroom opposite his own.

"Any luck with the police, Theresa?"

"No, but I don't think we're likely to get through." She stopped in the doorway, looked along the corridor and motioned discreetly for Doyle to come over. "There's something you need to see."

Doyle frowned but followed her through into the room. This classroom was opposite his own and looked out over the main road. The windows had been replaced a few years ago with thick, sound-proofed glass due to the growing distraction of the traffic outside so the room was blissfully quiet when he entered. Theresa strode over to the window but didn't look out, turning instead to watch Doyle approach.

"I don't think we can expect help anytime soon."

Doyle knotted his eyebrows in confusion but Theresa merely pointed towards the window. Doyle shrugged and looked out. The road was filled with cars, unusual at this hour but not completely unknown. The silence of the scene before him left him feeling disassociated from reality. Car doors lay open; smoke spiralled from overheated engines where vehicles had crashed into posts or other cars. People ran aimlessly, their mouths open in silent screams as other, slower figures pursued them relentlessly. Bodies lay on the ground or slumped in their cars, unmoving and oblivious to the carnage around them.

"They must have come from the graveyard. Jesus, there are so many," Theresa continued to keep her eyes away from the scene as she spoke. Doyle could hear the panic just under the surface in her voice.

Doyle merely nodded mutely as he studied the scene below with growing panic. Some cars were surrounded and the creatures pummelled the doors and windshields ineffectively. He couldn't see the occupants of the cars but could imagine their terror in such an enclosed space, almost like a living tomb.

There were hundreds of the things. Just as he was about to turn away he saw movement in a car across the road from the school. He squinted and gasped as he locked eyes with a woman in the vehicle. His heart missed a beat and he brought his hand to the window.

The woman suddenly bolted upright as she realised that there were people in the school. Doyle saw the car door open and the woman sprint across the road towards the school gates. A few creatures in the area turned towards her, attracted by the sudden movement and slowly began to follow.

The woman ran, weaving in and out of the abandoned vehicles. Doyle felt his heart quicken and leaned against the window to see how many of the creatures were in her path. He pressed his head hard against the glass but couldn't see the area directly in front of the doors to the school.

"Theresa," he said urgently. "Get someone down there to open the main door, we've …"

Just then he saw the woman stumble over the path, trip and fall heavily. She pushed herself to her feet but her leg collapsed under her and she fell to her knees.

"Get someone down the …" he began again but then saw the creatures loom closer. The woman started to crawl towards the school but they were moving faster than her now and soon caught up. There was a brief second where Doyle locked eyes with the woman again and then the creatures surrounded her. He knew the cries and screams must be horrific but he could hear nothing. He felt a tear well up in his eyes and drip slowly down the contours of his face, tickling as it fell.

"We couldn't have opened the door anyway," Doyle started as Atkins laid a hand gently on his shoulder.

Doyle felt like screaming at Atkins, at his callousness, but he knew that would be unfair. He was right, of course. That didn't help the feeling of guilt though.

Would the woman have made a break for the school if she hadn't seen him? Was it his fault?

He pushed the thoughts away as he looked once more at the circle of creatures. Some of them were already moving away, their hunger sated, while others still groped and pulled at the remains. Mercifully his view remained blocked. People were relying on him. He couldn't afford the luxury of falling apart. He balled his hand into a fist and turned away abruptly.

They had work to do.

"Okay, let's go over what we know." Atkins addressed the teachers. "Richard, you have some suggestions I believe"

Doyle looked around at the sea of familiar faces and uncertainty suddenly gripped him. They were all scared, some more than others. Everyone was pale, the strain of the last few hours had hit them hard and they looked at him for guidance and hope. Unfortunately, he didn't have a lot of that to give.

He crossed to the board and began writing headings, gaining confidence in the familiar activity. "Okay, we've got some food and drink downstairs in the school shop." He wrote two of the teachers' names under the first heading, "John, Peter I need you to raid the pantry and bring up everything you can find. The food will keep the boys quiet for a while. The important thing is to keep their attention away from what's happening outside; we're really not set up to contain a panic." The two men nodded and disappeared.

"Joanne," he turned from the board and walked over to the headmaster's personal assistant. The woman was in her late fifties and sat away from the others with her head in her hands. "Joanne, dear, I really need you to keep trying the phones, see if you can get anyone at all. Friends, family, anyone who can confirm if this is widespread or local. See if they can contact the police for us and get some help." The woman nodded and began punching numbers into a mobile, the distraction of something to do giving her strength.

Doyle wrote the word 'Weapons' on the board.

"Keith," he looked over at the diminutive English teacher. "I need you to break up a few of the desks; those wooden runners make good clubs. Get a few of the boys to help you. Oh, and confiscate any knives that might be around, I don't want some fool stabbing himself."

He turned back to the board and wrote 'Communications'. "Bill," he turned to the Chemistry teacher, "I need you to go down to the office and bring up the radio, we need to get an idea of what's going on."

"We have to assume and plan for the worst case scenario. There are too many of them out there and I don't think we can stay here indefinitely." Doyle paused to catch his breath. He was avoiding discussing his theories on what the things outside were. He had to keep everyone busy and focused on keeping the school secure. They could broach the subject of what they were and how it had happened when they had more time. "The doors won't hold if enough of them gather but the windows are probably our weakest point."

"Agreed, so what should we do?" Atkins prompted. Doyle was amazed at how the man was comfortable to let him lead in this and not feel the need to be in control all the time.

"We need to close and lock all of the classrooms downstairs. Luckily, all of the side doors are situated at an angle at each end of the building so they shouldn't be able to get too many pushing against them at the same time. They should hold."

"The main door is a problem though." Atkins mused.

"I don't think it can hold," Doyle agreed. "We can pile desks, tables and anything else we can find against it but if their numbers grow then their sheer weight will break through."

"Right," Atkins joined him at the board and added to the growing list. Bill Masters arrived with the radio and set it up in the corner. He looked at the board and started for the door again.

"I'll begin at the far end and work my way back. I'll get the keys from Peter," Masters said and disappeared.

"Bill," Doyle shouted after him. "Take a few of the older boys with you, you might need the bodies." Masters popped his head around the door, nodded and disappeared.

Theresa walked over to the radio and began to look for a station with news.

"... Nothing is confirmed at the moment but there are reports coming in of multiple accidents and traffic jams throughout the city. There have been some reports of attacks in the city also but details are sketchy at the moment. Police have asked for calm and have requested that motorists park their cars off the main routes to allow emergency services to get through."

"Either they know less than us or they're playing it down," Atkins said. "Regardless, it looks like it's pretty widespread. We need ..."

The sudden shattering of glass downstairs interrupted him and all three of them rushed to the stairs.

They met Bill Masters on his way back up the stairs.

"They've broken through."

Doyle grabbed a wooden runner from the pile that Keith Purcell had compiled and he rushed down to join Masters. The two teachers returning from the food run dropped the food into the eager arms of a few seniors, armed themselves and ran after them.

Doyle could hear Atkins ordering the food to be distributed as he ran towards the breach and the faint sighs of disappointment from the seniors.

The main doors were wide open. As he had thought, the sheer weight of the people pushing against them had been too much for the old hinges. As he reached the corridor Doyle could see a swarm of figures pour through the gap. Many of them fell under the weight of those behind them and disappeared beneath the flood of dead flesh.

The figures varied greatly; he could see grey desiccated figures, barely able to move and fresher corpses, their wounds still puckered and wet from where their flesh had been torn in life.

They slowly filled the corridor and began to creep forwards, slowly but ineluctably; unstoppable like the incoming tide.

There was no way they could stop this many.

"Back upstairs," Doyle shouted. The others didn't need to be told twice and sprinted back the way they had come.

"It's useless, we can't hold them," he panted as he reached the top of the stairs. Atkins nodded and took him by the arm, leading him over to one of the rooms.

"Bill," he called behind him, "get the boys ready. We're going to have to make a break for it."

"We don't have much time, Richard" Atkins still held his arm but seemed to be oblivious of the contact. "I've had a quick look outside and the north yard seems to be the best chance. Those things seem to be congregated mainly around the doors at each end so if we go out through the middle windows we should be able to get most of the boys clear before they realise what we're doing. What do you think?"

Doyle looked at the headmaster as if he was mad. We're on the first floor, the thought screamed into his mind, what is he talking about?

246

"The pole vault cushion is still in the storeroom from last month's sports day," Atkins explained patiently as he saw Doyle's confusion. "I need you to get it and drag it into place below the window. We'll hold them off as long as we can, but please hurry." Doyle felt a key pressed into his hand and then Atkins was gone, shouting orders to those around him and organising what delaying tactics they could.

Doyle ran to room 14, ignoring the confusion around him. He saw Bill Masters and grabbed him, explaining what was happening on the way. The windows on the first floor were allowed to open outward for six inches before they reached a metal support that had been put in place after the tragic loss of a student a few years ago who had fallen out while opening the window.

"We'll have to break it," Bill offered and went to get the board duster to smash the glass.

"No, they might hear it," Doyle said and then wondered whether they could hear at all. They knew next to nothing about these things and their lack of knowledge could get them all killed. "We need to get as many away as we can before they notice what we're doing. Hand me that pole would you?" He pointed at a wooden pole used to open the top windows and immediately jammed the end under the metal support and pulled down on the pole.

Nothing happened for almost a minute and then suddenly there was a loud pop and the metal support flew outward and landed on the concrete below with a loud clang. Doyle held his breath as he waited but after a minute went by and he could still see nothing in the yard below he allowed himself to exhale. He nodded to Masters and one by one they slid out onto the ledge.

There was a small gutter running along the roof above them and this fed into a metal pipe that ran down the centre of the building and into the drainage system beneath the school. The pipe looked stable enough but it creaked and groaned alarmingly as the men climbed down. At one stage the screws above them pulled right out from the wall but the lower supports held until they reached the ground. There was no way the pipe would support anyone else though. Masters looked at the screws and then at Doyle. He didn't have to say anything. This plan would have to work or the people they had left in the school would be overrun. And there was no way they would be able to get back to them to help.

The storeroom was situated at the back of the school and across the yard. To get there they would have to pass close to the east wing's door. This proved easier than they had thought on the way to the stores but on the way back the two men would be struggling with a heavy canvas cushion and the scraping of the material along the ground was sure to alert the creatures.

The two men reached the storeroom without incident and rushed inside. Doyle looked around frantically. It wouldn't take the creatures long to overrun the others and every second saved could mean the life of another boy. In some part of his mind he knew it was unlikely that they would save everyone but he forced himself not to dwell on it. He could only do so much. It was really a matter of best effort at this stage.

He heard an urgent whisper and looked over at Masters who was pulling at the corner of a bright blue material.

"Good man," he rushed over to help and they began to drag the cushion out. By the time they had succeeded in dragging it outside they were both exhausted, although Doyle's watch indicated it had only taken five minutes.

"We'll never manage it," Masters wheezed as he scanned the yard to see if their activity had attracted any attention. Doyle looked over the cushion and frowned; it was some ten feet wide and twenty feet long. By far the most awkward element was its thickness though. It wasn't that it was particularly heavy but it was filled with foam and sealed tight to allow for the weight of an athlete to drop safely from a great height so it was difficult to get a firm grip on the material.

Suddenly he had an idea.

"Bill," the words came out louder than he had planned and he saw Masters look up in shock. Doyle ignored the other man's motion of silence, he was too excited.

"We'll use the canoe oars." Doyle disappeared back inside and reappeared with a long, double-bladed oar. It was shorter than the cushion but if they bundled the material they should at least be able to keep it off the ground. Masters nodded and ran into the room to get another. By the time Masters had reappeared Doyle had already positioned the first oar under the cushion. Masters quickly followed suit on the other side and together they lifted their ends experimentally.

It was a little shaky and the oars were bending alarmingly but the large cushion remained wedged on top of the make-shift splint. It might just work.

Once Doyle had left, Theresa stayed close to Atkins to be best placed to help. She could see Johnson and a few others throwing desks down the stairs. They had already cleared out one full room and had begun on another. As she passed the stairs she looked down and could see the jumble of broken desks that filled the stairs from about half way down right to the bottom where they pooled in a mess at the foot of the stairs.

The resulting obstacle course should keep the creatures busy for some time. With their crude, stiff movements they would find it difficult to work their way up and it would buy them some time. But would it be enough?

Everything had happened so fast. It was only eleven in the morning. Two hours had passed since she had come into Richard Doyle's classroom. Two hours since the world ended. She looked over at the frightened faces of the boys as they looked to their teachers for re-assurance. She tried to smile at them but her lips wouldn't move. She dropped her eyes. How could she offer them the strength they needed when she was so terrified? Her stomach was wound so tightly, her head throbbed and her heart was beating so hard that she was certain she was going to have a heart attack. She hid her hands in the pockets of her jacket before anyone noticed how badly they were shaking and looked down the stairs again. She could see the first of the creatures appear at the end of the stairs. The first of them fell on the broken desks but the ones behind simply clawed their way over them. They were slow and awkward but it wouldn't be long before their sheer numbers made it up to the first floor. She prayed silently that Richard Doyle would hurry.

Doyle nodded and the two men began to make their way back to the school. The return trip was easier than they thought but it still took another five minutes because they had to stop a number of times when the cushion slipped off the oars. They quickly dragged it into place beneath the first floor window and the first boy began to drop down before they had actually finished.

"How's it going up there?" Doyle asked one boy as he pulled him clear and moved him to safety.

"I don't know, sir. There's a lot of shouting but I couldn't see much from where I was."

Doyle nodded and moved to help the next boy as he landed with a whoosh.

After an hour they had the line working quite well. They averaged about three bodies a minute but that still meant another two hours before they cleared the school. Theresa and two other teachers had already come down and they had taken charge of getting the growing number of boys out of sight and safe. They had been lucky so far.

About twenty minutes ago one creature had appeared around the corner and had shuffled towards them. They had easily taken care of the thing and had crushed its head with one of the wooden runners they had made into weapons. The most unnerving thing about the incident had been the eerie silence of the action.

Doyle assumed that the creature was not capable of speech as there was no air going through its windpipe to make any noise. He'd always wondered how films could portray these creatures as moaning zombies when they were dead and didn't breathe. He shrugged, was there any point in looking for logic in the first place? It was what it was. If he got out of this alive he'd write Romero a letter.

The creature had been alone and the rescue had continued. Twenty minutes later Guy Fallon leaned out the window and shouted down.

"They're almost at the top of the stairs," he panted. Doyle could see the blood on the man's forehead and felt guilty for his own relatively safe position.

"Send then down two by two," he shouted up and Fallon nodded and disappeared. They had delayed as long as they could but now the risk of injuries with two jumping at the same name far outweighed the certain death of the alternative.

They ran out of time a half hour later. As if they were working to some diabolical timetable, the creatures inside the school reached the top of the stairs at the same time that another crowd appeared around the eastern end of the yard and finally became aware of their presence. Doyle was helping two boys off the cushion when three more suddenly dropped on top of them, crushing one of the boys and snapping another's arm with an audible crack.

He looked up, ready to shout his annoyance when the window suddenly shattered and rained shards of glass down on to them. The boy beside Doyle cried out, the cry cutting off abruptly as a large sliver of glass sheered half his head clean away. Suddenly the ledge above became crowded with screaming boys as they all panicked and jumped together.

Doyle grabbed the boy with the broken arm and threw him off the cushion just before the first wave hit the cushion. The boys hit the material hard, one missing it entirely and landing on his ass with a sickening thump, his body seemed to stay upright for an age before he fell over and lay still.

The other boys hit the cushion together and the seal along the end burst with a loud tear, like sails on a ship being ripped in two. The stale air within the canvas rushed out and made Doyle gag. The material was already slick with the dead boy's blood and everyone on it was coated in red. Screams filled the air as panic reigned. The appearance of blood-stained boys screaming in terror sent those around them into a panic and many of them ran straight into the approaching hoard. The smell of blood was heavy in the air, cloying and the creatures shuffled faster towards them as if they could smell it. Already the next wave of boys was jumping and he screamed at those still on the canvas to move. There was already too much screaming and his warning was lost in the mad cacophony. Many of the boys sat rigid on the canvas as they looked dumbly at the blood on them and at the near headless body of the boy beside them. More boys fell from

251

above. For a mad moment he thought that it was raining children as they fell in ever greater numbers. Many of those who miraculously managed to survive the fall were crushed by those falling after them. Doyle tried vainly to pull the boys from the canvas but there were too many.

The cushion was completely flat and offered no cushion for the falling tide but the boys above were too panicked to notice. They continued to jump, oblivious to the carnage below, anything to get away from the creatures above. There was a pool of dead and injured boys on the ground and Doyle just couldn't get close enough to help the injured.

The dead bodies, however, did serve a macabre purpose. With the air gone they acted as a soft landing for those still trying to escape.

The boys that did manage to survive stood in shock as they watched their classmates die before them. Some of the stronger ones tried to help but the constant flood of bodies from above made it impossible. Doyle was so focused on the carnage in front of him he didn't notice how close the creatures had managed to get to them until he heard a high-pitched scream behind him. He spun towards the noise and saw four creatures right beside him. Two of them were tearing at a boy who stood mute as they tore his flesh from the bone, his mind so frozen in terror that the pain, mercifully, barely registered. Jesus, that could have been me, Doyle paled as he saw the other creatures reach for him.

He ducked below the swipe from a desiccated arm. The stench hit him like a blow and he retched as he reached down for the weapon at his feet. He brought the wooden runner up hard and caught the creature under the chin sending it sprawling into the things behind.

That gave him a few seconds and he used them to order those survivors he could reach to get to the outer field where the others were gathering. He grabbed a boy from his class; dimly aware that it was the ever optimistic Henshaw, and instructed him to tell Theresa to start the group moving and that they'd follow as soon as they could. Henshaw didn't have time to ask questions as another creature came up behind and Doyle pushed him away with a shouted command to move.

Doyle was vaguely aware that the rain of bodies was slowing, either they had gotten most of the boys out or the rest were dead. He saw Atkins appear on the ledge above and saw him drop and then Doyle was swept away by the crush of undead bodies.

He swung the runner from side to side, hitting dead flesh with each strike but he only succeeded in driving them back a little, and even that effect was reducing as more bodies forced them forward from behind. Before he realised it they had closed around him entirely and Doyle decided to make one more push and bet everything on the vague hope that he could power his way through and use his speed to get past them.

He took a deep breath, lifted the runner in front of him and launched himself with a scream at the creature in front of him. His speed and momentum carried him past the first creature, pushing it back against the next one and caused a domino effect. He felt his heart lurch as he saw a clearing just past the last few creatures and he kept his legs pumping against the wall of cold flesh. His arms ached from holding the runner out in front but it served to keep them at arm's length and kept those gaping maws away from his skin.

For just a second he thought he would actually make it but just as he cleared the way through he tripped over one of the creatures that was struggling to rise. He felt his leg buckle and then collapse as he stood on the creature, knocking him off balance.

He fell with a thump and the air gushed from his lungs leaving him gasping and wheezing on the ground. He tried to move but he just couldn't. He couldn't even look up to see them come for him. He felt a hand snatch at his shoulder and he tried to move away from it but his strength was gone. He closed his eyes.

He felt himself lifted off the ground and thrown back down some feet away. He opened his eyes in shock and saw Atkins standing over him.

"Get up, man," he wheezed as he tried to regain his breath. "We're the last. Come on."

253

Doyle would have laughed if he had had the energy. Instead he raised his hand and allowed Atkins to help him to his feet.

"To think," Doyle panted as they ran away from the creatures, "up till now I thought you were a useless, smug bastard."

"The feeling was mutual, I can assure you," Atkins replied with a grin.

They caught up with the group an hour later. They had found a deserted office block some twenty minutes walk away. The light was fading from the sky rapidly and the absence of street lighting threw the area into darkness much earlier than usual. They would have to hole up in the building and see what tomorrow would bring. They found limited food supplies in a canteen; not much but enough for the night.

Teachers and pupils alike sat stunned in the growing darkness. No-one asked questions, they were too afraid that they might not like the answers. They had lost forty two boys and had another twenty injured. Some of the injured had bites that were already looking infected. No one said anything but most had seen and read enough to suspect what might happen to those. Atkins had quietly organised a guard detail to watch the injured for any signs that they might become dangerous to the rest of the group. Despite this they had been very lucky that the numbers had been so small. Four teachers had died; at least they weren't in the building with them so it was assumed that they were dead.

Boys cried as quietly as they could for parents, family or friends. The feeling of despair was almost palpable. Doyle struggled with his own worries and growing fears. He hadn't been living with Jill Moroney for long but his heart ached for her touch and her quirky smile. Was she still alive? He hoped so. He would search for her but he had a responsibility to these boys for now. He gently pushed his thoughts aside. He had to remain positive. If he survived, then Jill could have as well. For all they knew the army had already regained control of the streets, though he doubted it. He knew that if they gave into despair then they were really done for. He desperately searched for something to say to lift everyone's spirits. Anything to give them hope, but nothing came.

"Hey guys," he heard one of the boys suddenly shout. "School's out for summer."

Doyle looked up but couldn't make out who had spoken. It sounded like Henshaw but he couldn't be certain. It didn't really matter. The faint rustle of laughter that swept over the group was like a pressure valve opening and he looked around to see boys wiping away tears. Already the riff from the Alice Cooper song spread through the group with some taking up the sounds of guitar while others played drums on their legs and the vocals began, quietly at first but then stronger until everyone joined in. He looked over at Atkins and Theresa and smiled.

It didn't change anything, they would still wake up tomorrow and have to deal with the nightmare that awaited them but for now it was enough to keep them sane.

THE END

GUISES
By
S. Michael Nash

... One times two is two.
Two times two is four.
Two times four is eight.
Two times eight is sixteen.
Two times six ...

A firm knock on the front door interrupted Mira's mental gymnastics. She closed her eyes, blocking the stucco ceiling from her sight. She was tired, so tired. Given everything, she just wanted to lie on the hardwood floor and let it's coolness soak into her skin. *Maybe if I just ignore it ...*

A second knock assailed her ears. She sensed the determination in it this time. Sighing in annoyance, she pulled herself off the floor by holding the arm of the couch.

"Just a minute!" she called.

Even the end of the world doesn't stop the automated calls or Jesus freaks from knocking on the door. Dodging into the bathroom, she dropped the jeans and t-shirt that were covered with four days of dirt and gore. She ran water in the sink until it was warm, then began scrubbing her face and body.

The knocking became more insistent.

"I said in a minute! I'm not fit for visitors!"

I haven't donned the uniform of the happy, young mother yet. She was always wearing a uniform. For years she wore the short skirt and fashionable boots of the 'perky grad student.' Then the layered outfits of the 'blushing newlywed.' And finally, she had morphed into the loose dresses of the 'new mother.' Even when naked she wasn't really naked, she was then the flirtatious lover. When completely alone, she would just stand, staring blankly. Unsure of whom she was when nobody was around to define her.

Quickly, she began dragging the brush through her long, raven hair.

The knock at the door was changing just as she was. It

was becoming less of a 'knock' and more of a concerned 'pounding.'

"Ma'am! I'm going to have to insist you come to the door!"

She had pulled on her pink and white summer dress and was staring into the mirror, trying to raise some colour by pinching her cheeks. It wasn't working. She was simply not going to be a beauty today. Her eyes were set in deep, pained sockets and her skin was sallow white.

Well, it had been a rough couple of days. They were going to have to take what they got and be thankful for it. Chuckling at her own folly, she walked to the door and pulled it open, leaning casually against the jamb.

"Can I help you?"

One week ago the sight of her visitors would have panicked her. Today, they were refreshingly armed and dangerous. That was a good thing. The walking dead didn't use tools or weapons.

She smiled her obligatory smile, revealing those peroxide-whitened teeth that so offset the black of her hair. Her gentlemen callers could have been termed the police, she guessed. Not that there was any formal civic organization anymore. There were two of them, and as always she thumbed through the mental Rolodex of character types to file and categorize them. Must know your audience before you can cater to them. Mustn't step out of character, not even for a second.

The closest of the two – the knocker – was the easiest. An older man, he wore a trim and tailored uniform, fully matching, and had a cool, competent manner. Cinched around his slightly enlarging belly was a thick belt and holster containing a heavy-looking revolver. The man's sweat-filmed hand never drifted far from it. She pegged him as a real cop, probably the only one on this tiny island. He had likely worn that uniform for years before Armageddon, and really didn't think much about it at this point. He had a carefully trimmed moustache and the wide, expressive eyes that bespoke of years of 'being a friend to the community.' She would've been happier if he had taken that hand away from the gun, but other than that she instinctively trusted and liked him.

"Good afternoon Ma'am. Do you have a few minutes?" The voice was crisp and clipped. He had questioned strangers like this a million times.

Do I have a few minutes? Buddy, I have the rest of freaking time!

The second man fit even more firmly into one of her predefined social pigeonholes. He was just out of high school, not educated and not likely destined for any. He probably worked out furiously and ineffectively, trying to keep the pounds somewhere south of 'obese.' With little self-control, dieting was out of the question. If she went to his gym and opened his locker, she knew there would be a nude picture pinned up on the inner door. Not that he was really attracted to this girl, but he wanted the other guys to know he was the type of man who likes a naked woman. Probably listened to the twangiest country music he could find. Or maybe he's a rocker, his CD collection divided between new heavy metal and old Lynyrd Skynyrd. The shotgun he still held jammed against his shoulder was both a weapon and part of his personal disguise. The gun made him a man, even though he clutched it the way a child holds a security blanket.

"I do. What can I do for you gentlemen?" Again, the disarming white teeth came out.

The knocker smiled back, just for a moment before catching himself. He then carried on in his carefully crafted, easygoing formality.

"Well, first of all, we were wondering who you are? Do you know this is private property?"

"Yes. It's mine. Or rather, it was my husband's parents. So now … I mean there is no will or anything. But I have a right to be here, I think. I'm Mira Effayant."

The knocker looked at her extended hand carefully; trying to judge its pliability and warmth. Finally, he smeared his palm down his pant leg to rid it of most of the damp and deftly took her hand.

"Sheriff … Well, just Roger Wilkins, now. Pleased to meet you Mrs. Effayant. You understand, of course, that we want to check on anybody who shows up suddenly on this island. Given

258

. . ."

"Yeah," she agreed. "Understood."

"So, if I might ask. How did you get here? I've been watching what's happening from the church bell tower with a telescope. Tough to tell from this distance but, I was fairly sure that there'd be nobody coming from the mainland anymore. Are there any more survivors?"

She inhaled deeply, and then let it out rather sharply. "Maybe. But not with me. I arrived alone."

He nodded, giving her time to elaborate. Instead she turned to more immediate matters.

"Having survived this long, I'd really appreciate not being blown to bloody ribbons by your friend." Her eyes glanced over his shoulder to the left.

He turned and snapped his fingers at the heavy kid, who shifted the muzzle of the gun a little, but didn't lower it.

"I dunno. She don't look too good to me."

Briefly, Mira's eyebrows knitted. *I don't look good! The fourth horseman just passed the Norman Rockwell painting of my life through its digestive tract, and you don't think I look good! At least I once looked good, fat boy.*

"She's fine, you damn dolt! She can talk. She hasn't attacked us. Put it up."

The kid gritted his teeth, clearly not happy about being dressed down in front of Mira, and he slid into an even more specific notch in Mira's mental Rolodex. The category she called 'the little big man.' A large part of his self-esteem comes from his perceived position in the male hierarchy. She should have guessed from the outfit. Clearly, he felt he had been 'deputized' by Roger, but he had to come up with his own uniform. He had a white t-shirt, with a camouflage coat over it. There was a badge affixed to the left breast and he had a black hunter-style hat with a second badge of some sort attached. Clearly, he couldn't find anything for below the waist, so he had just grabbed something that was at least part of a uniform, even if not the right one. Brown shorts. She wondered if he had worked for UPS himself or if he had stolen them from someone who no longer cared so much about his modesty. He was the kind of kid who always took boxing or karate, but never got good at them. He surely had a collection of knives and pointy, Chinese looking things. He dropped the stock of the gun from his shoulder in a swinging, underhand arc and caught it with his right hand. Clearly a well-practiced manoeuvre. He probably practiced it in front of a mirror the way she practiced her disarming smile.

Wilkins looked sour as he turned back.

"I'm sorry. But I'm sure you understand we've had a difficult couple of days ourselves. There was a small cemetery here on the island. We had some work to do to secure the island for the living."

"Of course." Mira replied, acutely aware of how desperately they were applying layers to the thin veneer of civilization that coated the current reality. *Of course I understand being threatened. If fat boy had shot me, my last words would be forgiving and sympathetic. Because my own uniform doesn't come off. Not until I'm cold and ... Dead?*

"I'd invite you in but I have nothing to offer. And I wasn't exactly clean when I arrived. I'd like time to get in order before I have guests."

"We'll be fine right here, ma'am. But if we could steal some of your time, it would be appreciated. We've talked to nobody from the mainland since this started. The Internet went down almost immediately, and the news was very confused and uninformative before it went off the air. You'll know things we won't, and if nothing else would offer a fresh perspective on what we already know."

She was not really in the mood for a talk, but it was a nice June day. Blue skies, dotted with white clouds. The sound of sparrows filled the air, along with one cardinal, all puffed up in his scarlet finery, chirping out his dominance over this area of the island. The concrete smile nearly cracked with tears as she listened.

The birds are singing.
The dead walk the Earth and the birds are singing.

But she gestured to the two chairs perched about the small drink table on the porch. Wilkins made a 'ladies first' gesture in return.   She sat, sweeping her skirt beneath her primly as she landed. Without even offering to the boy, Roger sat in the other chair, sighed deeply, as if dreading what was coming next, and spoke:

"Is it safe to assume your husband will not be joining us?"

Her eyes slammed shut suddenly. Blunt. Very blunt. But then, how could he have phrased it? Her cold breath hitched as disjointed flashes of her journey here projected against her lids.

The long, weeping drive with that horrible smear of Jeff's blood on the part of the windshield the wipers won't swipe. The sick baby that wouldn't stop crying. Jeff pounding on the moving figures, holding them at bay as the tank filled. And the bites. Oh, Jesus the horrible bites on his arms as he smashed their bones with the baseball bat. But they didn't stop. You could shatter them down to skin bags of broken bones and they just ... Won't ... Stop.

"Mansfield," she whispered, staring at the wood planking of the porch. Then, clearing her throat, she spoke more clearly. "We came from Columbus. A huge city, full of ... We had to go. It was death to stay there. We made it to the car ..."

She and Jeff and ran from the house. She had the baby and he had that old wooden slugger Jeff's father had given him a few years back. A week ago that bat had been worth more than a thousand dollars. It was signed by Johnny Bench, Tony Perez and Pete Rose (whoever they were). Now it was worth nothing in dollars, but if it could just get them to the car it would be worth all her remaining possessions and a thousand times more. Their little suburban neighbourhood had become a horror show. Friends and neighbours, all came. It was like they knew. They knew there was fresh meat in the house. The car was parked on the street. Thirty feet of shambling feet and blunt teeth away from the front door. They ran for it, Jeff smashing the walkers out of their path with the bat. She running behind, head low, the baby wrapped like it was the dead of winter, though it was unusually hot, for June. They made it to the car, and they left their little three-bedroom single family home with city taxes but a good, suburban school district behind.

"Jeff was an airline pilot." She shook her head, realizing she was speaking in a disjointed manner. "Jeff is my husband. Was my husband. We g-g-got in our car and started driving north. His folks were from Shaker Heights and they owned this vacation home here." She looked up at Roger, as if seeking approval. "We thought it might be safe here. You know, sixteen miles off the shore ..."

"Yes," Wilkins soothed. "It was a good plan. Please continue."

"But we didn't have ... I mean who thinks of these things? Keeping your gas tank full in case the dead come back? That would be crazy. It *still* sounds crazy." Her voice started to hitch.

"So you ran out of gas?"

"No. We saw immediately that we were low. But to stop and take, how many minutes outside the safety of the locked car? To fill the tank? We'd have been dead in seconds in the city. So we drove, figuring we would find something outside of town. Where the population was lower. And the number of-f-f-f ..."

Calm and easy, Wilkin put a hand on hers.

"Yes. Again, you were very smart."

"But we weren't! Once we left town there was no power anywhere. Hundreds of gallons of gas in those big tanks under the parking lots, and no way to get it. How were we to do it? Siphon? Get out and look for a hose? Then find a tool to pry up the covers. There were fewer walkers out of the city, but there were some. We couldn't leave the car for long enough to do all that. So we kept driving. We kept driving and the gauge kept getting lower and lower. Finally there was a place with power."

"Mansfield," he offered.

She nodded. "I've always thought of that as a small town, but ... how many walking death factories constitute a lot? It was as bad as Columbus. The walkers were everywhere. But we had no choice. The baby was sick, had been since before this all happened, but now she was untreated and on the run. We had to get to ... stable ground."

Jeff had left the safety of the car to pump the gas. He still had to pay for it! How's that for irony? He swiped his card but it wouldn't work. He had to smash into the station itself and flip on all the pumps. How he knew to do that she had no idea, but he did. But all the breaking glass was a hell

262

of a racket ...

"They can still hear, you know," she observed. It was out of the blue, from Roger's point of view, but he accepted it.

"I never thought about it. I suppose they can."

She looked at him more intently. "No. You don't get it. They can *hear*!"

The walkers came from all directions. They weren't fast, but they were relentless. Jeff got the nozzle in the tank and started pumping before the first one got near. He battered it back with a hit that would have been a home run even in a major league park. It actually flew about five feet then landed skidding for another five. Its face was smashed and oozing blood. Not really bleeding. Bleeding requires a beating heart. But oozing. Its jawbone was broken and hanging from the left side of its face. Its tongue, the colour of a day old bruise, lolled below its face ... and then it stood up, and came for him again. He battered it again, then spun to pound the one coming up behind him. The numbers on the gauge spun, .731, .854, .967, 1.001 gallons ...

"If they can hear, can they feel? Can they see and taste and feel?"

There were about six of them now. Jeff spun from one to the next, battering them away, going through the whole bunch of them while the first recovered it's feet and came toward him again. It was a game of who can last the longest and it was a losing game. Jeff was getting winded, tired. But whatever drove the muscles of the walkers was inexhaustible. They would just keep coming and coming and coming. And there were lots of them. More arriving every second. 1.98, 2.07, 2.84, the numbers spun. "That's enough!" She screamed. "We have enough! Come back in! Please come back in!"

But that wasn't going to happen. She could see that clear enough. There were dozens of them now. Most were going for the pungent, sweaty meat of the man with the whirling bat, but some came to the doors of the car, sniffing and looking at Mira and the baby. Veal. She couldn't help giggling crazily. They see the baby and want VEAL.

"Can they feel pleasure? Can they feel pain?" she asked Roger. Her eyes wide, needing this important piece of data. Needing it more than anything else in the world.

A face was pressed against the passenger door. A woman's face. Well, the face of something that had once been a woman, bloated and

263

mottled purple. The sickly tongue tracing sticky trails of clotted saliva along the glass. And then she heard a loud thump on the windshield. Jeff. His face was bloody and contorted with pain, his hand slapped the windshield, two fingers already missing and his agonized face cried: "Go! Go you stupid bitch! Get out of here! Take my baby and get to safety!"

And then his eyes rolled up in their sockets, and he began to slide, lifeless, down onto the hood. In blind, unthinking panic, she slid across the seat, slammed the car in gear, and mashed the accelerator. The car lurched forward, bodies, including Jeff, flew from the car as she moved about ten feet and slammed headlong into the brick of the small convenience store that all modern gas stations had become. The nozzle was still lodged firmly in the tank, the hose pulled and wrenched loose where it was weakest, at the point where it joined the pump. Gasoline continued to surge from the tank, spilling to the ground and flowing along the concrete. She threw the car into reverse and backed out, then jammed it back into gear and, tires spinning, she shot out of the lot and onto the road, dragging the hose behind her.

"Tell me Mr. Watkins. Can they suffer?"

"I don't know, Mrs. Effayant. I honestly don't know."

"He was all torn up. He was bitten and bitten. And now ... he walks. Do you think he feels the pain? Do you think he is hungry? I know they eat, but do they *starve*?"

Roger took her cheeks in both hands and forced her eyes to look into his.

"Listen. I cannot tell for sure. But I've killed dozens of these things, and ... I've shot them, and bashed them, and broken their bones, and if they feel it, they don't feel it like we do. That, I can promise you. Things that would hurt a human so badly they couldn't move, they just stand right back up and come back for more."

She leaned back, a little calmer. But hardly comforted.

"You killed them? They can be killed?"

"Yes. Sort of. Killed might not be the right word. Whatever it is that makes them move seems to be centred in the head. If you destroy the brain, they go down and don't get back up. We can just bury them normally at that point."

Her eyes widened at that.

"Then we can go back! We can go back and put Jeff down! Just in case he feels. Before he has to starve."

But Roger was already shaking his head.

"We can't Mira. Think about it. Think about the North Coast. Cleveland on one end and Toledo on the other and nearly non-stop urban area in between. Millions of people. Now most of them aren't people, but still millions. I don't know how you made it through that gauntlet once, but we can't do it twice more. Once down and once back. Mira we just can't!"

Calming again, she leaned back in her chair. She spent a few seconds smoothing her skirt back into 'pretty young mom' position, than looked back up at him.

"Why not?" she asked. "What else do I have to do with the rest of my life?"

"That is an excellent question. It's on my list of things to talk to you about. The answer is rebuild. We survive first, and then we rebuild civilization. You said your husband was a pilot, but what about you? What do you bring to us?"

She laughed.

"Nothing! I was a freelance writer! I write technical and science articles. Nothing we can use now."

His eyes brightened.

"That is fantastic."

She looked at him blankly.

"Really? How so?"

"Are you kidding? If nothing else you can write down the basics. As much as you can remember. That way, when our descendants start rebuilding the world, they won't have to start from square one. They won't need to wait for another Archimedes or another Newton. They'll already know."

"How can we survive in a world where we can't even die in peace! We will always have the walkers. They aren't going away. Even if they did, people are still going to die, then walk."

"Maybe the situation will change again. This virus or whatever ..."

Her laugh cut through his words like a harpy's screech.

"This is no virus. This is nothing natural. When this started it was very interesting. I figured there would be an article in it. I called some of my medical contacts. Do you know when it all started? Between 9:50 and 9:54pm last Thursday. That is as

265

close as I could narrow it down, but that's a pretty damn narrow window. So I called a friend in Los Angeles. When did it start there? 6:50pm or so. Do you know what that means?"

Roger looked at her, very intent on learning, but he didn't get it. He shook his head.

"It means this is not a virus. It's not a disease. It's not anything like that. There was no 'patient zero.' There were no disease vectors. One minute, the dead laid still. The next they walked. Instantly, everywhere. All over the world. All at the same moment. This is not a natural process. There is nothing natural about this."

Roger looked up at the boy. Little big man. Did she get his real name yet? She couldn't remember. This distressed her. It meant an awkward social situation was impending. Can't have that. God forbid.

"Well," he said at last. "That is distressing, but even if it is supernatural, it seems to follow some rules. It's in the head, whatever it is. So we can ... make them stop walking. We already know how to do that from trial and error. In the future we'll have to come up with new funeral practices, but we can do that. Cultures change over time, as new needs arise. But you are wrong about them never going away. And think about this, as it may comfort you about your husband. They are well and truly dead. They rot. They have trouble sneaking up on you because you can smell them a mile away. This thing that is happening, whatever it is, it's tied up somehow in the brain. In the meat. And it's rotting. So the shambling millions will ... Just rot away. And the living will inherit the earth."

She stared distantly out at the slate coloured surface of the lake, and the sharp line where it met the blue sky at the horizon.

"I don't want to inherit the earth. They can have it. I'm finished here."

Suddenly, Roger lunged forward and seized her shoulders.

"Don't say that! Don't ever say that. You don't have the right! Do you know how many people are on this island? Twenty-six. Twenty-seven now that you are here. Eleven women and sixteen men. And you may be the smartest and best educated of the lot of us. Do you

266

understand?"

"Stop hurting me!"

Just as suddenly, he released her. He held his hands, palms open, as if struggling to regain control. Then, he sat down again, coolly.

"I'm sorry Mrs. Effayant. That was uncalled for and unforgivable. I'm ..."

He paused. Breathing deeply a couple of times.

"I'm the Sheriff. I'm the guy everyone looks to. You see, it's my job – my duty – to keep the people safe. To make them secure and happy. That means, in this case, I have to bring it all back. Forgive my lack of tact here, but eleven Eves is not a very broad breeding base. Even if we didn't have your wonderful brain, we still need your womb. A horrid thing to say to someone I just met, but you have to understand what's at stake here. This is much bigger than any one of us."

But she was still staring, not at all startled by his poorly-timed honesty.

"No." She spoke so quietly that it was almost impossible to hear. "There are others. Other little islands. Other mountaintops. Other little heavens. It's not all on us."

"I'm sure you are right. But in the meantime, the only place I know for sure humanity has survived is right here. Until we know for sure, about others, we have to behave as if the whole future rests on us. We simply don't have a choice."

They sat in silence for a long time. Her eyes were lost, fixed to the horizon. Then, without warning, she pitched forward and vomited copiously on the wood planking of the porch.

The battered car plunged right through the gate at the little dock when she had run out of 'north' and came to the endless expanse of Lake Erie. The drive had been eventful, but easier than she imagined it would be. The roads were mostly clear, as people had taken to hiding in their homes when it all started going to hell. She did manage to run over one walker that seemed to be blundering along the centreline of the highway. The tank had just over four gallons in it. Not even half full, which was good because the gas cap was lost and the valve was held open by the nozzle. She was damned if she was going to stop to remove it now. She wasn't getting out of this car till the last possible second. Twelve feet of hose had danced along the ground behind her the whole trip.

Like most docks, there was a fence around it to keep out thieves, but that was a different time. A different world. Thieves wouldn't just drive through the gate because it would make noise and wake the locals. Phones would dial, and the constabulary would come running. Not now. Mira didn't give a tinker's damn who heard, and she mashed through the wooden planked gate without slowing down.

She knew where she was. Jeff's folks had a large powerboat that took them to the island. It was still carefully tied at its dock. She ignored it. Mira didn't even know how to start the damn thing, and now wasn't the time to learn. Abandoning the ruin of the car, she made her way down the short dock at the end, clutching the baby to her chest. A long line of small outboard motor boats — fishing boats, her father would have called them — lined the wood. She hopped into one after another, until she found one that was a pull start. She eyed the three walkers that had answered all the commotion. They were still minutes away. Mira pulled the start cord again and again, cursing each time. On the sixth pull, the little Evenrude sputtered to a coughing life. She slipped off the two ropes and kicked away from the dock. It had been years since she used her father's little boat, but it came right back to her. She twisted the handle and sped about forty feet away from the dock, then stopped to watch what happened.

Could they come after her? They just wandered around, seeming lost. One of the walkers fell in the water, but it seemed to be stuck; as if unable to let its head go underwater. It didn't need to breathe, but it didn't seem to realize it, so it couldn't follow her out into the lake. Saved by stupidity. Actually, that made sense, she guessed. It was, by definition, brain dead. How clever could it be? This thing was never going to take up a career in poetry or particle physics. Idly, she wondered how long it took the brain to die. Are there walkers that could still think for a period of time? She didn't know.

"God, if you are there, I beg you. Don't let Jeff still be able to think!"

She picked up Susie and touched her tiny cheeks and lips again. The child was so hot. Burning with fever. She had been sick for days, hell, Mira was sick, but she had a hundred pounds on the baby. She barely noticed, but the baby ... Oh, she needed to get the baby to a doctor.

Mira put up a hand, arresting Roger's forward rush to

help. That hand spoke without words: *Please. The polite thing is to pretend I didn't just do something disgusting.* She wiped her lips with her bare hand, trying to maintain what dignity she could.

"Breeding," she said, straightening up. "You want me to have babies."

The GPS still worked. She was puzzled by that for a second, then realized she shouldn't be. Nothing could touch those satellites; they just sit up there and beam out a carefully timed pattern of data. All the magic was in her handset, which ran on battery and needed little maintenance. Hell, GPS may well be the last sign of intelligent life on earth, sending out its signals long after everyone is dead. The thing was still programmed with the location of, not just the island, but the dock nearest the house. Turning up the throttle, she turned the little boat toward the island.

Will I find life there? A doctor? God, Susie was so hot! She had been screaming and crying most of the way up, but the last ten miles of the drive she was pretty quiet. She drove the boat with one hand and held the baby to her chest with the other. Susie made the nibbling motions she always did when she was hungry. Without really thinking about it, she popped the buttons on her blouse and offered a breast.

With inhuman power, the toothless, bony gums mashed the tender nipple. Mira screamed and pulled away from the child. Nearly tipping the boat as she scampered to the far end. Susie fell to the damp bottom and, thrashed with far more strength than an infant should have. The tiny fingers hooked into clumsy claws, digging at the ribbed bottom of the boat. Her little body writhed, her head and feet came up and down as she tried to move. To come after her mother. Mira screamed and screamed as the thing wreathed horribly, it's eyes lolling about in its sockets, unseeing. It actually made some progress toward the front of the boat where Mira was crowded.

Screaming, Mira lashed out with her left foot, catching the child in the stomach, and kicked her in a high tumbling arc through the air. She landed with a small splash and sank like a piece of granite.

Mira must have spent two hours weeping in the bottom of the boat as the motor took her in circle after circle after circle …

She exhaled sharply, and looked up at Roger. His features looked very concerned as he watched her.

"I am afraid," she spoke, very slowly, "that if you want any deliveries, you are going to have to call FedEx. Because this girl is out of the baby business."

269

Roger reached out toward her for a moment, then pulled back, as if realizing touching her might not be wise. Too soon. He should have brought up the 'rebuilding' on his second visit, or third. Too late now.

"Of course, Ma'am. I didn't mean to imply ... I'm sorry. I'm just trying to keep things going here. Progressing. You know. We'll take our leave now. Forgive the intrusion." He slipped a hand into a hidden pocket on the inside of his coat and took out a small boat horn.

"The phones don't work anymore, I'm afraid. But if you have an emergency of any type, just give a blast or two on that and we'll come running. We haven't come up with a non-emergency method of communication yet, but we are working on it."

She smiled thinly, her hand still on her belly.

"Before we go, ma'am. Is there anything we can do for you? We don't have a doctor, but we have a guy who is a retired EMT."

"I'm fine. I'm more heart sick than stomach sick."

Roger began patting down his pockets. "I may have an aspirin or something."

"I'll be fine. I took something before you got here. Just waiting for it to kick in."

He smiled at her.

"I'm so sorry I upset you."

"Think nothing of it. It was either today or later. What has happened ... isn't going away."

"Well, you have a good evening." He turned, heading down the walk to the golf cart he and little big man had arrived in.

"I will." She smiled back. And she was already starting to feel better.

She had taken something a little before they knocked on her door. Two Tylenol, washed down with twenty ounces of drain cleaner. Burned like the fires of hell, but the pain had gone away soon enough. And she had satisfied her curiosity about how long it's possible to think after you become a walker. A good long time, it turns out. That conversation was even better

270

than her multiplication tables plan.

Yeah, she was starting to feel better. She licked her dry lips as she watched little big man's chubby bare legs climbing onto the back of the cart.

Her appetite was even starting to come back.

THE END

LADYKILLER
By
Ricki Thomas

Ted arched his back, his spine complaining from the hours of weeding he'd just finished, and he surveyed the garden, the neat rows of marigolds lining the fence, the well pruned bushes and trees cleverly arranged to give a range of greens throughout the year. He smiled, proud of his work. But it wasn't the beautifully landscaped scene that gave him such a sense of pride. It was his other job. As a ladykiller.

Mindlessly plucking the dead leaves from his begonias, Ted thought back, a gentle smile appearing as he recalled the first girl, seven years before. Well, someone had to do it, rid the world of scum, it might as well be him. He'd been in his car, parked at the side of a winding country lane, eating a chicken sandwich, when he'd seen her. Oh, she was pretty, but he knew that beneath the long charcoal coat she had tied tightly, she had no clothes on, and that made her a prostitute. And prostitutes were filthy creatures, preying on men for their carnal pleasure.

So he slunk down in his seat until he'd heard her pass, then quietly collected the wheel nut wrench from the boot of the car. With a stealth he could still muster, he ran up behind her, and smashed her over the head, manically heaving the tool on her until her body slumped, broken and bloody. Always taught by his mother not to leave a mess, he couldn't just leave her there, so he'd carried her to his car and placed her in the boot, alongside the murderous tool.

When the darkness fell and the lights in the neighbours' houses died, he took the body and buried it securely in the garden, but not before removing her coat, and he was amazed to find she wasn't naked after all: she was wearing a business suit. A tinge of guilt flooded over him, maybe she hadn't been a prostitute after all. But with her safely in her grave, as he mused to himself with a whisky in the early hours, he knew he'd have to do it again. The sheer adrenaline rush had been so great, the feeling of empowerment, the cracking sound of the skull. It had given him too much pleasure not to continue in his newly found career.

The first problem he came across reared its ugly head three months later when he couldn't ignore the compulsion to kill anymore. Finding the girl. He'd been so lucky the first time, she had just appeared. But women walking alone weren't easy to find in this day and age. He was going to have to select a target this time, choose who to live, and who to die.

He'd heard through an article in the local newspaper about the prostitute problem in the centre of the nearest town. Apparently, although they plied their trade on the streets, kerb crawling was more of a problem, holding up the traffic, and lustful men propositioning innocent women who just happened to be in the area. He would have to be careful.

His next target wasn't as pretty as the first, but that didn't matter really. She had a twisted expression, hardened by her trade, steely eyes and a mouth crinkled from too many years of smoking. He pulled the car into a lay-by and watched as she tried to solicit her goods. Unsuccessful in her attempts, Ted decided to get out and approach her, suggesting she get into the car. She refused, cautious of the dangers her job entailed, but with the promise of cigarettes, alcohol, and a hefty payment thrust into her waiting hand, she reluctantly agreed after some coaxing.

Ted was aware that his demeanour was gentle, an aging, small man with grey hair and glasses for his myopic eyes, and he concocted a dramatic story about losing the wife he'd never had years before, now needing to seek his pleasure elsewhere. His tale took the entire journey to relate, and by the time he had reached his tiny village, she'd become comfortable in his presence. He'd stopped on the way to buy the cigarettes, and she was happy to stay in the car, which gave him relief.

As soon as he'd led her into the kitchen through the back door she started to remove her clothes, and he halted her. After all, it wasn't sex he was after. He suggested they shared a whisky, that she had a couple of cigarettes, and afterwards he would let her lie on the bed and give her a calming back massage. She thought she'd died and gone to heaven, how lucky was she to find a generous and caring punter. But very soon she did die.

And heaven became a small plot next to the first victim in his prized garden.

Ted gained so much pleasure from both of the killings, he adored the sound of the flesh splitting, of the muted cries as he extinguished their lives, of the only power he had ever managed to wield after growing up, an only child, with his oppressive mother. So it became a pattern. Every few months when the desire overwhelmed him, he would select his victim, entice her back to his house with his amiable manner, and make her pay with her life for her sordid career. Luckily the garden was big enough to withstand so many graves.

A voice brought Ted back to the present, and he turned to see his neighbour by the fence. "Bob, hello."

Bob laughed, he rarely spoke to Ted, but when they did interact it was always with pleasantness. "I see you've been gardening again." Ted was standing beside the latest grave he had prepared for his next victim. "Is it more roses you're planting?"

Ted nodded, his hands expressive. "Yes, another English Rose. I shall be going out soon to get a few more."

Bob chuckled once more. "So many rose bushes, you must have at least twenty blocks of them."

"Yes, I think they're befitting of such a pretty, well fertilised garden, don't you?"

He didn't know why, maybe it was because she was there, or maybe it was because he fancied something new, but the next victim Ted selected was just a girl. Maybe around the age of ten. She seemed vulnerable, there was a sadness in her eyes, not because she was unhappy, just an underlying torment that he soon came to understand was due to the loss of her mother at the age of three, which she informed him of in the car when he was bringing her back to his bungalow. She'd been easy to lure, a promise of sweets, some pocket money, and maybe a McDonalds later, in return for her company. She was to be the first victim he'd ever asked the name of, and she happily introduced herself as Maisie.

He revelled in her innocence, the bright blue eyes and trusting nature, and such a pretty little face, and he even contemplated letting her go at one stage. But the burning desire to rip her apart won the battle, and now he had her in his lounge, waiting for her sweets and fizzy drink. He had no need to have her facing the other way, even though he was in his sixties now, and even though he was a short man, he knew it would be easy to overpower her. He laid the tray, laden with chocolate and cans of pop, on the coffee table, and she dived in greedily.

With her attention purely on selecting which goodies she should start with, he grabbed the poker and came at her, cracking it around the right side of her head. The questioning eyes as she took the beating almost broke his heart, but he was too far into the excitement now to stop, and gradually her body faltered and she was limp. He'd give it a couple of hours into the dead of night, when witnesses would be unlikely, and let her join the others outside.

The noise was horrendous, deathly moaning, groans from the grave, and at first Ted thought he may be having a nightmare, but as his eyes slowly opened, adjusting to the soft light in the room, he could hear that the bad dream was real.

A quick glance at the girl's body on the floor reminded him of the previous day, or was it still the same day? But this had never happened before. The wailing, the crying, the guttural sounds. He jumped up from the sofa, as fast as his aging body would allow, and checked the young girl's pulse. She was definitely dead. So the television was next on his list, switching it off hastily in case the racket was some kind of interference with the signal, but still the gruesome clattering continued. He had to find out where it was coming from.

Opening the door to the kitchen, Ted took a step back, his eyes filled with horror, mouth agape, fear shaking his body. More than twenty women were in his kitchen, but they were horrendous. Eyes missing, heads crushed, clothes rotting, teeth brown, hair thinning and unkempt. He felt a pain in his chest, down his arm, and a terror he'd never experienced before. But still he didn't know what to do.

He backed away, trying to close the door, but the multitude of bodies compared to his fragile fighting was hopeless, and they soon all staggered into the room to join him as he edged further away. He had no idea why, but he lifted Maisie's little dead body, slightly stiffened with the onset of rigour mortis, and held her in front of him as a worthless shield, and suddenly one of the zombies lunged at him, fleshless fingers clawing at him, faceless teeth grinding, soundless screams echoing, and soon the others had joined the assault.

He was terrified now, aware that they wanted to kill him, a poor, defenceless old man, a man who had done nothing wrong, leading a peaceful life, tending his flowers, passing the time of day with the villagers. The pain in his chest grew; a clenching, gnawing, relentless torture that threatened to take him before the creatures attacking him did. He could feel his hair being dragged out, his arms being bitten, skinless mouths tasting his flesh. It seemed to go on for a lifetime, his death, and eventually it was there, his body slumped on the floor, a death mask of sheer agony, fright, and panic.

The most vicious of the zombies smiled a lifeless grin, her revenge now complete with the help of the spirits she'd shared her grave with. She dusted the mud from her rotting business suit, bending down to scoop Maisie from the floor, tenderly stroking the curly hair from her eyes. She kissed her, and Maisie returned, glad to finally be back in her mother's arms.

THE END

DADDY DEAREST
By
Dave Jeffery

Daddy was mean. Not in the fiscal sense like keeping his money secure behind the impregnable doors of a city bank. He was mean in the way he fetched bright blood with his small hard knuckles, or the manner in which he'd laugh when tears cut tracks through the gore on his kid's faces.

Our faces.

Lindsey and me.

Lindsey is twenty three now, a woman with yellow hair and a slightly crooked smile. But I'll always remember her as a gangly thing with freckles and a sense of mischief. Even with all the beatings Daddy Dearest doled out. Gangly, yes. But weak? It was never a word I could associate with my sister. Even when she lay on her bed, bloodied and bruised as Mickey Mouse peered down from the walls, that grin saying more than those black, black eyes. Daddy's birthday gift for her tenth birthday was three fractured ribs. Yes, he put tears on her cheeks and bruised her pale freckled skin; but he never took the light from her eyes.

Lindsey.

My Lindsey.

Never ceasing to amaze, to rise above the adversity of parental abuse. Taking the blows that had my name on them, giving me comfort in the dark as Daddy Dearest slept off another bottle of Ol' Jack, his thundering snores hiding my sobs and Lindsey's soft 'shushes' as she stroked my battered body.

Never ceasing to amaze.

Until the day came when she had the opportunity to leave and said 'no'. Me, of course, that was the reason. She was my protector, my champion. I was her dependent, a ten year old, under weight boy who flinched when a chair scraped the floor boards or a car horn sounded in the street. A boy who still pissed the sheets when he heard the dull thud of a whiskey bottle hitting the rug and the click of his bedroom door as it slowly opened wide, allowing the demon that was Daddy loose in the room.

She'd said 'no' and remained my armour, and I swore that as I grew older, stronger I would take the baton and protect her as she'd protected me. But the opportunity never came. Ol' Jack turned Daddy old before his time, made him decrepit and impotent and in this Lindsey, amazing Lindsey, dumfounded as she usually did by giving up any hope of college to support Daddy in his long suffering journey. I suspected pleasure in her actions, retribution. I told her my thoughts once. And she'd slowly shaken her head.

"I'm not looking after the man who beat on us, John," she'd said. "I'm looking after the man before Momma died. The kind and gentle man who loved his family."

A man I didn't know.

Mother had died before I could walk. She was a shadow in my mind, given form in the pictures hidden in the cellar for a lifetime, until Lindsey rescued them and placed them on the dresser in her room. Initially Daddy Dearest was too consumed with his grief to allow it. Then he became too consumed by Ol' Jack to care. For him it was medicine. For me it was just an excuse to camouflage the meanness.

When I heard he was sick at his own hands it pleased me. No one, it seemed, was immune to Daddy's abuse. Over the years he'd even managed to fuck up his own body as well as ours. The night Lindsey called and told me that she thought Daddy was dying part of me screamed out with joy. But another part, the part still wearing the bruises and the fear and the guilt, began whimpering like a hungry, mangy cur searching for scraps.

We had occasional respite. How else could we have come through it so well adjusted? The one day a year ensuring we didn't allow history to repeat in all its medieval glory: Father's Day. 24 hours where the beatings and the bullying ceased as Daddy Dearest spent the morning post-oiled and coiled in duck and down, and the afternoon reclined in his old squeaking chesterfield, the man who would be king, allowing us to serve him ribs and fries, a root beer or two. And then there was the cake. Lindsey's handiwork, of course. A square slab of fruitcake, coated in white icing and adorned with a single candle and the words "Happy Father's Day". It came with pride and misplaced love, but it meant there would be no fresh cuts that day.

One day a year and Jesus fucking Christ how we all revelled in it. Not even Ol' Jack could turn Daddy Dearest sour. But the bile would always return. And the blood. Constantly, consistently. Just like Father's Day.

I expected Lindsey's call, it was Father's Day after all, that hollow holiday for daddies everywhere, acknowledgement of their contributions to family holism. If my stomach wasn't so empty I would probably puke. I usually leave Lindsey to bake the cake and nurse the monster.

So, yes, I expected the call. But not the content.

"You need to come, John," her soft voice said through the grilled plastic of the receiver. "He's really sick."

"The guy has always been sick." I toyed with the Zippo in the pocket of my jeans and wondered if I'd used all my smokes.

"Funny guy," she said, the static not disguising her sarcasm. "You know what I mean."

I knew she was sitting in Daddy Dearest's old Chesterfield, just as I knew that on a small walnut table scarred with silver half moon coffee-cup stains and butt end scorches there would be that motherfucking cake, with its armour plate icing and lone candle. It was a ritual. A harking to the too few good times.

"Yeah." I rubbed at my brow and closed my eyes. I was fighting against the effects of half a bottle of Ol' Jack. The legacy of Daddy Dearest, his one and only lasting gift: dependency on a bottle. "We knew it was happening, Lindsey. The quacks told us as much last month."

"This isn't cirrhosis, John," Lindsey said. Her voice was hushed, almost conspiratorial. "I'm talking about The Sickness."

The world did a jig, and I grabbed at the wall, disorientated by the booze and the shock of her words.

"You got to get the hell out of there, sis," I said. "Just get gone and don't look back."

"But what if I'm wrong?"

"Then you're wrong."

"I can't, John." The voice was non negotiable, the kind of voice she'd used when the offer of college came through several years ago.

"You owe that shit nothing, Linz," I said sourly. "He's lucky you're still there for him."

"That's as maybe," she said through the fizz. "But you know why I stayed. I made my bed."

"You don't have to die in it," I said quickly. "You know how this thing works. You know what The Sickness does."

She knew. We all did. But no one knew why it happened or how to stop it. The Sickness came and went. But it always stayed a while. And when it did it played merry and it played hard; victims floored with a fever and then the bone quaking agony of multiple convulsions until they died, clawing at their throats as though attempting to rip it open and allow in precious oxygen.

Then the real problems began.

When those who had succumbed to The Sickness came back from the dead.

I could remember the first time it had happened. Hell, I was there now, my mind swirling back in time; no longer in the hall of my cramped apartment, but in a rail car; hand clamped to a smart phone watching the news, watching a small town on a small screen, cordoned off by a fleet of green military vehicles. Then shaky footage, the news crew letting the cameras roll; capturing the terrible yet incredible events and sending them out to the world.

"As you can see," the news reporter said off camera, "it's quite incomprehensible, but the dead are walking, ladies and gentlemen, the dead are walking!"

The screen filled with shuffling shapes, they came from homes, from stores, from vehicles scattered about the streets. These things were once human, but no longer. They were broken and malformed, each emitting a low pitiful mewling sound that combined to make an eerie sound track that drifted ominously from the speaker in the smart phone.

"The medical teams are going in, ladies and gentlemen," the commentator continued. "Oh, thank the good Lord! The doctors are attempting to deliver any aid they can to these poor, unfortunate souls."

On screen, medics moved amongst the military; white coats amid a sea of green fatigues. Tentatively the medical team approached the shambling throng of people heading towards the cordon.

I'm aware of people around me, other passengers peering at the screen, united in their fascination and, if they were totally honest, their revulsion of the scene on the screen.

And this was before the screams began.

They were thin and long, even in the confines of the rail car, but they were the sounds of agony and fear, bleeding into one another to create a cacophony that chilled the bones of those huddled around a smart phone five hundred miles away.

"Holy Jesus!" The commentator was back. The excitement in his voice gone, replaced by a hoarse rasping whisper, vocal chords taut with horror. "I can't believe it! Oh, Christ on a bike, this is the most hideous thing I've ever seen. They're attacking the medical team, wrestling them to the ground, biting them."

Not biting the medical team, I noted. Eating them. White coats made red with gore, skin torn and ripped as cloth, in strands, in chunks, by mouths that were wide and mewling. I watched, dumbfounded, as the crawling image of a middle aged medic screamed silently at the camera as his head was pulled away from his body by a teen in a bloodied school uniform.

The screen shuddered and it was not the camera man this time. It was my hand shaking so violently I almost dropped the phone.

"Hey, keep the thing still, man," a large black guy said; his eyes wide with fear. "We gotta know how this happened."

But we never did know, did we? No, all that came out of it was a town cordoned and burned by the army. And "The Sickness", a term that rendered the ultimate act of inhumanity into a sterile noun, two words to be whispered for fear they should suddenly become aware and return, reaping their terrible wrath.

"John? You still there?"

"I'm here, Linz."

"So what do we do?"

"You're asking me?" I said. "You're the practical one, remember?"

"I need you here," she said, putting the obvious into words. "I need your support."

There it was, Lindsey cashing in her dividends, recouping her investment when she needed it the most. Years of protecting her younger brother from the monster who was now destined to become a monster right there in the family home.

"What stage is he at?" I said; voice low. Accepting.

"Early," she said. "The fever and tracking."

Tracking. The veins coming up to the surface of the skin, blue tributaries that would turn rose red, morphing the skin into a lattice of livid wheals. Then the shakes would begin. Vicious and final.

And death would come, followed by rebirth and the quest for flesh.

"Ten hours tops, start to finish," I concluded. "Two hours to get to you, traffic being good. When did the tracking start?"

"Three hours."

"Then time's ticking. Okay, Linz, I'm there."

"Okay, John," she said, relief clear in her tone. "Thanks. I'm not sure I could finish it."

I now understood her dilemma; the reason why she was determined to call in her chips from the past. Lindsey's memories were forgiving enough to stay and play nurse maid to mean Daddy Dearest. She was dutiful enough to put aside her hate of him and mix in some duty to sweeten the taste and make her life more palatable. But when the man died and the monster emerged she couldn't say with certainty she could do what needed to be done. She didn't trust herself to go to the wood shed and get the axe from the shelf, next to the tacks and screws and cobwebs, and take it to Daddy Dearest, take it to his head until it was cleaved from his quivering, shivering body.

No she knew she may not be able to do such a thing. But she was sure that I could.

My sister knows me well.

The city lights were a memory, winking out on me over ninety minutes and a hundred and fifty miles ago. The view from the window was that of white lines in the yellow haze of my head lights and the twinkling blues and greens of the car's interior dash splashed against the wind shield.

As I drove I listened to news reports and weather bulletins, flipping between channels to listen to any announcement suggesting that The Sickness had returned to our fair land. I found nothing. But I knew all too well that this meant little. There had been sporadic incidents since the village of the damned had chowed down on the three medics on national TV. The Sickness was often popping up, but the incidents were isolated, townsfolk raising the alarm as well as their axes and shot guns before things got out of hand.

The military would come, scientists in tow, and neutralise the site, either spraying the locale with a clear liquid that gave off the sweet aroma of liquorice, or the flame throwers would come and raise the site of the occurrence to the ground.

My mobile purred into life and I activated my Bluetooth.

"Linz? You okay?" I swallowed the panic trying to climb out of my throat.

"Not Lindsey," a voice said. "Dr Conlon."

The family doctor. Our family doctor. The one who had resided over our cuts and bruises and breaks and said not one fucking word to the world.

"What you doing there?" I said coldly.

"Your sister called and said your father is sick," Conlon said carefully.

"First, he ain't my father," I said. "Second, since when did you come runnin' when someone says they're hurt?"

"Now, son, I'll be the first to admit that things were misinterpreted. But that stuff is done. We have to look at what's being dealt out to us."

"Keep an eye on Linz," I replied, my words greasy with malice. "When I get there I want you gone, got that?"

I hung up, the road and a pack of cigarettes becoming my companions for a while.

The house appeared from behind a group of maple trees, the car headlights giving the broad leaves a sheen that writhed like flames as they were tousled in the breeze.

Its omnipotent image brought the kind of memories that I'd sought to bury over the years. The kind of memories that had driven an eighteen year old kid to bail and put distance between this house and its secrets. But the miles did nothing to blunt the experiences, not really. Not in a way that really mattered, the way that would allow me to move through life without the booze.

I pulled the car onto the short drive, alongside a blue Ford I presumed belonged to Conlon. No sooner had I switched off the engine, the porch door opened and the slim figure of Lindsey appeared and ran to me. I held onto her in silence, the moment filled with the tick ticking of the car's engine blocks cooling down after their late night drive.

"Thanks for being here," she said into my shoulder. I could smell her perfume, something cheap from the local store.

"Why the doctor?" I said.

"He dropped by. I needed the company until you got here. Better than being on my own, I guess."

"You should be used to it," I said pointedly.

"Maybe. But this is different." She stepped away from me, her face wan with embarrassment. I felt guilt pulse through me and I feigned a smile to soften the moment. She bought it, but only just.

"Come inside," she said. "He's in his bedroom."

Lindsey turned and walked into the house I'd left behind years ago. I followed, stepping reluctantly into the past, hoping that I'd have enough in reserve to stop me going to the dresser in search of some comfort from Ol' Jack. Maybe I'd get lucky and my sister who fought for me, took the hurt for me, sacrificing her heart and soul in the process, wouldn't see just what a disappointment I'd become. And if all else failed, there was always the hip flask I kept in my pockets.

The lounge was as I remembered it, the heavy leather sofas were soft with use, the big cushions moulded in the shape of our asses over the years. Threadbare rugs covered the beaten floorboards and in the fireplace flames licked at the kindling of a recently lit, half assed fire.

The cake was there, no surprise, still with the "Happy Father's Day" lie emblazoned in blue icing. The candle wasn't lit. Seems there was always darkness around Daddy Dearest.

I scanned the walls, my mind making a conscious effort to block out the drinks cabinet in the corner of the room, where bottles lay imprisoned behind leaded glass, muting the temptation, but not stopping it from calling, calling to me.

It was the axe that silenced them as abruptly as a concrete path silences the screams of a high rise jumper. A wedge of bright metal rested on the tattered rug, its long wooden stave dull against the highly polished rosewood cabinet. It seemed fitting that the tools of daddy's demise should keep company. The axe, it seemed, was a statement; our salvation fashioned from iron and oak. And in its shadow things would end; Lindsey's life of blind servitude; my life of guilt and self loathing.

And Daddy Dearest? Well he'd die twice today, though he deserved more. I would cleave his head from his scrawny neck, retribution wearing the face of mercy. And as the blood pumped out onto the floor I would see the red tide was turning and life would be so very different, life would be right.

"What stage is he at?" I asked her as I stared at the stairs just visible beyond the lounge doors.

"The doctor says it's advanced," Lindsey said. "He hasn't long to go."

"Conlon needs to leave," I said. "For his own good."

"I was hoping that you'd be there before it comes to that," my sister said slowly.

"That's not what I meant."

She looked at me for a second yet in that moment we exchanged a lifetime; Conlon's disregard of the Hippocratic Oath on his road to become hypocrite incarnate. All the years of abuse selectively shelved in lofty positions, safe from prying eyes. And part of me knew that the doctor's presence was an extension of the family need to keep the dirty linen in the basket for fear the stink brought too much attention, for fear that people would need to see exactly what kind of stain was soiling the air.

285

"Let's go take a look at him," I said heading for the stairs, which were in deep shadow.

"Maybe you should take this," Lindsey said dragging the axe away from the cabinet. "You know, for later?"

"For the cake?" I said, my voice tight.

"Funny guy."

"Yeah," I said without enthusiasm.

I took it from her without comment. It was heavy and the weightiness gave me assurance that it would do the job and save us all.

I mounted the stairs leaving Lindsey to stare after me, her bright blue eyes muted by the darkness. Ahead, a slab of light appeared; a door opening in the gloom. But not just any door.

His door.

The sanctum of Daddy Dearest, the place where he kept company with his new companion: The Sickness. In the doorway a figure wavered in the light. I held my breath, stopping my advance mid way on the stairs, my hands lifting the axe in a subconscious act of preparation. I sensed danger. But it was muted, as though drifting through a thick mist.

"Hope you're not planning to use that on the living, John."

Conlon's tone was passive, but far from cordial. I lowered the axe, but only a little.

"I hadn't intended to but who knows? It may give those not willing to take a hint a little incentive."

Despite his age, Conlon was a big man. He had height, a good head and shoulders over me, and he had weight, his waist an inner tube of flesh that was barely contained by the belt of his pants. In the light of the doorway he stood a bloated bell shaped silhouette using the frame as support.

"Maybe we should accept that in this we're on the same side?" he suggested.

"Just leave," I said. "Then I'll accept whatever you want."

His shape sagged a little, his belly bouncing. "Maybe I should call the authorities?" he said softly. "Maybe I should let folk know that The Sickness is in town and it's stopped to pay you guys a visit?"

"Maybe I take this axe to you and say it was a piece of mercy, that Daddy Dearest chowed down on your lard ass and you begged for someone to end it?"

It started out as a bluff, the ego rising from the ashes like a phoenix ready for magnificent rebirth. But as the words formed, becoming real in the gloomy stairwell, I considered it. And as fleeting as the thought was, it felt so right I became numb with shock that I even paid it any mind. I ushered the errant thought into a dark corner where it glowered, resentful and defiant.

"A boy left here," Conlon said. "And a man has returned. Time works its magic doesn't it?"

"Not on everything."

"Happen that's true," the doctor said.

The silence rolled in the way a sea fog clogs the coastline in spring. I felt someone far away lower the axe, a sign that nothing changes. Not really. There's no end to the war but there is always place for a cease fire. And that time was here, now, in the gloomy stairwell of a house choked with bad memories.

"You gonna help with this?" I said.

"Yes."

"You know I hate you, right?"

"Yes," the big man said. "The shine might come off of that hate once this is done."

There was hope in his tone, absolution seeking out a chink in my armour. But why now? Years of regret perhaps? Years of guilt eating him away like a cancer?

"You coming to do this John? You coming to do the deed?"

Not Conlon this time. No resonance to the voice. Just a hiss, reed thin and gasping for air.

Daddy Dearest.

My skin crawled and my balls shrank. The hairs on my neck played host to goose flesh and the little boy who wet his pants when he heard the door click open at midnight, bringing Daddy Dearest and the stale sour odour of Ol' Jack, screamed soundlessly in the locker chained shut at the back of my mind.

"Yes," I said. But my voice was a small thing, lacking real conviction. "I'm coming to finish it."

287

There were only seven steps separating the landing and me, yet there may as well have been ten storeys. My legs were uncooperative cylinders of leaden flesh, jittering with each footfall, and my heart was pumping way too fast.

My bravado had taken a vacation, gone off to console itself with false promises that it may return sometime soon with new vigour. I called out to it, but it was useless. The little boy was here, his bladder a ball of hot steel getting ready to flow.

"You need to hurry Johnny boy," Daddy Dearest whispered. "My times almost up. And I don't want to be coming back. Oh, my. No, I don't, but I can feel the hunger, like a hard day on Ol' Jack, the need to feed."

I was on the landing now, my feet shuffling across the heavy pile. The axe, now a sudden weight against my arm, trailed behind like a lame third leg, its steel heel bringing with it fibres and dust devils. My lungs were steel and my throat, fire. I fought to stay focused but the world wanted to flip, and send me screaming into a pit of fear.

Conlon watched my trial, his face a mixture of bemusement and remorse. In that moment, as I realised that perhaps bridges, whilst not returned to their former glory, may be patched up just enough to allow safe passage, a huge cry punched through the air. It was agony vented into the ether, agony coupled with anger that is born from the last vestiges of hope.

Daddy Dearest was dying. It was the sound that in another time, another place I would have celebrated. Hell, I'd have probably cranked up the dial and danced to its tune. But this wasn't the dark corners I found when Ol' Jack was hauling the shots. I was stone cold sober and Daddy Dearest was in the room barred only by a doctor stewing in the juices of guilt.

"Time to do the do, John," Conlon said. "Then I'll sign the certificate. And no one knows."

"Your price for absolution?" I said.

"I already paid that this evenin'."

He stepped aside and the light played on a large damp stain on the arm of his shirt sleeve. Blood. Soaking into the cotton fabric.

My face acted puzzled on behalf of a dawning mind and he nodded sadly.

"The hunger starts early." His words explained more than just the chunk Daddy Dearest had relieved from the bad doctor's arm. It also gave an answer to his sudden change of heart. The Sickness was in him. And soon he would follow Daddy Dearest into its endless world of hunger. The Dear Doctor needed out.

And he needed me to do it. I was taken aback that my earlier thoughts of murder would now come with sanction.

"I'll help you to help me," Conlon said, his smile slack and forlorn.

I never thought the time would come when such an enemy would become an ally. But that time had come knocking; dressed in its Sunday best.

I stepped into the room, where a small part of hell played out before me.

Daddy Dearest lay still upon his bed, the bedding a ruffled mess, streaked with blood. His limbs, twig thin and bare save for the crimson wheals cross-crossing his skin, jutted out from his pale blue pyjamas, toes and fingers clawed by the agony that had taken him to his momentary death. My eyes traced his gaunt stiffened outline until they alighted upon Daddy Dearest's face, which was twisted into a mask of pain, mouth clamped in a crimson, oval grimace, cheeks sallow, and his eyes so wide they appeared to be without lids. I had seen those eyes many times, looked into them, and they were as terrifying in death as they were in life: piercing blue, devoid of expression or remorse, love or morality, rolling back into his head like a shark about to take a bite.

The blood on the sheets belonged to Conlon. I felt both disgusted and relieved by this knowledge. After all, it could so easily have been Lindsey with a chunk missing from her forearm.

"You're going to have to do it soon. John," Conlon said beside me, "I can support you through it. Then you know you'll be able to do me."

I know that now, I thought.

"Got to take his head clean off. No other medicine for The Sickness."

"If you're the expert, maybe you should do it?" I hissed.

"I can't swing that axe hard enough," Conlon said holding out his bloodied arm towards me, just in case I wasn't getting the message. "No, John, this is your duty."

I was about to respond, saying anything that would get the time passing without having to focus on what was unavoidable, but then I saw Daddy Dearest move. Only a finger at first, the one that used to have a wedding band as a sign of his eternal love for the mother I'd never known. It was a slight and deliberate movement, the clawed digit unfolding as though it were a flower seen through time lapse TV. The other fingers followed suit, accompanied by the protesting pop and snap of seized knuckles.

"Oh sweet Jesus," Conlon whispered. "Ain't that the damnedest thing?"

Damned alright. No doubts about that.

Even knowing it was coming to this made no odds to my ability to act swiftly. Last time I saw such a thing it was blunted by a TV screen. But up close and personal it was something else. It needed something to happen. It needed something from me.

"Do it, John!" No whisper from Conlon this time. Daddy Dearest was jerking into life like a mannequin bouncing down a stairway, arms and legs tight angles, C3PIO wearing a flesh suit.

I lifted the axe just as the first piteous moan wavered from Daddy Dearest's throat. It was a sound at once woeful and deadly and turned my heart to ice.

"For Christ's sake, do it!"

Another voice, loud and shrill: Lindsey's voice from the doorway. I yanked my head towards her, caught the blend of shock and fear in her eyes. It held her gaze for a moment longer than I intended.

The next thing I knew, Conlon was screaming.

Daddy Dearest had hold of the doctor's shirt, dragging the hem from out of his pants and exposing his big belly. Daddy's reanimated corpse was using Conlon to haul itself up from the bed, dragging the bad, bad doctor forwards, towards its yawning mouth. Before I could take aim with the axe, Daddy Dearest was clamping down on Conlon's flabby cheek and tearing him a new mouth.

I heard Conlon's high pitched protest shortly before Daddy Dearest ripped the wad of flesh away with a sickening purring sound. Lindsey retched in the doorway.

"Get out of the way!" I yelled, stepping back so that I had room for a decent swing. But such instruction was fruitless, since the big man and Daddy Dearest were now intertwined. I clamped a hand over my mouth as daddy's hands sought Conlon's navel and the hooked fingers yanked open his abdomen, exposing a visceral kaleidoscope to the world.

Conlon wore a quasi-comical expression of disbelief and agony, his breath a prolonged hiss. His big frame flopped forwards, his ample innards slopping out onto the bed linen, and for a time the world stood still, punctuated by the greedy slurping of Daddy Dearest getting to know the doctor really well. Inside and out.

I fought to gain composure, barely able to stand. Daddy's feeding had punctured something other than Conlon's abdomen, and the room was beginning to fill with the reek of vomit and shit. I gagged but swallowed hard. I hefted the axe and stepped up to the bed where ol' DD was buried up to his shoulders in the cavity he'd opened in the doctor's belly.

"Heads up, you asshole!"

Daddy Dearest pulled his head out of Conlon with a sucking slurping sound. The ice blue eyes peered out from a crimson mask, and he was suddenly interested again. But by this time the axe was slicing through the air, and my arms prepared for steel to make contact, which it did seconds later, shearing one of his arms off at the elbow. Even for me, this was a spectacular miss.

"Shit!"

The arm struck the head board where it writhed like a mottled pink and red snake. Daddy Dearest pumped his blood onto the doctor, but neither was in any state to be concerned by it. Seemingly invigorated by his recent feed, daddy came at me, forcing himself upright, his remaining arm reaching out, his bloodied mouth hanging open.

Again I swung the axe, this time making contact with his forehead, but I was off balance and it was a glancing blow, knocking his head fiercely to one side, and lifting a piece of his scalp so that it waved in the air before slapping back into place like some macabre pedal bin. I tried to create more space, moving away from the bed towards the doorway, but Conlon's legs got the better of me. I went down hard, going so far over on my right ankle that I heard the tendons shear shortly before the bolt of hot fire shot through my calf.

I cried out and clutched at my fractured ankle, the pain now the centre of my universe. And in the melee the axe went spinning away from me, skittering under a bed that was now seeping with gore, dulled only by the cloud of bright spots speckling my vision. And through this, the shape of Daddy Dearest emerged to say "hi" in the only way he knew how.

Through the pain I raised a hand to fend him off. It was feeble and resulted only in his teeth ripping off two fingers and a thumb. The pain in my ankle, the knuckle splitting agony flaring in my right hand, were nothing to the knowledge that even if I got out, even if I could do what I did so well and run away from the clutches of Daddy Dearest, The Sickness would soon be coming to pay me a visit. And all I could think of was Lindsey, standing in the doorway watching her world come apart, and making sure that she would be okay, making sure that she didn't have to do the do.

Daddy Dearest was on top of me, possibly far stronger in death than he ever was in life. But I fought. Even with the severed fingers and the shattered ankle I fought, driving him off, shoving him so hard he pin-wheeled backwards and into the dressing table where his head struck the vanity mirror turning the glass into a tangled web of cracks. Then I was at the door, where Lindsey was wan with despair.

"Oh God, John. What do we do?"

I knocked her sideways onto the landing and reached for the key jutting out of the door. I'd yanked it out before Lindsey could realise my intention.

"Time for me to take care of Daddy Dearest, Linz," I said as she scrambled back to her feet. "Time for you to get the hell away from here."

I shut the door on her screams and jammed the key into the lock, turned it and yanked it to one side so that it snapped in the tumbler.

Heavy pounding on the door now as Lindsey called my name over and over, and Daddy Dearest climbed to his feet; his stump weeping, echoing the tears coursing down my cheeks. He stumbled over to me and I reached into my pockets, the Zippo and the hip flask becoming wet with my blood.

"Well how about it, Daddy?" I said hoarsely. "How about you an' me share a little Ol' Jack?"

Of course, Daddy Dearest was way past such things. His poison was very different these days. I sparked the Zippo, its flame a testament to the searing heat in both my hand and ankle. Daddy loomed, the hip flask blessed us both, splashes of alcohol maybe not enough to endure under the touch of flame, but enough to help it take hold, enough to send us both to the places we were destined to be.

Never to return.

Daddy lunged and I sparked him up. His nylon PJ's roaring into a blistering heat, the burning material hanging like fireflies in the air before landing on the alcohol splashed about my own clothes. Even as the flames licked at my skin, I felt different, I felt The Sickness going to town on me. I rolled about the floor, ensuring the fire took hold of the room, of the house. The world became a blinding place of fire heat and pain and I knew that of all the people in the house only one truly deserved to be free of it.

Lindsey.

My Lindsey.

Never ceasing to amaze.

THE END

HOME FOR THE ZOMBI-DAYS
By
A.P. Fuchs

There was no other tree like it.

Roy Davies swore up and down it had been reserved just for him. Or, at least, a guy like him full of Christmas cheer, blood pumping with hot cocoa, images of his family and their smiles dancing in his head.

Ol' Sammy Dean said he had something special for him when Roy called in to Sam's Treetop Top Trees Christmas Lot early that morning. The plan was to get a jump on all the other tree-buyers by hitting the place early, even wait outside the fence a few minutes before the lot opened with anyone else who was crazy enough to get there at 7am, and forfeit a Saturday's sleep-in.

Except Roy didn't count on Old Man Winter sending a dilly of a blizzard, covering the town of Dellisburg with two feet of snow. The white stuff came down in sheets for most of the morning, but the sky had cleared by early afternoon.

Roy's truck wouldn't budge out of the driveway, so he spent an hour shovelling to clear it up. Sure, after that the truck moved, but only got to the bottom of the driveway before hitting a snow ridge that it couldn't clear.

Roy had no choice but to wait.

The afternoon wore on. He sat on a fold-out chair in the landing of his house, looking out the window of his screen door, waiting on the town to send a few street cleaners through.

The first showed up around two.

Roy got in the truck and headed out to Sammy's lot, hoping to snag a tree before anyone else did, wanting to get it home in time for when his wife and kids returned from visiting his mother-in-law in Alberta. He just hoped the storm had been localized and they'd still make it through on schedule, getting here just after midnight tonight.

It was slow-going getting to Sammy's. Most of the time Roy was stuck behind a street cleaner, waiting for the big bulk of a machine to clear the road before he could even drive on it. It didn't matter. The wait was worth it and he had plenty of time.

He checked the rear-view mirror. No one was behind him. Either no one else was coming out to claim a tree or they were taking an alternate route. According to his GPS, he was taking the fastest way.

Suckers, Roy thought. *See you at the finish line.*

Twenty-five minutes later, the street cleaner turned off at the yield. Roy continued in a straight line, the road still covered in snow but packed down. Looked like dozens of other cars had already been up this way, having come in from the south.

Mr. GPS had lied. At least, in terms of time. It was still the fastest route but the street cleaner slowed Roy down a whole lot.

"No matter," he muttered. "Another ten minutes and I'm there."

He drove on.

Only a few minutes in and the sky went gray. A few minutes more and the snow came down. Another minute and there was nothing but white in front of the windshield.

Roy had to pull over almost immediately the snow was so bad. He tried his cell to call ahead to Sammy's and let him know he was coming. No signal.

So he waited, running the heater intermittently, hoping the snow would die down soon.

It didn't. Roy got out of his truck and hit the road, toes frozen. So were his fingers. His nose, well, he lost feeling on that hundreds of meters back; same with the tips of his ears. He was never one to dress for the snow. Car heaters, he figured, had a job to do and he was more than glad to let them do it. Besides, he hated all those layers anyway. Now he regretted not listening to his wife's naggings about dressing for the weather and even wearing an extra layer "just in case," especially since his heater conked out on him as if it knew he was counting on it to stay warm in this stupid blizzard.

Sam's Treetop Top Trees Christmas Lot had to be up there just ahead, somewhere behind the veil of white that made it near impossible to see more than five feet in front of him.

He just hoped he'd get there in time and get warm before he became a Roy-sicle forever.

* * *

They say that mirages only happen in deserts. Something about the heat draining all the moisture from your body, even drying up your brain so you start seeing things that aren't there. No one ever said you started seeing things in the cold, namely a blizzard where there was only white, white and more white.

There was a shadow up ahead, looking something like a fuzzy rectangle with a spotted triangle made from mozzarella. There were other triangles as well, fluffy and somewhat transparent behind the snow.

Roy, forehead frozen, pressed on against the cold wind, hoping to God he'd make it to … to … He didn't know where he was supposed to make it to.

Tree Samtop Christmaslot Tree Stop or something.

Fuzzy, fluffy mozzarella. Fuzzy, fluffy toes; numb and fat. Fingers that were probably very well blue.

Treestop Samlot StopChristmas Tree.

Roy blinked – then couldn't open his eyes, the bits of frost from the wind-caused tears freezing his lashes shut. He squeezed his eyes, hoping the skin-on-skin from doing so would be enough to melt the ice so he could see again. It helped, but only a little.

Stoplot Tree ChristmasTop Trees.

Too cold.

So cold.

* * *

A sharp rod of pain spiked through Roy's heels, drove right through his shinbones and slammed into his knees. His thighs ached just above the kneecaps as warmth blasted through his system.

"Yaaaahh!" he shouted.

"Hold it steady, mate," an old, pebbly voice said.

296

"No, no fries for me, thanks," Roy said. A flashback to the mozzarella. "Two slices for a buck? Okay, but hold the chocolate."

"Love to, friend, but I don't think you're thinkin' straight. No, surely not."

Roy's head went warm, then fuzzy, then warm again.

His legs pounded from the knees down. There was no way he was walking.

The old voice again: "Hurts, I know, but you'll thank me later. This here ain't just hot water. If I did that I'd probably ensure you'd lose a toe or something. Maybe more. What you got here is what I called 'The Blend'. At least, that's the name I'm thinking of giving it. Never made it before, but have thought of it for years. Call me crazy, but warm water and some of the sap from my trees will make you just fine and dandy. Sap's supposed to have magical properties, so says some legends I heard. I don't buy it, but it sure is fun thinkin' it."

Roy groaned.

The old voice went on. "Maybe I should call it 'Sam's Warmer Upper Before Supper'?" He let off a whooping chuckle then followed it off with an old-timer's cough. "Nah. 'The Blend' works just fine for me. Listen, you're blue in the legs, my friend. This stuff'll help. Sap's supposed to be good for all sorts of things. You know, kind of like honey – syrup stuff – and killin' colds is one of honey's big things. So Mama used to say back in the day."

"I don't ..." Roy started but the words slipped off his tongue and a moment later he forgot what he was trying to say.

"Anyway," Ol' Sam said, "I know you came for the trees. Saw you hobbling up the road. Saw you fall. 'No good weather to be out in,' I said. So I come and got you. Still blowin' up a snow cone out there. We're gonna have to just wait 'er out till she's done. Then I'll take you home. Know where you live?"

"Manersh sha blin errr ..." Roy said.

"No matter. I'm sure you got a wallet on you somewhere."

* * *

297

Roy's world was black. The fresh scent of pine and burnt wood hit his nostrils. Despite wanting to open his eyes, he couldn't. The smell from the pine and wood filled his nose, went down his throat and hit his lungs. He tried moving, but the best he could do was wiggle his toes. They were in something liquid, something warm and sticky.

A craggily voice hung over his head like a wet blanket, each sound it made just that: sound without meaning.

Head hurting, confusion setting in, the sound of his heartbeat began to fill his ears and pulse away, each *thump-thump thump-thump* getting louder as if it was pumping inside his head instead of in his chest.

Muscles aching, he tried to move again, but like before the most he could manage was wiggling his toes. The sticky liquid sloshed over his feet, its warmth sending goosebumps up and down his skin.

A hot tingle, then extreme relaxation as he felt every muscle in his body turn to quivering jelly.

His heart pounded, the beats growing slower apart.

Roy thought he was shaking, but couldn't be sure. That voice sounded overhead and still held no meaning.

The beats slowed even more, and the inside of his chest began to feel hollow, as if something inside was slipping away.

The sticky fluid splashed up and hit his legs. He realized he was indeed shaking.

Thump.

Thump.

Th—

* * *

The sweetness of the pine's sap rested on Roy's tongue, every inch of skin inside his mouth coated with the sticky stuff.

When he opened his eyes, a man's face was before him, the fellow with his hands on either side of Roy's head.

298

"You there, mate? Your colour's gone. All pallid, you are. 'The Blend' was supposed to warm you, not freeze you out again."

"Hrrrmm …" The sound trickled out of Roy's mouth.

"That's it. Wake up. Let's get you out of—" The man glanced down at Roy's feet. "The bucket's empty. Where's 'The Blend'? It's as if you sucked it right up through your feet and—"

Roy put his hands on the man's and held them there. The fella's old face looked familiar, but no name came to mind. Roy licked his lips, the sweetness of the sap gone.

Where was it? What was he drinking that was so good, so sweet? It had to be around here, had to be—

The texture of the man's skin beneath his palms, tender, appealing. He smelled good, too, the scent stirring his stomach, making it rumble. Slowly, Roy brought the man's hand off one of his cheeks and dragged it across his skin to his mouth. The man's hands smelled of the delicious sweet stuff. Roy stuck out his tongue and licked inside the man's palm.

"Now, hey, there just a second. You can't—" The moment the man pulled his hand away, Roy jerked it back and couldn't help himself but bite into it. Warm blood spurted up into his mouth. The man howled and ripped his hand away, cradling it against himself like a baby.

Roy stood up, whatever that red stuff was that came out of the man's hand was even sweeter than the sap of a pine. He had to have more. Had to have that delicious sweetness on his tongue all the time. Legs heavy, head tipped to one side no matter how hard he tried to straighten it, Roy slowly moved toward him.

With the tears in his eyes, the man said, "Roy, it's me Sam. What're you doing? What's happened? Why are you—?"

Sam took a step back. Roy forced his legs to move faster. He raised his arms and reached forward. The old man looked like he was going to turn away from him, so Roy fell forward, his hands landing on the man's shoulders, Roy's weight was enough to set the old guy off balance and pull him to the floor.

"Mrrrr …" *More.*

He let his head flop onto Sam's and he started biting into the old man's face. His teeth tore away the flesh from the cheeks despite Sam's open mouth screaming in pain. If anything, the old man's screams made it easier because it stretched the skin and made a larger surface area for him to bite in to.

Roy slurped the slab of chewy skin into his mouth, relishing the sweet flavour of the blood upon it. These two combined made him go into a frenzy. He grabbed Sam's head, torqued it to the side, inadvertently snapping the old man's neck.

Roy ripped into his throat and tore out his trachea, crunching down on it like corn on the cob. Every mouthful made him want more and he ripped away Sam's clothes and dug into his abdomen like a dog burying a bone. Intestines boiled over the rim of the bloody cavity like noodles and sauce over a pot. Roy gorged on them, their slick texture sliding down his throat like squid.

With each mouthful, he wanted more. He dipped his hand into the old man's body and pulled out the liver and bit down on it like a pizza.

Growling, he chomped it down and knew that once the flesh from this man was gone, he wanted more. But where?

He'd find something. He had to.

When he was finished, Roy got up, let chunks of meat and strings of bloody skin roll off his mouth and chin and down his body. Eyes fixed forward, he stumbled to the door and left. While outside, something pulled him to the right. He didn't know where he was going, but heading this way seemed the right thing to do. The partly-covered tracks in the snow said someone else had been this way before.

He walked on.

* * *

"Roy?" Elena called from the front door. "Roy, we're home!" She looked down at Stephanie, their daughter. "Why don't you take your boots off and find Daddy?"

"Okay."

For a six-year-old, Steph was already adept at putting on and taking off her ski pants and parka. Still needed help with the wrap-around-the-head scarf though.

Before Steph left the foyer, she asked, "Should I tell him about Grandma and Grandpa coming over, too?"

Elena smiled. "Let it be a surprise."

Steph grinned, mimed zipping her lips shut, locking them, and throwing away the key. Elena gave her a wink. The little girl ran off into the house.

Elena hoisted the two duffel bags from their trip over her shoulders and climbed the stairs to the master bedroom so they'd be ready for unpacking later. As much as she wanted to see her husband right away and plant a big, wet kiss on that face of his, it was more important to her that their daughter spent a few minutes alone with him first because she had been so excited to see him. It was all she talked about on their trip home.

Elena dropped the bags on the bed then made her way back down the stairs. When almost at the bottom, a high-pitched shriek shook her to the core.

"Steph!" she screamed then jumped down the last step and headed for the kitchen. "Where are you?"

The girl screamed again.

Downstairs!

Elena ran down the stairs to the family room. Her foot caught on a step about halfway down and folded under her. She was on her butt instantly and slid down the stairs. She hit the bottom in a heap.

The screaming turned to a wet gurgle.

Then nothing.

The family room was empty. Just the sofa, the loveseat and the big, microfiber chair that she and her husband fought to sit on all the time. The flat screen TV was there, turned off.

There was no Steph.

The laundry room!

Foot hurting something fierce, she forced herself up and limped to where the small room ran off the TV area, just beside the bar. The light was off, the door slightly open.

301

Call the cops. Call the cops. Call the cops, she told herself. *Steph!* She had to know her daughter was okay.

She slowly neared the door and debated saying hello. *Stay quiet. Just see what's there first.*

Elena crept up to the small opening and listened.

A soft sound came from the dark room: wet and slurpy.

She pushed on the door; it opened with a whiny creak.

The slurping stopped and a pair of drooping, white eyes gazed up at her from the dark.

"Roy!" she said and flicked the light on. "Roy?"

Her husband sat on the floor, their daughter in his lap, chunks of Steph's face dangling from his lips. Blood dribbled off his chin, the droplets splashing against the open flesh of what was once Stephanie's cheekbone. Their daughter gazed up at the ceiling, eyes open, never blinking.

Screaming, Elena turned and ran. *Grab her! Get Steph out of there!* But her legs refused to turn her around. She tumbled over a few steps later, her bad foot giving out from under her.

"No, no, no ..."

Roy appeared in the doorway then hobbled toward her, dragging Stephanie's limp body by the foot behind him. Her husband's skin was blue, and bruised in nasty blotches all over his face and neck. He still had on his jacket and boots. His hands were blue as well, with dark sores on his fingers. Blood coated his face, chunks of moist flesh dotting his cheeks and forehead, as if he had stuffed his face into a bag of hamburger like a dog did to a snowbank.

Elena crawled along the ground, trying desperately to get her legs underneath her.

When she finally managed to get up and get most of her weight on her good leg, Roy grabbed her from behind. She swung around and backhanded him, but not before he tried to snap the hand off with his mouth. Fortunately, he didn't.

Breaking loose, Elena quickly limped to the stairs and, tears in her eyes, began the brave ascent to higher ground.

As she hobbled up the stairs, the *thump-slap* of Roy's footfalls pulsed behind her.

"Come on," she said through gritted teeth, "move it!" A few more stairs and … she was at the top. She desperately wanted to catch her breath but a *thwoomp-bump* behind her caused her to glance over her shoulder. Roy had fallen face first on the stairs, his blue-gray hands with black fingernails clawing at the steps as he tried to regain his footing.

The front door. She had to get to the front door. Elena ran as fast as she could through the house. Her heart leapt in her chest when the front door came into view. Elated, she ran even harder for it, hand already reaching out for the knob. She quickly snapped it back when another blue-gray man appeared in front of her, his eyes dull, green mucus oozing from between his lips. The portly old-timer reached for her. She slapped his hand away and did a one-eighty, heading back down the hallway in the hopes of making it to the patio door off the kitchen.

The old man behind her groaned, his clumsy footfalls thumping the wooden floor in heavy *wumps* as he followed suit.

Roy reached for her with both hands the moment he got to the top of the stairs. Elena hugged herself as she twisted by, narrowly avoiding him. She entered the kitchen, slipped on the linoleum, and hit the ground face first. A dull, echoey spike of pain blasted through her nose and into her forehead and cheekbones. Tears suddenly springing from her eyes sent the kitchen into a blurry mosaic of brown rectangular shapes dotted with silver.

Low moans droned somewhere behind her.

Elena pushed herself onto her feet, her head immediately swooning as she stood. She stumbled back a step … and into a pair of waiting blue-gray hands behind her.

Screeching, she tugged herself away, but not before a burst of wet warmth gushed onto her shoulder, soaking into her shirt. The pain came after, and there was no feeling in her right arm from shoulder to fingertips.

"Stop! STOP! STOOOOOPPPPPPP!" she shrieked as she made her way to the patio door. With each footfall, pain shot through her arm, the swinging motion only adding to the agony.

At the sliding patio door, she found the handle with her other hand and pulled. The door opened about a foot. Elena went to open it some more, but Roy slammed up against the glass right in front of her, his weight against the door making it impossible to open any further.

"Get away! Getawaygetawaygetaway ..." she screamed and instinctively lashed out at him with her left hand. Roy caught it and yanked her fingers to his mouth, ripping them free from her palms. Blood spurted out of the stumps like geysers; throbbing pain shot up her arm and seemed to punch her in the face.

Dizzy, Elena swung herself sideways through the foot-wide opening in the door, doing everything she could to get herself outside and her hand from Roy's mouth. The creature held on, his grip solid, fighting her every effort. She pulled and pulled and ... her arm dislocated in its socket. Pain shook her upper body and she fell out of the house and onto the patio.

Crawling along the deck, wriggling her hips and legs to move forward, eyes still blurry from tears, panic accelerating her heart with every moment – her first thought was how the deep snow didn't feel that cold at all. If anything, it felt as if it wasn't there.

White snow.

A series of sharp pricks hit the rear of her calves. A second later, red rained around her, dying the snow just in front of her a rich crimson.

Off in the corner of the yard was an old evergreen, one that she and Roy had planted there back when they first moved in. She loved its colour. Always had. Its green matched the red on the snow.

Something heavy landed on top of her. Then something else.

She thought she heard Roy whisper something. Then again, it could have been her imagination.

"Merry Christmas," she thought she heard him say. "Glad you're home for the Holidays."

But it wasn't Roy's voice or the old fellow's.

A little girl's head landed in front of her; Steph's wide eyes wrapped loosely around her skull was all that remained of their princess.

Elena couldn't feel her legs anymore. She still didn't feel the snow.

The evergreen looked on.

A bruised hand knocked some snow over her eyes.

Everything was blue-gray.

THE END

ROMAN HOLIDAY
By
David Dunwoody

"... Again, President Ford is expected to address the nation in a matter of moments. Authorities in a number of major cities have already confirmed earlier speculation that the erratic and violent behaviour of the affected is only an early symptom—"

Eric reached for the radio dial. He'd already heard all this, and he knew the President wouldn't have anything new to say. Martial law had already taken hold, with or without his blessing. What Eric really needed to know was the conditions ahead, in Napa, but every frequency seemed to be simulating this network patter.

The world darkened. Glancing up, Eric saw the sky had turned dull gray. He drove a 1970 Cadillac Convertible. It was a boat, and difficult to handle on these narrow and winding country roads. As such, he was making slower progress than he'd intended, and it didn't look like he was going to beat the bad weather. He hoped Liv was sitting tight. The winemaker probably had her on a short leash; that was good, in this case. As he rumbled onto a paved road and saw the entrance of the winery up ahead – a gate set in fortress-like stone walls – for the first time, he was genuinely glad for Liv's situation. He saw the winemaker's home in the distance, a sprawling villa atop a hill, and knew she was safer here than she would have been in the city. And he would be, too. That was why she'd called him, why she had probably begged and pleaded with the winemaker to allow Eric's intrusion.

"It's nice here," she'd said. "Just think of it like going on holiday. Like we used to."

The sky rumbled. Eric slowed to a stop before the gate. A young man with a rifle slung over his shoulder appeared on the other side. Putting the convertible in park, Eric sat up and shouted his name. "I'm Olivia's friend!"

The man began to unlock the gate, then stood erect, staring past Eric. Eric looked back and saw two of them, ambling down the road towards his car. They were both men, dressed in blood-spattered t-shirts and jeans, and their movements were slow and jerky as they advanced on the vehicle. One's neck was bent at an unnatural angle, clearly broken, forcing his eyes skyward; he was hunched over so that he could see Eric. A thin stream of blood and spittle ran from his lips. He almost looked like he was smiling.

Eric had only seen a few of them since leaving the city, lurching along the shoulder of the PCH. This was the last stage of it, whatever it was. Eric glanced back at the gate. The man with the rifle watched impassively. Eric began, "Aren't you going to—"

The man raised the rifle abruptly. The gun was pointing at Eric – he threw out his hands with a scream—

The round tore past his ear and into the head of the broken-necked man. Eric dropped below the windshield and heard the rifle's crack a second time. It was answered by a peal of thunder. When Eric sat up, both of the men in the road behind him lay dead.

Dead again.

He lifted a hand in thanks to the man at the gate. "Good shooting," he breathed. "Good shooting."

Something lunged out of the trees at his left. An old man seized Eric's arm. There was no life in his eyes. His mouth opened, revealing a modest collection of brown teeth, and he clamped them down on Eric's driving glove.

Eric howled and shoved the man back, breaking his grip. He fell across the passenger seat and scrabbled across the floor for his .38. The old man pulled open the driver's door and clawed at Eric's thigh. "Maaaaaa."

Eric's fingers snagged the butt of the gun, and he fought to get a hold of it while pushing at the old man's head with his own. "Help!" Eric screamed. The old man's jagged nails dug into his leg. He kicked hard and the man stumbled back into the open door. Eric sat up and shot him through the cheek.

The old man cocked his head, sputtered, then dropped to the ground.

Eric leapt from the convertible and ran at the gate. "Why didn't you shoot?" he yelled at the young man.

307

"I thought he got you," the man said, and shrugged.

Eric ripped off his gloves and showed his hands to the man. "He didn't get me! All right?" He lowered his shaking hands and cast a glance over his shoulder. "Open the gate. Please. Let me in. I'm the professor, Olivia's friend."

The man complied. "Salvatore."

"Pleased to meet you." Eric stuffed his pistol in the waist of his slacks and turned to go back to the car. The man caught his elbow. "I'm going to drive in," Eric explained.

Salvatore shook his head. "Leave it."

"Fine." Eric trudged through the gate. Salvatore shut it quietly.

"They hear the car, that's why they come. Better we walk."

"Good point. Okay." Eric shoved his hands into the pockets of his sport coat, and as they walked up the road toward the villa, cutting through the middle of the vineyard, it began to drizzle.

"Anyone else here?" Eric asked. He eyed the rows of grapevines as he spoke, thinking of the old man's shadow bursting from the woods. He'd scarcely seen his attacker's face before his hand was in the bastard's mouth. "Besides Liv, of course, and the master of the house."

"No." Salvatore picked at his coat. "Anselmo is my cousin. So I stay. The others, he send away."

The villa's porch was shrouded by olive trees. Eric took shelter from the increasing rain while Salvatore unlocked the entrance. They passed through a small courtyard with a disused fountain – a stone handmaiden looking heavenward, hands clasped – and entered the house proper.

Salvatore took Eric's coat and left him alone in the front hall. Eric shook the water from his hair. He felt more than a little awkward here, in the home of Olivia's new lover with a revolver in his pants. His heart was still pounding. I shot a man out there. Jesus, he would have never thought he had that in him. Of course, the man was already dead, but … Nothing to be proud of, he told himself. She wouldn't be impressed.

Would she?

308

No, no. He was hardly St. George. She'd called him here because she knew he would have died in the city. Simple as that.

He heard an unfamiliar voice from within the house and tensed. He'd hoped to see Liv first. The winemaker, however, wouldn't allow that. Eric knew enough about him to know he was always in control. They'd actually crossed paths a few times before, at university functions – the winemaker, the wealthy benefactor, wearing his plastic smile and a young woman on his right arm. A different girl every time, with a different look. Whatever was in fashion. Though Eric and Liv had been over long before she took up with the winemaker, Eric had still tried to talk her out of it – but he was hardly an impartial observer, was he?

"Anselmo Guglielmetti," the man boomed as he strode into the hall. He caught Eric's hand in a vice grip. "Sal tells me your trip was eventful."

Eric had hoped the man would look older and more haggard than he had at those functions. He didn't. Eric knew Anselmo was in his fifties, at least five years his senior, but he didn't look it, not even close. They had the same salt-and-pepper hair – more salt than pepper on both accounts – but Anselmo's hair was thick and his flesh was pink and that smile of his made Eric feel like an underclassman in an ill-fitting suit.

He hadn't yet spoken a word. "Olivia's in her room," Anselmo said. "She'll be with us shortly. It's been a hectic morning, as you can imagine. You look as if you could use a drink."

Eric followed Anselmo into the kitchen. Gesturing to a small table set in a winnowed alcove, Anselmo ducked behind the counter. Eric took a seat. He adjusted the .38, then took it out and set it on the table. "Have anything stronger than wine?" he asked.

Anselmo laughed. "I took you for a Scotch man the moment I saw you." He filled two tumblers, dropped in a couple of cubes, and brought the drinks to the table. Sitting across from Eric, he moved aside a vase of pink lilies – Liv's favourite. "I finally turned the TV off," he said.

"What's that?" Eric took a sip of his drink. Warmth spread through his belly, and he sighed. Better to come down a little from the chaos outside before he saw Liv.

"I mean I've been watching TV all night and morning," said Anselmo. "She doesn't care to see it. But I can barely look away. Saw footage of them staggering through Times Square, all stiff-legged and white. Some of them had awful wounds. Mortal wounds. But they just keep going. Anyhow, she wouldn't come out of her room so I shut it off." Anselmo drained his glass. "You're a professor of what, again?"

"Astronomy," Eric answered, knowing damn well that Anselmo knew it.

The other man nodded and clinked the ice in his glass. "My, looks like I need a refill already." He got up and walked back behind the counter. "So where do you think it came from, Professor? The stars, maybe?"

Eric ignored the jibe and said, "More likely our own people made it. I'm sure they didn't intend this, but ..." He took another drink and decided to humour the winemaker, wax poetic a little. "Everything outside this world is Creation yet unfolding. We seem to search for the means to undo it."

"Hmm." Anselmo returned to the table. "Never known a stargazer to be so cynical. Not like Liv. But she's young yet." He tilted back his glass and swallowed down its contents. Anselmo's face flushed. He set the glass on the table with a bang. Eric jumped in his seat.

Anselmo's wet eyes narrowed. Eric realized the man had been drinking long before he got there. Anselmo's hands curled into beefy fists, and he said softly, "She was your student. Do you really think you're better than me?"

Eric stared at him, searching for words, for some sort of exit strategy. His back was against the windows. Anselmo was between him and the front hall. The winemaker had a peculiar smile on his face, and it wasn't the one he wore to parties. The revolver sat on the table in front of Eric ... they both looked at it, and Eric's stomach turned. His hands twitched in his lap. What did this maniac want him to do?

The lilies' petals moved ever so gently. Anselmo frowned, and his hands relaxed upon the table. "Do you feel a draft?"

He barked into the front hall. "Sal! Check on Olivia!"

Eric's hand took the .38 from the table and stuffed it into his pants pocket. He barely noticed. His heart was pounding again, and he was rising, willing his legs not to break into a run as he went into the front hall. Anselmo followed after him. There, they heard Salvatore's cry.

Anselmo raced ahead of Eric, down the hall and into the rear of the house, through the last doorway. He stopped beside Salvatore, both of them looking at something in the room; Eric broke through the pair and let out a strangled yell.

It had been a month since he last saw her. They'd run into each other in the city – he couldn't remember where just now, couldn't remember anything but the way she had looked, and how kind she had been, and how it had stirred him just to make her laugh again. Now she was pale and lifeless on the floor beneath an open window. Raindrops pattered on the carpet and drew tears on her face. She was wearing no makeup, and her dark brown hair was damp and matted to her brow and neck and shoulders. She wore a thin dress with a floral print. She was beautiful.

(She's dead)

Eric vomited on his shoes.

Salvatore pulled him back as Anselmo knelt beside the body. "Why are you – let me go!" Eric shook Salvatore off and fell beside Anselmo. Liv's eyes were closed, lips parted slightly. She smelled like the rain. Eric's stomach heaved again, and he let Salvatore draw him back.

Anselmo rose and went to the window. He caught the fluttering curtains in his hands and ripped them away, looking out and down the hillside. "They got in," he said quietly.

"You see them?" Salvatore asked.

"No." Anselmo looked down at Liv. "I see her."

He touched her face and neck. "No bite. Just choked the life out of her." Anselmo's fist pressed into his teeth.

Salvatore released Eric and went to shut the window. Eric and Anselmo stood on either side of the body. Eric didn't know

311

how to feel. He wanted to rage, to sob, but she had not been his in the moment of her death. It was Anselmo who needed to break the silence. But he didn't.

"She called me three hours ago," Eric breathed. "She was alive." His eyes lit upon the phone beside the four-poster bed, and he went to it. When he touched the receiver to his ear, a hollow clicking filled his head.

"Phone's been out for an hour or so," Anselmo muttered.

Eric sat on the bed.

"It must have tried to drag her out the window," Anselmo said.

"Don't."

"She couldn't scream ..."

"Don't. Just stop. Please."

"Search the grounds," Anselmo told Salvatore. He tugged on the bed sheet under Eric. "Stand up."

Eric numbly complied, and Anselmo covered the body. Then he sat at the foot of the bed.

Eric had seen so few vehicles out on the highway. People were staying home, where they felt safe. He had come here – not because of the remoteness of the villa, nor the great stone walls that surrounded it – but because of her. She'd always made him feel safe. And she'd known that.

"She still loved me," he breathed.

Eric realized what he'd said aloud and looked up with a start. Anselmo was gone. There was only the body. He went to her and stood over the bed sheet. He knelt, one last time, and pulled the cover back to see her. He studied the lashes of her eyes, the curve of her jaw, her slightly opened mouth. He smelled lavender. She often bathed in lavender-scented water. He knelt closer, sniffing at her mouth.

He turned her head ever so gently to the side and watched as water trickled from her lips.

"She still loved you," Anselmo said.

He was in the doorway. Eric stood. He felt the weight of the gun in his pocket, against his thigh. But he only said, "Why?"

Something struck the window, rattling it in its frame. Eric spun to see an amorphous silhouette moving behind the curtains.

The pane rattled again. Thunder sounded. Glass exploded into the room, and a pair of mottled gray hands tore through the curtains like they were wet paper.

"They did get in," Anselmo mumbled.

Eric barrelled into the winemaker, sending him tumbling head over heels into the hallway. Eric clambered over him and raced into the front hall, where his shoulder connected with Salvatore's chest with such force it threw the young man into the wall. Eric slipped, righted himself, and plunged through the door into the courtyard. Through the rain, past the stone maiden, through the outer door – Eric came at last to a halt and stared into the vineyard. It seemed to be alive, moving with the rhythm of the falling rain. He looked from row to row. There could be dead men lurking in any one of them, waiting to pounce on him as he ran for the gate. Then he remembered the gun, and shoved his hand into his pocket – found nothing.

Where had he lost it? The hall? The courtyard? Eric looked back at the villa and saw Salvatore taking aim. The sky roared. A rifle round whizzed past his head.

Eric broke right, down the hillside. He heard yelling. Anselmo, giving orders. The man was a coward. He must have killed her in a rage. Now Anselmo was back in control, clear-headed, and he wouldn't dirty his hands again. Eric ran around the side of an enormous barn and skidded through a slick of mud. He banged against the barn wall and splashed down. Filthy water entered his mouth and eyes. Anselmo had drowned her in the bath. She'd been utterly exposed, completely helpless. She'd trusted him. Eric's blood ran hot.

"Come out!" Salvatore shouted.

Eric sat up and pressed his back to the wall. "He murdered her!" he shouted. There was no response. "A girl! A poor girl!" Eric cried. His voice broke. Then the response came, but it wasn't Salvatore.

"You know how she was!" Anselmo called. Eric couldn't tell which side of the barn the man was on. The rain was coming down in sheets, and he could barely hear the winemaker above the din. "She told me she called you – we'd never discussed it – she gave me that look, you know the one. Witch!

313

"Then I had her in the water. Under the water. There was no going back then, Professor! I must have been as scared as she was, believe me. But it was HER OWN GODDAMN FAULT!" Anselmo was slurring heavily, and the occasional stutter in his voice told Eric the man was stumbling closer. But he still didn't know from which side! And Salvatore might be advancing silently from the other. Eric saw the stone wall through a line of olive trees. He could try and climb it. No. It was soaked and so was he. He'd take a bullet in the back. Better to face the bastard head-on.

Someone rounded the corner at his left. It was Salvatore, but his rifle dragged in the mud at his side, and through the downpour Eric saw blood pumping from a ragged wound in his neck, gushing through his fingers. Eric watched in horror as the brimming blood was washed away by the rain, only to instantly return. Salvatore sagged to the ground, and the rifle fell before him.

Eric stepped forward to reach for it. A dead man appeared at the corner. Eric dove for the gun.

The dead man jerked back as a bullet punched through his ribs. Eric had only just caught up the rifle; Anselmo was behind him, with the .38, and he knew the bullet had been meant for his back.

It happened quickly. Eric rose. The rifle kicked in his hands. Anselmo fell with a scream.

Eric staggered away, toward the wall, away from both Anselmo and the walking corpse. The dead man looked from him to Anselmo. His eyes met with those of the latter, the wounded one. Anselmo rolled onto his bloody stomach and clawed at the earth. "NO! NOOOOOOOOOOOOOOOOO!"

He didn't make it so much as a foot before the man fell upon him. He screamed like a child as he died.

Standing beside the wall and the olive trees, Eric had a clear view of the other corpses shambling down the hillside. They came around the barn on both sides, falling on their knees over Anselmo and his cousin. But a few pushed past the feeding frenzy, their eyes on Eric.

He looked down at the rifle. He didn't know how to chamber a new round, or if he even had to. He didn't even know if there <u>was</u> another round. He was a stargazer, for Christ's sake, and today every star had been blotted from the sky.

"Liv," he moaned.

The dead moaned in return.

Though without a star, Eric pressed the barrel to his chin and made a wish.

THE END

LARRY AND HANK'S BIG DEAD FISHING ADVENTURE
By
Eric S Brown

"Vacation. Such a simple concept. A break from the routines of work and day to day life. Fun in the sun and all that. Beach balls, fishing rods, and big breasted women in bikinis. Tell me, Hank, do you see any women here?" Larry growled as he jerked the bolt back on his rifle and a spent casing popped into the air.

"You just shot one through the head, Larry," Hank said innocently, not comprehending Larry's sarcasm.

"No, you idiot! Dead ones don't count! I am not looking to get my privates chewed off. I mean real, wet, breathing women."

Hank leaned closer to the edge of the roof the two of them had sought refuge on. He looked down into the sea of hungry corpses. Hundreds of gray, rotting faces stared up at him as the dead snarled and raged, pawing at the walls of the Burger King below them. "I don't think so Larry. There's a lot of dead ones though."

"Oh, why don't we take the weekend off?" Larry mimicked Hank's words from the day before. "We can drive down to the beach. Get in some deep sea fishing and see the babes in their swimsuits. Maybe we can even go to one of them nude beaches. It'll be fun!" Larry chambered another round and took aim at the skull of a fat man in a John Deere cap with a ripped open stomach which leaked a continuous stream of black pus. Larry squeezed the trigger and the man's head snapped back as the high powered round reduced his brain to mush. "Do you remember saying those words, Hank? I remember you talking me into this," Larry grunted. "Well let me tell you, this is just loads of fun, buddy! You talked me into driving right into the middle of the apocalypse!"

Hank's forehead creased in thought. "Uh … I think the apocalypse would've happened whether we came down here or

316

not. Besides, we're getting great tans, stuck up here on this roof."

"Oh, Hank ..." Larry shook his head.

"It's true," Hank assured him. "We're going to look awesome for the girls back home. You just have to look on the bright side of things, Larry. There's always a silver lining. My dad said so."

Larry's rifle clicked empty as he tried for another shot. Sighing, he lowered the weapon and began to reload it with the loose bullets he'd stuffed inside the pockets of his shorts. "We can't shoot them all. I don't have enough ammo and, sooner or later, those monsters are going to find the stairs that we used to get up here. Mind telling me what we're going to do then?"

Hank shrugged. "I don't know, Larry, but you always think of something. Remember that time the boss figured out someone was taking money from the registers? You framed that mean guy, Pete, for it. Not only did we get to keep our jobs but that bastard got fired and couldn't make fun of me no more."

Larry struggled for a way to explain to Hank the reality of their situation. "Those things on the street aren't human, Hank. I can't con them or put on my charm with them. They're only interested in eating us. Nothing else."

Hank smiled at him. "No worries, Larry. Things will work out. You'll see."

Not far away, Erin was straining with her back against the door of the beauty salon's office. All her strength and the full weight of her slim, one hundred and twenty pound form was shoving into it, trying to hold back the dead on the other side. Bloody, broken and mangled fingers lined the edges of its frame, clawing at her. Melissa helped with one hand, her other busy stabbing at the fingers with a pair of scissors.

Beth stood watching the two of them as she held two pairs of scissors of her own. "Did you hear that?" she shouted over Erin's constant wailing and the hungry moans of the dead outside.

"Little busy here!" Melissa snapped as she hacked at another groping hand. Two severed fingers plopped onto the floor at her feet.

"That was a gunshot!" Beth exclaimed. "Someone else is still alive!"

"Beth!" Melissa snapped. "Some help!"

"Don't you get it? We're going about this all wrong. That door will never hold those things. We need to fight our way through them and make a run for it!"

"You're insane!" Erin shrieked.

"No, I'm not," Beth said firmly. "Let them in. We can take them."

"Fine. Have it your way," Melissa conceded and backed away from the door.

Erin's screams grew higher in pitch as the weight and fury of the dead on the door slowly pushed her aside. A teenage Goth girl in fishnets half staggered, half fell into the office with them. Beth stepped up to meet her and buried a pair of scissors into her face above the girl's nose. The girl's eyes rolled into their sockets as her body slumped forward.

"Follow me!" Beth ordered as she threw herself into the several creatures blocking her path. The creatures were slow and uncoordinated and Beth used that to her advantage, kicking, punching, and shoving her way through them. Blackened nails clawed at her skin and teeth snapped at her from all sides.

Beth paused in the salon's atrium, waiting for Melissa and Erin to catch up. A cop with one arm missing lunged at her. She planted her remaining pair of scissors straight into his right eye, ramming them in up to the hilt. "Cover me!" she yelled as she knelt over the cop's corpse and tugged at the pistol holstered on his hip.

Melissa rushed forward, shoving a shirtless, unkempt surfer-type with several bullet holes in his chest through the salon's large glass window as he came at Beth. Erin slapped at an elderly dead woman, but stumbled over its walker and fell against a cabinet, casting cans of hairspray and bottles of shampoo in all directions. The old woman leaned over her and sunk her false teeth into Erin's shoulder. As the creature pulled her head away,

318

trying to take a chunk of Erin with her, her teeth remained embedded in Erin's flesh. Erin stared at the nicotine-stained things with wide, terror stricken eyes and screamed again.

At last, Beth tore the gun free. Getting to her feet, she shot the old woman in the face, spraying Erin with black pus and gore. She then spun about, dropping two more of the creatures with quick headshots. "Come on!" Beth jumped through the salon's shattered window into the street.

The parking lot was full of cars waiting to be taken. She hoped one of them had keys in because she had no idea how to hotwire one. Dozens of the dead wandered among the vehicles and they all turned in their direction as Melissa and Erin appeared at her side.

Beth spotted a bright green van with its side door open. "The van!" she cried, already sprinting for it.

Larry silently brooded, waiting for the dead to come pouring onto the roof. It was only a matter of time and he knew it.

"Larry!" Hank said, suddenly jumping up and down where he stood by the edge of the Burger King's roof. "I found us some!"

"Not now," Larry muttered. "Can't a guy even get a few minutes to make peace with his maker before he dies?"

"There's three of them Larry! They're making a run for a van." Hank rushed over and yanked him to his feet. "We gotta save them!"

"What are you rambling about?" Larry snatched his arm away then he saw her. The red-haired girl jumped into a van across the street. Two more girls hopped in after her and the van's door slammed closed as several creatures reached it just behind them and began pounding on all sides. The van shook and rocked where it sat as more dead huddled around it. With the image of the red-head burnt into his mind, Larry jerked up his rifle and started shooting. She was hot. Sure, he'd only gotten a glimpse of her, but all he needed to know right now was that she was the kind of girl he wanted to get to know.

319

His first shot splattered a dead hotdog vendor's brains onto the van's front windshield. His second dropped a paramedic with one half-eaten leg trailing behind him. Larry kept firing as the van's engine roared to life.

Hank whooped beside him. The girls in the van must have spotted them because it ploughed through the dead towards the Burger King. "They're coming!" Hank squealed like a kid on Christmas morning.

The van came to a stop below them. "Jump for it!" Larry yelled and jumped off the roof. He landed on the van's roof with a dull thud. He looked back to urge Hank on as his friend fell on him. The impact jarred the rifle from Larry's hands and it went flying into the ranks of the dead who were surrounding the van once more. Larry shoved Hank aside and slapped the van's top loudly with his palm. "Go!" he shouted. "Get us moving!"

The van's tires screeched. It shot forward as Larry and Hank clung on.

Inside the van, Beth kept her eyes glued to the road, spinning the wheel left and right, trying to dodge both the dead and the wrecked and abandoned vehicles that filled her path.

"We have to kill her!" Melissa was telling her. "You know Erin's infected. She got bit!"

"I'm right here!" Erin pointed out. "I can hear you, y'know?" Erin held a hand pressed tightly over the bleeding wound on her shoulder. "That old bitch had false teeth! Can you even catch whatever it is from dentures?"

"I'm not taking any chances!" Melissa grabbed Erin by her hair and bashed her head against the metal wall.

"Help!" Erin wailed through a mouthful of blood as she spat two teeth onto the floor and flailed, desperately trying to shove Melissa away from her.

"Girls!" Beth shouted, keeping her eyes on the road. "Stop it! If we don't stick together we're all dead!"

Melissa reluctantly let go. Erin offered a crooked smile and then grabbed her by the arm. Melissa's eyes widened as Erin's teeth tore a chunk of flesh from her wrist. "You witch!"

Erin laughed as Melissa's blood dribbled down her chin. "You gonna kill us both now?!"

320

"I'll kill you both, and you *know* I will, if you don't stop it right now," Beth warned them. Melissa and Erin glared at each other, but they both sat still and kept quiet.

Larry breathed a sigh of relief as the van finally came to a stop in front of wrecked military blockade. Beyond it were the docks. There were only a few creatures milling around on the street and the closest was a good minute's shambling away. Flexing his aching fingers, Larry jumped down from the van's roof. This time, Hank managed to scramble down without injuring his friend.

The van's side door slid open and they came face to face with the three girls. Two were pale and bleeding. Droplets of sweat glistened on their foreheads and one was emitting a low guttural moan.

"Erm … Nice to meet you ladies. I'm Larry and this here is Hank. Thanks for the save."

"Beth," the red-head nodded at him. The other two just stared.

"Are they okay?" Hank asked.

Larry opened his mouth to speak, but that's as far as he got. With a snarl, the petite girl sprang at Beth. Beth rammed the butt of her pistol into the girl's nose and sent her reeling backwards. With two well aimed, lightning shots, Beth sent her former friends to Hell.

Larry's mouth hung open in shock. He snapped it shut then said, "That … that was brutal. I am utterly and totally impressed."

"Stow it," Beth grunted at him. "I say we grab what we can, find a boat, and make for the islands."

"What islands?" Hank asked dreamily.

"Does it matter?" Beth replied with a thin smile.

"Suppose it doesn't," Larry agreed.

The blockade was littered with decaying, properly dead and half eaten corpses. Most of them were soldiers and there were weapons scattered around them. Larry whistled in appreciation as he helped himself to an M-16. He tossed Hank one as well.

"Bad ass," he commented as he saw Beth test the weight of a discarded USAS-12 automatic shotgun. "Now that's some firepower."

"Didn't help these guys much though, did it?" Beth said as she examined the boats moored up in the distance. "Either of you guys know how to sail? We don't want something that'll run out of fuel on us and leave us stuck in the middle of nowhere."

"Larry knows everything there is to know about boats, lady. We're going deep sea fishing," Hank informed her.

Beth's expression was a mixture of pity and hope as she offered him a smile. "I hope so," she said. "I really do."

"Wait up a sec!" Larry ordered them as they started for the docks. He disappeared into a nearby gas station and emerged a few minutes later with his M-16 slung over his shoulder and carrying two cases of Bud Light and a bag of ice. "If we're taking a fishing vacation, for who knows how long, by God, we're going to do it right!"

The docks were clear of the dead as they boarded a small white fishing boat by the name of *Seahorse*. Larry cast off its lines as Beth and Hank loaded up what few supplies the three of them had been able to loot from neighbouring boats. A lone dead man came shuffling down the dock towards them at the last moment as the boat drifted free of the dock. Beth raised her automatic shotgun and put five rounds into its chest, cutting it in two.

"That's for the girls," Larry heard her whisper under her breath. He put a hand on her shoulder. Tears rolled down her cheeks. Larry pulled her to him and hugged her tight.

"It's going to be okay," he assured her. "We're safe now. It's all over."

As the sun set over a dead world, the sail boat glided across a languid sea. Larry and Beth reclined in lawn chairs on the deck with cold beers in hand as Hank stood at the boat's side railing, his line cast, and fishing pole in hand. "You see, Larry," he told them. "Don't you feel better now? This vacation rocks!"

THE END

HOME IS THE SAILOR,
HOME FROM THE SEA
By
William Meikle

I smoked too many cigarettes, sipped too much Highland Park and let Bessie Smith tell me just how bad men were. For once thin afternoon sun shone on Glasgow; the last traces of winter just a distant memory. Old Joe started up "Just One Cornetto" in the shop downstairs. I didn't have a case, and I didn't care.

It was Easter weekend, and all was right with the world.

I should have known it was too good to last.

I heard him coming up the stairs. Sherlock Holmes could have told you his height, weight, shoe-size and nationality from the noise he made. All I knew was that he was either ill or very old; he'd taken the stairs like he was climbing a mountain with a Sherpa on his back.

He rapped on the outside door.

Shave and a haircut, two bits.

"Come in. Adams Massage Services is open for business."

At first I thought it was someone wandering in off the street. He was unkempt, unshaven, eyes red and bleary. He wore an old brown wool suit over a long, out of shape cardigan and his hair stood out from his scalp in strange clumps. I've rarely seen a man more in need of a drink.

Or a meal.

He was so thin as to be almost skeletal, the skin on his face stretched tight across his cheeks. I was worried that if I made him smile his face might split open like an over-ripe fruit.

"Are you Adams?" he said as he came in. He turned out to be younger than I'd first taken him for, somewhere in his fifties at a guess, but his mileage was much higher. "Jim at the Twa Dugs said you might be able to help me."

I waved him in.

"It's about time Jim started calling in some of the favours I owe him. Sit down Mr ...?"

"Duncan. Ian Duncan."

He sat, perched at the front of the chair, as if afraid to relax. His eyes flickered around the room, never staying long on anything, never looking straight at me.

"Smoke?" I asked, offering him the packet.

He shook his head.

"It might kill me," he said.

I lit up anyway … a smell wafted from the man, a thick oily tang so strong that even the pungent Camels didn't help much.

Time for business.

"So what can I do for you Mr. Duncan?"

"I'm going to die sometime this weekend. I need you to stop them."

I stared back at him.

"Sounds like a job for the Polis to me," I said.

He laughed, making it sound like a sob. He took a bundle of fifty pound notes from his pocket and slapped them on the table. I tried not to salivate.

"No. This is no job for the terminally narrow-minded," he said. "I need somebody with a certain kind of experience. *Your* kind of experience."

Somebody put a cold brick in my stomach, and I had a sudden urge to stick my fingers in my ears. I got the whisky out of the drawer. I offered him one. He shook his head, but his eyes didn't stray from the bottle. I poured his measure into a glass alongside my own and sent them chasing after each other before speaking.

"And exactly what kind of experience do I need to help you?"

A good storyteller practices his tale. At first, when he tells the story, he sounds like your dad ruining his favourite dinner table joke for the hundredth time.

Oh wait … did I tell you the horse had a pig with him?

But gradually he begins to understand the rhythm of the story, and how it depends on knowing all the little details, even the ones that no one ever sees or hears. He knows what colour of trousers he was wearing the day the story took place, he knows that the Police dog had a bad leg, he knows that the toilet block smelled of piss and shit. He has the sense of place so firmly in his mind that even he almost believes he's been there. Once he's done all that, he tells the killer story, complete with unexpected punch line.

Then there's the Ian Duncan method ... scatter information about like confetti and hope that somebody can put enough of it together to figure out what had happened to who.

I raised an eyebrow, and that was enough to at least get him started.

"It was four years ago we bought the hotel in Largs," he started.

"Well there's your first mistake," I replied, but he didn't acknowledge me. Now that he'd started the story, he meant to finish it. The tale he told would have been outlandish to anyone else's ears, but like he'd said, I knew better, from bitter experience.

I let him finish – sick customers, ancient curse and all, before asking the important question.

"And how do you think I can help?"

Just telling me the story had taken it out of him. I forced a glass of whisky on him – it was either that or watch him die in the chair. He almost choked on it, but managed to keep it all down before replying.

"Come down for the weekend. There's a room I need you to see. Maybe you'll be able to make sense of it where I can't."

I *wanted* to say no, but he'd put his money on the table, and that got my attention. Besides, his story had me intrigued, and I hadn't been *doon the watter* to Largs since I was a lad.

What better time than a holiday weekend?

Largs is where old people go to die – a Victorian seaside resort that is itself dying slowly of neglect. The Vikings tried to sack it eight hundred years ago. Maybe it would have been better all round if they'd succeeded.

I'd spent many long weekend trips here as a lad. My parents couldn't afford to go any further afield, and to a young boy one beach was as good as another, even if the weather was rarely good enough to take advantage on the long patch of golden sand to the south of the town. As I got off the train I could already see that the place hadn't changed much. It was raining, that steady drizzle peculiar to the west of Scotland, the kind that you just *know* is going to last all week.

Luckily I didn't have to go far. Duncan had given me instructions before leaving me in the office, but I could have found it with my eyes shut as it was on the sea front, two hotels down from the Barrfields Theatre and next to the putting green where my dad used to swear for Scotland.

The Seaview Hotel lived on past glories from the days when the middle class of Glasgow filled it every weekend of the summer. Back in the twenties it had been the height of fashion, but now it exuded the faint whiff of decay. It was a rambling, Edwardian building, with thirty rooms and nearly as many corridors. The décor was all mock-Scottish; dark furniture, stuffed stag heads and heavy on the tartan for wallpaper and carpets; a hideous red and yellow that clashed with everything else in the hotel.

Duncan met me in the hallway and led me through to the dining room. There were six patrons sitting at a table by the bay window, and not one of them looked like they were going to last out the day, being as thin and wasted as Duncan.

"What's going on here?" I asked.

Duncan led me to the far side of the room.

"I told you," he said. "The curse …"

I waved him away and lit up a smoke. It improved the smell, but not by much.

"Aye. The curse," I said. "Some time in the Twenties you said?"

He kept his voice low.

"Jim McLeod was an old Navy man. He retired to Largs with his wife and had this place built. It was to be their dream home, but she died before it could be finished. After that McLeod became a collector," he said. "And he wasn't fussy about where he bought his pieces. Many of them were stolen to order from other collectors or museums. The story goes that someone took umbrage and laid a curse on the whole hotel."

I nodded.

"But here's what I don't get. Why now?"

Duncan didn't reply, but I saw a look in his eyes I recognised. He was hiding something. And he was afraid to the point of abject terror. I took pity on him.

"Let's cut to the chase. Show me this room you told me about, and we'll see if we can get to the bottom of this."

The room at the highest point of the hotel was packed wall to wall with antiques. Even to my unpractised eye I knew that there was a small fortune just lying there in the accumulated dust. From the look of things McLeod's passion had been African tribal masks, and a variety of them leered down from the walls interspersed with weapons and beaded necklaces. But the thing that Duncan had brought me here to see was spread out under a pane of glass in a long display case.

At first glance it looked like a crude map, tracing a journey across Africa, ending at the mouth of the Zambezi River.

"McLeod thought it belonged to David Livingstone," Duncan said. "But I can't see it myself. Livingstone was a devout man of God. He wouldn't have anything to do with this depravity."

I saw what he meant as I leaned for a closer look. What I had taken for paper was in fact skin, so thin as to be almost translucent. I didn't have to ask the question.

A map made on human skin, drawn in blood.

I had a good look at it, but it seemed I had already got as much information as I was going to get. Duncan was looking at me expectantly.

"Well, what do you think?" he asked.

I was still unsure exactly what he wanted from me. Sure, the curse *seemed* to be working ... residents in the hotel were certainly wasting away beyond even what you'd expect in a pensioner's graveyard like Largs.

But how could I find out why?

I only knew one man who might help, and I was loath to involve him. I'd damaged my good friend Doug enough in too many cases. He was at his happiest right where he now spent

327

most of his time, deep in the stacks of the Hunterian Museum storerooms.

I sent him a couple of pictures by email from my mobile phone, knowing even as I hit *Send* that it might be some time before he got back to his desk to receive them. In the meantime, I needed to maintain the illusion that I knew what I was doing.

"Let's have a chat with your guests," I said to Duncan. He looked shocked at the suggestion.

"That might not be such a good idea," he said, but he allowed me to lead the way back downstairs.

My plan to interview the guests came to nothing, mainly because two of them were dead face down in their soup, and the other four were too far-gone to notice.

Duncan showed little concern, and only became agitated on my mention of calling the Police.

"There's no need for that Mr. Adams," he said. Once he'd written me a cheque for an extra five grand I came to agree with him. I helped him drag the bodies out of the dining room. It took little effort – the old folks weighed no more than a small child at most.

Duncan had me take them out the back of the hotel and left me alone for a minute – long enough for me to wonder if the five grand was enough.

To either side the adjoining hotels had bowling-green flat lawns, lush and verdant. The Seaview on the other hand looked like someone had ploughed the lawn over, leaving lumps and bumps across the whole surface. It was only when Duncan came back with two shovels that I realised why.

Duncan held out a shovel but I ignored him.

"Just how long have you been burying guests out here?"

He wouldn't meet my gaze, and mumbled, but I caught the vital word.

Years.

"Please," he said, holding the shovel out to me, his eyes pleading. "No one need ever know."

But I will.

I left him to it and went in search of a drink.

One advantage to an almost empty hotel is that the bar is quiet, and a man can smoke with impunity. I helped myself to a large scotch and lit up a Camel. By the time I got on to the second scotch I was starting to feel more myself, and the large cheque in my pocket had me feeling much more sanguine about the situation. I thought matters had improved when my phone beeped and I got a text message from Doug.

"No real idea beyond burning it," it said,

Burning it. There's a thought.

I took a third Scotch upstairs with me. I checked out the window when I got to the top room. Duncan was still out on the lawn, knee-deep in a growing hole. I was about to burn his property, but then again, he'd brought me here to stop the curse, and that's what I intended to do.

I had to take a spear from the wall to prise the glass case open, having to slice and chip at glue that had gone rock hard. I'd finished the third whisky by the time I was done, but finally I was able to lift the lid.

The thing felt slimy to the touch, almost warm. It got warmer still as I flicked the Zippo and applied the flame to a corner. It took fast – so fast that it went up with a *whoosh* and I had to drop it to avoid getting singed. I stood back as it blazed itself down to a charred black mass on a now equally charred carpet.

I was feeling pleased with myself ... right up until the screams rose up from out in the back garden. As I moved to the window my phone rang. I answered it on the way, just in time to read the full transcript of Doug's text that had been split into two messages.

"No real idea beyond burning it ... would not be recommended."

Bugger.

Things got even worse when I looked down from the window.

Duncan had backed away, holding a shovel like an axe, smacking it again and again on the head of one of the recently deceased.

Or maybe not so deceased.

The withered thing pushed herself upright, shakily at first, then more sure of herself as she started to stagger forwards. There was more life in her now than there had been before she *died.*

Duncan hit her again, screaming in fury.

"Die you old bitch, die," he shouted. The old woman tripped, but didn't fall. She opened her mouth and clacked her teeth together. The effect was spoiled when the false top set slipped out and fell wetly to the grass, but she didn't slow. Duncan screamed one last time then fled for the back door of the hotel.

I should have gone to his aid, but I was dumbstruck by the view below me.

The whole lawn seethed and roiled, as if a great beast struggled to break through the blanket of grass. But this was no single beast. The first indication was a pale arm bursting with some force through the sod, grasping for a hold. More arms pushed through; some pale, some grey, some green and moist with decay, but all grasping.

I remembered Duncan's answer when asked how long he'd been burying bodies.

Years.

Even as they dragged their re-born bodies up out of the lawn, screams rose up through the hotel from below. I grabbed the spear I'd used to open the display case and made for the stairs.

Duncan was once more the source of the screaming. I found him in the rear scullery, fighting to hold the back door closed against a press of bodies. They were packed tightly around the door, a crowd of what looked like over twenty, coming forward slowly. At first all that could be seen were silhouettes, dark shadows against the strong daylight beyond. But when they approached the glass door, it became all too clear what they were.

They had once been pensioners, but they'd been too long in Largs ... far too long. Some of them were in better condition than others were, but all shared one common, open-mouthed expression, teeth and gums working in expectation of food.

The outside door of the bar crashed open and the press of bodies fought in a scrum trying to reach us.

"Bastards!" Duncan shouted, as the first of them pushed into the scullery itself.

It had once been a woman, dressed in an expensive tweed two piece suit and Gucci shoes. Now she missed one of her heels. She lurched from side to side like a drunken sailor.

I stepped forward and slammed the spear into her chest.

She staggered backwards, but only for a second. By the time she came forward again three more of her kind had pushed through into the scullery.

I felt something tug at my arm. It was Duncan.

"Mr. Adams," the hotel owner said. "I really think we should be going."

I shoved the old man ahead of me and headed for the door at the far end of the scullery. We barrelled through it at the same time. Duncan kept going down the corridor beyond, but I stopped, trying to lock the door behind us. The handle turned in position, all the way round three hundred and sixty degrees. There was no way to lock the door.

Well, this just keeps getting better and better.

I backed away down the corridor. The door swung open, slowly, revealing the scullery beyond. The undead already filled the room. Unblinking stares looked for fresh meat … and found me.

They shuffled forward. I stabbed with the spear, twice, thrusting deep into dry flesh. The attackers didn't flinch. I thrust again, deep into the belly of a fat thing that had once been a formidable woman. She *sucked* it in, and the spear was torn from my hands. I turned and ran catching up with Duncan in the dining room. He was backing away from the table by the window where four more of the *things* shuffled from their seats. Alive or dead, I didn't know, but it made no difference – they all looked at me with that same *hunger* I was coming to recognise.

"Outside or the stairs?" I heard Duncan say. "They're at the front door already."

"Take the stairs," I said.

Once more we took the stairs almost together, all the way up to the collections room at the top of the building. I slammed the door behind me, but again there was no lock to secure it.

"Shit."

We were *trapped*.

Outside, footsteps thudded as the undead came up the stairs.

I threw my weight against the door.

"Find something to wedge it. Quick."

I locked out my legs and leaned into the door, trying to put my weight just over the handle. Something heavy hit the other side, hard enough for the door to open by two inches then slam shut again.

Behind me I heard clattering and smashing.

"If you're going to do something, now would be a good time," I shouted.

The door slammed against my shoulder, opening almost three inches this time.

"Let it open further next time," Duncan shouted.

"Open further? Are you mad?"

"Trust me. I have a plan."

The next time the door slammed against me I let it open slightly wider.

Duncan stepped forward and threw something through the gap, something that smashed in the hallway beyond.

I put my shoulder to the door and slammed it shut. This time Duncan helped me.

"Okay," the older man said. "Now I need your lighter."

I managed to dig inside my jacket, came up with the Zippo and handed it to Duncan.

"If I say duck, don't ask 'Where?'" Duncan said.

The door slammed hard on my shoulder. My feet slid on the floor as the door opened, six inches, then nine. A long dry hand at the end of an arm clad in thick blue serge gripped the inside edge and pulled. A head followed, grey hair hanging lankly over a face further obscured by a full salt-and-pepper beard. The blue serge was a heavy jacket, done up with silver buttons

332

A naval man.

I heard the distinctive sound of a Zippo being fired up.

"Duck," Duncan shouted.

I ducked. Something flew past my ear, something that burned yellow.

The hall beyond the door exploded into flame. The blue-serge clad figure fell away from the door. I slammed it shut and Duncan wedged a chair under the handle. Even though the door was firmly closed the smell of cooking meat seeped through the gaps.

"Good plan," I said when I'd caught my breath. "What did you use?"

He looked sheepish.

"A bottle of Smirnoff. Blue Label. I hid it up here so the missus wouldn't catch me at it."

That was the first I'd heard of a Mrs. Duncan. I wasn't sure I wanted to ask, but I had to.

"And where is she now?"

He waved at the door, fresh tears in his eyes.

"Out there for all I know. I put her out in the garden nearly a year ago now. But if I know her she'll be up and about – she never missed a chance to give me a hard time."

My phone rang, saving me from having to get deeper into the conversation. It was Doug.

"How's it going?" he asked. In reply he got a thirty-second diatribe on the merits of not splitting up text messages. I may even have used several words my mammy wouldn't have liked very much. Even then, he wasn't particularly contrite, but I couldn't afford the satisfaction of hanging up on him – Doug was our only chance to get out of this.

"Come on then," I said when he showed no signs of replying. "I know you. You wouldn't have phoned if you didn't have something for me."

"McLeod was a naval officer," Doug began.

I didn't have time for the long version. Something had started pounding on the door again, rattling it in hinges that looked old and rusted.

"I know," I said. "I've met the man. Very sprightly, considering he's been dead these many years."

I heard Doug's sharp intake of breath.

"And have you seen the collection?" he finally said.

"Seen it? I'm standing in the middle of it."

I didn't have to see him to know he was smiling.

"That's good," he said. "You need to find her hair."

"Her?"

"Mrs. McLeod. He had her scalp and hair made into a headpiece after she died. There was a great scandal and ..."

"Enough," I said, feeling as if I'd just kicked an excited puppy. "Just get to the point Doug. The undead are at the door, and they're worse than the bible-thumpers."

The pounding at the door got louder as if to emphasize my point. The top hinge squealed, the screws starting to loosen in the sockets.

I sensed his smile had faded, but he did speed up.

"It's a talisman," he said. "Part of a Zulu necromancy ritual. It's used in conjunction with ..."

"Let me guess... a map written on human skin?"

"Right first time. And now that you've burned one, you have to burn the other. If you don't all those affected by the curse will arise and walk the earth and ..."

"Yadda yadda yadda. I've seen the movie," I replied. "Anything else I need to know? Like why this is happening now?"

"Well old McLeod has been in the ground a while now. Maybe this is a last attempt at bringing his wife back before he is too far gone?"

Just at that moment the door decided it had taken enough of a beating and gave way beneath the assault. The first thing to come through was an arm clad in blue serge – badly singed, still smoking, but unmistakably belonging to McLeod.

"I'll get back to you on that one," I said. I threw the phone aside and tried to put my shoulder against the door. "Find a wig," I shouted at Duncan. "It belongs to his wife."

Then I was too busy to talk for a while.

It felt like someone was hitting me on the back with a large lump of wood … in fact, someone was. McLeod's hand gripped at the edge of the door and *tugged*. I had to slam my weight back against the door, hard, to keep him out.

Too far-gone my arse.

"What exactly am I looking for?" Duncan called.

"How the hell should I know? Just burn anything that looks like hair."

The weight behind me pressed even harder and I buckled. A withered hand grabbed at me, and I had to leave a clump of hair behind as I pulled away. The door fell in with a crash.

"I've found it," Duncan shouted at the same moment.
I had to back away as McLeod came through the doorway, those who had paid for his obsession shuffling close behind.

"You'd better be right wee man," I said. "Quick. Where's the Zippo?"

That was when I remembered.

He threw it out into the corridor.

But hardened nicotine addicts aren't stupid enough to be out without a backup plan. I held McLeod off with one hand and fished a box of matches out of my inside pocked with the other.

McLeod's teeth *clacked* perilously close to my fingers.

I threw the matches in Duncan's direction, hoping he was quick enough to catch them.

Then I was in a fight for my life. McLeod showed no sign of being too far-gone for a fight. He took my best punch, right on the point of the jaw. His head rocked and a split appeared in the skin of his neck, gaping bloodless and grey. It didn't slow him any. He came inside my swinging arm and grabbed me. He forced my head to one side and exposed my neck. Then he sniffed, twice, close together, as if checking my after-shave.

"Where is it?" he said.

His voice was rough, harsh, almost a bark.

I tried to speak, but the grip around my throat was so tight that all I could manage was to keep breathing.

"Where is it?" he said again, almost shouting this time. His breath smelled, of stale food and stagnant water, but I guessed now wasn't a good time to tell him.

With his spare hand he went through my pockets; fast and methodical, like a pro. When he didn't find anything, the hold on my throat tightened further still. I tried to break the grip, but my strength was going fast. I punched him, hard, just below the heart, but he didn't even wince.

He laughed in my face.

"Is that all you've got lad?"

He threw me away, like a discarded rag. His hand barely moved, yet I flew, a tangle of arms and legs, crashing hard against the far wall and falling to a heap on the floor. Something gave way in my lower back; a tearing pain that I knew meant trouble.

I hoped I'd live long enough to see it.

I turned to see him coming for me again. I held up an arm, but in truth I had no fight left in me. McLeod came on, teeth *clacking*.

Duncan saved my life.

Just as McLeod reached for me, his minions right behind him, a forest of arms my only view, I heard Duncan shout.

"Is this what you're looking for?"

McLeod turned away from me, and I had a clear view across the room as the case came to its denouement.

Duncan had what looked like a long wig in his left hand, and a burning candle in his right.

"Burn it," I shouted.

But it looked like I was in no immediate danger. The undead were all focussed on Duncan. Nobody moved, the only sound the sputter of the flickering candle.

"Burn it!" I shouted again.

Duncan had other ideas.

"I know how you feel," he said to McLeod. "Every day, I want her back. Every day I miss her. But look at yourself man. Do you want her back like this? Could you stand it? Here ..."

"No!" I shouted, but couldn't stop him handing the wig to McLeod.

"Let her go," Duncan said softly. "Set both of you free."

McLeod didn't move, just stood there stroking the hairpiece as Duncan put the candle under, first the wig, then the navy man's long beard.

He went up like a piece of dry paper, consumed to ash in less time than I would take to smoke a cigarette. At that point I expected the others with him to fall to the ground, or wither and turn to ash themselves.

That's how it works in the movies.

But this was Largs, on a holiday weekend. Things didn't work like in the movies around here. The undead milled around the room, seemingly devoid of purpose, maybe twenty of them in various states of decomposition.

"We should burn these too," I said, but I knew already my heart wasn't in it, and I was glad when Duncan disagreed with me.

"Just leave them to me," he said. "I'll take care of them, like I've always done."

By the time I left he had them all in the dining room, sitting over cups of tea that would never get drunk, fancy teacakes that would never get eaten.

That's Largs for you.

THE END

BURJ
Chelsea Tractor
By
Nigel Hall

The following events were recorded by the Laikoseimas on November 5th, 2019 A.D. (Gregorian) and July 11th, A.Y. 31 (Tangential). Broad persistence of events is classified as Very Low (no documented reoccurrence).

I

I guess I had come to say goodbye. Fuck knows there was no other reason – plenty of authorities, even the Foreign Office, had advised against it. Abu Dhabi was fine, they said; but not here.

The thing is, we're gathered at a safe distance, so it's not like we have our noses pressed against the scene. We know the virus dies under the conditions that are about to occur, too. And if the worse comes to the worst, we're indoors, at least protected by walls and floors, and ventilation shafts that can seal up in seconds, and the relevant breathing equipment. We've switched off the air conditioning, making this the sweatiest party any of us have been to since any of us graduated. We're more than prepared. We're even on a damn *island*, for fuck's sake. We're going to be fine. Unlike the poor bastards in the centre of our view, if they're still moving in that dhow-shaped building we've got our eyes occasionally trained on.

Nothing's kicking off for about an hour, anyway, so I focus on the occasion at hand, which is somewhere between a wake and party. With any luck, the world's seven-year nightmare ends this afternoon, so that's the party; on the other hand, more people have died than arguably needed to.

Mourning the dead are the six of us – in here, anyway; there are probably loads of others, hundreds, maybe thousands, ghoulishly scattered outside the city, taking up temporary residence on all the abandoned artificial islands. There are media helicopters needlessly hovering over the scene, whilst reporters back in London, New York, Shanghai, Delhi, and Doha explain

338

with an apparent lack of irony that their viewers are watching the news and nothing is currently happening.

So there are six of us: there's me, a survivor from the incident that set all this up, there's my partner Laura – I say "partner", but we've been together about seven months. It felt awkward dragging her here, actually, but having just moved in together, I'd have thought it would be even more awkward to bugger off for several days. So she's here, and it's awkward.

There are my fellow survivors Tim and Zemyna; there's Zemyna's sister Ruta, and finally Tim's brother James, who by a not-that-amazing coincidence happens to be a medical researcher with specialist knowledge of the virus, as well as a survivor who spent three days in the hotel before devising a sufficiently intelligent (and hence decided uninfected-like) plan to break out; those enforcing the quarantine took a chance on not shooting, and had their faith rewarded.

Of course, now he's out, and he's spent a year not under the dominion of the Sombra virus, he is, today, naturally relieved at the thought of never having to experience what he's experienced ever again, but also naturally a little peeved that science and willpower, the most grudging partnership in all of international politics, is quite possibly going to make a second virus dead, and of all the ones it chose, it chose his.

"So Tim," Ruta says, "how did this all start, anyway?"

We've got an hour, so when the small talk lulls, we turn to Tim for, well, not big talk, exactly, but medium talk. Talk with a 32" waist, so to speak.

"You mean my story or the virus generally?" he replies.

"Well, the virus, I guess. It's like it appeared from nowhere."

And with Laura's verbal encouragement, Tim is given the legitimacy to take us on a lecture of how it all happened.

II

"It's like you say, Ruta; these things do sometimes appear to come from nowhere. Even now, scientists are safely putting their best bets on HIV being from zoonosis—"

He gets hit with a five-panel wall of blank faces.

"From animals," he translates, "but it's still uncertain, even seventy years or so on. And it'll be the same with Sombra. Much of what we have about the history of it, especially the origins, is rumour, is speculation, is idle talk amongst the masses. I remember when the first mention of it turned up in the lab; it was the first day back after Christmas; I'd claimed as much as holiday as possible, so it was after New Year. Anyway, rumour – not really much more than that – had passed from South Korean intelligence to the WHO of disruption on the DMZ, and of course, the weird thing was that it had gone to the WHO, not the Security Council."

He has all of our attention now; to the point where I am only dimly aware of the helicopters being ordered to move a safe distance away, out of the flight route.

"As you can imagine, the rumour gets out, and the Internet's all a-twitter, in a total fucking frenzy, because of course a deadly new virus may or may not have emerged and it's–"

"December 2012 when it happens," I interrupt, because stupidity on the Internet happens to be my expertise, and whilst there's an endless amount of it, it all falls into very finite patterns.

"Exactly. And of course, it's not the end of the world, just like SARS, just like H5N1 or H1N1, just like they all weren't. But the rumours keep building. The virus, of course, moves into South Korea, and therefore the open, where we get a good look at it. And of course–"

He's moving into the bit we all know, but of course, he's simply got to tell it again.

"We eventually get the video, once the problem hits Shanghai. This grainy phone footage shows the victims walking around, apparently normally, but something isn't right with them, there's that blank-eyed stare, and where they should be speaking normally, they do so in a flat monotone.

"We were clearly dealing with something that attacks the brain, and whilst the victims attacked in the late stages, by biting and tackling, it transpired that this was simply a death throe."

"How do you mean?" Ruta asked.

340

"It's like the way Ebola victims go into fits in their final stages, which can often conveniently throw a lot of infected blood around. They get the urge to bite people, sometimes even bite animals, which has the convenient effect of passing the disease around more directly. But it's airborne anyway, which is how the trouble really kicked off."

The media choppers are still pushing their luck with that flight path, and the BBC and Al-Jazeera – why we have two televisions on I have no idea, but we do – are still pushing for some news out of none, all the while ignoring the infinitely more informative tickers in the lower tenth of their screens.

"And even as Shanghai gets a quarantine slapped on it, cases are exploding all over the world, in America, Canada, Brazil, Russia, India, and it starts creeping into the Middle East and Europe too. The UK government goes into overdrive – they might be imbeciles but they're not complete and utter idiots, and so we're allowed to bring in as many experts as we can get. So we bring them in. Virologists, neurologists, philosophers ..."

"*Philosophers?*"

I think it's me who says it, but it could be anyone of us in the audience of five.

"We were working on the theory that ... well, I dunno. But it wasn't entirely pointless, anyway. But that was what happened, you know the rest, it went worldwide, it killed about three million, we got it locked down and then for four years it was in recession and the global economy finally wasn't."

"Yeah, those were good times," I quip. It gets a bit of a laugh.

Outside, the skyline remains the same, for now. From our vantage point, we can see to the north-east, when we're not dizzy from the heat, the hotel that most of us had to escape from; beyond that, the hypodermic spire of the Burj Khalifa and the surrounding skyscrapers are unmissable.

Or at least, you'd bloody well hope so.

III

So we pass stories around the room, and for that matter pass around the vol-au-vents and beverages with them. Alcohol's kept

341

to a minimum, in part because of local law but also because we'll need to be fully alert if it all goes wrong.

The hour is ticking round swiftly and the stories are almost all told, helped in part by Laura and Ruta being a rapt audience without a story of their own.

"You know," Laura begins, before attention swivels round to me properly, "Jack never properly told me this story he's about to tell until just before we got on the flight."

"Well, it wasn't one I wanted to recollect too often," I reply.

"Yes, but ..." she gives me a funny smile, pitched halfway between about-to-laugh and about-to-hug-me. "It's like when we went camping, and you were really keen not to stay in a hotel, or go abroad. Had to wrestle this out of you."

"Well, OK. I guess after it's shared once it's easier, right?"

I get a few nods to this notion. Behind me, the BBC has turned to a profusion of CGI in order to cycle through the 2014 pandemic and the vaccine that was developed at its peak. No doubt the Dubai incident – which Al-Jazeera is naturally more focused on anyway, will come up shortly. In fact, it does, and so with that neat parallel in place, I begin my story.

IIII

Even by last autumn, the Burj Al-Arab was still probably the most extravagant hotel in the world. And why wouldn't it be? The 2010s as a decade had been a zigzag of recession, the brief recovery from it, the pandemic, and the recovery from both of them. Beaten senseless by these twin blows, the world had perhaps become a slightly more cautious place, one where all these overblown gestures suddenly paled into insignificance. Dubai now stood as the last outpost of excess, the final place where architects and designers could deliver nonlinear and post-modern civic indulgences in wholesale batches. London, Shanghai, Mumbai and New York had given up this nonsense; there was no place left for it in their economies.

And so, as a wealthy man, I had to go, and I had to experience this last outpost, before it also joined what similarly conservative-minded punters liked to call the Dourist zeitgeist. And I had to book into what I thought was its finest specimen.

So I did, and for three days it was the standard holiday experience, albeit blown up to ridiculous levels. What wasn't marble in there was glass, and what wasn't detailed down to a sub-molecular level was probably a dumpster round the back. I could've spent half a day fiddling with the room settings or losing tennis balls over the side of the court, and in fact, I probably did. Those were three fantastic days, even if on some deep level they were probably a little empty. But I could stump up £5,000 a night, so I was well within my rights and it's what I chose to do.

It was the fourth night when things deteriorated.

It was also in the early hours of the morning. I had gone to bed but not slept; not necessarily because of insomnia – well, maybe – but more because as soon as I stopped walking around, my head buzzed with thoughts. Not really relevant thoughts, to be honest, just my mind, skipping over all manner of things, making all kinds of tenuous connections, wondering about this, about that, about life, about work, for some sad reason. You can take the City out of the man, and all that.

Naturally, I got tired of being tired and I wasn't going to listen to my inner monologue's bullshit all night, so I got up and left the room, in my pyjamas. Because why the hell not? That's why. I moved around the floor I was on, came across the reception desk and stopped.

Something was wrong with the receptionist; the phrase *uncanny valley* threw itself in front of my train of thought, a half-remembered phrase from my investments in computer games studios earlier that year. I spent a bleary couple of seconds wondering how they were doing before coming to my senses. That woman behind the desk? She wasn't right.

"Can I ..." she said, paused, and then repeated it, over and over, like there was a glitch in her system. I should be fine, I told myself – I was vaccinated. But then, why was I worried? And why hadn't the Burj Al-Arab vaccinated their staff? Of course they had. They must have done. Most of the whole damn world had got one.

"Can I ..."

343

I kept at least five metres back, and looked behind me for extra walking space. She was probably in the mid-phase of the disease, if it was still the same disease. It quite possibly wasn't.

"Can I ..."

You fucking can't, I thought to myself, and took a couple of steps back. She didn't chase, she merely gave that weird, faded stare. She didn't have to chase. If she coughed, sneezed or even breathed heavily, at least some of those viral spores would be out in the space of the room. They could've been already, I realised.

"Can I ..."

"Shit," I whispered, and made a run for it, all the way back to my room, slamming the door and locking it. Outside I heard a shout, and then another.

I bolted to the bathroom, locked that, just to be sure, and pissed over the toilet seat. Better there than where it was going. I then found myself in the bath, simply lying down, having forgotten how exhausted I was. But I couldn't sleep now, and I knew it, and my mind was still digging for thoughts, and it was working like a diamond mine, moving tonnes of shit and earth to find grams of rock that had to be chipped away in order to find something of value, or even, for that matter, the startlingly obvious.

Like the way that I was now behind two locked doors.

In every zombie film – not that I claim comprehensive knowledge of Russo and Romero; I have, at best, moderate knowledge of Boyle, and that'll do – but in these films, there's a theme, and that is that confined spaces are counter intuitively bad for the uninfected. And this knowledge had applicability, I decided, because the symptoms of mind-rotting debilitation minus accompanying loss of physical strength had worrying similarities. In the end, I concluded that like Lyndon Johnson, victims of the Sombra virus, or whatever the hell this mutation was, should be inside the tent pissing out, causing an expansion of welfare programs and direct intervention in proxy wars in south-east Asia.

Well, that was a bad analogy, but it'd have to do.

I unlocked the bathroom door and looked around. I was safe, and I heard no banging on the door, just a noise from upstairs I couldn't figure out. I decided I wouldn't bother to, either. It was hard enough to figure out what was in front of me.

I got dressed. That much was sensible. I walked over to the window and glanced out at the view below me. It could've been a water landing, maybe, if I flung myself out far enough. The thing was, it was also a huge drop down, at least – was I halfway up? At least a hundred metres. Dropping that far onto a bouncy castle would break a leg. The window exit was a no-no.

So I opened the door instead.

"Can I …"

I kicked her in the crotch and shut and locked the door again, then slowly, slowly let go of my breath.

I needed a gun, I thought. Or even a longbow. Just some sort of range weapon. But I wasn't getting one. It was down to me and the equally unarmed infected, the brain-addled versus the brain-rotted in the ultimate showdown, the rumble in the … hotel.

I slapped that thought away too, and tried the door again. The corridor was empty; the receptionist had apparently wandered off.

From the room, I found my way to the balcony overlooking the lobby. Along the way I checked the ventilation systems. No luck there; most of the time it was hard to tell what they even looked like. When I found a shaft, it was too small even for a baby to crawl through.

Looking over the lobby revealed it to be a mess; debris was scattered across the floor. I heard gunshots, saw shadows sweeping across the floor. Someone had a gun. Someone was also on the ground floor, making me wonder why they hadn't simply left.

This changed things. Blinking hard and jabbing my fingers at the grit in my eyes, I realised that the man with the gun in the lobby's motives were ultimately impossible to predict, so I'd have to have a plan for him. People who were asleep were probably wondering about the noise people like him were making, and hence were waking up, exposing themselves to infection earlier, so I had to have a plan for that. And obviously I had to get out, and have a plan for that.

I got out, obviously. In fact, ninety per cent of the escape was easy; finding a lift, exhaling weary relief as the doors opened to nothing and then riding it down to the ground floor was simple enough. The ground floor, though, had turned into a warzone, and this was the hard part, where my journey had to become so indirect. This is the bit that both stays with me and becomes so incredibly hard to describe.

It wasn't that shit I saw that was the problem, although there was enough of that to keep any sane person at night with their eyes jammed open and their cheeks flooded. Chunks were shot out of the walls and doors. Bodies were strewn about the place. What I hoped was blood was smeared on the walls that weren't pockmarked. In front of my own eyes, I watched in real-time as the man with the shotgun was hoist with his own petard and then processed, for want of a better phrase.

No, what really troubled me was what I had to do. Or what I justified as necessary, at any rate; the late-stagers are obvious enough, and there's no cure – I had no qualms about that. The early-stagers, though, that's a different matter. I found the weapon I was looking for, and I used it, but I could never be sure that I had been one hundred per cent accurate, or that I'd judged every case correctly.

And when the massed authorities outside announced the quarantine, I found myself dashing past a definitely uninfected woman in the corner of the lobby. The man with the shotgun had been somewhat indiscriminate and hit her across both thighs. There were seconds to go on the deadline, it was a borderline case; certainly, I didn't have to time calculate how much I'd be slowed down. I just had a gut decision to make, and I hesitated, but the injured, crawling mid-to-late stager heading my way sealed the deal.

So I left the building and reached the massed ambulances, soldiers, police and press with less than a minute to spare, holding up my hands and shouting anything that sprang to mind as eloquently as I could. They lowered their guns on me as the barriers went up. A set of temporary metal panels, they were going to be replaced in due course, and work on the more permanent barbed-wire wall started within the hour.

I was still shaking, though. The Sombra victims hadn't laid a finger on me, and the choices I made I could probably justify, but that didn't matter. What was trying to kill me was child's play; what I had to live with was a different matter.

V

I tell the group all of that. What I don't tell them is what happens next; how, having escaped from the hotel and jumped on the emergency flight back to London, I quit my job, moved down to a smaller house and spent quite some time in there, going out perhaps twice a week at most. After about three months, I gave this up, and that's when I met Laura.

There was something I just found intriguing about Laura, from the off. And it took me about a date or two to figure it out, but it came to me in a half-remembered flashback in the midst of a dream. She was the spitting image of the young woman in the lobby. I wondered briefly whether it was my memories and my thoughts mixing, but no, that didn't seem right. The similarity was definitely real; it resonated with me too much.

I have never told Laura this, and I'm especially not going to tell her now, ten minutes before the big event, as we whittle down those minutes with the world's most impossible blame game.

"Accident."

"No, Iran. Definitely Iran. Or some sponsored Islamist movement."

"Mossad. They have previous."

"CIA, if we're going there."

"Lockheed Martin. Weapons testing. Apparently there's some experimental shit going down today, what better test than this, right?"

"The Qatari government," Tim suggests.

"What?"

"You name me a bigger rival in this part of the world in the whole 'building expensive hotels and stadiums' business. Aren't they hosting the World Cup in four years?"

"Eight, I thought. They postponed one of them," I point out.

347

"Oh, right, the pandemic."

"How could you forget that?"

"Yeah, true enough."

"Anyway," I say, raising a flat diet coke, "never assume malice when an event can be explained by incompetence. Hanlon's Razor."

"Well said, Jack."

"Something I had to constantly tell any non-colleague in my old line of work."

Well, that lightens the mood.

VI

"And so we come to this footage now, of the combined force of F-16s and B-52s about to come in, and hopefully they will be destroying whatever remains of the Sombra B virus, the Sombra A virus of course being contained by the widespread vaccination in 2014 and 2015. Now, Guy, I hear there is something different about this mission."

"Yes indeed, Alan, and it's the new weaponry in particular, the High Utility Lethal Kinetics, or HULK bombs and missiles. The American military is hoping that this will demonstrate a new paradigm in military power, the stepping stone between conventional ordinance and tactical nuclear weapons …"

The television – we decide that having two on is stupid – continues to burble away, but Guy has to be interrupted and the whole thing is drowned out as the first of the F-16s flies over our balcony, heads off to our left and lets off the first of those HULKs. The missile streaks towards the Burj Al-Arab and hits.

The building flares with an almost blinding white light and collapses forward into the sea, with the wind taken out of the sail on that dhow shape. More jets fly in, singling out specific buildings, the taller skyscrapers and the grander projects that break up the homogeneity of the city.

And then the B-52s drone in, they drop open their bellies and let loose, with steady, metered rhythms, those new HULK bombs. We can feel their detonation resonate through the balcony, and see mushroom clouds sprout up in place of the skyline.

"It's over, Jack."

"I know."

I embrace her and feel the tension slowly leave me.

"Shit, you can really feel the heat from those things."

She laughs. The whole city centre is pretty much levelled by now, and the parts that aren't are almost certainly filled with an inhospitable heat. Pundits on the news talk about how Sombra B as a virus should now be extinct, but they're guessing as much as I am.

Ruta gets up from her seat and heads inside. She pauses and turns. "Can I ... can I ..."

I start to panic.

"Can I get anyone anything?"

"A diet coke and a kick up your ass," I reply. Laura laughs again, and suddenly it's all OK again.

Mostly.

THE END

A DARK MOON HONEYMOON
By
Rob Smith

I

They had been married for twenty-seven hours and nineteen minutes.

It had not been time wasted, Susan thought, alone now in the bed. There had been the ceremony, and she remembered every detail of that, even if Roy claimed it had all gone by in a blur. There had been the post-wedding meal, where the budget-constrained food had been redeemed by some excellent speeches. Mick, the best man, had told some long and rambling joke. It had culminated in the most feeble punch line known to man, at which point Roy had almost collapsed laughing, but other than that the speakers had all done well. The whole evening reception thing had been tiring, and Susan was dimly aware that she had got rather drunk and made a little bit of a fool of herself. But as she'd told her mother, 'It's my wedding, and I'll get absolutely steaming shit-faced if I want to.' She'd have to ring and apologise later.

By contrast, the night in the hotel had been fairly quiet. They'd not consummated the marriage at that time, if only because Roy was past the stage of optimum efficiency and Susan had developed a very close relationship with the toilet bowl. They'd made up for it since, she thought, looking up at the ceiling and smiling to herself.

It had been so nice of Uncle Ben to lend them his holiday cottage. It had given them the chance to have a half-decent honeymoon. They could have gone for a cheap package holiday abroad, but instead they had jumped at the chance of a week here, rural Wales, as far away from the city as it was possible to be. Both of them loved the quiet little villages, the bleak moors, the cold hills. Roy had been brought up in an area like this, though hundreds of miles further north. Susan was a city girl, but she loved the sense of peace that the hills brought her. It had been a lovely drive up, despite her worries that their old banger

350

of a car would not survive the journey. She'd told Roy that they needed a new one. He'd just laughed and told her that the old thing had plenty of good miles left in it. Maybe that was true, maybe not, but it had got them here. Tomorrow they planned to go walking, following the stream that trickled past the back of the cottage up into the thinly-wooded heights behind. She was already looking forward to that, just as she looked forward to every moment they spent together.

"We ought to get Uncle Ben something nice, to thank him," Susan mused aloud.

"Yeah," Roy agreed, emerging from the en-suite bathroom into the darkened bedroom. "Not too nice, though. That shower is a pain in the backside to get working. I bet the old bastard has never had it looked it since he's owned this place. What time is it?"

"Quarter past seven."

"No wonder I'm so hungry." He pulled on a pair of creased trousers and dragged back the curtains. Neither had expected a beam of brilliant sunshine but it was still a little disappointing outside, dull and overcast, with the hills all but obscured behind fine drizzle.

"Typical Welsh summer evening," Roy muttered.

"Never mind," Susan said gently. "I'm sure it will be nicer tomorrow." She ignored his answering look. "What do you want to do about dinner?"

"We could go into the village. There's a nice café there."

She shook her head. "I don't really want to go out. I can't be bothered to make myself look beautiful."

"I'd starve to death before then anyway," he said, smiling as he expertly dodged a viciously flung pillow. "So you want me to go out and get something then? What do you fancy?"

"Anything."

"Kebabs it is then."

"Except kebabs. I wouldn't have thought there would be a kebab shop around here anyway."

"There must be," Roy told her. "I haven't seen a single cat or dog since we got here."

"How about fish and chips?" Susan suggested. "We drove past a chippy on the way in. It can't be more than a five minute walk."

Roy looked out again at the steady drizzle. "Five minutes," he sneered. "Maybe you should go."

"Take the car," Susan suggested.

He shook his head, reaching for his coat. "Fish and chips, yeah? Salt and vinegar?"

"Of course. What are you having?"

"Same, I reckon. Seeing as I can't have kebabs."

"I'm only thinking of you," she protested, and then, glancing down at his increasing-noticeable paunch, "and that." He followed her gaze and patted his stomach contentedly. Pulling up the collar of his coat, he walked over to her and leaned down.

"You just stay there," he said, kissing her gently on the forehead. She reached up and pulled his head down for the sort of kiss more befitting a new bride.

"Don't be long," she breathed heavily. "Have you got your mobile?"

"I'll only be gone a few minutes," he said, smiling as he tapped the phone in his pocket. "I've got a great new ringtone on it, though. You'll love it when you hear it." He winked, and left the room. A few seconds later she heard the front door slam behind him.

II

Ten minutes later the telephone rang. Susan, newly dressed but still looking like someone who had just got out of bed, raced across the room and lifted the antique-looking receiver. "Hello?" she said brightly.

There was no answer.

"Hello?" she repeated. "Roy?" Through the phone she thought could hear the gentle patter of rain. Susan shrugged, and put the phone down.

Almost immediately it rang again.

"Hello?"

"Hi, it's only me."

"Did you just ring?"

"No. I'm outside the chip shop. Is something wrong?"

"Just a wrong number or something," she said lightly.

"Wouldn't surprise me if the phones around here are a bit missed up," Roy told her. "We used to have problems at home. I'm only ringing to see if I can get a signal. Plus I wanted to make sure you're alright, all alone there."

"Fine," she told him. "You've only been gone ten minutes."

"I know," he said, and there was a pause. "You realise this is the first time we've been apart since we got married?"

"Go and buy the food," she told him firmly.

"OK. Bye."

III

Quarter of an hour had passed when she heard the front door open. "I've got some plates ready in the kitchen," she called, rinsing the last of the toothpaste from her mouth and wiping it with a horribly brown-hued towel.

There was no answer.

Susan draped the towel over the radiator and walked out of the bathroom back into the bedroom. "Roy?" she called. Outside the rain was still gently drumming against the window.

She slowly opened the bedroom door, and looked through it into the living room. The kitchen door was slightly ajar, and she could see the plates and cutlery that she had laid out on the table. There was no sign of any food, and no sign of Roy. She sniffed. The room smelt of disuse, of being left empty nine months of the year. She could faintly smell the air-freshener she had sprayed about the room on their arrival. There was no hint of the distinctive odour of fish and chips.

"Roy?" she repeated, quietly. There was a slight tremor in her voice, she knew. Her heart was beginning to beat more quickly. She felt cold, the fine hairs on her arms rising in sympathetic unison.

From the part of the kitchen that she could not see, behind the thin wooden door, there came the faintest of noises.

Susan stepped forward, very slowly edging towards the kitchen. Another noise came, causing her to breathe in sharply. She reached out with one hand and gently pushed the door open.

There was a flash of movement, and suddenly there were hands upon her, tightly gripping her waist. She screamed.

"Got you!" Roy shouted triumphantly.

"You bastard!" she shouted, punching his arm with as much force as she could muster.

"Steady on, it was just a joke."

"You almost scared me to death!" she snapped at him, her eyes flashing with anger.

"That was the idea," he said, slightly defensively. He kissed her, despite her best attempts to turn her head away. Then he began to laugh.

"It's not funny," she told him, trying to stifle a smile that was half-amusement, half very genuine relief.

"It is," he disagreed. "But not as funny as what just happened to me."

Susan looked around the tiny kitchen. "Where's the food?" she demanded.

"That's what's funny," he told her, continuing to laugh. "Sit down and I'll tell you."

It took Roy a few moments to compose himself, while Susan watched him, still a little angry but mostly just bemused by his behaviour. She probably should have guessed that it was him waiting to scare her, she decided. It was just the sort of thing Roy did. Once he'd bought an empty fish-tank and told her there was a pet tarantula in it. When she said she couldn't see it, he had very convincingly panicked and told her it must have escaped. She hadn't been able to sleep that night. He hadn't been allowed to sleep with her that week.

"OK," he said finally. "I just went into the village and found that chip shop. I rang you just before I went in, yeah? Just to make sure you weren't scared on your own. If I'd known just how jumpy you were ..."

"Get on with it."

"So I go into the chippy and I ask the bloke behind the counter for fish and chips twice. And do you know what he says to me?"

"No," Susan replied, trying to sound bored. "Enlighten me."

"He says, get this, I can't give you fish and chips twice, or the zombies will get you!"

"What?"

"That was what I said. I asked him what he had said, and he repeats it."

Susan looked at Roy, and his giggling face. "Don't joke around," she told him sternly. "I'm not in the mood."

"No, honest," he replied, somehow managing to look hurt and amused at the same time. "That's what he said. He can't give me fish and chips twice because the zombies will get me. He repeated that twice. I thought he was joking but he just wouldn't budge. In the end I thought sod it because there was a queue forming behind me."

"OK, whatever," she told him exasperatedly. "What are you going to do about dinner?"

"I asked some woman, there's another chip shop a mile or so up the lane. I just popped in on my way past to tell you about this. It's pretty weird. Maybe they just don't like the English."

"Maybe they just don't like you," she suggested. "Go and get my fish and chips."

IV

The smile was gone when he came through the front door again.

"What's up?" Susan asked, sitting up in her seat when she saw his expression and his empty hands.

"OK, once was funny."

"What are you talking about?"

"I went up to that other chip shop, and asked for fish and chips twice. It was a woman this time, but she said the same thing."

"What? That rubbish about zombies?"

355

"Yeah." He put on a high pitched voice. "I can't give you fish and chips twice, love, the zombies will get you!" He shook his head. "This is probably some local wind-up trick. I bet your bloody Uncle rang them up and arranged all this."

"I doubt it," she said firmly. "Uncle Ben is a right sweetie but he has no sense of humour whatsoever." She looked at him closely, still suspecting that Roy was winding her up, but the look of annoyance in his eyes and the low rumble that came from his stomach at that moment suggested otherwise. "Did you try ordering anything else?"

"No. I want fish and chips. If they don't want my custom, sod them. I'll go somewhere else."

"Roy, don't get stubborn about this."

"I'm not getting stubborn."

"You are," she told him gently.

"I'm not," he replied, not quite so gently.

She put her hands up, placating. "All I'm saying is I'm happy to have something else. A fishcake, maybe. I'm not sure I could eat a whole fish anyway."

"That's not the point," he said sharply. "Where are the car keys?"

"Why? Where are you going?"

"Llannisa … Llanas … whatever it's called. The next village. There's bound to be a decent chip shop there."

"Roy," she began, then saw his look. "OK, have it your way."

"I won't be long. Where are the keys?"

V

Despite the fact she was waiting for it, and that she had deliberately sat by it, the ringing of the phone still caught her by surprise.

"Any luck?" she said as she picked it up.

There was only silence at the other end.

"Roy?" she called. "Can you hear me?" She listened carefully. Again there was no reply – just the sound of rain beating against something. Then the line went dead.

356

She put the phone gently down and dialled 1471, hoping to find out the number. The emotionless, disembodied voice of the computerised operator told her the number was unavailable.

Susan cursed aloud, and put the phone down, harder this time. She still suspected it was Roy playing silly buggers, just as she still had a faint suspicion that this whole thing with the zombies was just a wind-up on his part. But then again, Roy liked his food, enough so that he would have ended the joke a while ago in order to get some grub down him. Maybe she was being unfair to him. Maybe it was Uncle Ben developing a sense of mischief late in life.

She picked up the phone again and clumsily called Roy's mobile number, unused to the obsolete manual dial. The number rang seven times before it was finally answered.

"Hello?"

Roy's voice, sounding annoyed.

"It's me. Where are you?"

"I'm in the car. I'm getting a bit pissed off now."

"Why? Don't tell me you're getting the same thing there?"

"You guessed it," he replied shortly. "The same old shit about zombies. I've already tried two places here. The last place had a girl behind the counter, only about eighteen. When she started to talk about zombies I got quite annoyed, and a couple of blokes in the queue behind me told me to get out. I was going to kick off but I'm too bloody hungry."

"Roy, just forget it. I'll have a battered burger or something."

"No!" he almost shouted at her. "You're having fish and chips. I'm having fish and chips. We're having fish and chips twice if I have to go behind the counter and serve them myself. OK, I can see another chip shop. I'll call you soon."

"Don't do anything stupid and get yourself hurt," she half-hissed at him.

"Oh, don't worry about me," he replied firmly, and hung up. She didn't care much for his tone of voice. She glanced at her watch. They'd been married for twenty-eight hours and thirty-six minutes, and they were having their first argument.

The phone rang. Answering it only confirmed her suspicion that there would be no one there.

VI

It was dark outside now. Susan stood by the window, looking through the rain towards the shadowy bulk of the hills. She could see lights in the village, though she could not make out the individual buildings. Occasionally a car came down the lane, past the drive of the cottage, and with each new set of headlights she prayed that it was Roy. But it never was.

She was worried. She knew how Roy's mind worked. He was stubborn. Sometimes that was a good thing. The fact that they were together was largely due to his stubbornness, his refusal to accept that her family's dislike of him should stop them marrying. He had eventually won them over, even Uncle Ben. Uncle Ben had hated Roy from the start, but something must have changed because by the time the wedding date was announced he had been only too keen to lend them his beloved cottage. But that same stubbornness could also get Roy into trouble. He could be aggressive, and would almost never back down, regardless of the odds. When he said that he would get fish and chips twice, that's what he would do. She loved him for it, even as she wished he could just back down and get something else. She was hardly even hungry anymore. She was simply too worried.

She had tried his mobile twice, and each time she had got his answer-phone. That in itself meant nothing, she told herself. In these hills, in this weather, the mobile signal could come and go. If anything had happened, if their ageing car had finally given up on life and died on him, if he'd got in a fight, he'd have found a way to tell her. She told herself all this.

It didn't make her feel any better.

The phone had rung twice more. Each time she had picked it up, wanting to hear his voice in the darkened room. Each time there had been no one there. This time, when it rang, she didn't answer it, not straight away. She ignored its annoying tinny noise, looking out of the window. There was no moon, she realised. It was heavily overcast of course, but Susan still felt she should have been able to see some sign of it, some faint glow behind the shadow of the cloud. Dark moon, Roy had called it. She had once admitted to a little trepidation when it was a full moon, childhood nightmares of werewolves and demons coming to mind. Roy had told her not to worry, that the moon couldn't hurt her. It was when there was a dark moon, no moon at all – that was the time to worry.

He'd always been able to frighten her. He'd frightened her then. He'd frightened her in the kitchen earlier. He was frightening her now.

The phone continued to ring.

Another car passed, its headlights briefly illuminating the darkness in front of the cottage, the low rumble of its engine penetrating into the room before fading into the encroaching darkness.

The phone continued to ring.

Susan watched as several drops of rain coalesced into one which slid down the window frame, gathering speed before dashing itself to pieces on the windowsill. A night bird called somewhere in the darkness.

The phone was in her hand. She did not remember picking it up.

"Susan?"

"Oh God, Roy? Are you OK?"

"I'm fine," he told her. "Why, were you starting to worry?"

"No," she lied, sniffing. She realised for the first time that she was crying. A tear rolled down her cheek and dropped onto the phone. "Where are you?"

"I've just turned into the lane. I haven't been able to get a signal until now. I've got dinner with me – hope you've still got an appetite."

"You mean …?"

"Yep," he told her triumphantly, "fish and chips twice."

"You found somewhere, then?"

"Well, no. I just got bored and pissed off and thought enough was enough. Finally I went into this chip shop and asked the guy for fish and chips twice. He starts to give me the usual about I can't give you fish and chips twice and I interrupted him and said, look mate, I don't want to hear this crap about zombies. I've heard it all before. You've all had your little joke and it was very funny, but now I'm sick of it. I just want two lots of fish and chips and I honestly don't give a flying fuck about the zombies. And that was it. He asks me if I want salt and vinegar, he serves it all up, I pay him and that was that." He laughed.

"What do you think that was all about then?" Susan asked.

"God knows. Like I said before, maybe they just don't like the English. Maybe it's some bizarre local custom. They all look a bit inbred around here, don't you think? I keep expecting to see some kid playing the banjo. I'm back now, anyway."

Susan looked up, towards the window, as two shafts of light illuminated the room. The car pulled up into the drive.

"I hope you've got those plates warmed and ready," Roy said. She heard the engine die, and a second later the lights were extinguished. Silhouetted against the faint glow of the village she saw him step out of the car, his mobile tucked between shoulder and ear, two grey-white bundles in his hands. "I'm starving," he told her. "I could eat ..." and his voice stopped abruptly. Through the window she saw him stop moving.

"What's up now?" she asked him, jokingly exasperated.

"Hey!" he suddenly shouted, and it was a moment before she realised he wasn't talking to her. "What are you doing over there?" She watched him walk away from the car, disappearing from her view. "Hey, I'm talking to you!"

"Roy, what's going on?" she asked, feeling the fear begin to come back again.

"There are some people around the side of the house," he told her. "Probably kids from the village. I'll ..."

He fell silent.

"Roy?"

"Jesus," she heard him mutter. "Oh, Jesus Christ!"

"Roy, what is it?" Susan said, her voice rising in pitch. She strained at the window to try and see anything, but he was out of vision to the left. In the shadows on the right, something moved. A figure.

"Oh God," she mumbled.

360

"Susan," Roy said. His voice was a harsh rasp. "Susan, lock the door."

"Get into the house, Roy," she begged.

"I can't. They've got me cut off. Lock the door!"

"Roy, please!"

"Do it!" he shouted. "I'll get in the car. Please. Jesus!" There were more figures in the shadows now, moving towards the car. There was something odd about the way they shuffled, limping, advancing as if in pain, shambolic. She saw Roy reappear, his back to the car, phone still clasped to his ear.

"Behind you!" she screamed. She saw him turn, watched the look on his face as clearly as if it were daylight as he dropped the bundles and grabbed the phone in his left hand, his right hand fumbling to unlock the car door. The figures were getting closer. She felt more tears on her cheeks. She wanted to lock the door, but she could not move. She was transfixed as surely as if she were paralysed, her eyes on the scene before her, the phone pressed so hard against her ear that it would have hurt if she had been capable of feeling pain right then.

Roy wrenched the door open and got into the car. "I'm going to get help," he said. "I'll be back for you. Lock the doors!"

"Just go, Roy. Go!"

She heard the noise of the car, of the starter motor vainly trying to start the engine. She heard Roy muttering between sharp breaths. The figures had almost reached the car, and for the first time she heard another sound, a sound that she could not recognise. It was a low moaning noise, like an animal in pain, and it was a moment before she realised where it was coming from.

"Roy!" she screamed.

"It won't start!"

More figures appeared from the left of the car, from the shadows behind it. She could not count them all. She could only watch in sobbing terror as they surrounded the car. The sound of breaking glass shattered the night.

"Susan!" Roy screamed, and then his scream became louder, became shockingly high as the car became obscured from view by the dark bulk of the creatures.

"Roy," she sobbed. She couldn't look, turned away and collapsed to the floor. The phone hung loosely by its cord, a series of grunts and wet tearing sounds emanating from it until finally it, like the night, was silent.

VII

She couldn't have said how long she lay there, too scared to move, too distraught to think. Nothing came through the door, although she had never locked it. Nothing smashed through the windows to take her the way it had Roy.

It took the frantic beeping of the phone to rouse her from her near-catatonic state. Left off the hook too long with no signal left, the alarm had come on. Numbly she picked the handset up and replaced it in its cradle. The phone let out one sharp ring and was quiet.

She could barely bring herself to look out of the window, but eventually she managed it, wiping away the tears that blurred her vision. The car was still there, the last faint light from the village sparkling on broken glass. Nothing moved. No shambling shapes in the darkness. No Roy.

She was still not thinking, not in any real sense. Had she been able to think she would not have gone outside. She would not have turned the interior light on as she left to cast its revealing rays across the driveway. She was on autopilot. The fear that had so completely overtaken her had gone, leaving a void inside her. Only a compulsion, a need to know what had happened, powered her body as she walked out into the night.

The rain had at last stopped. The ground was sodden and thick with mud that embraced her naked feet. She did not notice. The driver's side door of the car was closed, the cheap plastic of the handle wet beneath her hand as she reached out to open it.

It took her a moment to realise what it was, the dark, unrecognisable shape that tumbled from the car. It lay there in the mud, one limb outstretched, dead fingers seemingly grasping

362

for something. She could see hair but there was no face, not anymore. Something that might once have been called an eye stared blindly up at her from a half-shattered socket. She did not scream. There was no emotion left in her. Her eyes followed the line of the arm as it reached towards two shredded bundles of paper and food, two greasy masses that glistened dimly in the light of the house.

From inside the car came a noise. It took her a moment to realise it was a tinny mobile rendition of *I Just Called to Say I Love You*. She reached into the car, found the phone. It felt slippery and faintly warm as she pressed it to her ear.

"Susan?"

"Uncle Ben?"

"Yes, it's me. Is everything alright? I've been trying to ring for hours but the phone was always engaged. It only just occurred to me to ring Roy's mobile."

"Oh, Uncle Ben," she sobbed, his voice bringing her back from the edge. "It's, "it's Roy. They ..." She tried to speak but the words stuck in her throat.

"Easy, Susan," he said soothingly. "Tell me what's happened. It's something to do with Roy. Yes?"

She looked down at the corpse at her feet, at the wedding ring on one finger that seemed to glow in the darkness.

"Roy's dead," she said simply.

There was a long pause.

"Yes," Uncle Ben said finally. "Yes, I know."

Susan continued to stare at the body. She had said the words, she knew he was dead, and yet something inside her wouldn't accept it. She kept expecting him to jump up and laugh, so that she could scold him for scaring her. That was just the sort of thing Roy would do. Like the thing with the tarantula. It was funny now, looking back at it, but at the time ...

She was suddenly cold.

"What do you mean," she whispered. "You know?"

"They tell me they tried to warn him," Uncle Ben said reasonably. "Poor Susan. I always said he was too stubborn for his own good. I know you agreed. You always said one day it would get him into trouble."

"What are you saying?" she said, numb again, knowing the answer.

"You can't have fish and chips twice. The zombies will get you. But he had to have something he wasn't supposed to have, didn't he? Like you, Susan. You were always too good for him. If only he could have just walked away. Still, all's well that ends well, eh?" He began to laugh. Slowly, other voices began to join him, each laughing, some recognisable, others not. Each new voice added to the cruel merriment.

Susan lowered the phone from her ear and then, as if it were suddenly burning, hurled it away. It landed ten yards away, but the noise seemed louder than ever. Susan screamed, holding her hands to her face, leaving handprints of mud and blood on her cheeks and forehead. Again and again she screamed, trying to drown out the mocking laughter in the darkness.

Lights began to blink on in the village, but interest in the screaming soon faded when it became apparent where it came from, and one by one they disappeared. In the darkness that followed, the fish and chips began to sink into the mud.

THE END

THE LAST TRIP TOGETHER
By
John McCuaig

"Dad ... Jack ..." her hushed little voice was barely audible over the high pitched, whistling wind. Tip-toeing between the lines of almost identical caravans Katie searched for her family as those rows of metal boxes seemed to draw in all around her. Passing one of those faux white picket fenced gardens her eyes spotted the door of a light coloured caravan slowly creep open. Gingerly, a well aged woman appeared from out of the darkness and descended the three small steps before stopping to stare at the young girl.

That deep groaning escaped from its blood drenched mouth as the pensioner suddenly made her way towards the rain soaked teenager. Edging herself backwards Katie only stopped when she felt a hand grab a hold of her shoulder.

Six hours earlier
"For the last time, can you *please* get yourselves moving," his voice was booming as he stepped outside. "I want to get over to Hastings before dark."

Sharing a little look, the sixteen year old twins Jack and Katie watched as their dad Gordon started to pack up the gear from outside their camper van. If the truth be told, they were glad that this would probably be the last holiday they'd have to endure with their father and his rickety old mobile home. Every single year it was the same old thing, they'd head down to the south coast of England, travelling around the quaint little towns for a full, and very long, two weeks. Now however, they dreamed of the delights of the music bars of Ibiza or swimming off one of the Greek islands.

"This stuff isn't going to move itself," Gordon attempted to smile to his only children. He failed, he saw the look in their eyes, he knew himself that they were growing up fast and he'd already guessed they were just building up the nerve to let him know.

"Sure thing, Dad," Jack mumbled as he stood up and folded up the tatty, old table while his sister grabbed the chairs and stacked them up inside. "I take it we're heading for the usual site?"

"Yeah, of course we are, son. I know how much the two of you love it down there."

Katie stood right behind her dad; a huge smile spreading across her face. Yeah, they *did* love that site, but that was back when they were about eight and building sand castles down on the beach. Turning away quickly Jack did his best to hide his own little smile from his father.

Soon enough they were back on the road and heading east along the coast to the old fishing town of Hastings. All during the two hour trip the camper van was filled with songs from the sixties as tape after tape was shoved into the slot on the dashboard. The twins shared their I-pod; each had an earpiece in, the fancy little machine was trying its best to block out the sounds of the Beach Boys and the Monkees.

"Okay kids we're here," Gordon said as they turned off the main road into the rain swept complex and saw that all was quiet. "Let's find our slot and get parked up." Driving straight by the Office they headed for the very back of the site. The owners had let him book online but although he had been a good customer over the years they still wanted his grubby old caravan well away and out of sight. They sure as hell did not want to chance any prospective new customers catching a glimpse of it, even if the sun was just slipping down behind the horizon.

Reversing into their bay right by the rear wall, Gordon set about connecting the park supplies to his van — water, gas and electric. All the while the twins kept themselves dry and warm inside.

"Well sis, this sure is fun," Jack said as he grabbed a deck of cards from a drawer.

"Hey, keep your voice down," Katie snapped back. "He's doing his best."

"Yeah ... he's doing his best to kill us with boredom."

"Please Jack," peering out the window she checked their dad was still out of earshot. "Just keep smiling and try and at

366

least look as though you're enjoying it. We've only got a few days left, and then we'll be back home."

"Whatever," Jack mumbled as he dealt out the faded cards to play a game of patience.

"Will sausage and beans be alright for now?" Gordon shouted as he ran back inside and quickly removed and shook off his well drenched coat. "We haven't got much else; I'll need to pop down to the store in the morning."

"Sounds good, Dad," Katie said as she kicked her brother in the shin under the table.

"Yeah, that'll be just fine," Jack shouted out as he glared at his sister while rubbing his throbbing leg.

It was Katie's turn to wash the dishes while Jack dried them up with his usual enthusiasm. Huddled around the cramped little sink they watched as their father spread his map out on the table, no doubt already planning the next day's adventures.

"Do you hear that?" Jack whispered, grabbing hold of his sister's arm and stopping it from splashing around in the water. "There's something at the door, sounds like a dog."

On hearing the light scratching behind them, Katie wiped her hands dry. "Well then you big scaredy cat, are you going to see what it is or do you need a little girl to have a look instead?"

Chucking the damp towel at her face and grumbling under his breath he made towards the door. Flicking over the lock he'd only managed to open it an inch before it flew open. It was however no dog; a balding middle aged man dressed in grubby blue overalls thrust himself in through the opening. Grabbing a good hold of Jack by the collar they stumbled backwards towards the sink.

"Dad ... Help us!" Jumping up on the man's back Katie screamed as she wrapped her arms around the rabid attacker's neck while Jack pushed his snapping jaws away with all his might.

Instinctively grabbing the frying pan up from the draining board Gordon smashed it into the head of the man that was attacking his children. The force of the blow sent the twins and the man sprawling across the floor towards the bedroom. Jack was first to his feet.

"What the fuck's up with him," screaming he pulled up his sister and dragged her away.

"Watch your mouth, boy," Gordon said as he looked down at the unmoving man. With the frying pan still tight in his hand he got himself a little closer. "It's Conner Hobbs; he's the handyman around here. I've known him for years."

"And what's that all over his face and hands? He's covered in fucking blood!"

"I said stop the swearing, Jack!" Grabbing him by the shoulder Gordon looked at his son right in the eyes, and then he lowered his voice. "Will you please get on that fancy phone of yours and call for an ambulance, and you'd better get the police over here as well." Going over to Katie he kissed her head gently and moved her even further away from the still body. "Come and sit over here, love, there's no need to worry about him anymore."

"No damn signal," Jack muttered as he slid the lid of his phone back down. "What can you expect in the arse end of civilisation?"

Before Gordon could berate him again all the lights in the caravan blinked out. Katie grabbed hold of her father, just in time to hear the moans, the low pitched moans coming from deep in the darkness. The handyman Conner was slowly getting back up on his feet.

"Get behind me Jack," Gordon stood up and held the frying pan high and waited for Conner to get close. He found it hard to see him in the dark but he could sure hear him approach. One more swipe sent him sprawling back down to the floor, but Gordon did not stop there this time. Again and again he rained down blows onto the skull of the man who had dared to threaten his family, only stopping his attack when he heard his daughter's screams. Spinning around he saw she'd hid her head in her hands, unable to watch her Dad as he smashed in the brains of another man.

Dropping the weapon to the floor he sat down and wrapped his arms around his girl. "I'm sorry love, but I had no choice. I couldn't let him harm you or your brother." Rivers of tears soaked into his t-shirt as she buried her face deep into his chest.

368

"Dad ..." Jack was peering out of the window. "You'd better get over here and have a look at this."

Breaking free from his daughter's grip he joined his son. Pulling the curtains slightly open they saw two men in their thirties staggering down the gap in the caravans. Even at distance and through the heavy rain, the moonlight shone on them just enough for Gordon to see they were not quite right. Like Conner, they were soaked through in blood. A woman out walking her little terrier bumped right into them as she came hurrying around the corner, no doubt trying to escape from the rain. Pouncing on her as soon as she appeared they pulled her to the ground and tore at her flesh with their teeth and hands. The screams of her pain and desperate calls for help brought another half dozen more men to the scene. But they were not coming to her aid but to join the party, to join in on the feast. Even that yapping, little excuse for a dog was picked up and devoured by one of the eager monsters.

"We need to get the hell out of here now, Dad," Jack whispered. "It's like we're stuck right in the middle of some frigging zombie movie."

"For the last time," Gordon snapped back. "Will you quit it with all the swearing?"

"Please tell me you're kidding me on," Jack just stared at his father in disbelief. "We're watching someone being eaten alive, you've just brained a man with a frying pan and all you're worried about is my shitty language?"

"What's going on out there, Dad?" Calling out from the seat, Katie tried to break their angry eye contact. After the last couple of years of them locking horns she had become an expert at breaking them up.

"Don't you worry honey," he said as he pulled the curtains tightly closed. "Just stay nice and quiet please."

"We need to go now," Jack carried on as soon as his father turned back to face him.

"It's not that easy son," Gordon slumped back down on the seat and stared at his kids. "They shut the gates after dark for security; they don't want anyone sneaking out with one of their caravans. The only way to open it is from inside the Office itself.

369

If we drive over there we'll never get out, you saw how quickly they appeared when there was some noise."

"So what are we gonna do then? We can't just stay in here."

"You and your sister will be staying right here. I'll sneak over to the office, open up the gates then get back so we can all drive out."

Staring at each other; the twins could not believe what he was saying.

"I'll only be gone for about twenty minutes," Gordon said as he put his heavy coat back on. "Just keep quiet and out of sight and you'll be just fine, trust me." Opening the kitchen cupboard door he tripped out all the little circuit breakers. "Just in case the power comes back on," his eyes glanced up the lights.

"I'll come with you, Dad," Jack grabbed his own coat. "You'll need someone to watch your back."

"No son, I need you stay here with your sister. I promise I won't be long."

Without another word he peered out the window and made for the door, silently opening it and soon disappearing deep into the rain and darkness.

"Where the hell is he?" Jack's glare was still stuck on the outside. "He's been gone for over an hour."

"Do you think they got him?" Katie whispered.

"I don't frigging know sis," he snapped back. "But I do know I ain't hanging around here just waiting for them to find us." Standing up he grabbed his coat again. "I'll be back in about five minutes, just gonna have a little look around and then come back."

"No ... please Jack, don't you *dare* leave me alone."

"Don't worry, I won't be long."

"Yeah, that's what Dad said."

Katie sat alone in the darkness for nearly another hour. They had both now left her and not returned. On hearing the beasts mulling around outside with their deep moaning filling the air, she knew it would only be a matter of time before they found her. And she knew only too well how that little meeting would end. Throwing on her own coat she peered out through the frilly curtains again. The blood and rain drenched beasts still wandered up and down the lines of caravans searching out fresh victims. She would never be able to get out the door without being seen, she needed to find another way.

Squeezing herself out of her father's little bedroom window, she gently dropped down onto the heavy mix of mud and grass. Inch by inch, yard by yard Katie worked her way through the maze of metal trying to get to the Offices while keeping out of sight of the undead. Dozens of them lumbered to and fro as they peered through the windows of the caravans and fumbled away at the doors in a usually futile attempt to get inside. The surrounding storm provided Katie with the cover of noise from the thunder and poor visibility through the rain.

Peering ahead she saw them, her father in that well worn yellow windcheater disappearing around the side of a caravan and following about a dozen feet behind was Jack. Both her heart and her legs sped up as she hurried to catch them, Katie called out but she was too loud, the old zombie inside the caravan had heard her.

Moving itself towards the girl the undead woman's eyes seemed to widen with delight at finding some fresh meat, but it too stopped for a second as it saw its prey being grabbed.

"Keep quiet," Jack's voice whispered in Katie's ear. "Just keep frigging quiet girl. I'll deal with her."

Marching forward he swung the lump of wood in his hand down on top of the woman's skull. Just like he had watched his father do earlier, he pummelled his weapon down again and again on their attacker's head as it lay twitching on the ground.

"Where's Dad gone?" Katie said as she joined her twin, trying not to look too closely at the mashed up brains that were gently oozing out over the ground.

Grabbing her arm he pulled her away before the noise attracted any more company. "I'd almost caught up with him when I heard you. Come on, we'll find him again."

"Why didn't he come back for us?"

"How the hell do I know?"

371

"Is he okay ... I mean is he still our Dad?"

Jack never answered.

It took another fifteen minutes of silent searching before they came across their father. Kneeling down in a huge puddle he may well have had his back to his children but they instantly knew it was him.

"Stay here," Jack whispered. "I'll check him out and be back in a second."

"No way," growling back she strode up alongside him. "I ain't getting left alone again."

Knowing that he could never change her mind Jack slowly carried on. As quietly as they could they got closer and closer but then they entered the deep puddle too. Both stepped into it at the exact same time, the sounds of the splash and the movement of water alerted the kneeling man before them.

Slowly standing their father turned and came face to face with his children again. All the love had long since disappeared from his widening eyes, and his silly smile had been taken over by a blood soaked snarl.

"Jack," edging backwards Katie grabbed a hold of her brother's arm. "We need to get out of here now."

"Not yet," Jack mumbled as he marched towards his dad, the lump of wood now held high above his head. "We can't leave him like that."

This time Katie did let Jack go on by himself, she even closed her eyes as the first blow was let free. She did not open them again until the crunching noises had ceased and the distant moaning had gotten louder.

"It's done," Jack grabbed a hold of her arm. "We can go now."

Katie looked down at the lump of wood Jack still carried; little rivers of blood raced along its length and dropped down into the puddle. It was drops of her father's blood.

"How could you do that?" she said, glancing over her brother's shoulder. "We could have just left him be."

"Fuck him," he said as he pulled her away. "He was one of them, we can't show any mercy."

"You're bloody enjoying this aren't you? Eh Jack, you ain't so frigging bored now."

"Shut it, sis."

"Or what?"

Pulling up to a halt he turned to face his sister. "Please just be quiet, we can finish this later."

"Jack ..."

"I said shush. Now come on, we need to keep moving." He did not have to tell her twice, she was already pulling away from his grasp.

"Jack ... look behind you."

Three of the monsters had spotted them. On seeing some fresh victims, they screamed out and raced towards them.

"Back to the van, come on," Jack shouted, pushing his sister ahead of him.

All around them the air was now filled with the sounds of the undead, the call was being answered and the twins were being surrounded.

"Are the gates open," Katie shouted. "Can we drive out?"

"No, but I've got another idea, we just need to get back to our van."

There was no more time to be careful, no more time to peer around the corners. All they could do was run as fast as they could.

Throwing the thin door open the twins scrambled back inside their faithful old holiday home and slammed and locked the flimsy door behind them.

"We need to get up on the roof," Jack shouted as he dragged a chair over to underneath the skylight.

The second he finished talking the window blew in as an array of hands burst through the thin glass after their prize. A snarling face pushed through the curtains as the first beast got a good look at the siblings.

"Fucking move it," Jack screamed as he set his chunk of wood to work on the intruder. Sprays of blood shot up in the air and painted the ceiling. "I'll be up in a second."

Perching up on the wobbly chair Katie released the two clips and pushed open the stained hatch. This allowed a few gallons of water that had settled on the roof to rush inside. Her little arms pulled with all their might and she dragged her body up and outside. Glancing down she saw that the caravan had been completely surrounded by the hungry monsters. Scores of the undead had encircled them.

"Jack … Jack," she hollered down into the darkness. "Come on, *please*, get the fuck up here now."

Just as she was giving him up for dead his hands appeared at the opening and he pulled himself up to join her. Right behind him a forest of hands followed as they tried in vain to pull him back down.

"What the hell are we going to do now?" she sobbed as she watched her brother scramble to his feet.

His hand rose up and he pointed to the wall behind them. "Over there, the beach is right on the other side. You should be fine once you get over there."

"What are you on about?" she said as he turned to set his weapon on the invaders again, the wood crunching into the flesh as he fought to keep them back. "Why are you talking like it's just me?"

Turning slightly to face her, the last of the moonlight caught his face. His cheek was a bloody mess, all ripped and torn the bite mark was still clearly visible.

"I'll watch your back, sis," he smiled. "Looks like I'm destined to be stuck in this shithole forever. One of those fuckers got me good and we both know how that'll end."

"I can't do it! I can't go out there alone Jack. You can come with me, you'll be fine."

"Sorry sis," he shouted as he went back to his wild attacks. "You know I can't, now fucking jump over there and get the hell out of here." Turning back again he gave her a little smile, "Yeah, and you were right as usual, I sure am enjoying myself now."

Katie could look at her brother no longer, blowing him a little kiss she ran towards the wall and jumped. Slamming her body into the bricks she just managed to hang on as a group of the undead eagerly waited below for her fall. Scrambling up she slumped over the other side and dropped down onto a grassy dune.

She did not try to run; she just lay down and cried. All she could hear was a heady mix of those deep undead groans and the high whoops of delight as Jack defeated yet another of the beasts. The sun beginning its rise over the horizon brought her to her senses and she too rose up and headed towards the beach.

As she was almost at the sea she saw where a child must have played the day before. A slightly collapsed sand castle became sheathed in the rapidly approaching sunlight and Katie dropped to her knees beside it. She picked up the little pink bucket and spade that were carefully placed alongside it.

She never even realised that she was not alone; her mind was oblivious to the sounds of the undead as they raced towards her from both ends of the beach. The beasts were everywhere, she would never find safety.

Patting the moist sand firmly down into the bucket she set about finishing the castle. Her mind drifted away but she no longer dreamed of those fancy foreign lands.

All that she dreamed of now was those long ago but happier days with her father and brother. And how she wished they were back.

THE END

THE DAY THE MUSIC DIED
By
Joe McKinney

"But this changes everything," Isaac Glassman said. "You see that, right? I mean you gotta see that. We can't ... I mean, Steve, you can't ... I mean, shit, he's dead. Tommy Grind is dead! How can you say nothing's changed?"

"Isaac," I said. "Calm down. This isn't that big of a deal."

He huffed into the phone. "Great. You're making fun of me now. I'm talking about the death of the biggest rock star since The Beatles, and you're cracking jokes. I'm telling you, Steve, this is fucking tragic."

I let out a tired sigh. I should have known Isaac was going to be a problem. Lawyers are always a problem. He'd been with us since Tommy's first heroin possession charge back in 2002. That little imbroglio kept us in the LA courts for the better part of a year, but we got *The Cells of Los Angeles* album out of it, which went double platinum, so at least it hadn't been a total disaster. And Tommy was so happy with Isaac Glassman that he added him to the payroll. I objected. I looked at Isaac and I saw a short, unkempt, Quasimodo-looking guy in a cheap suit in the midst of a school girl's crush. 'He's in love with you,' I told Tommy. 'And I mean in the creepy way.' But Tommy laughed it off. He said Isaac was just star struck. It'd wear off after a few months.

I knew he was wrong about Isaac even then.

Just like I knew Isaac was going to be trouble now.

Behind me, closed up behind the Plexiglas screen I had installed across the entrance to Tommy's private bedroom after he'd overdosed and died from whatever the hell kind of mushroom it was he took, Tommy was finishing up on the arm of a groupie I'd brought him. The girl was a seventeen year old nobody, a runaway. I'd met her outside a club on Austin's 6th Street two nights earlier. "Hey," I asked her, "you wanna go get high with Tommy Grind?" The girl nearly beat me to my car. And now, after two days of eating on the old long pig, Tommy was almost done with her. There'd be some cleanup, femurs, a skull, a mandible, stuff like that, but nothing a couple of trash bags and some cleaning products wouldn't be able to handle. As long as the paparazzi didn't go through the garbage, things'd be fine.

I turned my attention back to the phone call with Isaac.

"Look," I said. "This isn't a tragedy, okay? Stop being such a drama queen. And secondly, The Beatles weren't *a* rock star. They were *four* rock stars. A group, you know? It's a totally different thing."

"Jesus, this really is a joke to you, isn't it?" Now he sounded genuinely hurt.

"No, it's not a joke." I looked over my shoulder at Tommy. He was at the barrier, looking at me, bloody hands smearing the Plexiglas, a rope of red muscle – what was left of the girl's triceps – hanging from the corner of his mouth. I said, "I'm deathly serious about this, Isaac."

"Yeah, well, that's comforting."

"It should be. Look, I'm telling you, I got this under control."

"He's a zombie, Steve. How can you possibly have that under control?"

Tommy was banging on the Plexiglas now. One hand slapping on the barrier. I could hear him groaning.

"He's a rock star, Isaac. Nothing's changed. He's a zombie now, so what? Hell, I bet Kid Rock's been a zombie since 2007."

"So what? *So what?* Steve, I saw him last night, eating that girl. He looked horrible. People are gonna know he isn't right when they see him."

For the last three years or so, Tommy Grind and Tom Petty had been in a running contest to see who could be the grungiest middle aged rock star in America. Up until Tommy died and then came back as one of the living dead, I would have said Tom Petty had him beat. Now, I don't know. They were probably tied.

"Nobody's gonna know anything," I said into the phone. "Look, I've been his manager for twenty years now, ever since he was a renegade cowboy singing the beer joints in South Houston. I sign all the checks. I make all the booking arrangements and the recording deals and handle the press and get him his groupie girls for him to work out his sexual frustrations on. I got this covered. The show'll go on, just like it always has."

"Yeah, except now he's eating the groupies, Steve." I thought I heard a wounded tone in his voice. He didn't like to hear about Tommy's other playthings, even before he started eating them.

"True," I said.

"How're you gonna cover that up? I mean, there's gonna be bones and shit left over."

"We'll be careful," I said.

"Careful?"

"Get him nobodies, like this girl he's got now. Girls nobody'll miss. The streets are loaded with 'em."

I turned and watched Tommy picking the girl's hair out of his teeth with a hand that wouldn't quite work right. No more guitar work, that's for sure. But then, that was no big deal. He had a cameo in *Guitar Hero XXI*. Tommy Grind's reputation was secure, even if he never played another note.

Finally, Isaac said, "Did he finish that girl yet?"

Good boy, Isaac, I thought.

"Yeah," I said. "Just a little while ago."

"Oh." He hesitated, and then said, "And you're sure we can do this? We can just go on like nothing's happened?"

"Absolutely," I said.

Tommy was always prolific. He wasn't much for turning out a polished product – that part we left to the session musicians and Autotuner people to clean up – but the man had the music in him. He'd spent fifteen hours a day playing songs and singing and just banging around in the studio we built for him in the west wing of the mansion. Just from what I'd heard walking through the house recently, I figured we had enough for three more full length albums.

It'd just be a matter of having the studio people clean it up. They were used to that. Business as usual when you work for Tommy Grind.

Isaac said, "Steve?"

"Yeah?"

"Can I ... can I come over and see him?"

"You're not gonna screw this up, are you? No whistle blowing, right?"

"Right," he said. "I promise. I just want to see him."

"Sure, Isaac. Come on over any time."

"And this is how he's gonna live? I mean, I know he's not alive, but this is how it's gonna be?"

"For now," I said.

Isaac didn't look too happy about that. He was watching Tommy Grind through the Plexiglas, bottom lip quivering like he was about to cry. He put his fingers on the barrier and sniffled as Tommy worked on another groupie.

"He looks kind of ... dirty."

"He's a rock star, Isaac. That's part of the uniform."

"But shouldn't we keep him clean or something. I mean, he's been in those same clothes since he died. I can smell him out here."

He had a point there, actually. Tommy was really starting to reek. His skin had gone sallow and hung loose on his face. There were open sores on his hands and arms. The truth was I was just too scared to change his clothes for him. I didn't want to catch whatever that mushroom had done to him.

"How many girls are in there with him?" Isaac asked.

"Two."

"Just two?" Isaac said, shaking his head in disbelief. "But there's so many, uh, body parts."

"His appetite's getting stronger," I agreed. "He regularly takes two girls at a time now, sometimes three. So, when you think about it, he's actually back to where he was before he died."

"That's not funny, Steve."

I didn't like the milquetoast look he was giving me. I said, "Don't you dare flake out on me, you hear? Between the record sales and the movie deals and video game endorsements and all the rest of it, Tommy Grind is a one hundred and forty

379

million dollar a year corporation. I'm not about to let that fall apart because of this."

"Is that what this is about to you, the money? That's all you care about? What about Tommy? What about what he stood for?"

I laughed.

"Tommy stood for sex, drugs, and rock and roll. That was the world to him."

"His music was the soundtrack for my life, Steve. It means something."

"Bullshit," I said. "It means he liked his women horny, his drugs psychotropic, and his music loud. That was all Tommy Grind ever wanted. Now, all he wants is food. We're good the way I see it."

"We should let him out. Let him get some sunshine."

"Yeah, right," I said. "Isaac, the paparazzi hide in the bushes across the street just praying for a chance to shoot Tommy Grind while he's smoking a joint on the lawn. You have any idea how bad that would be to take him out for a stroll? No, if we're gonna bring him out into the world, we need to do it under controlled circumstances."

He nodded, then leaned his forehead against the barrier and watched the love of his life pop a finger into his mouth. Smaller parts like that he could eat whole.

"Listen," I said, "you want a drink?"

"No, thank you. You go ahead. I'm just gonna sit here for a while and watch him."

I shrugged. "Whatever. I'll be out in the hot tub."

I made myself a whiskey over shaved ice and dropped in an orange slice for garnish. Then I stripped and climbed into the hot tub and let the jets massage my back. The hot tub was outside, but the little courtyard where it was located was covered with ivy to prevent helicopters from peaking in on Tommy's private parties, which were the stuff of legend. One of last year's parties had included half a dozen A-list porn stars and a pile of cocaine the size of an old lady's hat.

I took a couple of phone calls and arranged for a cover of Eddie Money's "I Think I'm In Love" that Tommy had done in his studio a month before he died to appear on *That's What I Call Music, Volume 153.*

As was I finishing, I heard screams coming from the front lawn. I told the guy from Capitol I had to go, hung up, jumped out of the hot tub.

Fucking Isaac, I thought. *You better not have …*

But he had. The little idiot had gone and let Tommy out of his bedroom and taken him for a walk down on the front lawn.

When I got there, clothes soaked through and my feet squishing in my shoes, Tommy was staggering around in the middle of the street, a team of terrified paparazzi gathered around him, snapping pictures. The flashes were making Tommy disoriented and he was swiping the air in a futile attempt to grab the photographers.

I waded into the crowd and grabbed Tommy by the back of his black t-shirt and guided him toward the lawn. I looked around and saw Isaac standing on the curb, a drooping question mark in a cheap blue suit.

"You get him inside," I growled at Isaac.

"I'm sorry," he said. "I just wanted to –"

"Go!" I said. "Now."

He led a reluctant Tommy back to the house. I watched him get most of the way to the front door, my mind scrambling for a way to explain all this, then I turned to the crowd and said, "Okay, people, listen up. Come on, gather around."

Thirty photographers just looked at me.

"What the hell, people? You don't recognize a press conference when you see one? Gather around."

That did it. Soon I was standing in the middle of a tight ring of bodies, cameras rolling.

"All right," I said, "we were hoping to save this announcement for the Grammy's, but clearly Tommy Grind wanted to give you guys a sneak peak. Tommy has just completed his first screen play. It's called *The Zombie King* and I've just got word from our people in Hollywood that it's a go for next fall. We'll be shooting here in Austin starting around the end of next September."

"A horror film?" one of the paparazzi said.

"That's right.   And it's gonna be Tommy's directorial debut, too."

"So, that was … what? A costume?"

"Look," I said, and sighed for effect, "what do you think is gonna happen when you give a rock star access to a stable full of professional makeup artists?   I mean, we've all seen Lady Gaga, right?"

That got a few laughs.   I passed out business cards to everybody and told them to send me an email so I'd have their addresses for future press releases.

They scattered after that to email their photos to their contacts and I went inside to kick Isaac's ass.

A few days weeks later, in early February, I was back in the hot tub, helping another untraceable young lady out of her bikini for a little warm up before she went in to see Tommy. I was sitting on the edge of the tub, and the girl came over and positioned herself between my legs and put her cheek down on my thigh. The drugs in her drink were already starting to take effect, and I had to nudge her a little to get her to pay attention to what she was supposed to be doing.

She had just gotten to it when Isaac Glassman walked through the sliding glass door.

"Jesus, Isaac," I said, covering up my junk.   "What the hell, man?"

"Sorry," he said. "But we have to talk."

The girl had pulled away from me and sunk down to her chin in the water. She wouldn't look at either one of us, even though it was a day late and a dollar short for any pretence at modesty at that point.

"Do you mind?" Isaac said, and pointed at the girl with his chin.

"Just wait for it," I said.

The girl's eyelids were drooping shut. I jumped in, caught her just as her face slid under the water, and pulled her out.

"Help me get her out of here," I said to Isaac.

He reached in and took one arm and I took the other. We pulled her onto her back on the side of the tub. She had great tits, I thought absently. A pity.

I climbed out and slid into my trunks.

"This better be good," I said.

"What are you gonna do with her?"

"What do you think? You're gonna help me drag her into Tommy's room. Then he's gonna eat her."

"But you were gonna have her first?"

"I think Tommy's past the point of jealousy," I said.

He was uncomfortable, stared at his shoelaces, then at the ivy-covered walls behind me. Then, finally, at me. "That's what I want to talk to you about," he said.

"Oh?"

"Yeah. I don't ... I don't like the direction you're taking Tommy's career. The Eddie Money cover —"

"Has been number one on the Billboard charts for two weeks in a row. What are you trying to say?"

"That's not the point," he said.

Not the point? *Not the point!* I couldn't believe it. The little geek had the gall to stand there and tell me he didn't like my decisions. Christ, what did he know? The song was doing great. The critics were calling its stripped down acoustic arrangement and gravelly-voiced lyrics a masterstroke from one of rock's greatest performers. Industry experts were already anticipating Tommy Grind's fourteenth Grammy, which I would accept on his behalf in just a few weeks.

"Tell me, Isaac. What is the point? I gotta hear this."

"It's a cover song, Steve."

"Yeah, a fucking successful one, too."

"But it's a cover song. Tommy Grind never did cover songs. It was always *his* music, *his* vision. That's what made him so special. That's why people loved him."

"Oh Jesus," I said.

"Seriously, Steve."

"You're so full of shit, you know that? You don't live in the house with him, Isaac. You never heard him playing in there in his studio. The guy would sit in there and play cover tunes all day long. He loved 'em."

"That's because he loved the music, Steve. He played what made him feel good. But when he put his music out there for the world, it was always his own stuff. Don't you see?"

No, you little dweeb, I don't see.

I had managed to get together a lot more original songs off of Tommy's studio tapes than I first thought. We had enough for another eight, maybe nine albums. More if I included the cover tunes he loved so much. And it was good stuff, too. Plus, he had tons of live recordings from the heavy touring he did from 2003 to early 2008. I was thinking of putting together a double live album to go along with a DVD release of his Hollywood Bowl concert last August, maybe a viral marketing campaign on the web. Michael Jackson had been a bigger hit dead than alive, and it was looking Tommy Grind was going to be even bigger.

"What is it you're accusing me of?" I said. "You think I'm selling him out? Is that it?"

It took him a moment to work up the courage, but finally he squared his shoulders at me and said, "Well, yeah, I do. I guess that's exactly what I'm saying."

It took all the self-control I had to keep from killing him right there where he stood. I felt my face flush with anger.

Maybe he saw it too, because he took a step back.

"You listen to me," I said. "Nobody accuses me of selling Tommy Grind out. Nobody. You don't have that right. You jumped on this gravy train after it had already worked itself up to full speed. But me, I've been with him since the beginning. I was with him in Houston when he was working two daytime jobs and playing all night long in the clubs. I'm the one who got him his first radio time. I'm the one who made the club owners pay up. And when he got drunk and wanted to fight the cowboys who threw beer bottles at him in the middle of his sets, I was the one who stood back to back with him and got my knuckles bloody. So don't you stand there and think you know more about Tommy Grind's vision than I do. I'm the one who told him what his fucking vision was."

That cowed him. He stood there with his eyes fixed on

his shoes and it looked like he was about to cry. For a second there I thought he was going to run from the room like a scolded hound. But he suddenly showed more backbone than I knew he possessed. He raised his almost non-existent chin and looked me square in the eyes.

"What?" I said.

"You're the one telling Tommy what his vision is?"

"That's right."

"Well, good. Because I just talked Jessica Carlton's attorney over lunch. She heard your bit about *The Zombie King*, and she wants in."

"*The Zombie King ...*"

"Yeah. The movie you told the press Tommy had just written. Remember that?"

"Yeah," I said, and looked down at the naked girl at my feet. I had almost forgotten she was there.

Jessica Carlton, damn. The bubble-headed blonde who broke onto the scene a few years back claiming to be as virginally pure as Amy Grant, but had no qualms whatsoever shaking her ass for every camera from LA to Hamburg. The claims to virginal purity passed away unnoticed right about the time her first movie came out, and she rose to the status of tabloid cover starlet, which if you ask me was a brilliant piece of marketing. Now she was on the cover of just about every magazine in the grocery store checkout line. The last I heard she was dating an NFL quarterback, was doing a new album, and even had another movie deal on the table. She had the goods, definitely. And if she said she wanted to be in Tommy's movie, well, there was no easy way to refuse that. People would ask questions. *People Magazine* would ask questions.

"That's a problem, right?"

"Yeah," I said. "That's a problem."

And a week later, I still didn't have a solution. The Eddie Money cover had slipped down to number fourteen on the countdown, but we were prepping a new single – a Tommy Grind original – and that would be out in another three weeks, so at least his name would stay out there.

385

But the Jessica Carlton thing was bothering me. She had come to Texas to see her jock boyfriend, and her people had been calling to set up a meeting. No surprise there. I just didn't know what to tell them.

I started smoking again. Cigarettes, I mean. I never quit weed. That was almost impossible when you hung around Tommy Grind. I quit cigarettes back in 1998, and never felt better. But the stress of dealing with Tommy's unique needs — he was up to four girls a week now, and it was getting increasingly difficult to dispose of the garbage in a way that didn't attract dogs of both the canine and human variety — and the Jessica Carlton situation conspired against me. In a weak moment, I bummed a smoke off of Isaac and within a week was back up to a pack a day.

It made me feel ashamed every time I lit up. Like I was some kind of pansy or something, but, to quote Tommy, a need is a need and it has to feed, like it or not.

The situation reached a head on the night of February 14th – Valentine's Day.

I was in Tommy's fully restored 1972 Triumph TR-6, headed back to the mansion from the store where I'd gone to buy another carton of smokes. It was a cool, crisp night, full of stars, and I had the top down and Tommy's 2003 album *Desert Nights* cranked up on the CD player. The night was cool and clear, and the little Triumph handled the Hill Country roads like a dream. Any other night, I would have been in heaven.

But, like I said, I was troubled.

The feeling got worse when I pulled into the driveway and saw the lights on upstairs.

I had turned them off when I left. Tommy was usually calmest when the lights were off.

"Fuck," I said, and in my mind I was already throttling Isaac.

I parked and went inside, just to make sure. But I wasn't surprised to find Tommy gone. Isaac hadn't even done a half-assed job of cleaning up Tommy's latest meal. Nice enough girl. Said she was from Kentucky, I think.

I went to the security room and replayed the tape. There

was Isaac, talking to Tommy through the Plexiglas, opening the door, coaxing him outside. Tommy staggering toward Isaac, hands raised in a gesture that almost looked like supplication.

And then they were off camera until they got downstairs and out the front door.

I turned on the GPS tracker – basically a glorified version of what veterinarians use to track the family pet – that I had injected into Tommy's ass after the last time Isaac walked him outside. Then I called the signal up on my iPad and got a good fix on him.

He was heading down to the west point of Lake Travis. There was a secluded little pocket of vacation homes down there for the uber wealthy. Sandra Bullock and Matthew McConaughey both had houses there not too far from Tommy's. It was his private little retreat from the world. Tommy didn't often like to disconnect, but when he did, that was where he went.

And then, a terrible thought.

Please dear God. Tell me he's not taking her to meet Jessica Carlton. He can't be that stupid.

I called Isaac's cell, and to my surprise, he answered.

"What the hell are you doing?" I said.

"Can't talk," he answered. I could hear Tommy moaning in the background. Car noises. Isaac struggling to keep Tommy off him.

"Isaac. Isaac, don't you dare hang up on me!"

But he did.

Damn it.

I got in my Suburban – the one I'd specially modified with a police prisoner barrier in the back so I could transport Tommy if I needed to – and headed after them.

Thirty minutes later, I was looking up at an eight thousand square foot mansion done up like a Mediterranean villa – red tile roof, white adobe walls, fountains and hibiscus everywhere. I had parked off the main road, in a small gap in a cedar thicket that concealed the Suburban just perfectly, and tried to figure what Isaac was doing. What possible reason could he have for bringing Tommy here? If Jessica Carlton saw him, we were done for. Despite the constant upkeep, Tommy was looking pretty rough these days. Worse than Willie Nelson after a three day whiskey binge. Which I've seen, by the way. It ain't pretty.

And then it hit me. Valentine's Day. Today was Valentine's Day. Isaac Glassman had no chance of ever becoming Tommy Grind's lover. Not anymore anyway. The pathetic bastard's heart was probably breaking. He couldn't give Tommy flowers, or candy, or stuffed animals, or any of that worthless shit people give each other on Valentine's Day. But he could give him something pretty. Something that Tommy *did* still care about.

I heard shouting from the house. It was muffled, but definitely shouting.

Then gunfire. Three pistol shots, one after another.

That lit a fire under me.

I reached behind the driver's seat of the Suburban and took out a badly scuffed Louisville Slugger, the one with nicks in the business end that went back to the Houston beer joint days.

Old School persuader in hand, I advanced up the driveway and tried the doors and windows until I found an unlocked servant's door off the kitchen.

I looked up and saw a camera in the corner, pointed right at me.

Same system as at Tommy's. I could deal with that.

I looked around and noticed the stove. A huge Viking gas range with a dozen burners.

I cranked them all up to full and walked into the living room, where I could hear a man whimpering.

I didn't recognize him, which probably meant he was part of the legal community. Maybe one of Isaac's lawyer friends. He wore a light gray double-breasted suit with a canary yellow silk shirt and no tie, both of which were torn and splashed with blood. He was clean-shaven and fit-looking, but his eyes were crazed.

Had to be Jessica Carlton's lawyer. He must have brought her here so the talent could play while the lawyers talked contracts.

He turned his insane eyes on me and that's when I saw the pistol in his hand, the slide locked back in the empty position.

"Help me," he pleaded.

I grabbed him by the shoulders. "Who else is in the house?"

"To-Tommy Grind. Oh Jesus. He … something's wrong. He attacked Jessica. He bit her leg off. I … I think she's … I think she's hurt real bad."

Then he held the gun up in front of his face like he had never seen it before.

"I shot him. I emptied the whole magazine into his chest. He just … he just kept coming. He's … oh Jesus."

"I see. Listen, what's your name?"

"Leslie Gant," he said. He was in deep shock, functioning on autopilot.

"Great. Listen, Leslie … you mind if I call you Leslie?"

"Huh?"

"Leslie, I want you to kneel down right here, okay?" He let me guide him to his knees. "That's right," I said. "Just like that. Now put your arms down at your side. Look over there."

"What? Why?"

I pointed his face toward the sliding glass doors that led out to a beautifully dappled swimming pool.

"Perfect," I said. "Now I'm gonna tee off on your head with this bat."

"Wha—"

I swung for the fence. Laid him out like a sack of rocks.

Then I went to find Isaac and Tommy.

Isaac was standing in a hallway outside the master suite. He turned when he heard me approach, and his eyes went wide as the bat came up.

"No!" he said, showing me his palms. "It's okay. Stop, Steve."

"Like hell it's okay. I ain't gonna let you ruin us, Isaac."

"No," he pleaded. "You don't understand."

I was close enough now to see into the master suite.

Jessica Carlton, blouse torn off, exposing her absolutely amazing tits, skirt hiked up high enough to give a peek of a white, lacy thong, was pulling herself across the deep pile, honey-coloured carpet. There was blood on her face and a huge big bite mark on her right leg. From her expression, I could tell she'd been drugged.

Tommy was staggering towards her, moaning like I'd never heard him do before. There was fresh blood on his face and hands and chest, but if I didn't know better, I'd have sworn he was aroused.

"What the hell?" I said. I turned to Isaac. "Did you drug her?"

"Yeah. GHB."

"How much did you give her?"

"The usual."

"The whole dropper full?"

"Yeah."

"And she's still moving around?"

He shrugged.

"Damn," I said, and whistled. "The girl must be in pretty good shape."

"Yeah."

Tommy caught up with her, fell on her and started to feed. She let out a weak scream, but there was nothing behind it. In less than a minute, she had stopped thrashing.

Feeling stunned, I said, "Isaac, I'm not sure if I'm gonna be able to unfuck this situation."

"I was ..." he said, and drifted off feebly. "It's Valentine's Day."

I didn't even bother to respond.

"I wanted to give him something, you know? We just take and take and take from his talent. Nobody ever gives back to him. I wanted to give him something special."

"So you gave him Jessica Carlton? Jesus, Isaac, how did you expect to pull that off. This isn't some two bit groupie chick. People are gonna notice she's gone."

"She wanted to meet Tommy. Leslie Gant called me. He said she was going to be in town. He asked me if we could

390

set up a private meeting between them. You know, a little romantic Valentine's Day dinner the paparazzi wouldn't know about. She's still with that football player guy."

I took a moment to absorb all that. Then, "So no one knows she's here. Is that what you're saying?"

"Leslie Gant knows too."

"I'm not too worried about him," I said.

But I was worried about Isaac. In his mind, he must have felt he was making the supreme lover's sacrifice. He must have felt almost like a martyr, giving someone else to Tommy Grind so that they could satisfy him the way Isaac only wished he could.

"This must have been really hard for you," I said.

He looked at me, a suspicious note of caution in his eye.

"I mean that," I said. "I know you've been in love with him for a long time."

Isaac started to object, but then he hung his head and nodded.

"Listen, come with me. Let's go have a drink and let him eat. What the hell, right? There's nothing more you can do here."

I put my arm over his shoulder and led him back to the living room. He balked at Leslie Gant on the living room floor, but I guided him away from the body.

"Don't worry about him," I said. "Here, we got time for one drink. Then, we got to think about how we're gonna clean all this up. Can't afford any loose ends."

He looked back at Leslie Gant and grunted.

I handed him his drink. "To Tommy Grind," I said. We clanked glasses. I downed mine in one gulp. He sipped his, but managed to get most of it down just the same.

"Hang tight here, okay? I'm gonna go get Tommy and put him in the car."

About five minutes later, I was done with Tommy and back in the living room. Isaac was nearly passed out on the couch.

I slapped his cheeks to rouse him. "Come on," I said. "Don't face on me yet."

He stirred.

"Okay," I said, "here's what we're gonna do. You got your lighter on you?"

He reached into his pocket and held up a pink Bic.

"Pink?" I said. "Seriously?"

A corner of his mouth twitched. As close as he was going to get to a smile at this point.

"Well, it'll work. Start lighting those drapes on fire, okay?"

He nodded.

I took the whiskey and a couple of other bottles back to the master suite and lit the bodies on fire. Once I had it going, I came back to the living room and grabbed Isaac by the shoulder.

"Come on," I told him. "Gotta stay on your feet until we get to the car."

We passed his car in the driveway, and though the drugs I had slipped into his drink had made him so groggy he could barely walk, he was still able to point at his car and groan.

"Don't worry about it," I said.

At that very moment – and I mean it was cued like something out of a movie – the house behind us blew up.

And I'm not just talking a part of the house, either.

The whole fucking thing exploded.

The shockwave nearly knocked me down.

Isaac stared at me, stupidly. His mouth was hanging open, a thick rope of drool hanging from the corner of his lips. Some people don't handle the GHB well at all.

"What did you do?" he managed to say, though it came out all as one syllable, slurred together.

"This is your big chance," I said. I leaned him up against the front fender of the Suburban, reached into the driver's side window, and turned up Janis Joplin's 'Take Another Little Piece of My Heart.'

One of Tommy's favourite songs.

Then I helped Isaac Glassman to the back and balanced him on my hip as I opened the door.

Tommy was waiting inside, watching, his dead eyes locked on Isaac.

Isaac groaned and slapped at my hand in a futile show of resistance. Poor guy, he knew it was coming.

Janis was singing *never never never hear me when I cry*.

"She's playing your song," I said. "Happy Valentine's Day, Isaac."

Then I chucked him inside, closed the door, and drove out of there before the first sirens sounded in the distance.

I listened to the sounds of weak screams and tearing meat coming from the back seat, but didn't look back.

Instead, I turned up the radio.

It ain't easy being the manager for the biggest rock star on the planet. Sometimes you gotta get your hands dirty. But what the hell? I mean, the show must go on, right?

THE END

WABIGOON
By
James Cheetham

I can still picture our surroundings. Above me the sun sparked bright while in the distance the sound of songbirds painted a picture entirely innocent and removed from the horrors of the day. Today should have been filled with fun, fish, and brotherly bonding; a beer in my hand, a line in the water, sunscreen on my nose. Things don't always turn out the way one expects them to however – and I can appreciate that, but never would I have believed a day as beautiful as this one could have ended as tragically as it had.

Even now, the cloudless sky remains a constant reminder of normality. The beer still waits in the cooler and my line remains forever in the water, along with my tackle box, my rod, and my cell phone.

The boat still has power too, but the outboard refuses to turn over. I've done everything in my limited mechanical ability to change that fact, but it has not been enough. I am not blessed to be so inclined, and the person who did have that know-how – my brother, Jerry – lay on his back in the hull of the boat, inhaling tiny gasps of air, his skin slowly turning a shade of shocking blue as his eyes gazed past the infinite sky above.

I was uncertain what to do with Jerry, my mind snared by thoughts of our mother – God rest her soul. She'd have rolled over in her grave if she knew I'd considered rolling my only sibling over the side of the boat.

The last time I heard Jerry say anything coherent he'd been directing me on how to get the motor started again while he busied himself applying pressure to a gaping bite taken from the meat of his left hand, just below his thumb.

"Take the filleting knife, and dig that shit out of the propeller," Jerry had said as small streams of deep red trickled down his forearm only hours earlier. He removed the towel he'd been using on the wound and held it over the lake, squeezing the blood from it the way one might squeeze a chamois while drying a car. The motor was heavy but I managed to pull it up and tilt it back, bringing the propeller blades out of the water. I was repulsed by what I saw as shades of fleshy pink and crimson dripped back into the lake and tiny remnants of the morning's catastrophe floated upon waves of water so crystal clear, you could see to the very bottom.

"Dig it out with the knife. It won't turn over because it's blocked up with all that ... crap."

The filleting knife wasn't enough however. It was sharp certainly – which was fine for cleaning Pickerel, but was useless when utilized in the process of digging, like a spade or a spoon. The blade was too thin and it bent to the point I worried it might snap altogether, the blade-tip lodging in my eye leaving the both of us injured – two helpless fools drifting along in a boat that refused to start. Perhaps that was our punishment for wandering off the beaten track.

Jerry had mentioned Raindance Island on the very first night spent in Wabigoon, Ontario five days earlier. Our wives were inside our rented cabin getting the kids off to bed while my brother and I sat in the screened porch enjoying a few drinks as the sun set over Wabigoon Lake.

"I wouldn't mind taking a look – might be interesting," Jerry said after mentioning the isolated island with strange anticipation in his voice.

"I imagine they'd have it all blocked off from the public somehow ... wouldn't they?" I'd asked.

Jerry sipped at his whiskey and shrugged. "No need to block off a place nobody knows about."

"What's the big deal anyway?" I asked him. "You see dead bodies all the–"

Jerry motioned for me to be quiet. I looked up to see our wives, Andrea and Jackie, coming out through the patio doors – Andrea still nursed the vodka cooler she'd had with our late supper of barbequed hotdogs.

"They all tucked in?" I asked, watching Jackie – my brother's wife, pull the patio door closed behind her.

She smiled. "Sort of ... Jonathon has Joshua convinced there's a deranged lunatic in a hockey mask lurking in the woods.

I wouldn't be surprised if he crawls into bed with you guys tonight."

"That's my boy!" Jerry said, toasting his son with his glass while the rest of us shared a laugh.

"Some things never change." I said. How ironic, Jerry's son had my kid terrified – we hadn't even unpacked yet. "You think he'll be alright?" I asked, as Andrea sat down on my lap and wrapped her arms around my shoulders.

"We're here for two weeks, I hope so," Andrea said with a chuckle.

Jackie pulled up a plastic chair, sat down, and rested her bare feet on Jerry's legs. "I feel so bad. Jonathon's become a horror fiend – no thanks to his father."

"Ah, it's just first night jitters – tomorrow night will be easier," Andrea said, waving Jackie's worries away with her hand before turning her attention to me. "You guys planning on unloading that boat at some point tonight?"

"We were thinking we might head out tomorrow morning," Jerry said, flirting with the possibility, forever a braver man than I.

"Head out where?" Andrea asked, giving me the look only a wife could give a husband.

"Fishing," Jerry said and gestured with a flick of the chin, "out on the lake."

That was of course not what we'd been talking about, not exactly, but it was enough to make the girls groan nonetheless. I could imagine their reaction had my brother told them the honest to God truth.

Jackie – struggling to get the twisty cap off her beer, shook her head. "Tomorrow's our first day here … you guys aren't getting off that easy!"

My brother's ambitions were left in the porch that night along with several empty beer bottles. Jerry was smart enough not to push his luck. There would be plenty of time to get out on the lake, though I could still see his mind churning as we continued to enjoy our vacation together. By the time Monday rolled into Tuesday and we'd spent the day with the kids hiking, and Tuesday rolled into a Wednesday full of swimming off the local dock, I'd all but forgotten my brother's anticipation of Raindance Island …

Back on the boat still trying to dislodge the mess in the propeller, I realized I'd been right about the blade of the filleting knife too. The tip snapped off leaving me little blade left to work with, and in the process of breaking it, I knocked my tackle-box into the lake along with my cell phone. Not that the phone had worked worth a damn on the lake anyway. Though beautiful and cloud free, service remained unwilling to cooperate with my obvious distress. Not wanting to risk getting the phone wet and after numerous futile attempts to call the girls at the cabin, I'd finally stuffed it in one of the many plastic drawers of my tackle-box – one of many terrible decisions I'd made that day.

It wasn't until Jerry suggested I try the broken paddle instead of the filleting knife that I noticed how truly pale my brother had become.

"I don't know if the paddle would do any good," I said disgusted. "Its wrapped in there pretty good."

"From when we hit the–"

"Yeah," I said, interrupting my brother as I studied the mess lodged around the blades of the propeller. My stomach climbed up into my throat as I tried to understand just how we ended up in such a horrible situation in the first place …

I know by Thursday I'd forgotten about the island altogether though I'd not forgotten about going fishing with my brother. In fact, I was chomping at the bit to get out on that beautiful lake after the six of us had dinner at a local restaurant called The Lakeshore Inn. They served the best pickerel I'd ever tasted. Even Andrea, who refused to acknowledge fish was even edible, enjoyed the mouthful I insisted she at least sample. Breaded in a delicious beer batter, it took all my strength not to get in Jerry's boat the moment we arrived back at the cabin.

Jerry was suffering from the same itch that Thursday evening, I could tell. "Saturday is Man-day," he'd said cracking a beer open while our sons set up a game of Monopoly in the screened porch. Moths danced on the screen walls, attracted to the light of an antique lamp as I listened to my brother tell our wives of our plans to spend Saturday fishing. The girls gave us a hard time, but it wasn't long before we realized they were taking great pleasure in pulling our chains.

"You go have fun with your little boat," Jackie had said sarcastically, "while we do our woman work, cleaning and a scrubbing, and a tending to the children ..."

After the kids went to bed, and the wives retired to the living room to watch a movie, Jerry and I reminisced over past fishing trips – finishing off one of two twelve-packs that had been sitting in the fridge. It was good to be with my brother again, and it truly felt just like old times. Thinking back now, I guess I realized for the first time in my thirty-nine years alive that he was not only my brother, but my very best friend as well.

Though both born and bred in Manitoba, my brother had since taken a job in Boulder, Colorado. He worked for a group called Genecore Cryonics, a company that took the money off those who could afford it, and offered them the possibility of immortality, freezing the deceased's body with the anticipation that they might someday be reborn once technology found a way to catch up. This was right up my brother's alley of course – though to meet him, you'd never know the intelligence he hid under the guise of a simple man, who still found farts funny and the last beer in the fridge irresistible.

It had been two years since our families last rendezvoused, and I was happy that night to finally be with him again, only then realizing how much I missed him. The beers flowed freely and our wives appeared willing to give us a distance they suspected we required to reacquaint ourselves – the last time Jerry and I were together was our mother's funeral two years earlier.

Still lying in the boat, Jerry moaned – tearing me from my thoughts. My mind was wandering when I should have been trying to get us out of our mess. I brought a flask of water over to where he still lay in the boat. "Here," I said, lifting his head up as I held it over his dry white lips. "Drink something, you'll feel better."

Jerry let out a cough and water splashed onto my hands. He was no longer able to swallow. I pulled the flask away, frightened by the strange colour of his eyes then gently, I lowered his head back down.

398

I took some electrical tape I'd found earlier while searching for tools I could use to unclog the motor, and taped a fresh towel around Jerry's bite. The bleeding had stopped but I wanted to protect him against any infection, surprised that I could think straight at all after everything that had happened. Not far from the boat a fish jumped – a flash against the sun, before disappearing once again.

The lake itself remained hauntingly peaceful throughout the horrible ordeal and as we drifted along, serine waves licked the hull while I searched the shoreline of distant islands wondering if I could get to one of them using the paddle still available. The question was: what waited on those islands? I'd seen enough on Raindance to change my mind immediately for as they say – once bitten, twice shy. In the distance, a loon cried out, breaking my concentration. I chewed nervously on my bottom lip, debating what I should do and pondered just how much time I had left to do it. The daylight wasn't going to last forever, and I was becoming frustrated.

"It wasn't worth it, Jerry," I finally mumbled to my brother frustrated, but silence answered me and nothing else. For a man who loved to talk, my brother had so little to say now – a far cry from his excitement only days earlier when the fishing trip still seemed like a good idea.

"They have what's called a body farm on the island," Jerry had said Thursday evening when he was still very much alive and well. Midnight soon came to pass while we drank in the screened porch. Jerry turned on a small transistor radio and found a station broadcasting Coast To Coast, a paranormal talk radio program we'd both been fond of over the years.

"What the hell is a body farm?" I'd asked, as host George Noory talked through radio hiss about unidentifiable flying objects spotted above Phoenix years earlier.

"Well, they study the environment's effect on corpses," my brother explained. "At one time, they used dead pigs; they even dressed them up in clothes to make them seem more realistic, more human ... but now they're using actual bodies." He rocked in his chair, balancing on the back legs when he slapped his neck suddenly, bringing the annoying buzz of a mosquito to an abrupt end.

"Who are *they?*" I'd asked, feeling light and inquisitive – a perfect buzz with perfect company. Everybody inside the cabin was fast asleep by then, and we did our best to whisper our slurs.

"The U.S Government," Jerry said.

It seemed odd to me at the time. Why would the U.S government want to study rotting bodies? What more, why did they have to study them up here in Canada? "Where do they get the corpses?" I asked, wondering if my brother was pulling my leg, something he'd taken pleasure in doing on several occasions in the past.

"Where do you think?" he replied getting up. "You want another one?"

I shook my head and finished what was left of my beer then handed him the empty bottle. "I don't understand."

"How do you think I know about the island?" Jerry asked. If he winked, I couldn't see it in the dark, but it seemed an apt way to end his sarcastic question. I looked out on the lake and watched a long thin reflection of the moon as it danced upon drifting waves. I tried to imagine an island out there in all that tranquillity, lined with the bodies of people who'd spent large sums of money under what I could only assume were false pretences. A short clamour was followed by the sound of my brother sliding the patio doors closed. He sat back down next to me and handed me another beer.

"That's highway robbery," I said and then added, "If you aren't full of shit, at least what they're doing is."

"I swear on Mom's grave little brother," he said, twisting the cap of his bottle as he leaned towards me. He whispered, "It's a military operation under the guise of a private corporation." I could smell the beer on his breath as I searched his eyes for sincerity, but like the imaginary wink I was certain had been there only moments earlier, the sincerity had remained hidden in the night. "Think of it like a post-mortem tax donation of sorts."

"Why would the government have to do something out here that they could just as easily find out in a laboratory?" I asked, cracking my beer open.

"You can't recreate Mother Nature's effect on a dead body in a laboratory." Jerry said tapping his fingers on the table. "You have to put them out in the environment."

"Is that why you chose this place for our vacation?"

"Shh," Jerry slurred, "you're going to wake the kids."

I calmed down but the thought remained in my mind. This, my brother could see.

"You don't think Wabigoon is beautiful?" He asked, holding a vague hand out toward the lake in the dark.

"Of course I do but—"

"I won't deny I'm intrigued, but it in no way lessens the fact that it's great to see you and your family again. You can pick our vacation spot next summer, on one condition of course ..."

"What might that be?" I asked as I took a swig from my bottle. Beer ran down my chin onto my shirt.

"There's somewhere for us to go fishing ..."

We spent yesterday lolling around the cabin; our original plans to tour the local goldmine quashed by a rash of intense thunderstorms that all but tore the roof off. Our two families had become one again, and we rode out the storms playing Uno and Mousetrap with the boys – the power remaining out for hours at a time. Jerry continued on, drinking beer like a trooper, but I was too hung over after the late night prior, and chose to cleanse my palette on a bag of pretzels and a six-pack of Orange Crush, much to my brother's chagrin.

'What a pussy', he'd muttered.

At one point during that afternoon, Jerry took me aside and showed me something he made me promise to forget I ever saw. It was the photocopy of a military map he'd brought with him from Boulder. It was a satellite image that looked like something you could get off of Google Earth though he insisted Raindance Island would never appear on such a public search engine, as it was not for schmucks like me to see.

On the black and white map Jerry circled our cabin with a highlighter. He unfolded the paper two more times and pointed at a small island approximately thirty-two miles from the shoreline where we were staying.

"That's a long way to venture," I said

"I got a GPS, don't worry," Jerry insisted. "We'll have to bring an extra container of gas though, just in case ..."

I should have known at that point that Jerry's excitement was an indication there was more to the detour than my brother was letting on. He saw dead bodies all the time at work so why the insistence to see more, especially while on holidays? I considered that perhaps he felt this was somehow a gift to me – a gesture of sorts, two brothers on some kind of *rite of passage*, some Tom Sawyer-like adventure. Maybe if we were thirteen – but now, as both of us flirted with our forties – I was no longer so certain.

It was just last night that we retired early to bed, each of us anticipating what I can only assume were very different outcomes of our fishing trip. Early Saturday morning we awoke to find individual lunches packed by our wives. They'd been left on the shelf in the refrigerator, and under each paper bag lay a drawing in crayon, our kids' renditions of what two fools might look like pretending to be outdoorsmen. Jerry's son Jonathon – the fledgling horror fanatic, drew my brother frantically fighting to get a fish off his hand, little drops of crayon blood dripped from his yellow fingers. Beneath it Jon wrote *'Don't get bit by the piranhas'* in bright green marker. The pictures gave us both a good laugh as we made coffee in the quiet of the cabin. I felt like a kid again, back in St. Norbert Manitoba, where the two of us often woke early as boys to sneak out to the Red River, launching our canoe just as the sun came up, rods and reels – cheapies bought at Canadian Tire – resting in the length of our vessel.

The gentleness of this morning had put my mind at ease, and my paranoia of Jerry's preoccupation with Raindance Island subsided with the arrival of a spectacular sunrise – the taste of coffee still fresh on my tongue. We loaded the boat making sure we had all the essentials: the beer to feed our pleasure, the music to induce our memories, and each other's company to re-establish what had always been, the most influential relationship in all my years alive. I packed my lunch bag into the cooler and closed the lid, placing the picture my son drew in my pocket with the map of our pending journey.

On the way to the boat-launch Jerry explained what he had in mind for the day.

"We'll head out to Raindance Island first, just to take a look. I can't imagine they post any security there. As I said – it's out of the way and doesn't even show up on most maps. Which reminds me, did I bring the map?"

"I got it – good thing I'm here, eh?" I said, pulling it out of my pocket. Jerry switched his satellite radio to a Blues station and we listened to Muddy Waters while I unfolded he map to take a better look. In the top right corner of the page were the words: **Operation Prairie Flood**.

"I brought my camera too, not too often you get to see a body farm. There should be a dock there where we can anchor and take a look around." Jerry said; his eyes remained on the road.

I didn't like the sound of that. "You look around all you like. I'd sooner stay in the boat."

"What are you twelve? Come on little brother, live a little."

I studied the map until we arrived at the boat-launch. Jerry turned off the radio and adjusted his mirrors as he backed the truck down the cement ramp in the early morning light. "That's weird," I said noticing something peculiar on the map. "I think I can make out a couple of tiny boats near the island – they're marked with X's on the bows." I put the map down and leaned my head back, realizing I was in Jerry's line of view. "You sure they don't have any security sitting on that corpse farm? They are military …"

"The satellite takes a new picture every four hours. Someone could have been there dumping bodies off or taking decomposition readings at the time the photo was taken but it's the weekend now, and it's early. Worst case scenario – we see people walking around, we just cruise on by."

"As simple as that, eh?" I said, always amazed at his ability to avoid concern.

"You worry too much," Jerry said, putting the truck into park. He opened the door and as he stepped out onto the cement pad, he smiled. "Live a little bro. There's a container of gas in the back of the truck, you mind grabbing it?"

Jerry made it seem logical at the time. I am a worrier by nature though I have to admit, as we put the boat in the water, I felt no such anxiety. I was in no hurry to see dead bodies certainly, but above that – I was feeling rather excited about the adventure we were embarking on. We would go to the island, Jerry would see what he needed to see, and we could get down to some fishing. Still, looking back I struggle, wondering if there'd been any inkling of instinct that I'd ignored, not that it really mattered anyhow. I suppose what happened – happened. Dwelling on it was becoming a pointless endeavour, no help to me at all. Nothing would change the fact that Jerry – my only brother, was no longer amongst the living.

It happened rather fast actually; one large gasp of air and it was over. Jerry's chest remained extended; his eyes open, his stiff fingers appearing to clutch imaginary weapons. A tear formed in my eye as I glanced down at my watch. Jerry's son and wife would be sitting down to supper with Andrea and Joshua and they'd be wondering where we were. I reached for one of the paddles and found the broken one covered in blood and matted hair. I dropped it and found the good paddle resting beneath Jerry's leg. With a gentle tug, I pulled it from under his body and placed it in the water. Pointlessly, I attempted to paddle in the direction of the cabin, thirty-odd miles away. It was insanity to think I would be able to get us anywhere at all with the limited amount of time I had left, and as my mind continued to race, the boat went nowhere. I dropped the paddle next to my brother's body and placed my hands atop my head utterly defeated. Around me, the lake stretched for miles. I collapsed into the driver's seat of the boat feeling helpless.

The venture to Raindance Island had taken longer than we'd first anticipated. On the map you could not make them out but in order to get to our destination we had to manoeuvre through two separate narrows – one of which took almost an hour, the other just under twenty minutes – but still a setback nonetheless. The cattails were so high, we could not see over them, and if not for the GPS we may never have found our way through the maze of tributaries at all. I doubted now that I could make it back to those narrows before sunset, even if I could get the motor going again – and if by some miracle I did manage to get back there, I'd likely get swallowed by those narrows and lost forever anyway.

It certainly didn't help that the GPS started acting up shortly after we arrived at the island and had not worked properly since. Jerry thought maybe it had been zapped by some kind of military surveillance or anti-radar – I don't quite recall just what he said now – all I did know was that one good paddle did me no good at all. I was stuck, along with my dead brother, in a hellish nightmare I wanted out of desperately.

I eventually concluded I had little choice but to wait out the approaching darkness and try and make it until dawn. Certainly by morning, Andrea and Jackie would have a search team out looking for us, maybe even an airplane. Mind you, we were miles from where we were thought to be fishing, but boats drift ... right? I left my faith in that single notion as a swarm of mosquitoes had their way with me. With every inch the sun dropped below the tree line came a thousand more buzzing attacks. Frustrated, I rifled through my duffel bag until I found some bug spray and coated my skin with it, feeling the sting as it came in contact with my sunburned flesh.

Surveying the horizon one last time I let go with a desperate holler for help and listened to my own pathetic voice echo off the endless water. In the distance a Raven took flight from a tree as I watched, wondering like a child if it was leaving to tell the others of the meal my brother had become for the taking. My eyes fell on Jerry's body and I sat back down as the boat rocked to and fro.

"I don't want to throw you overboard Jerry, but what you said scared the hell out of me. If you're planning on turning into one of them things, do it now. I don't know if I can handle it in the dark."

Jerry did not respond, though his body released a gassy belch to which he showed no sign of embarrassment, nor did he chuckle the way he would have had we still been kids, and he'd still been alive. I covered my nose and made a desperate attempt not to inhale the foul odour as I juggled the few options I had left. I had to get that motor started or I would be in for a long and traumatic night – the odour alone was enough to change my mind.

I stepped over Jerry's body and tilted the outboard back up out of the water, lifting my nostrils disgusted as the decapitated head wrapped between the blades of the propeller snarled at me.

"Hello Dolly ..."

Her good eye focussed on me as I locked the motor in place and found the broken paddle, flipping it around so the jagged wooden edge could be utilized as a spear. Holding my breath, I began poking at the fleshy mess. Her mouth – all teeth but little left of lip still managed to let out a gruesome howl as I jammed the paddle into her cheek, chopping her face ragged but not loosening it in any way that would be advantageous to my situation. As I worked on her I sweated, and as I sweated, the bug spray wore off and the swarm of mosquitoes had its way with me all over again. Wearing on my sanity even more than the annoying hum of the swarm was the glaring eye of the woman; still so very much alive and beautiful. The green iris followed my every move, judging me and sizing me up. Had I the nerve I would have stuck the broken handle right through that eye, but I could not. I concluded that what was left of her could not harm me in any way, for it was nothing more than a crushed and ribbon-cut piece of rotting meat. I found out quickly how wrong I could be.

As I poked the broken paddle against her head one last time, I came into direct contact with bone and felt the pain reverberate up the handle of the paddle into my wrists.

The pain was excruciating and I'd had enough. The eye – the remnant seer of someone's daughter, or mother, or sister ... seemed to enjoy my distress. With a temper saved for madmen, I lost it. I raised my foot up and with one solid kick dislodged the head from between the blades of the propeller nearly slipping into the lake as a consequence of my success. Grabbing onto the edge of the boat sweaty and angry, I regained my composure and watched the mangled head flop into the water and slowly float by, the eye forever gazing back at me like a large insect nesting in a scalp of curly black hair.

The motor was free of human waste. When I'd had enough time to successfully catch my breath, I dropped the outboard back in the water and went to the front of the boat, stepping over my brother's body once again so that I could sit down in the driver's seat. With a shaky hand, I turned the ignition.

Though the outboard struggled and wheezed, the propeller finally coughed up water and the air filled with the odour of fuel as the engine began to hum.

"Success Jerry!" I screamed, looking back at my brother's body – black flies were having their way with him, cleaning their legs, crawling in and out of his nose. The sun was almost gone when I hit the throttle and directed the boat southward, my mind full of bitter regret.

It had been a stupid idea going to Raindance Island and I won't deny that I tried to talk Jerry out of continuing once we'd reached the second narrows earlier that day, but he made it clear how important it was not only for him to see the so-called body farm, but for me to see it too. When he talked about the island it was like he'd become a child again – he was convincing, and I wanted as bad as he did to recapture a little of that feeling again too. I was a willing partner in that fatal misstep and can still recall that fateful moment when everything went wrong ...

"You remember when we were kids and we stayed up to watch Night of The Living Dead on the late night movie?" Jerry had hollered as I watched the narrows disappear into the horizon behind us earlier in the day.

"Sure!" I screamed over the sound of the boat crashing hard against the water. By that point we were on the move again and Jerry was making up for lost time. "It scared the hell out of me," I'd mumbled.

"And you remember that night at the Odeon drive-in when Dad and Ma took us to see Dawn of the Dead – the one with the zombies in the mall?"

"Yeah, it was your birthday present wasn't it?" I asked. We had failed to stay for the second feature because the movie had made me so sick. "Why?"

I don't recall what my brother said after that. I simply remember Jerry easing up on the throttle when I noticed the island of his preoccupation just up ahead.

"Is that it?" I asked. I stood up to get a better look, placing my sunglasses atop my head.

"That's it," Jerry said, letting the boat circle slowly. As we rounded the small island another boat soon came into view. Jerry saw it too and immediately cut the motor in case there was security there after all. Soon, he was squinting under his sunglasses. "Do you see that?"

Atop the bow of the other boat lay what appeared to be a naked body. It didn't take us long to realize it was female. The woman was strapped down, her ankles and legs tied opposite each other forming an X, her blonde hair matted and dry as straw.

"What the hell is that all about?" I asked bewildered.

"Well ... I know they do different experiments with the bodies. Put people in natural type surroundings and all, but it almost looks like she's—"

"Sunbathing," I said, crawling to the other side of the boat to take a better look.

"I'm going to move closer," Jerry said, starting up the engine again. With his free hand he pulled his camera out of his pocket.

"You think that's a good idea?" I asked, no longer interested and feeling suddenly queasy.

Jerry had an odd look on his face. I watched a trickle of sweat roll down his cheek. "We're here now. We may as well take a look."

Jerry inched the boat closer and startled me by calling out to the naked woman who turned her head toward the sound of his voice, her skin dark like leather from too many days in the relentless summer sun. The reflection of the water imprisoned her eyes and I saw a horror I hoped I'd never have to experience again. Orbs of baby blue – almost transparent, gazed back at us. She bared teeth no longer capable of finding shelter beneath lips, for the lips had all but rotted away. The woman was left with a permanent, sadistic grin.

"Why would they tie her up like that?" I asked my brother as the hair stood up on my arms.

On the island, just past an embankment formed by bedrock we soon found out the woman was not alone. In the trees I could see shadows moving, sombre creatures on two legs, dragging their bodies over the rough terrain. Distant howls and grunts reminded me of Mutual of Omaha's Wild Kingdom. It was as though Jerry and I had discovered some strange new tribe existing on one island alone – Raindance Island, hell on earth.

"There are more of them over there – do you see them? They're alive," I said transfixed.

Jerry shook his head. "They're dead," he said soberly, "just like in them movies."

"We should get out of here," I said as I tapped my brother's arm. I tried to shake him from his daze. "Come on, Jerry. We need to go – they're coming."

Jerry was debating – I could see it on his face. He surveyed our surroundings as if to ensure we weren't being watched by anybody that mattered, and then pointed toward the rocky bank where six of the dead began gathering. "They're tied up. If they go into the water, they're gonna drown." He turned his camera on as our boat drifted ever closer.

I looked toward the gathering mob and blocked the sun with my hand. Sure enough, five out of six of them had cinder blocks firmly attached with a chain and a shackle to their ankles. The only one that wasn't shackled had no arms whatsoever. The other five – three men and two women appeared to be in their early twenties to mid forties. One girl in particular stood out because of her Hooters t-shirt and orange short-shorts. One of the men donned a thick green sweater and cargo pants, not summer wear by any means, though it certainly didn't take a fashion designer to dress a rotting corpse.

Dragging the cinder blocks behind them, the walking dead were soon wading in the shallow water when our attention was drawn away from the island. A large clang erupted beneath our boat.

"What was that?" I asked, watching Jerry move cautiously toward the outboard motor. He picked a paddle up and gripped it tightly before hesitantly leaning over the stern of the boat.

"Jesus Christ!" He moaned, backing up.

"What?"

"There's a bunch ..." Jerry said.

I moved toward my brother as the boat rocked back and forth, and tried to maintain my balance as I peered into the clear lake. I was astonished to see a dozen pair of eyes staring back at us from below the waterline. The living corpses were anchored by cinder blocks attached to their ankles and every one of them had their arms extended up toward us, the tips of their fingers jutting out of the water like fleshy aquatic plants, their hair flowing gently to and fro with the mild current. Even submerged and restrained, they wanted nothing more than to get at us.

"I bet they wander out here whenever a boat shows up with new specimens," Jerry said, watching spellbound.

"Why?" I asked.

"Well," Jerry said as a matter of fact, "probably because they're hungry."

That was enough.

"I don't think we should be here Jerry," I said. Several more corpses were approaching the water's edge; some of them struggled up to their waists while another ripped the chain off his ankle altogether, severing his foot in the process. He stumbled over the rocks, the fresh stump throwing him off balance and he finally fell to the ground in a growling heap.

"One more minute," Jerry begged calmly. "I want one more picture."

"No!" I insisted. "I'm done with this crazy shit, let's go."

I meant no harm to Jerry but will admit I was terrified when I chose to sit down in the driver's seat of my brother's boat and turn the ignition switch, coercing the motor back to life. I hit the throttle sending Jerry – who was busy aiming his camera – tumbling over the side of the boat. There my brother dangled, and there our fate took a dark and twisted turn. I turned the ignition back off and went to Jerry, helping him up, but not before one of those anchored bodies managed to take a nasty

410

bite out of his hand. The blood poured out of my brother's wound as he struggled to remain calm.

"I'm sorry Jerry," I insisted, over and over again. He stumbled about the boat, finally finding the towel which he wrapped around the deep wound. His blood coated my clothes as I helped him sit down. When I knew he was safe, I turned the motor on once again, my heart racing, my mind sputtering, the groaning dead playing symphonic havoc on my ears.

A horrible grinding noise filled the air when I hit the throttle and the entire boat jerked forward. The motor struggled until bubbling lake water turned crimson red. Smoke soon followed, and Jerry screamed over the chaos for me to turn the motor off, but I couldn't. Every time I looked over my shoulder I saw the blood pouring down his hand, every time I looked back I saw a dozen more dead bodies stumbling down the rocky embankment, and it wasn't long before I could smell them – their rotting skin, their insides putrefying. I looked up at the sky as the motor struggled – I glanced at the beautiful sun and wondered if I was only dreaming.

The boat went nowhere – we were stuck on something, and the dead were finding their way to the edge of our craft, the water shallow as we drifted closer. In the chaos I watched Jerry – he was using the paddle at the back of the boat, hitting something over and over until finally, I heard a snap. First it was the paddle that let out a sharp crack but then – something else, something far more ... human. The outboard broke free like a tether had been cut and we jerked forward, leaving Raindance Island in our wake.

I turned to see my brother cursing angrily at me but I could not hear him. He pushed me out of the way. I fell against the live-well and watched him struggle to reach for the ignition key. He switched it off and fell into the driver's seat, clutching his bloody hand as the boat came to a subtle drift once again.

"You're gonna fry it," Jerry gasped out of breath. He pulled the towel off the bite and cringed at the wound before crawling over to where I still lay. "You alright?" he asked.

I shook my head and got up glancing back at the island to make sure we were no longer in its grip. Jerry collapsed. I caught him, but he was bigger than me and all I could do was guide him down so that he didn't hurt himself again. In the moments we still had together he told me what to expect should he die and begged me to throw his body into the lake if I had to but I couldn't think about it. It was too much to process, he was telling me survival plots from late night movies, and even though I saw those dead people with my own eyes, I still had trouble believing it could happen to my own brother.

"I'm sorry about this," Jerry said as we drifted on the lake. "Bad idea ... stupid idea ..."

"I'll get us back to shore. We'll get you to a hospital – Dryden is only twenty miles away," I insisted. Jerry shook his head like he agreed, but I think deep down inside he knew of my capabilities. I was his little brother – even at thirty-nine, and in his mind it was still up to him to somehow take care of me.

"Take the filleting knife, and dig that shit out of the propeller ..."

Daylight died along with my sanity when the motor I had worked so hard to get started again chugged a final breath in the fading light of a horrid day. We would not make it back to the narrows because the boat had run out of gas.

In the glow of a full moon, I saw my brother's dead eyes stare back at me and I felt his disappointment. "I forgot to grab the extra fuel Jerry!" I said, laughing sheepishly. "You told me to grab it, but I forgot. What a pair we make, eh?"

I began to sob. I pulled my son's drawing out of my pocket and looked at it, hoping to calm my nerves. He'd drawn me standing in the boat with my arms out celebrating. Next to me was the crayon recreation of his Uncle Jerry, with his arms extended as he held up a large brown fish. I smiled, swallowing my emotion. When I glanced back up I realized Jerry was crawling toward me, emitting a low growl from the back of his throat. I stood up, dropping Joshua's picture into the water.

"Jerry?"

My brother reached for me, his thick fingers seeking my throat. He opened his mouth and released a snarl that came with an odour of death.

I fought with Jerry – I didn't want to, but I had little choice. I fought him and I begged him to remember who he once was as we struggled. In the ascending moonlight, his dead eyes failed to sparkle, and as I pushed him away from me he fell down, giving me enough time to grab the broken paddle. I used it on him the way I'd used it on the decapitated head that had rendered our outboard useless. I jabbed the jagged wooden handle into his body but it did little to stop him. He wrapped his hands around my leg and sank his teeth deep into my calf. I let out a mind-bending scream as I felt my leg muscle separate from my bone. I fell on top of Jerry and felt the warmth of my own blood as it pooled inside my sneaker. I closed my eyes against the pain and my mind faded in and out.

With what little strength I could gather, I pulled myself up to the front of the boat and crawled out onto the bow, separating my brother and myself with the windshield. I tried to stop the flow of blood from my wound, clenching my leg in desperation, when I was startled to hear the sound of a motorboat approaching.

Jerry struggled to find a way over the windshield as I balanced my weight atop the front of the boat while suddenly feeling terribly dizzy. With what little strength I had left I screamed out to the strangers for help.

A searchlight soon lit the area, and I waved toward it, feeling weak. I was so very thankful they'd come. Then I heard the first shot ring out. In my daze I heard Jerry's body drop out of the boat, and a second shot followed immediately. Cold lake water splashed on my lips and I savoured it, my throat so dry. I lay on my back, no longer able to feel my wounded leg as I overheard voices, military and formal.

"Two males, one deceased – one infected."

"Copy that."

I felt a shackle go around my left ankle and my wrists were cuffed. I asked them who they were as I drifted in and out, but nobody answered me. Above me the sky filled with millions of stars and I gazed at them for what seemed like hours as they towed Jerry's boat back to shore. I debated what I would say when I saw Jerry's wife, Jackie, and their little boy, Jon. Then I remembered that I'd been bitten too.

Perhaps I'd only been dreaming after all . . .

413

I awoke to sunshine. I could hear birds chirping, and could see trees dancing in the heavy wind, but my mind wasn't right. I was not thinking straight and my thoughts were strangely jumbled.

Confused, I glanced over to see someone strangely familiar. The naked dead girl stared back at me from the boat where she remained chained, just as I was now. Chained and naked, my body formed an X on the bow of Jerry's boat.

I struggle to move, but cannot.

In my confusion, I look over to the shoreline of a familiar island and see Jerry.

Jerry?

Jerry is lying on the rocks.

The others ...

The dead are eating his corpse.

Damn you, Jerry ...

Damn you for everything.

I want to hurt him so badly ...

He let me down, for he's over there with them, and I'm tied up ...

I'm chained up ... over here, on the boat.

 I want to eat too ...

I want to eat my brother ...

You let me down, big brother. You let me down when I need you most.

THE END

THE FOUR OF JULY
By
Shawn M Riddle

I wake with a jolt, dreaming of being lowered steadily into a thumping cement mixer. As I struggle back to the waking world, I realize that the sound isn't only in my dream; it's resonating throughout the whole cabin. Damn! Those helicopters again. They've been flying around here at all hours of the day and night for the past two days. Helicopters in Washington D.C. were common enough, but not all the way out here.

"I'm gonna find those flyboys and tear 'em a new one," grumbles Jack as he sits up in his cot and rubs his eyes.

"I don't know man. Something doesn't seem right," I say.

"We're in the middle of the Shenandoah Mountains, for Christ's sake! I expect this kind of crap at home, but I came out here to get some peace and quiet!" Jack's voice gets louder with every word.

"I don't know which is louder; you two or the damn helicopters! Will you shut the hell up? I'm trying to sleep over here!" Mike yells from his bed.

"This is starting to freak me out a bit," I say. "Maybe there's something wrong."

"We can ask at a gas station on the way back, if you like," Jack says with a shrug.

Since there's no cell phone reception out here, and the local radio stations aren't much better, it's about our only option. I nod in his direction.

"Why are you worrying about a few helicopters anyway? They're probably just on an exercise or something," Mike says.

"Well thanks to those damn choppers, we're already up, so we might as well get goin'," I say. "Let's get something to eat and pack up."

Jack and Mike mutter a few unhappy remarks, but finally get out of bed. We get the coffee pot going and load the car. We finish up, lock the cabin and head down the road. After an hour or so of hairpin turns and narrow mountain roads, we finally turn

415

onto the paved road that leads to the Interstate. Jack turns on the satellite radio. The speakers remain silent.

"Did you pay your bill this month, Einstein?" Jack asks me with a smirk.

"Yeah, I did. It should be working. Try the regular radio."

He switches the receiver to AM/FM and thumbs through about a dozen stations; nothing but a soft hiss. I lean back in my seat and light up a cigarette. I must be looking grim because Jack turns around and tells me, "You worry too much, man. It's probably just the antenna. I'll check it when we get to the gas station." Deciding that Jack is probably right, I hand him my MP3 player and he kills the quiet with some music.

There are no cars on the road, but that's not unusual for this remote area. Along the way, we pass a couple of people walking in the road, staggering back and forth. One of them is limping. "Looks like they've started nipping at the Kentucky sipping medicine a little early today," Jack chuckles as we pass them by.

We reach the gas station and hope to pick up a snack and fill the tank, as well as hopefully get a few answers. The lights aren't on inside and neither is the electronic display on the pump.

"Well, this sucks," Mike says as we get out. "Ten thirty in the morning and the place is still closed? What the hell's up with that?"

"Closed or not, I gotta take a leak," says Jack.

Jack walks around the side of the station toward the restroom. When he turns the corner, he stops.

"Hey man, what's up?" I ask. "Didn't make it to the can? Should we bring you some dry clothes?"

Mike and I chuckle, but instead of the expected sarcastic remark, Jack says nothing and still doesn't move. We start to walk over to him. Before we reach him, an acrid stench catches in our nostrils. Mike turns his head and retches and I gag and swallow back bile. With eyes watering, Mike and I turn the corner of the building and see what's rendered Jack speechless.

A few feet from the restroom entrance, a man is sprawled on the ground, his skull split wide open, pinkish gray remains of

416

his brain smeared on the sidewalk. On the wall, next to the body, there is a reddish brown stain. Maggots are crawling over the rotting flesh of his skull.

"Holy shit!" I gasp.

Mike gapes at the corpse. "What the hell?"

Jack's face is deathly white. He turns around, falls to his knees and throws up. I struggle to contain the contents of my stomach. Covering my nose and turning my head, I take a few deep breaths to compose myself.

"You OK, bud?" I manage to ask, as Jack regains some composure. He slowly nods his head, but says nothing. I help him to his feet.

"I'm OK, man," he says finally.

Mike pulls out his cell and stares at the display. "No Service. Hey, either of you got a signal?" he asks as he flips his phone closed.

Jack and I check our phones. "No dice," I say as Jack shakes his head.

"Well, let's not just stand here with our dicks in our hands. Let's get inside and call the cops," says Mike.

"What if the guy who did this is still here?" I ask, glancing around nervously.

Mike turns and heads towards the shop. "You gotta be pretty stupid to hang around after doing something like this." Jack and Mike, despite being the best friends a guy could have, can be impulsive and reckless at times. As if to prove this point, Jack follows Mike without a word.

"At least keep your eyes open, guys," I say as I hurry to catch up.

The shop is unlocked and the interior has been trashed. Packages of candy, chips and cans litter the floor. I go behind the counter and pick up the phone. It's dead.

I take a long look at the mess. "What the fuck is going on?" I ask. Neither one of them say a word.

I light up a cigarette and inhale deeply. Mike follows suit.

"Hey man, hand one over," Jack says.

"I thought you quit?" Mike asks.

"Just give me a damn cigarette!"

417

I toss Jack my pack and lighter. He lights up and inhales half the cigarette in one drag.

"What do you think happened?" I ask finally.

"Who gives a shit?" says Mike. Motioning in the direction of the corpse, he says, "All I know is someone popped that guy's head like a zit and we need to get the hell out of here!"

"You're right," I say. "Let's just go."

Before we get to the front door, Jack says, "First things first. Hold up." He heads to the cooler in the back and opens it. Pulling out a twelve-pack of beer, he frowns and then says, "Well, warm beer is better than no beer!" He opens up a bottle and downs it in seconds.

"What are you doing?" Mike asks, incredulous. "Isn't this is a fucking crime scene?"

After belching, Jack says, "Do you think the cops are gonna give a shit about a twelve-pack of beer? Are they gonna come in and take inventory? No, they're gonna walk straight over to dead Fred or whatever the hell his name is, stick a meat thermometer in his ass and vacuum up what's left of his brains."

Mike and I glance at one another then, despite the situation, we start chuckling and it doesn't take long before we're out right laughing.

"Fair point," I say and head for the door.

As I open the door, something grabs me by the arm and pulls me toward it. I stare into my attacker's face and nearly piss myself. The thing looks like a man, with pale greenish, bloodshot eyes, but half of the left side of its head has been torn away; its left eye bulging from its socket and dripping with thick yellow pus. The bones of its jaw protrude through the torn skin. It moans as it tackles me to the ground, opens its mouth and lunges forward. I lash out, yelling, "Get this fucking thing off me man!"

Mike kicks the creature in the head, sending it reeling across the floor. It stands up as I scramble away. Jack stares into its rotting face, his eyes wide with shock. Mike is fixed to the spot, staring in horror.

It begins to move toward him. Jack reacts first. He punches the thing in what's left of its face, knocking it back to the ground. Breaking the empty beer bottle against the wall, he jumps on its chest and jabs it straight down into its left eye. Thick yellow-brown fluid shoots out the top of the bottle, splattering his shirt. It twitches, and then lays motionless.

Mike helps me up. I stand there, shaking, staring open mouthed at the bloody corpse on the ground. My heart is pounding in my chest; every beat sounds like an earthquake. I'm sick to my stomach, sweat pouring off me. My friends look first at me, then at the body on the ground.

"Thanks, guys." Neither respond, just nod numbly. They're dazed, almost like they're moving in slow motion.

"What the blue fuck is going on?" Jack asks. "We're in the middle of a bad horror movie! That thing was a zom—"

"Don't even say it," Mike interrupts. "We all know what that thing was."

"We have to go. Now! Maybe we can find some help." Jack looks around and walks over to the service island to grab a few paper towels. After wiping some of the blood and pus from his shirt, he comes over to me and puts his hand on my shoulder. "Come on man. Let's get out of here."

A moan sounds from across the road. One of those things is running from the rear of a house, heading right for us. Its moan becomes an ecstatic howl.

"Get in the fuckin' car!" Mike yells.

As we race away from the station, tyres squealing, I look out the rear window and see the creature chasing the car. It falls behind quickly and then disappears out of sight.

Mike lights up another cigarette and, offering me one, says, "You gonna be OK, bud?"

"Yeah." I take a cigarette from him, my hand trembling slightly.

"I don't know about you two, but I need to get to my parents' house and check on them. I hope they're OK," Jack mutters, staring ahead.

"Me too," says Mike.

My family is Jack, Mike, and Jack's parents. I've known these guys since grade school. They're the closest things I have to brothers. Jack's parents sort of adopted me after my parents died. I spend holidays, weekends, and most of my spare time with

419

them. I'm just as worried about them as he is. If something's happened to them while we've been off screwing around in the mountains, I don't know if I could deal with it.

We drive for a long time. As we reach the outskirts of civilization, we see other vehicles, broken down and abandoned. At first there's only one or two, but then more and more clog the roadside. On the other side of the highway, we see another vehicle heading our way. It shoots by at high speed. Several more pass us before we merge onto Interstate 66, east bound towards Washington D.C., and home.

We all live in Rosslyn, just outside D.C. proper. We see signs of further carnage as we drive. Burning vehicles and numerous bodies litter the highway. Many appear to have been torn to shreds. Jack has to swerve several times to miss creatures that are wandering in the road. Some chase after us as we pass them, but most of them continue to stagger aimlessly.

"What do you suppose started this shit in the first place?" Mike asks the question we have all been wondering.

"Don't know and don't care right now," Jack says. "What I do care about is finding some gas for this heap before we end up walkin'. From what we've seen so far …" Jack pauses and points to one of the creatures stumbling in the road, "walkin' ain't exactly my preferred choice and we're damn near empty."

"We also need to start thinking about where we are gonna get supplies too," Mike adds. Jack and I nod in agreement.

Jack takes another look at the gas gauge. "Keep your eyes open, and let me know if you see anyplace we can stop."

A little further down the road, just outside the City of Manassas, we come to a rest area and coast into the parking lot, out of gas. Two other vehicles are here, one SUV and a large van with the markings of the Virginia State Police on the side.

The SUV's driver's side window is smashed; the half eaten corpse of a woman hanging out the door. Bite marks cover her torso and arms, and her severed head is lying on the ground a few feet from the vehicle, cheeks and eyes gouged away. The van appears to be intact, with the exception of one flat tyre.

The rest stop is a small single level building, with two separated sections for public restrooms and a lobby in between.

420

There's a small picnic area and a pet rest area at the side of the structure. Scanning the area, we see no signs of life or movement. Dismembered bodies are littered everywhere.

"Fuck me," Jack says as he takes in the scene. "It's a war zone."

A man, – or what used to be one, – staggers out from behind the building near the pet rest area. Its left arm is missing from the elbow and its torn business suit is covered in blood and gore.

"Shut up and get down," I whisper, pointing to the creature. We kneel down behind the car, out of the creature's line of sight. We and wait for a few minutes. The creature shambles on aimlessly.

Jack scans the area. "We can't sit out here all day, man. There's got to be more of those things creeping around."

"Well, we can't just walk by that thing," I say.

"I've got a plan." Mike leans into the open door of the car and takes out a long metal flashlight. "I'm gonna go around the other side of the building, sneak up behind that thing and crown its ass."

"Are you on drugs?" I ask him. "What if there are more of those things around back? They'll rip you to pieces!"

"What choice do we have?" Mike replies fiercely.

Jack and I look at one another and then nod to Mike. I don't like the idea at all, but it's all we've got. He is small and fast, so he has the best chance of the three of us.

He inches around the side of the car and takes a peek. The creature is standing motionless in the pet rest area, looking in the opposite direction. He takes his chance and darts around the side of the building and out of sight.

Several tense minutes pass before I see Mike appear around the other side. He crouches low and creeps up behind the creature. It seems oblivious. Once close enough, he swings the flashlight over his head and brings it down onto the back of the thing's skull. Blood spurts upwards and it falls to the ground with barely a sound. He jogs back with a big smile on his face. "Fucker never saw it coming."

421

"Don't bust your arm patting yourself on the back man," Jack says, but manages a smile.

We head for the building, stepping over bodies along the way. We see dozens of empty bullet and shotgun casings amongst the dead. I reach the front door first; it's locked and chained from the inside.

"Stop right there and put your hands up!"

Looking up, I see a woman on the roof with a machine gun pointing at us.

"Hold it lady, we're not armed! We just want to get inside," I say, putting my hands in the air.

"Are you bitten?" she asks.

Jack looks to me and Mike then to the woman on the roof. "What?"

"Are you bitten?" she snaps.

"No," Jack says. "We're not! Will you put that thing down before someone gets hurt?"

She stares at us down the barrel of her weapon. "I give the orders here. If you want in, you're gonna have to strip!"

"What the hell are you talking about?" I ask.

"Strip, now, or get the hell out of here!" As if to emphasize her point, she pulls back the charging handle of her weapon, chambering a round with a series of dry clicks.

We strip fast. We're standing there naked, in front of a rest stop off Interstate 66. Under different circumstances it would all seem pretty funny. "Turn around nice and slow; now!"

After we've turned a full circle, her tone more relaxed, she says, "OK, put 'em back on and get over to the front door. I'm coming down." We nod, getting dressed even faster than we stripped."

A short time later, she appears at the door, wearing the uniform of the Virginia State Police. She fumbles with her keys, unlocks the chains and gestures at us to come in. Keeping her eyes on us, she chains the door once more.

"Look, lady, if you wanted a date, there are certainly better ways to ask than that," Jack says with a smirk. Leave it to Jack to make a smart ass remark to someone who just threatened to shoot us.

422

She ignores his comment. "I'm sorry. You can't be too careful; I let some folks in here a few days after I got here and one of them had been bitten. In a couple of hours, she turned and chewed up her family and two of my men before I put the bitch down. You three are the first living people I've seen since then. My name is Sergeant Diana Ortiz."

After somewhat shell-shocked introductions, she leads us into an office and hands us some bottled water. A table in the centre of the room is cluttered with a variety of shotguns, pistols and ammunition.

"That's a nice piece!" I say, gesturing to the machine gun in her hands. "I didn't know cops were allowed to carry those."

"I'm a trooper; it took me a lot of hard work to earn this uniform." She scowled at us to emphasize the point then added, "It's an MGA MK46LE SAW; very useful as an attitude adjuster. We had a few back at the barracks. They're issued on a limited basis – crisis situations, terrorist attacks, that sort of thing."

"OK, sorry," I say. "Can you please tell us what the hell is going on?"

"Where the hell have you three been?" Sgt. Ortiz gapes at the three of us in astonishment.

"For the last three weeks we've been out at Jack's cabin." I gesture with my thumb toward Jack. "Out Shenandoah way. We went up there for the Fourth of July weekend ... and our yearly vacation. We heard helicopters flying around the past couple days, but besides that, we don't know a damn thing about what's going on. We come down from the cabin this morning and find the world has gone to hell."

Sgt. Ortiz nods at this and says, "About two weeks ago we started getting calls in like you wouldn't believe. Out of the blue, we were getting hundreds of them an hour. It gets busy at times, but never like that. Murders, attacks, looting, you name it. When people started describing the attacks, we thought we weren't hearing things right, thought maybe they meant dog attacks, an outbreak of rabies or something."

"Dog attacks?" Mike asks.

She takes a drink from her water bottle. "Yeah, we kept hearing about people being bitten. But it didn't take long to figure out it wasn't dogs doing the biting."

"Jesus Christ," Mike mutters, shaking his head.

"He has nothing to do with it. Within hours, all the law enforcement agencies in the Washington D.C. area were completely overwhelmed and simply couldn't respond to every call. It spread so quickly, there wasn't even time for the National Guard to be properly mobilized. A few units here and there were rumoured to have gotten moving, but we never saw any kind of help from them."

"Did anyone have any clue what was causing these things to walk around?" Mike asks.

"The same bullshit you always hear on the radio and TV, people talking like they knew what was going on, but no one had a fucking clue. After I lost my partner on a call, I decided not to ask any more questions. Before long I couldn't raise anyone on the radio anymore to ask. All the channels had gone dead. The few times I was actually able to raise someone; they were just as clueless as everyone else. Some were begging for help that I was no longer in a position to give. What's the point of knowing why or what anyway? The only thing we can do is deal with it! Those things have taken enough, they're not gonna take any more away from me!" She gestures to the table next to us, pointing out the small collection of guns and giving a curt nod.

"What happened to your partner?" Jack asks.

Sgt. Ortiz takes another drink from her water bottle, brushes her hair away from her eyes, and continues. "I was on duty in the Fairfax area with my partner. The call came through as a domestic dispute. We normally don't answer calls to residences, but the shit was hitting the fan and the local cops needed our assistance. When we arrived at the house, the lights were off and the curtains drawn. Knocking on the front door didn't elicit any response. My partner David and I kicked in the front door and went in. What we found there ..." She trailed off, her eyes glistening brightly.

I pull out my water bottle and say, "Maybe something to drink?"

424

She takes it. "Thanks."

Jack grabs a cigarette from the pack I had left on the table and lights up. "So you just walk up to the house and kick in the door? Not too bright if you ask me with those things running around."

"At that point we didn't know those things were the cause of this shit! Perhaps I wasn't clear on that point. Can I continue now?" Sgt. Ortiz snaps.

"Sorry," Jack says, looking as if he has just been slapped in the face.

"We saw the woman of the house – neighbours said her name was Wilma Simmons – dead on the kitchen floor. No, not dead, worse than dead. When I looked at her I thought she'd been torn apart by a wild animal. Blood was still oozing from her wounds, she hadn't been dead long. Nothing left of her face – it had been bitten ... ripped off. Blood was everywhere. Then like that," she snaps her fingers," a loud crash and David was screaming. I turned around and saw a man on top of him. It must have been Mr. Simmons; he had his mouth around David's throat and was tearing at him like a wild dog. When he pulled away ... well a mouthful of blood and David was dead. I shot the fucker in the chest. He jerked but he didn't fall. Then he ran right at me. I shot him right between the eyes, which put him down for good."

"Talk about fucked up!" I say.

She ignores me and continues. "I didn't even have time to take more than a couple breaths, and then the old lady ... just got up off the floor and came at me. I never thought an old lady could move that damn fast! I shot the bitch in the head before she got too far. I looked over at David lying on the floor. His eyes were wide open, blood still oozing from his neck. I checked for a pulse, I got nothing. Then he started to stir; I stood up and put my foot on his chest to keep him down. He began to moan and thrash, jaws snapping at the air, trying desperately to bite me. His eyes were a milky greenish colour, all bloodshot and cloudy ... I put a round in his head, there was nothing else I could have done. I'd known David Brown for ten years, and I put him down like a rabid dog." Tears roll from her eyes.

"I … I'm really sorry," Mike says, putting his hand on her shoulder.

She shrugs off Mike's hand. "It's done, and I can't change what happened." She wipes the tears from her face and takes another drink. "Shortly after that is when things just went to shit. Buildings were burning out of control, people in the streets with guns, shooting those things and each other. All order broke down, it was anarchy. I came back to my barracks and loaded up the van with as many guns and men as I could. I lost five men in the few hours after we left, two were torn apart by those things, and the other three were killed in a shootout with some looters. The whole world was coming to an end and these motherfuckers were out looting DVD players and shooting people? When it's all said and done, people will never change. It makes me sick. There were only three of us left when I decided to get us the hell out of the war zone. The situation had escalated far beyond anyone's ability to control. We heard reports on the radio of several local towns completely engulfed in flames. Other reports stated that the President had ordered non nuclear bombing runs on major cities. We were driving on Route 66 West, trying to get as far away from D.C. as we could when we saw a formation of bombers in the air, headed for D.C. It didn't take long for the city to be reduced to a steaming pile of rubble. The explosions and flames were incredible. Did it do anything but kill thousands of people? No, those things are still everywhere. What a waste."

I feel as if someone has just hit me in the chest with a sledgehammer. I stare at my friends and a look of absolute horror is etched on both of their faces.

"D.C. is gone? No … I don't believe … Mom? Dad? No! I've got to find them!" Jack shoots out of his chair. Sgt. Ortiz gets up, firmly puts her hands on Jacks' shoulders and forces him back into his chair. She brings her face up to his, so they're staring nose to nose. Speaking very clearly and firmly, as if to a child, she says, "I'm telling you … D.C. is gone, there's nothing left. All you're likely to find are those creatures." Jack begins to sob, slamming his head on the table.

Mike's eyes are wide with shock. He slams a fist down on the table. "I don't believe this shit!" I put my hand on Jack's shoulder, trying to offer him comfort; I do the same for Mike. I feel a burning hatred welling inside me. These creatures, they've taken everything from us, I want to kill every last one of them with my bare hands!

After a few long minutes of silent sobbing, Mike wipes tears from his eyes and looks at Sgt. Ortiz. "Excuse me offi–"

"Trooper," she corrects.

"Sorry, there's something bugging me about those things," Mike says.

Jack lifts his head from the table and glares at Mike, "You mean besides the fact our families are most likely dead because of those motherfuckers?" His eyes are filled with a rage you only see in movies.

"As I was saying," Mike continues, a little stunned. "The thing that kind of bothers me here is the one that attacked him." He pauses and gestures to me. "It didn't move very fast, but the other one we ran into at the gas station moved faster than a redneck seeing a 'free beer' sign. If these things are dead, they shouldn't be walking at all, but since they can obviously walk, shouldn't they be stumbling around, you know rigor mortis making them all stiff or something?"

"Didn't move all that fast? Try being at the receiving end of that bear hug and tell me it didn't move fast!" I snap.

Sgt. Ortiz puts up her hand. "From what I've seen and heard in the initial reports, the 'fresher' they are, the better they seem to be able to function. I've seen people get up and run, climb ladders, jump over barriers, and even use some basic fighting skills just seconds after they were killed. The ones that are a little older move pretty slowly, with no real co-ordination. You can almost walk past them. So it's the fresh ones you have really to worry more about. I wouldn't want to get caught with my pants down in even a small group of the slow ones though. I don't really know how long it takes for them to slow down, probably a few days or so."

His voice still rather weak, Jack looks at us and says, "I think it's time we all thought about what the hell we're gonna to do. We still need supplies and we sure as hell can't stay here forever."

I nod. "Man's got a point."

Just then I hear a 'whoop whoop' noise in the distance that can't be mistaken; a helicopter. "You hear that?" I ask.

Sgt. Ortiz bolts from her chair and yells at all of us to follow her to the roof. She runs out of the room and down the hallway that leads to the roof hatch. We follow her as quickly as we can. We climb the ladder and open the hatch to the roof. "There!" Sgt. Ortiz points to the helicopter. It's swaying back and forth and I see smoke coming out the back.

"Oh man, they're fucked," Mike says. Another larger puff of smoke erupts from the passenger compartment and flames become visible. It auto rotates to the ground about a quarter mile from the rest stop. We watch as it circles around and around, trying to keep some measure of control in its descent. It hits the ground hard, landing on its runners just on our side of the highway, near the edge of the woods fifty yards or so from the rest stop. Two people jump out before the chopper explodes, sending shards of metal and debris everywhere. We duck down behind the parapet wall for cover. The sound of the explosion is almost deafening.

The people who escaped from the chopper are on the ground, not too far from the building. They're barely moving. "They need our help! I'm going out there!" Sgt. Ortiz snaps.

"Me too," Jack and Mike say simultaneously. I hesitate for a moment, frozen with fear. I've spotted dozens of those things coming out of the tree line — about a hundred yards or so from the downed chopper.

"Holy shit! Look at all of 'em!" Jack yells.

"Downstairs in the office, there's more guns. Get down there, grab something to fight with and let's get out to those men before those fuckers do!" Sgt. Ortiz commands.

"Come on man, these guys need our help!" Mike shouts to me as he heads down the ladder.

I slide down the ladder and run to the office. I grab a 12 gauge shotgun, as many shells as I can manage to stick in my pockets and a 9mm pistol from the table. Jack and Mike grab some shotguns and pistols as well. Sgt. Ortiz holsters her pistol, grabs her SAW and leads us to the front door. After she unchains the door, we run as fast as we can toward the crash site and the injured people. It's an Army chopper; the men who made it out are wearing digital camouflage fatigues. They're on the ground, blood covering their uniforms. We bolt into the field as fast as we can, but it's too late. We hear the men scream as the things reach them first, tearing them to pieces. There's nothing we can do. Several creatures notice us and start to run toward us.

"Move it! Get your asses back inside!" Jack screams. The four of us turn and run towards the rest stop. Twenty more of the creatures have appeared as if out of nowhere, blocking our retreat. They're runners, explains how they closed the gap so quickly. Sgt. Ortiz opens fire. She cuts the first few of the things down in mid stride. The chatter of her SAW is deafening enough; the addition of our three shotguns in the mix makes my ears scream. The blasts keeps coming and coming. The creatures in front of us are falling – blood, bone, tissue, and every type of matter possible in the human body are being ripped apart by the hail of bullets and buckshot.

Once the last of the runners are down, we continue back to the building. "They're down, let's go!" Sgt. Ortiz yells to us. I'm surprised that I can hear anything at all with the ringing in my ears.

Before we get to the front door of the building several of the runners come around the opposite side of the building and grab Mike who's a few feet behind the rest of us. We hear him scream; all of us turn around at the same time. They have him down on the ground, sharp broken teeth sinking into his limbs and torso. He screams again and again as he lashes out, trying to fight them off.

Jack shoots two of them, but it's too late to save him. As Mike is being torn apart, I raise my pistol and shoot my friend in the head – his screaming brought to a sudden, brutal stop.

We enter the building and chain the doors behind us, barely making it inside ahead of the creatures. Looking through the glass doors, we see the area is now teeming with them. Some of them are the runners, but many of the ones that move slowly, making their way methodically toward the building, and us. They're everywhere, the sound of the crash and resulting explosion must have brought them.

I begin to panic. "Those things killed Mike! They're everywhere! We're fucked! There's no way out of here!" My vision flashes white and I feel a white hot sting on the side of my head as Jack slaps me hard across the face. I fall to my knees, stunned and sobbing.

"Get yourself together man! There's nothing we could have done for him. We have to stay cool!" Jack growls at me. Shocked, but gathering my senses, I rub my throbbing cheek and jaw, stand up and nod silently.

There's loud banging on the service entrance door in the back. More of the creatures have made their way behind the building. Sgt. Ortiz rushes towards the noise and yells, "Cover the front!" The back door begins to shake and buckle under the onslaught of the creatures.

After reloading, Jack and I look to the front and see twenty or thirty creatures pounding on the safety glass, desperate to claw their way in. Bloody handprints stain the glass. A loud crash signals the demise of the back door. Sgt. Ortiz's SAW begins to chatter. Another crash and the creatures break the safety glass and start surging into the lobby. Jack and I dive behind the information desks. We raise our shotguns and start shooting. A heady cocktail of rage and terror are burning through my veins; hate for these things, these murderous God damn things. I bellow and scream as the blasts tear apart the rotting corpses.

As I glance at Jack, his shotgun clicks empty. He raises it like a club and runs at the remaining creatures.

"You pus-brained motherfuckers! You want some, come and get it!" Jack screams as he charges them. He hits one in the side of the head, shattering its skull. He continues to wade into them as I fire into the crowd. Still hearing the chatter of the SAW in the back of the building, we continue to fight. One creature manages to get behind Jack and grabs him.

I aim at it and pull the trigger, but instead of a recoil, I hear a dry click. It sinks its teeth into Jack, tearing a chunk of

430

flesh from his arm. Howling, Jack discards the shotgun and lifts the creature off the ground. As it snaps at him, he twists it and slams it head first into the ground with a sickening crunch.

An arm tears away from its socket in his powerful grip and he uses it as a club; adrenaline lending him extra strength. He uses his improvised meat club and beats several others back before he's overwhelmed by them; they take him to the ground. As the things rip him apart, he yells "Hope you choke on it you fucks!" They tear him to pieces in front of my eyes. It takes less than ten seconds.

Screaming, I take out the remaining creatures near me using the butt of my shotgun, crushing skulls. The ones who have just murdered my friend get extra treatment, smashing their heads into mush. I turn to face another one; it lunges at me and sinks its teeth into my throat. I manage to throw it off and cave in its rotting skull with one final swing. I fall to the ground, choking on the blood pouring from my neck and into what's left of my throat. As the world begins to blur, I hear pistol shots coming from the back of the building. My final thoughts before all goes dark are of my friends ...

Blackness ...

I feel ... Strong ... powerful. I don't hurt.

I hear loud noises close by ... *What are they?*

My eyelids feel like lead, but I force them open.

Where am I? How did I get here?

I look around and see someone at the back of the building. Loud noises and screams are coming from her.

She looks familiar ... but ... I can't ... remember ...

She's holding something in her hand ... a gun ... she's shooting the others.

Rage ... searing, blinding rage ... and hunger, a burning, uncontrollable hunger. What's happening to me?

I stand up and run toward the woman in the room. She doesn't see me, her back is turned. All I can think about is this woman's flesh. *So alive, so warm. I want to rip it from her body, tear her to pieces ... hungry ... this hunger's unbearable! I must have her!* I'm so close, I can smell her, even taste her in the pungent air. She turns

431

around, raising her pistol. I see a flash of bright white light and the sound of thunder roars through my head ...

THE END

WHERE MOTH AND RUST DESTROY
By
Thomas Emson

Mya dreamed of her zombie father coming down the stairs to eat her.

In her dream she was six. Six like she'd been when the temperatures soared and the dead came alive to eat the living. Six like she was twenty-one years ago when her mum and a stranger named Sawyer came home just in time to save her from her zombie father.

But in her dream no one came. In her dream Mya's dad attacked and killed her. In her dream she was dead and then her eyes snapped open.

And she woke up.

"Nice nap?" said Zimmer.

She blinked, her eyes adjusting to the bright, brilliant sun.

"Lovely, thanks," she said. "Are we nearly there?"

"Nearly," said Zimmer.

"How far?"

He glanced at the HGV's dashboard. "Another hour, I'd say."

She drank water from the canteen and grimaced.

"You shouldn't leave the canteen out in the heat," she said. "Put it in the ice box, Zimmer."

"You giving me orders, now?"

"I'm just saying."

His face reddened. "I'm driver, you're escort. No way you tell me—"

"Okay, I get it."

Anything for a quiet life, she thought. Anything not to draw attention to herself. But Zimmer wasn't done.

"No way," he said, "you tell me what to do. No idea how you ran things up north, darling, but down here –"

"I get it, Zimmer."

They lapsed into silence. She tried not to think about things too much. She fixed on the grey and empty road. It had once been called the M20. Along its verges lay the rusting hulks

433

of army vehicles. Military Land Rovers and armoured personnel carriers ditched by soldiers. Even the charred wreck of a helicopter. All were remnants of the war against the zombies. A war humans had lost.

Zimmer drove past what had once been a tank. It triggered a memory in Mya. Twenty-one years ago, with her mother and Sawyer, Mya had fled a zombie-plagued London. They had driven out of the city and found an abandoned tank in the middle of the motorway. Surrounding it were the remains of soldiers, killed by the undead. Eaten to death. Like most of the population had been eaten to death.

Now as Zimmer drove, Mya scanned the road. A cluster of zombies were gathered up on the ridge. They were squatting over a pile of meat, clawing at it, scooping it into their mouths, their faces red with blood. It was probably human meat. Some poor sod stranded on the highway perhaps, hijacked as he or she made their way somewhere. Two decades after the dead had risen, the living were still trying to flee. In this new world of the dead, you were either food, breeder, or worker. You had to be. But some people tried to escape it. And they ended up like that poor sod on the ridge.

Zimmer said, "You're a pretty thing, it's a wonder you've not been hauled in for the breeding programme."

Her skin crawled. "I'm infertile."

"Right. They didn't just make you food, then? That's what they normally do, ain't it. If you ain't got a skill, I mean. If you ain't no use to them. At least you're of some use as food."

"Well, I've got a skill."

"Oh yeah."

"Yeah, Zimmer – I'm willing to die for my fellow humans." She smiled at him. He gawped, losing control of the truck for a second. The HGV swerved across the motorway. "Careful, Zimmer," she said. "I never said I'd die for you, mate."

"Hey, that's a joke ain't it? Yeah? You're joking. What you said, what you said there, that's what those Human First fellas say. You ... you ain't one of them nutters? You ain't ..."

"No, Zimmer, chill out."

"You sure?"

434

"Yeah, sure," she said.

"So ... so what skill you got?"

"I'm a mechanic. Why do you think I was assigned to you?"

"Who knows? Far as I'm concerned, you're just an escort. This needs two people, this lark. I'd never do it solo, never. You ever been to a Z-World?"

Mya shook her head. "Be first time today."

"Treat for you, doll."

"Not your doll, Zimmer."

"Being friendly. What's wrong in calling you 'doll'? You don't remember the time before the dead, do you?"

"A little. I was six when it happened."

"Political correctness everywhere – you couldn't say boo to a goose, let along call it a goose. Had to call it, I don't know, feathered sentient being, or something. Bollocks, it was. And women," he glanced at her, "you wanted to be like men, you did."

"You made sure we didn't after the dead, though," said Mya.

"What do you mean?"

"Crimes against women increased in those early days after the plague. Rape was –"

Zimmer shuffled in his seat and said, "Yeah, whatever."

She thought for a second, her gaze scanning the empty motorway as they drove north. And then she said, "Sometimes I think it was for the best the zombies took control."

"True enough," said Zimmer.

"Slavery agrees with us humans, don't you think?"

"Well ... keeps us on the straight and narrow. You step out of line, you're food. Simple, really."

After a few minutes of silence Zimmer spoke again.

"You know," he said, "before all this happened, I was a Christian."

"You were?"

"Yeah, a real Fundie-type. Creationist, you know? God made the world in six days and all that crap."

"Some people will believe anything."

435

"And evolution, well, I suppose I never understood it, but there was no way I believed in it – till the zombies showed me it was real."

"It's real."

"I mean, they changed so quickly. Every generation different. And now, look at 'em – they're running the country."

"Kind of."

"What d'you mean?"

"Zimmer, it's anarchy. Human society has collapsed. We're either food, breeders, or ... or people like us, workers."

"Least we're alive."

"I wouldn't call it living."

He glared at her. "You do sound like those Human First folk, girl. Are you sure you're not –"

"I need a pee."

"You what?"

"Pee, I need to pee."

"We're only half-an-hour away, can't you hold?"

"No, I can't."

Zimmer grumbled. He stopped the HGV in the middle of the carriageway. You could do that these days. At least the problem of congestion had been solved in the years after the dead.

"Thanks, Zimmer. Hey, you want a drink?"

"You what?"

"A drink. While you're waiting."

"A drink? What do you mean a drink?"

"You know what I mean."

"You serious?"

"I am serious."

"Where ... where d'you get booze?"

"Oh, you know. Plenty of moonshine around."

"They'll kill you if they find out. Makes the flesh taste bad. Pickles it and they hate that."

"They were never worried at the beginning. They'd eat anything."

"Bit more choosy these days," said Zimmer. "So where is it?

Mya leaned over the seat and retrieved her ruck sack. Out of it she pulled a dark brown bottle. Zimmer eyed it eagerly, licking his lips.

"What is it?" he said.

"I don't know? Booze. Just booze. You want it?"

Zimmer nodded and she gave him the bottle. As she stepped down from the cab, her heartbeat quickened and a cold sweat soaked her back.

She clambered up the slope at the side of the road, not looking back to see if Zimmer was drinking or not.

She went over the ridge and scooted down the other side on her backside. She sat on the grass, in the warm summer sun, and stared out over the remains of Maidstone. The city looked dead. Mya shivered, knowing its streets crawled with zombies. The inner city dead. Thousands of them still living on instinct as opposed to intelligence.

Most of the evolved zombies now inhabited the Z-World centres. Hundreds of them lived permanently at the resorts, while many more gathered there for the great feedings in December and June. Zimmer and Mya were going to the facility based at the former London Zoo in Regent's Park, London. It was the June feeding. It would be the first time Mya would witness the event. It would also be the last. She cried a little, mourning the things that would die that night.

She closed her eyes and thought, That's enough time.

She returned to the truck and found Zimmer slumped across the seat. She climbed into the cab and nudged him, saying his name. He snorted. Mya took a deep breath and got out of the cab again. She walked round to the rear of the truck, listening to the noises coming from inside the trailer. She tried not to listen.

She looked up the road. It was empty, clear, barren.

From her pocket she took a signalling device. It was the size of a key fob. She pressed the red button. A green light on the gadget blinked.

Mya sat on the side of the road.

Twenty minutes later a lorry appeared on the horizon, shimmering in the heat.

Mya got to her feet and waited for the vehicle. As it came nearer, she saw that it towed a trailer. It was the same as the one she and Zimmer were taking to London. The same apart from its cargo.

She waited and the truck came.

Three men leapt out and one came to Mya and they kissed, his hand gently resting on her stomach.

Then they went to work.

After what had to be done was done, the men and the truck left. Mya watched and pined for the man who had kissed her and touched her belly. She sighed and turned and went back to the cab to see if Zimmer had recovered.

She was about to nudge him awake when she spotted the manifest lying on the seat next to him. Mya picked up the clipboard and read the sheet of paper in the plastic sleeve. The words chilled her.

Delivery 472B/3
Dover to Z-World, Regent's Park
200 bred humans – A-Category/Norfolk
Aged: 12-40

"A-Category" meant the highest quality meat. Organically reared humans. Well maintained livestock cultivated in the countryside. Not the factory-bred flesh delivered to the inner cities where the zombie population had surged, and the less-evolved undead had settled. As the manifest noted, this batch had come from Norfolk. It had been delivered to Dover the previous day. Now it was on its way to London to be eaten.

Mya shook off the horror and poked the driver in the arm.

"Zimmer," she said, "Zimmer, wake up."

He jerked and mumbled something. Spit dribbled down his chin. His breath smelled of booze. He came to, blinking and scrabbling around.

"You all right, Zimmer?"

"How ... how long've I been ... asleep?"

"Not long," she said.

He sat up and groaned, holding his head. The sleeping pills Mya had powdered into the beer the previous night made Zimmer woozy, and they would give him a headache.

"Never felt so bad after booze," he said. "What the hell was that stuff?"

He kicked the bottle away. Mya picked it up and tossed it outside. It smashed on the road. Beer spilled. She smelled it and then shut the door.

"You want me to drive, Zimmer?"

"You can't drive."

"You want to bet?"

"I'm the driver."

"Get going, then."

"Christ," he said and started the truck. "My head feels like someone's drumming inside it. Can't believe I – shit, oh shit."

"What now?"

"Is that the time?"

"Probably."

"We're late, we're badly late."

Mya said nothing. She appeared cool, not bothered they were late for their appointment. Inside she trembled with fear. Part of her was relieved the trailer had been swapped, while another was terrified she'd be found out before getting to Z-World. The cargo trucks were always in danger of zombie attacks. They would be the less developed kind, mostly originals from the first days of the plague. They were brutal and mindless. They were relentless, and in days nearly wiped out the human population.

The country became known as Zombie Britannica.

Zombies do not reproduce through sex. They reproduce through death. Death gives birth to them. Their victims are resurrected, as is anyone who dies from natural causes.

As more zombies were made, mutations occurred in their genes. Some mutations produced intelligence.

As the undead regenerated, a few populations showed more brainpower than their predecessors.

Ten years ago, the first zombies with language abilities appeared. These were basic grunts, a few words, simple sentences.

But as the decade wore on, those communication skills grew more complex. The zombies evolved. They learned to think. They learned to control their nature. As a result, they became deadlier than ever. They became nearly human.

"Do I smell of booze?" said Zimmer. "Because if I do, they ... they'll ... Jesus, I'm dead."

"Here," said Mya, offering him a mint from a paper bag.

"You're a right black marketeer, ain't you? Booze, mints ... what else can you get us?"

She said nothing.

He glanced at her and said, "Well, you a black marketeer or not?"

"'Course I'm not. I got the booze off a mate, he's a moonshiner up in the borders. I bought the sweets at the market in Dover yesterday."

Dover. Hell on earth. A town that used to have a population of just under 30,000 now groaned under the weight of nearly 150,000. When the plague struck, thousands went there, hoping to cross to the Continent. But the ferries stopped sailing. There was no escape. And no one knew if the Continent was safe. Most of the people who came to Dover, stayed. And then more came. And more. Buildings were ransacked. Battles broke out between locals and incomers. There was no law to control the outbreaks of violence. Zombie attacks also caused panic and fear. But gradually, a fragile peace settled over the town.

It became what it was now – an enormous refugee camp.

Similar camps were found across Britain, mostly in the port towns – Portsmouth, Holyhead, Liverpool, Felixstowe, Hull, Leith, Aberdeen.

As the zombies evolved, they saw value in these over-populated, disease-ridden slums. They saw a food supply.

And in recent years, the zombie leadership realized that without humans, they would die out.

It was another development that made them more human – the ability to recognise their own mortality.

In the months after the dead came alive, the surviving humans formed small communities. Over the years, as the zombies evolved, they took advantage of this anthropological development. They appointed human leaders in these communities. Militias roamed the camps, maintaining order. The people despised the leaders and the militia because they were collaborators, working with the new breed of zombies.

But the work continued.

Warehouses were commandeered to store humans selected for food. They were usually troublemakers, or anyone the camp leaders disliked. Prisons housed breeding programmes. The healthier and genetically-blessed humans were kennelled at these sites to produce the next generation. Stock was selected from these programmes and sent to rural areas. These humans were housed in villages and small towns and were reared organically as food; zombies evolved enough to gain a place at a Z-World.

Every human was potentially food, but you could save yourself by either becoming a worker – you had to be fit and strong – or a breeder – you had to be attractive and healthy.

Mya and Zimmer had been handed their duties the previous night – a cargo of food for Z-World in London.

While she was listening to the foreman handing out the orders, Mya could hear the whimpers and cries of the humans in the trailer.

She tried to ignore them, just as she'd been taught to. But it was difficult. Her instinct was to open the trailer and tell those poor, doomed people to run.

Had she done that, she would have been zombie meat.

Best to wait. Best to stick to the plan.

And that's what she was doing as they drove along Primrose Hill near Regent's Park. This road used to be called leafy. Now it was overgrown, the hedges and trees unkempt and uncared for. The road was rutted and rusted vehicles lined the way.

Overhead, crows circled. Mya shuddered. The birds were there for food – and the way they croaked and wheeled suggested there was already meat waiting for them down below.

"Almost there," said Zimmer. "Now listen up, girl. Since you never been to one of these Z-World places before, there are things to remember, right?"

"I'm listening," she said.

Fifteen minutes later, after Zimmer's lecture, they arrived at the entrance to the old London Zoo. The sign depicting animals still remained, but it was now red with blood, and the words Z-World had been painted roughly across it.

Two figures armed with shotguns and wearing fluorescent bibs guarded the gate.

Zimmer rolled down his window and said, "Morning," to the guard on his side.

Mya looked out of her window. The second guard looked up at her. Half his face was gone. His bony hands grasped the shotgun. He grinned at Mya. Saliva oozed from his mouth.

Zombies with guns, she thought. What could be worse?

She looked away.

By that time, the first guard had checked Zimmer's manifest and waved them through the gates.

"Welcome to Z-World, London," Zimmer said. "Where zombies come to sunbathe and to slaughter."

Mya was shivering. Her fear grew. She was in hell, now – really in enemy territory. If she put a foot wrong, the zombies would kill her. No questions asked. No mercy given.

Zimmer drove the truck slowly along the road. On each side were cages and enclosures once used to house animals. Now people were stored in the pens and paddocks.

Mya thought her heart would burst when she saw a group of children, aged around nine or ten, reaching through the bars of a cage. Their little faces were creased with horror and tears stained their cheeks. For a moment Mya couldn't breathe, panic clutching at her chest. But as Zimmer drove by, and the children went past, she mastered her horror again. She had to keep herself together.

Zombies watched Mya and Zimmer as they drove. They had stopped to stare at the truck. They knew it contained food, their feast for the June feeding.

"Told you," said Zimmer, "don't look 'em in the eye – they'll take it as a challenge and might just go for us."

Hundreds of zombies were strolling along the paths that snaked around the resort. They moved in groups or individually. There didn't seem to be much interaction between them. Some leaned over to look down at the humans in the enclosures. The undead snarled and growled at the terrified people.

Mya's chest flared with rage.

She wanted to kill every zombie here. If she had a gun, she might just have leapt out of the cab and started firing, blowing the heads off those monsters.

But she wouldn't last long. She was one against many. Zombies cared little about their kind. So what if some died? As long as they got to you, that was all that mattered.

During the war, waves of zombies charged the army. The undead were mown down in their hundreds. But behind the first wave more came. More and more and more. The dead sea was unstoppable. Military action failed. Humanity was defeated.

"Here we are," said Zimmer.

He stopped the truck in front of some single-storey buildings. There was a swimming pool to the right. It contained no water, just bones and litter. Next to the pool a female zombie lounged on a sun-bed. She wore bikini bottoms. She had no need of the top because her breasts were gone. The whole front of her body was gone, and Mya could see into the cavity. The woman sat up and brushed her long, grey hair out of her face, and then curled back her lips and dribbled.

Mya followed Zimmer out of the cab. The heat was stifling. The smell of decay hung in the air. A rich, ripe odour that made Mya retch.

"Your companion feeling somewhat under the weather, Zimmer?" said a voice.

Mya turned towards it. Approaching them was a figure wearing a black fedora on his head, long black coat, black trousers, and black shoes. He wore sunglasses. His face was chalk-white. The skin on his hands was peeled to show bones and ligaments.

443

"I am Geller, I run this facility," said the black-clad. "Who are you?"

"Her name's Asher, Mr Geller," said Zimmer.

"Mya Asher," said Mya.

"Asher, I see. New to duties, are you? What skill keeps you from being food at my table?"

"I'm a mechanic," she said.

"Plenty of those around," said the zombie. "Well, you are late, Zimmer."

Zimmer rubbed his hands together. "We ... we had some trouble with the truck, Mr Geller."

"That's why you have a mechanic."

"Yes," said Zimmer, "and she ... she sorted things out."

Geller grunted. He was dribbling a little. Mya knew that was probably because he was near humans.

We're his food, thought Mya. His instinct is to eat us, and he wants to eat us right now – but he's evolved the ability to control his nature.

She trembled with nerves, and looked around.

The woman by the pool had lain down again.

"How many zombies here this summer?" said Mya.

"This summer?" said Geller. "We have three-hundred and twenty guests, seventy-eight residents. Why do you ask?"

"Interested. I've never been to a Z-World before."

"No? How did you not end up as food, Asher?" asked the zombie.

She looked him straight in the face. "I worked on the docks up in Leith. I was on a ground team, repairing trucks that ferried cargo to Scottish Z-Worlds."

"And you came south?"

"My family was from this area. Before the ..."

"I see," said Geller. He looked her up and down. "You could have been on the breeding programme. You appear fit, healthy – genetically-blessed."

"She's barren," said Zimmer.

Mya quaked but held Geller's stare. Her mouth was dry and she was terrified that she'd be found out.

444

The zombie said, "Take the truck into the vehicle bay, leave it there till tonight. Your quarters have been prepared."

Zimmer and Mya turned to go back to the HGV but Geller called after them, "Wait a minute."

Mya turned, dread chewing at her belly.

Geller said, "You didn't come across a crew of Human First scum on your journey did you?"

Mya could feel the blood leaching out of her brain, and it made her giddy.

"We didn't see anyone," said Zimmer and then turned to Mya. "You see anyone when I had a nap?"

Eyes on Geller she said, "There was no one."

He said, "Found them on the road, coming from your direction. They had stolen cargo them."

"Stolen?" said Zimmer. "Who from?"

"We don't know. You've not let the consignment out of your sight the whole journey, have you, Zimmer?"

"Absolutely not, Mr Geller."

"I would have the trailer opened to check –"

Mya stiffened.

Zimmer said, "But that would –"

"I know, I know," said Geller. "It would damage the stock, let some fresh air in." He licked his lips. Spit oozed from his mouth. "Humans are better when they're ripe. A nice odour of decay on the meat. And it makes it softer. Too much exposure to fresh air spoils that a little. Always best to keep them in that humid condition provided so well by your trucks, eh? What do you say, Asher?"

"I say ..." Mya's mouth was dry. "I say, of course."

"Of course," said Geller. "Follow me. I'll show you."

Geller led them behind the buildings and towards an enclosure. Zombies were leaning over the wall, snarling at something down below. Mya's skin goose fleshed. Her fear mounted.

"Here we are," said Geller as they reached the wall.

Mya had to use all the military training she'd received at the Human First camps in the north of Scotland to stop herself from screaming.

445

Down in the enclosure, three men had been tied to trees. The men were naked and they were screaming. Their bodies were covered in wounds. Blood soaked the ground. Chunks of meat torn out of their bodies were strewn around.

Mya wanted to leap over the wall and go to the men, to one in particular – the one who had kissed her and laid a hand on her belly.

But she controlled her emotions. It was difficult. Inside she was wailing.

Geller lifted his hand. A door opened at the back of the enclosure.

A huge zombie burst out of the entrance. The giant was naked and had enormous muscles. Its flesh was grey and parts of its scalp were missing, showing the skull underneath.

It was a 'roid zombie. One of the monsters this new, evolved zombie society had pumped full of growth hormone for their own entertainment.

The 'roid zombies were used in gladiatorial-style games, where they were pitted against the best of humanity – former professional fighters, soldiers, hard men.

There was only ever one winner in those contests.

Humans were no longer the alpha species.

The monster charged at the men tied to the trees. They shrieked. The zombie tore a chunk from one man's thigh. The victim howled in pain.

Mya stared in horror as the zombie grabbed the man in the centre – her man. The creature sank its teeth into her lover's arm. He cried out and caught Mya's eye. Seeing her intensified his terror, and she saw this. She wheeled away just as the zombie bit through her lover's arm, and all she heard as she staggered away was his squeals of anguish.

An hour later in their quarters, Zimmer said, "Why d'you run off like that?"

"We didn't need to see that."

"You know what they're like."

"I do know what they're like."

"They're just scaring us, that's all."

"They do that anyway. There's no need for …"

"What?" said Zimmer.

She was shaking, tears in her eyes.

"You knew those men," said Zimmer.

Mya rubbed her eyes with a towel. "Of course not."

"You did, Mya. You knew them. You're Human First."

She looked at him. He was sitting on his bunk. The cabin was bare apart from the two beds. A door on the back wall led to a toilet and washbasin. They would stay here till after the feeding, then, in the early hours of the morning, drive back to Dover.

Zimmer shook his head. "Don't believe it."

"What don't you believe?"

"You're arrogant, you lot."

"Arrogant?" she said.

"We're trying to get along, trying to stay alive, and you … you lot just spoil everything – you put the rest of us in danger. You're not Human First, you're *Me* First, *Us* First. Sod the rest of humanity."

"How old are you, Zimmer?"

"Fifty."

"Getting on, now."

"I'm all right."

"There'll be younger drivers wanting your job, soon. Younger, fitter."

"So?"

"What do you think happens to you when you're surplus to requirements?"

He said nothing.

Mya said, "You'll end up as food, that's what. And being you're overweight, older, bad skin, you'll be shipped to the inner cities. Tossed out in the streets with a bunch of other oldies where you'll be hunted down by first-born zombies. The originals. The ones you can't talk to, Zimmer. You can't beg and reason with them, you know that. They'll rip you apart. You're food. That's what we all are. Is that what you think you deserve?"

"I … I just want to live."

"You won't. You'll die in agony like those men out there today. You'll be eaten alive. No questions. You know that. It's how we all go. It's human destiny – to be devoured."

"Christ," he said, putting his head in his hands.

"We're at least trying to do something, trying to maintain human dignity," said Mya.

He looked at her. "Tell me what you're doing here?"

She told him.

"Christ," he said. "You failed, then?"

"Failed?"

"The cargo we were carrying, the cargo your friends stole, it's ended up here anyway. Those people *are* going to get eaten. You failed."

"No ... no, we didn't." And she told them why.

After they talked, Zimmer agreed to go with her to where the truck had been parked.

It was night. Howls and screams filled the air. Torches burned, lighting the resort. Humans cried and begged.

At midnight, the great feeding would begin. The human cargo would be released into the grounds of Z-World. Two hundred men, women, and children. Add to that the hundreds already caged at the old zoo, it would mean that nearly a thousand humans would be stampeding through the resort.

And then the zombies would hunt them. Nearly four hundred monsters unleashed.

The zombies would savage the humans. They would eat them. Kill them all. The screams of the dying would echo across London. Z-World would be swimming in blood and gore. Death would be everywhere. There would be no human survivors.

"Are you wearing your badge?" said Zimmer.

"Yes," Mya said, indicating the red, cotton square pinned to her jacket. It marked a human worker out from food. The identification was vital if you were delivering to a Z-World. Any human wandering around without the marker would either be killed on the spot or thrown into an enclosure or cage for eating later.

Zimmer and Mya stayed in the shadows and made their way to the vehicle bays.

448

"I can't believe you drugged me and swapped this trailer," said Zimmer, standing near the container that stored his original cargo.

Mya could hear the humans whimper inside.

"You put me in danger," he said. "I'm still waiting for an apology."

"I'll not say sorry for trying to save the human race."

"At the cost of human lives?"

"People die in wars. It's sad, but it happens. How many will die and suffer if we don't do anything?"

"Maybe I won't. That's all that matters to me."

She said nothing.

"You're not infertile are you," said Zimmer.

She looked him in the eye.

"In fact," he said, "you're pregnant."

"How do you know?"

"Just guessed. The way you were rubbing your belly when we were watching those poor buggers in the enclosure, the way – "

"One of them is the father – *was* the father."

"And you're going to sacrifice your baby for a victory you may never achieve? Is that what you're saying?"

"It's ... it's for the future. I have a younger sister. She was born soon after the plague. She's six years younger than me. She's pregnant, too, and I want her children to have a world worth living in."

"What about your child?"

"It's ... it's the price we pay for freedom."

"What did the dad think?"

"He understood."

"Now he's dead, and you'll be dead too."

Mya went over to Zimmer's truck and squatted next to the trailer her lover and his two companions had attached to it hours earlier.

She was reaching under the trailer, feeling for something. Something that had been taped there so she could use in an emergency.

"What are you looking for?" said Zimmer.

"For a –" She found it, and froze.

Two figures came from the shadows, one of them a giant.

"Busy are we?" said Geller, still wearing his hat and sunglasses. Behind him the 'roid zombie snarled. Its teeth had been filed into points. Mya imagined them ripping through her lover's flesh.

"Just ... just checking the cargo," said Zimmer.

"You should've done that at 5pm," said Geller.

"Thought we'd check to see where this came from," said Zimmer, banging on the side of the trailer they'd originally towed from Dover.

"Can you tell?" said Geller.

"Might be able to," said Zimmer.

Then Geller looked at Mya. "What are you doing there, Asher?"

Mya jerked at the gun and the tape tore away. She leapt to her feet and trained the weapon on Geller.

He said, "Oh, I see what you're doing."

The 'roid zombie growled and moved forward.

Mya shuffled nervously.

"You're Human First scum, aren't you," said Geller. "Both of you."

"Not me," said Zimmer. "I know nothing about –"

"Shut up," said Geller. "Asher, put down the gun. There's no escape."

"Then you're dead, too," she said.

"I'm already dead," said Geller.

"Well I'll kill you again," said Mya. "You know I can."

Geller smiled. "There's nothing you can do, Asher. Why do you fight? Your world is gone. It's our world now."

"We're taking it back."

"No you're not," said Geller. "Do you know why? You are too weak. You value things too much. You kept gold and money and antiques and art and cars, you stored these things. And did they save you? Jesus warned you, didn't he?"

"I don't believe in Jesus."

"You wouldn't," said the black-clad zombie. "That's why you ignored his warning: 'Do not store up for yourselves

450

treasures on earth, where moth and rust destroy.' But you did. And what for? Your money and cars are meaningless. Put the gun away, Asher. Give it up. Accept your fate."

"You're dying, Geller," said Mya. "All of you. Tonight. Z-Worlds across the country are being hit."

"Hit?" he said.

"We're blowing you away."

Geller snarled. "I am going to eat you, legs first. Make my way up your body, slowly. I'll make it hurt so—"

She shot him in the face. His sunglasses shattered. The hat flew off his head. His skull erupted in brain and blood and he hit the ground.

The 'roid zombie charged. Zimmer legged it. Mya, panicking, started firing. Bullets pummelled the monster's face, turning it into a bloody maw.

Mya kept firing but she'd emptied the clip.

The 'roid zombie stumbled towards her.

She backed away.

The monster was on her.

She cowered, screaming.

A gunshot made her ears ring.

She smelled cordite.

The ground shook when the 'roid zombie fell, smoke rising from where his head had been.

Mya looked up.

Zimmer was leaning out of his cab with a shotgun jammed into his shoulder. Smoke plumed from the double-barrel.

They looked at each other for a second and Zimmer must have read Mya's thoughts.

"I keep it for insurance," he said.

Mya nodded.

Zimmer said, "You get going, they'll be here any second."

"You what?" she said.

"Get in your' boyfriend's truck and take those people out of here, take them anywhere."

"Zimmer, you can't—"

451

"Just do it. You're right. This is my last drive, they've told me. I tried not to think about it, but it's over. I'm food. You've got your baby, now. Go, Mya, get out of here."

"No," she said, "I've got to set off the explosives."

In the distance, a siren blared. Shouts and screams filled the air.

Zimmer asked, "Where's the detonator?"

Mya gawped.

Zimmer said, "Where is it?"

"Under the trailer's rear wheels."

"How ... how do you ... you know ..."

"You ... you just open the cover and press the red button. You've got sixty seconds."

"Jesus, plenty of time for them to rip me to pieces."

"Zimmer, you don't have to do this, you –"

"Go, Mya. Just go. Time I did something for the human race. I did nothing before all this happened. Nothing when I thought I was good, when I went to church. Go. Get in that other truck, now. I'll give you a minute, then I'm detonating. How much explosives in that trailer?"

"Enough to make a crater out of Regent's Park."

He nodded. "Go, now."

As she drove along the roads of Z-World, running over zombies as she went, tears streamed down her face.

She hoped Zimmer would have enough time.

She hoped he would not suffer.

She hoped.

Armed zombies fired at her, but they caused little damage. 'Roid zombies tried to stand in her way, but she drove over them.

She put her foot down, the big truck roaring down the road, past the cages full of children, towards the zoo's entrance.

Mya felt sick. All these humans would die. But she couldn't save them all. She would save two hundred, those in her trailer. That would be something. She wept, hating herself for letting those people in the cages and the enclosures die. But as her lover said, this was war. She'd been ready to die herself. Sacrifice was necessary. And at least the poor sods wouldn't be eaten alive. Death would be very quick for them.

She smashed through the gates and hit the Outer Circle road.

Behind her, the sky lit up. An orange glow filled the darkness. And seconds later, an explosion deafened her and the lorry bucked.

Mya screamed as the trailer swung out behind her. For a moment, she thought she'd lose control of the HGV. But she managed to keep from tipping over. She accelerated.

If she failed to get far enough from the blast, the people in the trailer would be baked alive.

She felt the heat from the explosion now. The earth trembled. A dark cloud of debris and smoke suddenly started to spread from the epicentre of the blast.

It was catching her up, rolling down the road behind her like a wave.

But Mya kept driving. She had lives to save. Two hundred in the trailer, and one in her womb.

She drove without looking back.

Finally, as she left London, she slowed down and glanced in her side-mirrors. A great fire raged in the centre of the city, lighting up the night. The cloud of dust had covered Central London and was seeping into the outskirts now.

An hour later on the M1, seventy miles outside London at the Watford Gap Service Area, Mya stopped and opened the trailer.

The smell was terrible. Humans staggered out, crying and screaming. They were sweaty and dirty, covered in their own shit and blood. As they poured out, Mya noticed that some were dead. Dozens of them. They would have to be burned or soon they would rise up as zombies.

"Where do we go?" said a man, his bright blue eyes standing out against his dirty face.

"I ... I don't know," she said.

"Where are you going?"

"North. Scotland."

"Are … are you Human First?"

She nodded.

"Take us," said the man.

"How?"

"In the trailer. We've been in it for twenty-four hours waiting for death. I think we can bear it for a few hours more if we know we're going to live."

The crowd had gathered behind him. They murmured in agreement: "Take us, take us."

Mya thought for a second.

Then she said, "Take your dead out and burn them. There should be some fuel in the petrol station in the service area."

"Burn them?" said the man.

"Burn them," she said.

"But … you're Human First, you don't–"

"They're not human anymore," said Mya. "Do it. And keep watch. I'm going to have some shut eye in the cab."

Mya fell asleep to the smell of burning flesh, and she dreamed of her unborn child, a daughter, she was sure, waiting for her nine months in the future.

THE END

THE ZOMBIE WHISPERER
By
Bob Lock

'I've heard of a Horse Whisperer: a Dog Whisperer, even a Ghost Whisperer, but a Zombie Whisperer? You're yanking my chain now, aren't you?' Doug said with a grin.

I shook my head. 'Honest, I saw it myself; this isn't a second or third hand account. It isn't even an urban myth. I've watched the guy do it, more than once.'

Doug still looked at me sceptically. It's been nearly five years since we came to London for a short-break holiday and the world fell afoul of the zombie plague which has almost wiped out humankind. Doug and his great ideas, *a weekend in London will be fun,* he said, *a change from boring, wet Wales.* We're still here and Wales is one of the safest places in Britain, great. Anyway, no one has ever been able to get close to a zombie without the damn thing trying to rip your face off and shove it into its stinking mouth. I didn't blame him for not believing me. I hardly believe it myself and yet I've witnessed it.

'Go on then, tell me about it. I can't wait to hear the punch line,' he said with an exasperated sigh.

I rolled my eyes. 'It's not a joke, man. Honest, I *saw* a guy do it.'

He held his hands up, palms out towards me. 'All right, already. Tell me about it!'

I nodded. 'Okay. The first time was three months ago, after we had that bad spell of snow, remember?'

Doug nodded and made a hurry-up sign with his hands, he has an appallingly short span of attention.

'Right, right, calm down. I was on my way back from rummaging around Tesco – there wasn't much stuff left – I only managed to get a few tins of marrowfat peas and I bloody hate them but, hey, you never know. I could swap them perhaps ...' I shrugged and then carried on as I saw Doug's patience was wearing thin. 'So, I'm leaving the store when I see this guy just strolling along. He had his hands in pockets, like it was just another Sunday,' I frowned, 'or was it Saturday? All the damn

455

days just seem to meld together now. Oh, as I was saying. He stopped when he saw me and raised a hand to wave. That's when I spotted the zombie step out of a ruined car, which was wrapped around a lamppost, near the guy. I shouted to him and pointed.'

'Did he run?' Doug asked.

'Nope, he just turned around, easy-like, as if he had all the time in the world. Which he *didn't* because the zombie was only a few paces away and this was one of those fit types. You know the ones, no broken or shattered bones, no dragging leg, not too much damage done to it at all. It was a big bastard too, must have gone down with one hell of a fight before being bitten. Might have been a rugby player or something,' I said.

'And?'

'And, well this guy just stepped towards it and held up both of his hands in the air as if he was going to press the damn thing back. He was making some sort of mewling sound. Damn weird it was. I just stood there, didn't know what to do. I just expected to see him get his arms torn off and his stupid head kicked into touch.'

'And did he?' Doug asked, really interested now.

I shook my head. 'Nope. The strangest thing happened. The zombie just pulled up short. Stopped. Looked at the guy, tilted its head to one side, you know, like you see dogs doing, well like dogs *used* to do when they were still around.'

'Shit!'

'Shit yeah. I almost crapped myself and *I* wasn't even the one close to the bloody thing.'

'Did it get him?' Doug asked.

'No, it just stood there, head askance, like it was listening to him. Like it could understand what the guy was saying.'

'What the hell? He was *talking* to it?'

'Yeah, he'd stopped doing the mewling sound and was whispering to it, not talking. He had his damn mouth right up to the bloody thing's ear!'

'You're shitting me ...' Doug said with a shake of his head.

'I shit you not, Doug,' I replied and made a cross sign over my heart. 'Honest. The guy was whispering to it, right in the zombie's damn ear!'

'What was he saying?'

I looked at Doug open-mouthed. 'You *really* think I was going to walk up and put my ear close to them to eavesdrop? Are you out of your mind, Doug?'

'Weren't you the least bit tempted?' He shook his head. 'The first time someone's gone up to an undead, stopped it from trying to eat him and has *actually* spoken to it and you didn't think of getting a little closer to find out how he did it?'

'No!'

'No? Why not?'

'Listen, I saw a sword-swallower in a workingmen's club in Aberystwyth once. He stuck bloody great blades down his throat. Blades that he took out afterwards and stuck in the floor. I didn't go up to *him* either and ask him how he did it so *I* could have a go. So I sure as hell wasn't going to put *this* pretty face anywhere near that big zombie's gob, I can tell you,' I replied, pointing to my ugly mug.

'But *this* is different,' Doug said animatedly, 'don't you see? If the guy can stop zombies attacking, imagine if he could teach all us survivors how to do it too! We'd be safe at last. You have to admit that.'

I could see his point, but all I remember is at the time I didn't want to get close to them. It just seemed surreal. I expected any minute to see loads of blood and flesh flying all over the place. And besides, the last time I took on-board anything my best mate said I ended up getting stuck in the world's zombie capital. *We can spend a night in Soho, the red light district!* He'd said. Yeah great idea, only thing is after we'd gotten off the train from Swansea we found that *all* of London was a red light district and I don't mean it was full of ladies of questionable moral standards. Everywhere was splattered with blood and gore. A great holiday; we spent it running like fuck until we'd completed the London Marathon at least three times over. I explained to Doug how I felt, but he just couldn't get his head around it.

457

'God, you don't half moan,' he said with a shake of his head, then added, 'We *have* to find him.'

'The guy, you muppet, the guy!'

I stared at Doug. 'You want to give it a try, don't you?'

He nodded. 'Sure! If we can find him, and persuade him to let us in on his secret, then I bet we could do the same. Look, remember when they had those programs on the telly? You know ... the Dog or Horse Whisperer ones? They not only had the expert training the animals but they also had *other* people learning how it was done too. They even wrote damn books about it. Like a do-it-yourself guide to whispering.'

I remembered them. 'I suppose we could go look for him. He must live around there somewhere, I saw him quite a few times after the first meeting. Nearly every time I saw him he whispered to a zombie too. He was always at it.'

'Bloody hell!' Doug was excited now. 'So, after he whispered to them what happened?'

I shrugged. 'Not sure, but he got them to sit down,' I replied. 'Haven't you noticed any zombies sitting around doing nothing?' I asked him. 'Not even looking at you when you walked past?'

He nodded. 'Hell yeah, now that you mention it!' then he frowned. 'Some of them had died, really died. They looked as though they'd just rotted away.'

'Perhaps he just tells them to sit there and they do, until they die ...'

Doug grabbed my arm. 'Let's go over to Tesco. Perhaps we can spot him. It's got to be worth a try.'

'Okay, I guess. At least you can help me carry some more marrowfat peas back. They're the only tinned food left. The store's been emptied of everything else, but some bugger has got to be partial to them,' I said and picked up my trusty double-barrelled twelve bore shotgun. I never used anything else after reading a Dumb-Arse's Guide to Killing Zombies.

'It's strange seeing those zombies sitting around and knowing finally why the hell they're doing it,' Doug said as we made our way to Tesco's. We must have passed dozens on our way there. Some were dead, some alive – well, not alive, but not dead – you know what I mean.

'They're not even going into that hibernating-sort-of-phase, all dried up and kind of mummified like they do when they can't get enough nourishment. It almost looks as if they just give up and die,' I remarked.

'We need to find that guy …'

'I know, Doug, I know. I should have spoken to him sooner. We could *both* be Zombie Whisperers now if I had.'

Doug patted me on the back. 'Never mind. Once we find him I'm sure he won't mind passing on his skills to someone else. *Everyone* should be taught it, don't you think?'

I agreed with him and we pressed on. We'd almost arrived at Tesco's car park when I spotted the guy. He was ambling along just like the first time I saw him, hands in pockets, eyes cast down and, on the wind, I could hear him tunelessly whistling something.

'There he is!' I said and pointed him out to Doug.

'*And* he's got a stalker,' Doug noticed and he indicated a really decrepit-looking zombie that was shuffling along slowly behind the man.

'Well unless he stops, *that* walking wreck isn't going to catch him. It must have been ancient even before it was bitten. I swear I can almost see through its chest, the skin is so thin and papery,' I said as we drew closer.

'Our guy's stopping. He's seen us,' Doug said as the man looked up and waved laconically in our direction. I'm sure he recognised me, because he smiled. I waved back.

'He's waiting for that geriatric zombie. He's going to do his whispering thing,' Doug said, all excited by the prospect. 'We'll let him do it and then ask him to teach us, okay?'

I nodded. 'Sure. I feel better about it now there are two of us. We can watch each other's arse.'

Doug pushed me. 'I'm not that sort of bloke,' he said and laughed.

'Ha ha. Oh, look the bicentennial zombie has finally reached him,' I said as we watched the guy. As before, he raised his hands and made a mewling sort of sound. The zombie faltered and stopped.

'Bloody hell,' Doug said quietly. 'I have to admit that I still thought you were taking the piss, but you're right. The guy *is* whispering to it.'

We watched breathlessly as the man bent forward and whispered into the ancient zombie's ear. We continued to watch breathlessly as the ancient zombie tilted its head at an angle, dog-like – and then lunged at the man's exposed throat and ripped a huge lump of it away. Part of the man's windpipe dangled from the old zombie's jaws as it moved forward again towards the Zombie Whisperer, who was trying desperately to stem the outpouring of blood from the gaping wound in his neck. It was a futile effort and, as we held our breath, the man was down and the gutter was running crimson with his blood.

I raised the shotgun to my shoulder and drew a bead on the ancient zombie's head. It was pushing the remains of the man's throat into its gore-encrusted mouth. It surprised both of us by staying upright for a second or two after I blew its head clean off with both barrels. But then it collapsed in a messy heap of bones, rags and desiccated flesh next to the dying man.

We both ran towards him and then stopped warily as he held a blood-soaked hand out to us. Something was clutched in it, but we were afraid to get too close. Dark blood gushed out of his mouth. He coughed it away and with his dying breath he managed to gasp.

'The old fucker was deaf ...' and, as his hand fell to the floor, an ancient hearing aid fell from his lifeless fingers.

I reloaded and put two shells into the dead Zombie Whisperer's head ... just in case ...

THE END

THE DAY I DISCOVERED THE TRUTH ABOUT THE MAN IN THE RED SUIT
By
R. Phillip Roberts

Dedicated with all my love to Raven Rachelle Dozier

I had hardly slept a wink all night, when at nearly five o'clock in the morning, I once again opened my eyes. Another noise in the darkness of the night had me shooting straight out of bed and over to the window, only to discover that another branch had fallen, or quite possibly the barn door had blown shut again, as a result of the harsh blustery winter wind.

A fresh blanket of white covered the ground, hiding the tracks we had made over the last few days in the previous snowfall. In the light of the full moon everything took on an eerie cast, especially since the vast whiteness changed the appearance of all that I had grown familiar with over the last thirteen years of my life.

With disappointment in my heart, I returned to bed, just as I had all previous times, with a promise to myself that I would not jump out of bed again; that I would lay back down and fall asleep. Morning would come eventually, and if I could just fall asleep for a little while, then when I next opened my eyes, it would be time to go downstairs with the others.

Yeah, right! Like that was going to work. It was Christmas Eve, and all through the house, not a creature was … well, you get the idea. I was filled with the excitement and anticipation that any child has at this time of year. And, I wanted to catch a glimpse of Santa, of course, even though my older brothers had told me that he did not exist. Liars!

I know, I know! You wonder why a thirteen year old girl such as myself still believes in Santa Claus, right? Well, I believe in him because I actually saw him last year. But he did not fly through the air, nor did he have a team of magical reindeer to guide his sleigh from rooftop to rooftop; none of that nonsense. No siree! But Santa did come by sleigh, however.

It was one year ago today, on a night just like this, in fact. As I lay in bed, I heard a sound. It was a familiar sound to be sure, but when one hears the approach of horses in the middle of the night out here in the country, it usually means something really bad has happened. So of course, I jumped out of bed and threw on my robe. I ran to the window, and to my surprise, saw that it was in fact Santa, coming across the field.

Well, who else could it have been? The man wore a red suit, a red hat, with black shiny boots on his feet. His long beard was white, and his belly was big and round. Once he brought the team of horses that pulled the sleigh to a stop, he climbed out, pulling a large sack with him, which he slung over his shoulder before approaching the house.

As if he could sense my presence, the jolly fat man stopped dead in his tracks and looked up at my window. For a moment, I was too scared to even breathe, but when he smiled and shook his head, I sighed with relief. Then the man bowed his head and continued up the path to the front door. I swear that I had heard the faintest sound of laughter, as the wind howled outside my window, blowing the large falling flakes of snow aloft in the air as they descended gracefully to the ground.

Too afraid to go downstairs and meet the man face to face, I silently crept down the hall. Taking a seat at the top of the stairs, I listened to the front door creak open, then gently shut. The sound of scraping followed, as I assumed that Santa was wiping his feet on the carpet near the entry, laid out for just that purpose.

When I heard him walk across the hardwood floor, with a soft creaking in the floorboards every few steps, my heart began to race. The sound of his bag slumping to the floor almost made my heart jump straight out of my chest. Then I heard a soft chuckle, and then a clunk. When I heard the blaze of the fire in the hearth begin to crackle and sizzle, I knew that the jolly old man had added a fresh log to the fireplace.

By the sounds that followed, I could tell that Santa had begun to set the contents of his hefty bag around our tree. While he went about his business, he whistled. It was a familiar tune. I believe the words to it had something to do with being naughty or nice, making a list, checking it twice, or something like that.

After about fifteen minutes, but really, it felt more like an eternity, everything went silent. I sat there at the top of the stairwell, straining my young ears to hear something, anything, in the silence. Then Santa chuckled once more, before opening the front door and disappearing back out into the cold winter night.

In a dash, I was on my feet and down the stairs. I ran to the window and peered through the curtains, just in time to see Santa boarding his sleigh. With a crack of the reigns and a shout, the horses took off. Santa and his sled pulled away. I watched until he was completely out of sight.

When I turned around, grinning from ear to ear, I was amazed to see all the colorfully wrapped gifts he had placed under the tree. Then my eyes fell upon the table where we had set out a plate of cookies and a glass of milk. The plate held not a crumb, and the glass had been drained bone dry; not a trace that either had held anything.

More excited than ever, I dashed back up to bed, but I was way too anxious to sleep. I waited until I heard the others awake, then I went downstairs, as well. When I told everyone my story, no one believed me, except for my wide-eyed younger sister, and of course, my mother and father. My older brothers, twins they are, kept saying that I had been dreaming, because Santa was make believe, and only small children believed in him.

In response to their mean words, I stuck out my tongue and called them liars, then said that they were jealous because I had seen Santa, and not them. It had gone on like that all day, until my father finally got tired of it and told us all to shut up, or we would all get a switching taken to us in the barn.

I must have fallen asleep, because the next thing I know, Mom was standing in my door and whispering, "Wake up, Carol! You can come downstairs, now!"

"Did Santa finally come? I was up all night, but for this last hour, and I never saw him," I explained to my mother, but she never answered and went to wake the others.

I quickly donned my robe and slippers, then went out into the hall. I almost ran into my little sister, Carmen, who was stumbling her way sleepily toward the staircase; one hand rubbing her weary eyes, the other clutching her favorite rag doll. When she saw me, she took my hand, and together, we began descending the stairs.

As the sky had just begun to lighten on the horizon, it was still pretty dark inside the house, so I had grabbed the kerosene lamp from next to my bed, before entering the hall.

Once we were halfway down the stairs, however, I no longer needed it to see. When Sis and I were on the last few steps, we could see that Mom had lit all the candles on the tree. It was so pretty with all the wrapped presents spread out beneath.

It looked just like one of those picture postcards from long ago that Mother had stowed away in a dusty old shoebox under her bed.

With excitement in our hearts, we ran the last few yards over to the shimmering tree, where my mother and the twins were already beginning to huddle upon the floor, and we knelt down beside them. The boys were craning their necks with squinty eyes, each attempting to get a peek at the names on the tags to see which of the packages belonged to them, of course.

When they began arguing over who had the most, you can bet that Cadence Piper put an end to it. My mother slapped them each upside the head. "Now, behave! Or, I'm gonna send the both of you to your room! No presents! And no dinner! You got it?" my mother scolded them. And when Mother scolded you, you got the evil eye; the one that informed you that she meant some serious business.

Now the twins, my brothers Billy and Willy, were four years older than me, and they were fidgety boys. They found it hard to resist the urge each had to push and shove the other, spewing graphic verbal insults meant to get a rise out of one another. They were big boys who liked to rough-house and wrestle to see which one could get the other on the ground.

When they were younger, the boys were much smaller than the other kids their age. Billy handled it well, but Willy had been teased much more, and was branded with the nickname, 'Wee Willy Wanker'. My brother never forgot that, so when he got a little older and got much bigger from working out with

464

Billy, they both got their revenge on all those others who had taunted them in the past.

Well, even though they were some big boys now, with a lot of meat on their bones – very little fat – Mother did not let them intimidate her. It was she who now took the boys out to the barn for a god switching, when they needed it. Father refused, as he said they were now men. I think he was just a little afraid one of them might hit him back one day.

Once again, Mother raised her voice to the twins to get them settled down. My eyes wandered to the table; the one we always put the milk and cookies out on. The glass remained two-thirds full, and the plate of cookies still held the two large ones that had been placed there, with a single bite taken from just one.

Something was wrong. I could feel it. Santa never left anything behind, other than the gifts. The plate had always been clear of even the tiniest of crumb, and the glass always drained to clarity, as if milk had never touched the inside of it.

Mom told us that we would have to wait until after dinner to open the gifts. My brothers sighed and guffawed in unison, whining aloud, "Why not? Huh, Mom? Can we ... *pleeeaassssse?*"

Instead of scolding the twins, Mom said, "I will let you have your stockings! But, only if you promise to be good all through dinner, and then we can open the gifts."

With that, she got up and went over to the fireplace, pulling down each of our stockings, handing them out to the each of us. Greedily, we all shoved our hands inside, hastily pulling out their contents. There were a variety of candies, shiny little trinkets found on father's excursions, and best of all, fresh-made beef jerky.

I could tell by its thick smoky aroma that it had been cured quite recently. I took a bite, immediately tasting the freshness. Now this was a real treat. It had been months since there had been any meat to be had, and our stores had nearly run dry of the potatoes and apples picked from our fields, before winter had set in.

As we all sat their chewing on the beef treats, I thought about how it used to be, back before the plague had come. We led a simple farm life, and had simple family values, but we were aware of what was going on in the big cities. I mean, we did have cable, at least before all the electricity went dead everywhere.

The epidemic had begun two-and-a-half years previous, and had spread across the country like a brush fire. People were dying left and right as the result from the bites. Creatures that had once been human, like us, attacked anyone living with frenzied rage. The crazy thing was, those that had fallen dead, then began to get back up and walk around. But they were not living. They had become monsters, just like the ones that had bitten them.

Father said that we were safe in the country, so we had stayed, and never really had much trouble. The only time they came around at all, was in the warmer months, but there were never many. Father and the twins would use them for target practice, killing them dead with hunting rifle blasts to the head. In the winter months, when it was harshly cold, they never appeared at all. Father had started saying, 'If the monsters don't get us, we'll all die of starvation!' It scared me to think that he might be right.

Then it hit me. Father had not yet returned from one of his many foraging hikes. Sometimes they lasted for weeks, but he had always made it home for Christmas Eve, even when the world had been normal.

I asked my mother, "When will Father return?"

"You will see your father, soon, Carol! Now finish up, everyone! Dinner is almost ready!" Mother then disappeared into the kitchen to finish preparing for dinner. For the first time since I had turned nine, my mother did not ask for my help.

Not giving much more thought to it, I went back to snapping off another bite of jerky, while giving closer inspection to each of the little trinkets from my stocking. The twins and Carmen were also doing the same, while we all waited for mother to return.

When next she came into the dining room, carrying a large silver platter, Mother made the announcement. Each of us dashed over to the table and took our places, Mother setting the platter in the centre. By its sheer size and the strain that Mother had looked under while carrying it, there had to be something bountiful hidden under the shiny lid.

Mother finished placing a bowl of sliced apples, then another with steaming boiled potatoes, upon the table, and then she spoke. "We have been blessed this year, my children! Eat it up while you can, for who knows when next we will meet such good fortune! At least with what's been smoked, we're sure to see the coming of spring alive and well!"

Mother smiled, then leaned over, clutched the handle, and pulled the lid off of the platter. What lay before us was startling. With a loud gasp, my siblings and I were shocked to see our father; or what was left of him, anyway. His arms and legs were missing, but the rest of him was there. The skin was blackened and charred, cracked in places, the pinkish juicy meat bubbling within. Where Father's eyes were supposed to be, there were empty sockets, but for some residue of gooey looking gelatin.

The room was silent as we all looked at each other. Then finally, Carmen said, "Can we eat now?"

As hard as we tried, none of us could hold back a smirk, which soon turned to laughter. Pretty soon, we were acting just as normal as any other day. When my mother began carving off pieces of meat from Father's torso, and placing them on our plates, we took them willingly, and then began to eat as if it were normal to be feasting on your father for the holidays. It had turned out to be a good Christmas, after all, and we still had gifts to unwrap.

I later found out that Father had been stricken down with a heart attack, and died several days earlier while on his way home from delivering gifts to some of the neighbors in the outlying area around us. Mother had found him in the woods on the edge of the property, dead in the snow and all dressed up in his red suit and shiny black boots. I was unsure whether to be more sad about Father's heart attack, or the fact that Santa really was make-believe.

Anyhow, she told me she had thought she had heard someone calling her name off in the distance, sometime earlier that morning. She thought she was hearing things, but had finally decided to go investigate, just in case. Then when she found his dead body, quickly made up her mind what she was going to do about Christmas dinner.

That was four years ago, just shy three days. And, what I think happened was that Mother had finally cracked. True, we all ate from our father, but I have a feeling his death was no accident. Three years ago, we had Willy for the holiday meal; the next year, Billy. And I saw mother take the axe to his head from behind, though she had told Carmen and I that he had slipped and fallen on the ice, cracking his head clean open, dying as a result. Last year, however, I took the initiative, and got to Mother before she could get me, or my little sister.

When she least expected it, I snuck up behind her and smashed the back of her head in with an iron skillet. I made sure she would never get up again before I stopped pounding her pulverized skull with the heavy pan. With Carmen's help, I dragged her body into the smokehouse, and hoisted her onto the big hook hanging from the chain fastened to the rafter above.

By the time Christmas Eve came around three days later, we had the feast of our lives. With Mother's head propped upon a plate so she could join us, Carmen and I gorged ourselves on her steamy cooked flesh.

I knew that once this winter had come, that I was going to dread the coming of this day. There are four days left. And as I clutch my little sister's hand tightly, my mind is on tomorrow night, when I must stick her lifeless body inside the smokehouse, hoist it upon the hook, and secure the door shut. She will be ready in two nights' time, after that. And just in time for Christmas Eve dinner, too. So now, a Merry Christmas to you all, and to all, a good night.

THE END

CROSSOVER
By
Tony Burgess

There are two things on this stink-ass planet that I hate. I hate goddamn teenagers and I hate what the Dead have done to us. The Dead problem used to be worse, of course, before we figured out how to deal with them. One zap with a taser and they don't get up again for twenty four hours. All you gotta do is put a taser in every household and real incidences of fatal attacks by the Dead are reduced to a statistic lower than shark attacks. It's a waste disposal problem now. The Dead don't die; you can't kill them, so you gotta isolate them. For a while we did that by stickin' 'em in arenas and then pits and then weighing 'em down in the Pacific. The problem with the Dead is you get new ones every day. People cross over every fuckin' day. So now we load 'em into these giant barges, shoot 'em up into space and dump 'em into orbit. Bring the barge back and load it up again. Right now it's estimated that there are over 800, 000,000 dead up there circling the Earth. The thing that messes with me is that they're still animated. They float up there flapping their arms and rolling their eyes. Gives me the creeps. In fact, the sight has been deemed too disturbing by the authorities, so no images of this crazy outer space death party are made public. Personally I think that makes it worse. It means you can't stop thinking about it. You shiver when the sun comes up because you know what it's lighting up.

Why do I hate teenagers? Because teenagers will fuck with anything. They think they'll live forever. And that is precisely the problem right now. They call them crossover parties. A bunch of like-minded assholes get together, get high, hand out the guns and, at the appointed hour, they all blow their brains out. Not because life's too hard, but because they want to go to outer space. They want to be immortal and scare the shit out of everybody. It's tragically misguided, but that's what makes it irresistible. It's so grotesque that the media won't report on it for fear of spreading the idea. Same with schools. But despite that, crossover parties are here to stay and, thanks to e-society, they spread. In fact, the vacuum created by ignorance around these things has been filled with some pretty dangerous ideas. Many teenagers think that you are alive up there. That it's a party that never ends. That it's Heaven.

So it has become a waste management problem. That's where I come in. I work for WasteCo. I used to work for private security firms. The kind that the military hires to go in and do dirty jobs. It's ironic really; I used to infiltrate terror nests to kill and now I interfere with suicide parties. And I'll tell ya, I had more respect for those bastards committed to a desperate war than I do for assholes using death as a drug. I fuckin' hate teenagers. I think we should throw a few up there still alive. Scare 'em straight.

Before this dumb fucking gig with WasteCo, I lived in hot spots all over the world. I've smoked entire families at prayer in Peshawar. I wore a burqa for a month in Iran, so I could off a troublesome officer in the revolutionary army. I even helped make IEDs in Iraq, so I could get closer to a circle of mad clerics. The things I've done are dirty. Ugly. To keep western leaders and their shining armies on the highest road possible, I have slit the throats of children in their beds. Doesn't sound good, I know, but it was hardcore and it shifted the ground under superpowers. You felt potent. Now I sneak into suburban neighbourhoods, living out of a fuckin' suitcase in some of the most bland hotels ever built. I spend a lot of time pretending to be a teenager online. I hunt for a specific profile. Ring leaders. Usually an intelligent kid, artsy type you could say, who reads from a list of books we know that equate crossing over with native spirit quests. Of course, that's bullshit. The real allure in this culture is drugs. It's a major high they seek, and somehow, the fact that this is achieved by ending their life on Earth is part of the pitch. It's fucked up. And it has parents so scared that authorities have tasked me, not with rounding up these kids and making sure they're safe, but to identify the local shamans and put bullets in 'em. That's the part of my job that makes sense. That's the thing I like. Find 'em online, pretend I'm some gloomy thirteen year old chick clutching a unicorn stuffy in one hand and a swearlodge manual in the other, then I go meet him and surprise him with a .45 calibre slug in the head. He goes to the big party and the local suicide party get's sent to counselling or detention or who knows what the fuck. And I get to fire a weapon on a teenager. Everybody's happy.

Right now I'm in Playland, Ontario. Snow Valley. Blue Mountain. It's the beginning of March break and lots of fucked rich kids are making their annual migration away from cushy mansions to gin-soaked chalets. These are perfect conditions for a rash of crossovers. I'm in the small town of Dingwall, hunting a particularly nasty local douche known online as Starfucks331. This guy's supposed to have sent more than 900 kids to live in the space junk and all of them rich kids. He's running a lucrative con here. Some shamans are true believers and they cross when you cross. Others, like Starfucks331, take the money and run. WasteCo has given me an address for Starfucks331. Dingwall, Ontario. Tractors and churches and Main Street and henchman for a devil somewhere in one of these basements, probably, cookin' up death on a laptop, while his parents sit upstairs watching TV. I'm gonna find you fuckwad and I'm gonna toss your mind up against a wall.

There's a high school located at the top of town and I spent some days walking it, listening for a sign. I interviewed some teachers, a guidance counsellor and a couple of church elders. Not in our town. We trust in Jesus. That may be true, but I think the kids trust in getting laid and getting bombed on Energy Pop. You're lucky, Dingwall; the worst that'll happen to your kids is they'll be pregnant and obese before they're twenty. Starfucks331 is waiting for the brats. The spring break citiots and their BMW's, designer snowboards, and appetite for hardcore escape. So I walk Main Street. Where would rich kids congregate in a shit kickin' cow town like this? Antique shops. A chocoletier. Hardware. Feed store. Tractor lot.

I nod to folks as I walk. People from the city think small towns like this one are bastions of brotherly love, community and the easy tip of the hat. These are the places where you say 'Mornin' ma'am'. Not even close. Small towners are mostly assholes. So when I nod and smile at the little bald guy sweeping the sidewalk in front of his shabby pitchfork stand, I wanna see him wince. And he does. Gives me a dirty little sneer and turns his flat ass out to me. It's okay, pal. Your daughter's fine. She's drinking cough syrup behind the diner and nodding off on a big dick. Trust in Jesus, prick.

There's no obvious place for me to start. So, I guess I'll wait till the bitches start flowing in with their fuck off Saabs and Jaeger cup holders. There's a coffee shop on the comer. A drive thru. It's too busy to be much good. This bastard needs to be settled somewhere. But goddamn, I could use a coffee right about now. I decide it's a waste of time and stroll back to the other end of town, which is a block and a half.

That's when I notice a Starbucks sitting beside a bank at the edge of a parkette. At least I'll get my coffee. I reach for the door and hear a familiar sound. A car horn. Not pressed as a warning, more like a mad goose. Here come the kids. I squint, looking up the street to see if I can see what's coming. The sun is too brilliant and I shudder. Somewhere up there a one hundred million Dead children are spinning in a slipstream. Moaning without breathing. Chewing without eating. There's madness in that light and timeless order. The Earth, like Saturn, is a ringed planet. Another horn. I slip through the door.

I'm surprised to see that most of the people in here, in this most urban of franchises, are locals. Old folk mostly, retirees with nothing to do but try specialty coffees and predict how the run off will go this spring. It's not a city Starbucks. Smells different. Metal and concrete have a smell. Here, I smell the shit of livestock thawing up wind. It gets in everything. *Everywhere.* I order an Americano and blink the cow shit from my eyes. Pleasant enough girl makes my brew. Teenager. Oddly appealing person. I find myself a bit startled by this. I fuckin' hate teenagers. Maybe she's older than she looks. I smile and drop a quarter back to the counter.

I spend the morning here at a corner table watching Main Street through a vast panoramic window. Car after car full of white kids in sunglasses. Skinny hairless arms hung out windows slapping candy coloured shit cars. If nobody stops here then I'm

472

in the wrong place. Old men in tractor caps with shit lined shoes don't get horny and blow their brains out on Spring break. And as the afternoon crawls along I'm wondering where the fuck they are. Time to go online and find the flock. I'm amused that there's wireless here. I believe mine is the first laptop opened at this particular Starbucks.

Then it hits me. Starbucks. Starbucks. I thought Starfucks331 was making a joke about sending horny kids into the sun. Not the case. Starfucks331 is Starbucks and I bet its address is 331 Main Street. His name is the place. He comes here and this is where he meets his suckers. I am definitely in the right place. I look around again. Who's coming in and who's leaving? Six old farm boys. A table of paramedics reading newspapers. An old couple. A Priest with two farm boys. Probably trusting in Jesus. I just have to wait.

And wait I do. This is apparently a public works satellite office. Garbage men. Cops. Parking enforcement. Firemen and the paramedics. The little bible school moves on apace and then I notice this: Father Dopey over there has added four to his flock. Teenagers. Six of 'em. This ain't Starfuck331, is it? Can't be. Makes no sense. These are local kids and that old padre ain't gonna attract kids with the handle Starfucks331. But there it is. That's the teenagers. And look at them. There's something too intense going on over there. The kids keep sharing little conspiratorial nods, furtive glances back. One of the girls looks like she's crying. Holy Fuck. Holy Fuck. This isn't Starfucks331. This is a faith based crossover. I heard about these. Mostly in the southern states. Not here. But if it was gonna show up anywhere else it kinda makes sense that it's here. Trust in Jesus isolation. This is just disturbing. This is end of days crap. The padre stands and puts hands on shoulders. He lowers his head and mumbles with his eyes closed. His little crew's getting ready to leave. They don't want coffee. They wanna drink the kool-Aid. I stand. I have authority to act here. I pat my weapon, curl my thumb back and pop the snap. Gonna kill a priest this morning. In a Starbucks in front of the entire public utility. Sometimes a kill feels right. I launch the weapon, gangsta style, sideways. I'm showing off. The crew-cut closest to me turns in his chair and

473

there it is. Good fuckin' Lord. They got an actual bomb on the table. I unload and miss. I'm leaning in too hard and I fall. My elbow slams the floor and the gun pops off under the table sending a slug into the padre's shin. The leg and foot below tip away and lie down. Hands are pulling me back up. Strong hands. Farm Hands. How the fuck did I fall into this hornets' nest. I can sense movement all around me. Chairs falling and tables squawking across the floor. A big brick of a fist drops down on my head and I'm dropped. This is a bad place. This isn't where I wanted to be. It's one thing to put a hole in some asshole's forehead at a spin the bottle game from hell. This is just crazy. I feel a boot hit my upper teeth. Another slams into my hip. I try to clutch, but can't. My hip is broken. Son of a bitch. My pelvis is snapped in half. They keep laying into me and it occurs to me now that this ends with me waking up surrounded by assholes I've killed. Floating in space. I can't die. I'm not kidding. I can not die. I manage to drive my hand out from under a boot and snatch up my gun. If I could die … I mean actually die, like you're supposed to, then I'd blow my own head off right now. But I can't die. It's not an option. I roll over fast and shoot straight up. Blood drops down on me from trusted jaws and barrel necks. The mob is momentarily stunned and I throw myself under their legs toward the door. The door opens and I'm lying on the sidewalk.

And then the bomb detonates.

THE END

DECEMBER IN FLORIDA
By
Asher Wismer

Cal sat motionless, wedged in the space between the soda machine and the wall. It was an unusually deep space, the soda machine being a recent model, with many more brands of soda available in a wide refrigerator. Of course, with no electricity, the machine had been off for over a year, and while the soda inside wouldn't have gone bad, Cal hated warm carbonation.

Outside, one arm reaching through the space and waving up and down an inch or two in front of his nose, was Santa Claus.

He shivered, trying to keep his breathing steady. Even though he had been back from the Dead Zone for more than a month, he still got the shakes when he confronted one. He didn't like them, didn't like the way they pushed and stumbled and killed. Not that anyone else liked them either, but for Cal it was more about the civility of the thing. You shout a warning, or fire a shot over the head. You don't just attack. War has rules.

Had rules.

His bag, with his Kukri and guns, was out in the middle of the corridor. The zombies paid it no mind; it was dead and they only liked living things. His combat vest was hanging on a chair, alongside his pants and shirt, boots and socks folded neatly underneath.

It was getting dark outside. The mall had skylights and large bay windows, so he'd had plenty of looter's light despite the lack of electricity, but he'd been trapped here for over three hours now, and the sun was setting.

Outside, the red-clad arm wavered and withdrew. Cal took in a deep breath and waited. He knew better than to run blindly, and sure enough, a different arm pushed into the space and waved around, fingers opening and closing with the mindless need to grab and infect.

This arm was bare, with chunks of skin missing. The figure behind the arm was indistinct, but Cal could see Santa behind, pushing aimlessly at the zombie that had muscled him out of the way.

It wasn't really fair, Cal thought. If anyone deserved to get a present on Christmas, it was Santa. He spent the whole year planning for the holiday, and then while everyone else had a day off he was hard at work, giving stuff away for free to screaming kids who didn't appreciate the work he put in.

Not that it was too much of an issue these days. The mall had been open to the elements, most of the windows broken, but he needed to resupply and the area had seemed to be reasonably clear. Cal had found a few things – an untouched pair of socks was very nice – and had let his guard down.

The mall had a fountain, and in the year since the infection struck, it had long since ceased pumping. The water remaining in the basin, though, was clean enough, sediments and pollutants having settled in the interim. Cal was used to going days without washing, but the urge was too strong, and he had stripped down and started to wash and … well, here he was.

Santa wasn't the only one out there. Zombies tended to stop moving and wait without visual or auditory stimulation, and these must have gone into their personal stasis after the mall cleared out. Cal had made just enough noise, and they wandered in from their various hiding places, and he had barely made it to the hiding space in time.

It was a bad mistake, Cal thought. He wouldn't let his guard down like that again, if he made it out. He had nothing on but a pair of boxers, and he couldn't risk trying to bull his way through; too much skin exposed, too much risk of infection.

At least it was warm.

The arm waved.

The sun peeked over the first skylight, sending a gleam of light down into Cal's face. He hadn't slept, hadn't dared to take the risk, and the waving arms – two now, Santa and the other, side by side – hadn't faltered.

Cal had been awake longer than this before, and he wasn't too tired yet. At some point, fatigue would take over his mind and even if he could get out, he wouldn't be able to react fast enough to keep the zombies off. That would be the tipping point, where he had to sleep or risk passing out. As it was, his body was aching with the strain of stillness. He tensed and relaxed, trying to allow his body relief, but it wasn't enough.

With the light, he tried to evaluate his status anew. The space between the top of the soda machine and the ceiling was far too narrow to climb into, and the machine itself was set into a space between the wall and a partition, meant to allow patrons some privacy as they pondered how to best spend their buck seventy-five. The partition, on the other side, meant that he couldn't push the machine sideways, which would allow him room to move but also let the zombies in. He barely fit himself as it was, so it was nothing but luck and Santa's girth that kept them out.

A gunshot. The arms, which had grabbed and grabbed all night long, froze, and then withdrew. Cal remained utterly still. Out of his sight, he heard the distinctive moan, and then two more gunshots in quick succession. Footsteps. An airhorn, from outside the mall. Clattering movement and then someone ran past the soda machine, fast, not a zombie but human and Cal jerked towards the opening and stopped, torn between his desire to escape and the danger of mistaken identity.

Santa and a few more zombies followed the running figure, more slowly, and Cal waited for them to get past. He breathed as quietly as possible. The fourth gunshot preceded a volley, and then silence.

Footsteps again, slow and measured, not halting and dragging, and therefore human. Cal closed his eyes. He knew what would happen if they saw him, and if he couldn't make them understand fast enough ...

"Someone's been here." A female voice. Good; women weren't as likely to kill on sight.

"How long ago?" Male.

"Can't say. They were clustered over there, not by this stuff ..." Clanking. "Hey, put that down."

"This is a very nice knife," said the man. "Look how thick the blade is. If he got ganked, he won't miss it."

Cal took a deep breath and allowed his body to slump as far down as possible. He let his face relax, let his body go limp, and knocked gently on the soda machine.

Outside, the sounds changed from curious to wary. "Did you hear that?"

"Someone alive?"

"Some thing, anyway."

He knocked again, making it a pattern. Three short, three long, three short. S O S.

"It's coming from over there."

"Be careful."

"It sounded human."

Cal tapped again, and again, and a shadow appeared at the opening, blocking out the increasing light.

"There's someone here," the woman said.

"Alive?"

The woman had a hunting rifle – lever action carbine – pointing vaguely in his direction. Cal knocked again. "Are you OK?" the woman said.

Cal waved his hand, but didn't get up. He had a feeling, and wanted to seem less capable in case his feeling was right.

"He's alive, but I think he's hurt," the woman said.

"Infected?"

"I don't see any bites, and he's not acting like he's turned."

"Why isn't he speaking?"

"I don't know. Why aren't you speaking?"

Cal motioned to his mouth and neck, and then shook his head. He moved his hands, in case she knew sign.

"I think he's mute," the woman said. "Can you get up?"

Cal pushed against the walls, making each movement seem painful, and started to move out of the tight space.

"Wait," the woman said. She backed away. "Vin, come here and cover me."

With the space open, Cal crawled out, looking up. The man was short, hairy, and wore a hunting vest covered and filled with things. He had Cal's Kukri in one hand and a pair of revolvers holstered on each side. The woman was taller, but very thin; she held her rifle like a professional, not pointing directly at him but easily aimed if the occasion rose.

"He looks terrible," the man – Vin – said. "Stand up, if you

478

can, and turn around. Let us see."

Cal complied, still moving as if he was weak. He made a complete rotation and Vin said, "Take off the shorts."

"Vin, he's fine."

"We can't be sure unless we're sure, Candy. Stranger, take off the shorts and turn again. Slowly."

Cal understood; he would have done the same. At least he was clean; he dropped the shorts, raised his arms, and made a second, slower, circle.

"Fine," Vin said. "Put your things back on. You know, we saved your ass here. The least you could do is say thank you."

"Vin—"

Cal pulled his boxers back up and repeated his earlier motions at his mouth and throat. He finished by shaking his head and signing, "I can't speak."

Candy said, "Vin, he's mute. He can't talk."

"Well, I don't read sign. How's he gonna talk to us?"

"I never learned," Candy said. "Maybe he can write."

Cal nodded. He was used to people assuming the inability to speak vocally meant mental retardation, so he took no offense. He walked to the fountain, slowly, keeping his arms out from his sides. Vin and Candy watched as he pulled his pants and shirt on, socks and boots, and finally the combat vest. His pack was behind the chair.

"You got anything to write with?" Vin said.

Cal shook his head.

"There'll be something here in the mall," Candy said. "Vin, give him his knife back."

"Not yet," Vin said. "We don't know if he's safe or not. He might be one of those baiters, gets travellers to drop their guards and then kill them for their gear."

"He was trapped in there, maybe for days," Candy said. "Look at him. He can barely walk."

Cal didn't smile.

"Don't trust anyone, not these days." Vin pointed to one of the shops, windows shattered and rotting merchandise strewn across the tiles. "Stranger, get something to write with and tell us who you are and how you got here. We'll decide what to do after that."

"Vin," Candy said. "Give him his knife. You're not sending him into a dark shop without defence."

Vin hesitated, and Candy took a step forward. "Fine," he said. "Stranger, turn around. Don't move unless I say."

Cal turned. He felt the movement as Vin approached, placed the Kukri on the floor behind at his feet, and backed away.

"Now you can move," he said.

It was like a bizarre game of Red Light Green Light. Cal turned, picked up the Kukri, and held it loosely in his left hand. Vin pulled one of his revolvers and thumbed the hammer back.

"Go on," he said.

Cal turned and scanned the shops. Most of them would be empty, or close to it. Looters had long since ravaged through; perishable items had perished, and anything else would be useless or hard to carry. He chose the closest shop, a florist, with big open (and broken) windows letting in the light from the corridor.

He walked to the shop and peered inside. This, he knew, was where most people made their mistakes. Zombies were brainless, but accidentally cunning; one could be stuck behind a counter, throat cut so it couldn't moan and alert himself to its presence. That, he decided, was why the two travellers had blown the airhorn. It excited the zombies and brought them out where they could be dealt with. It was a good idea. He would have to find one somewhere.

Without that option, Cal settled for kicking in a chunk of unbroken glass. It shattered across the tile floor of the shop, making an enormous racket that no zombie could possibly miss. He waited.

There was no sound from the shop, and he walked in through the broken window, right to the counter. No one, it seemed, had bothered to loot the florist at all; the broken windows were the extent of the damage. All the flowers had died, wilted, and rotted, the dry ones crumbling to dust and the ones still in water turning to some sort of horrible slime. There were bouquets of plastic flowers here and there, looking uncommonly cheerful and bright among the wreckage.

480

Behind the counter, Cal found a pad of credit card receipts and a pen, which was dry. He rooted around and found a whole box of pens. He tested a few, stuck a couple in his vest, and took the box out with him. You never knew what items would be useful barter.

Outside, Candy was still covering the shop, while Vin rotated one turn every other second or so, keeping the open area under supervision. Cal walked to the chair and sat down. He put the box of pens down and started to write.

"He's been walking north," Candy said. "The last thing he heard was a talk radio station from New York, so he figures there might be people left alive up there."

"I doubt it," Vin said. "There's nobody and nothing north of Mason Dixon. Why would you stay in a cold area?"

"Maybe they're waiting for the zombies to freeze."

Cal tore off another sheet and handed it to Candy.

"He's been trapped there for two days? Wow."

"I don't buy that," Vin said. "He'd have shit himself a couple of times."

Cal made eating motions and shook his head.

"No food?"

Cal nodded.

"This is silly," Vin said. "He's a drifter, and I don't trust him. We should get out of here."

"Vin," Candy said. "You were the one holding the knife on him. He's been trapped. Cut him a little slack. I mean, he was here first."

"Well."

Cal tore off another sheet, handed it over, and stood up.

"He's leaving," Candy said.

"Fine."

"Wait," Candy said. "Calvin, you should come with us."

"No," Vin said.

Cal shook his head.

"We're heading west, once we get past the panhandle. We think if there's people alive anywhere, it would be Texas."

"Don't tell him that!"

481

"We've been walking a long time; gas is hard to come by and the roads are pretty well clogged. Would you like to come with us?"

Cal thought about it. It made a certain amount of sense to band together. Multiple people meant safety; it meant someone could stand watch while the others slept, it meant they could carry more gear; it meant they could help each other.

He didn't want to lie to himself, so he allowed the thought that it also meant the zombies would have more targets and thus he personally would have a better chance of survival.

Still, he'd gotten this far on his own. The last group he'd tried to join had splintered apart too quickly; quarrels over leadership were deadly, post-collapse.

"Candy," Vin said. "We're doing fine on our own. We don't need another mouth to feed, and we certainly don't need someone stupid enough to get trapped like that. Shit, he was naked. Why would you take your clothing off in the middle of a zombie mall?"

"I expect he didn't know they were there."

"How do you NOT know zombies are around? They're not known for their stealth!"

Cal knelt and tightened his bootlaces. He pulled his pack over and examined it. Nothing seemed to be out of place. He hoisted it, slipped the credit pad into his vest, gave Candy a salute, and started walking.

"Wait!"

"Let him go …"

When Cal was out of their sight, he could still hear them arguing. Their voices echoed in the mall, no talking customers or Muzak to drown them out. He looked around and focused on a drugstore, smashed and looted like the rest. He made some noise, enough to draw anything inside out, and then made a quick loot in and out. There wasn't much; a few candy bars, a single glass bottle of water, and – jackpot! – a full carton of Slim Jims. They weren't the most healthy thing to subsist on, but they had good calories for the size and they lasted forever. He stuffed the carton into his pack, poked his head out, and left the mall.

Outside, the sun was high in the sky. The days were shorter

in the winter, even this close to the equator, so Cal decided to get on the road as fast as possible. He froze under the mall entrance, listening for anything that sounded dangerous.

There was still a slight murmur from inside, but not enough to drown out anything shambling around. He couldn't see anything moving, and there were a number of zombie bodies in the parking lot that hadn't been there the day before; fruit of the traveller's battle, earlier.

His bike was untouched, sideways under the burnt-out wreckage of an enormous SUV. He'd figured nobody would bother examining the wreck; it couldn't have any value, charred inside and out on melted tires. There was decent clearance underneath, though, and he pulled the bike out, checked the tires, and swung on.

Cal's memory told him that there was an Army base nearby. He hadn't heard anything on his crank radio for days now, no shortwave, no HAM, no CB, and certainly no AM/FM since that last broadcast. If there was anyone alive in the base, they were keeping radio silence and waiting it out.

Behind him, he heard the clatter of footsteps. He dropped the bike, turning and whipping his Kukri out in a manner made smooth by too many roadside ambushes.

It was Candy. She was alone, coming out of the mall, rifle slung over her shoulder.

"Wait," she said. "Wait."

Cal checked the four directions, stepped back over his bike to keep it between them, and waited. He re-sheathed the Kukri, but kept his hand down over the handle.

She got within a yard and stopped. Her eyes were wet.

"That bastard," she said. "He won't budge on anything, not ever. It kept us alive, God knows, we would never have made it if he'd been more complacent, but he's just so stubborn."

Cal raised a hand at the mall, made two fingers, and then shrugged.

"I think you mean why did I come out alone?"

Cal nodded.

"He wants to stay and loot. I can't stand it; we don't need anything. I only wanted to stop to rest and stay out the night if

483

we could find a safe place in there. I know malls are dangerous, too many places for them to hide, but I just feel safer with walls and a roof. I don't mean to be insulting, but we didn't expect to find anyone alive."

Cal nodded and placed a hand over his heart. He left it there for a beat, then clasped his hands together and held them up, waving them at her.

"You're grateful we stopped to rescue you?"

Nod.

"I don't want you to feel in debt or anything," she said. "It's just ... we've been walking for so long. He keeps talking, won't ever shut up. He's right, they were wrong, look where it got them ... just over and over and over. I get so sick of him."

Cal shrugged.

"You don't talk," she said. "That's OK. I just wanted to spend some time with someone who wasn't him, you know? I'll go back to him, of course I will. He's good at this, he's just so ... you know?"

From inside the mall, two quick shots.

Candy whirled, Cal pulled his Kukri and they ran towards the entrance.

Two more bodies, fresh. Cal had long since stopped checking bodies to see if he could tell if they were dead or alive when they had been killed; one to the head, everything's dead. It made no difference. The chair by the fountain was knocked over. There was fresh blood in the fountain.

"Oh no," Candy said. "Please no, please God–"

Cal scanned the area. There was no sign of Vin, or his gear; a few shell casings littered the floor by the bodies.

"He must have stopped to reload," Candy said. "He must have got bit. Shit, please don't let him get infected, but they don't bleed–"

The florist shop was nestled underneath a staircase. This mall had no escalators, and Cal didn't see an elevator, not that they would be functioning. He glanced up at a skylight. Still plenty of sun.

"Vin!"

No answer.

Gunshot from above. Cal looked up and saw something falling; he dodged to the left and a body slammed into the floor.

Santa.

He'd looked bad enough already. The first bullet, the one from Candy and Vin's brief struggle while Cal was trapped, must have skimmed the edges of the brain without destroying it. Cal had seen it before; if any part of the inhuman brain remained, it could still direct the body to some degree. Now, though, Vin's second bullet had left a nice clean hole directly between the eyes. There was no chance of Santa returning next year.

A single shot boomed around the mall. Nothing else.

Candy broke for the stairs.

Cal followed Candy up the stairs, much more slowly, checking up and down with each step. He thought about Vin's holsters. Maybe he'd work on something like that for his own pistol, a small .22 currently empty and useless in his pack. He hadn't seen a horde for so long that he trusted in his own abilities with the Kukri, but now he thought about changing his strategy some.

At the top of the stairs, Candy was kneeling by Vin's prone figure. She wasn't speaking, wasn't making any noise at all. Cal walked over.

Vin was dead. A ragged bite in his arm showed his motive, the round hole in his own forehead showed the cause.

"I shouldn't have left him," Candy said. "But he made me so mad. It's not my fault. Not your fault; you couldn't have stopped this. He was careful, usually so careful."

Cal walked past them and looked around. No movement. He came back and knelt by Candy, watching her. She wasn't touching the body; it wouldn't have had time to become infectious, but there was no sense inviting trouble.

"I guess it's just me now," she said. "Unless you want company. It would make sense ... but you have that bike. I'd need something too. It's not going to work."

Cal shrugged. He didn't want to leave her there, but if she wouldn't go with him, it wasn't his problem. He had stopped thinking of altruism the day his superiors had sent him to Florida

485

to try and quell the outbreak before it tipped.

"Listen," she said. "Can you stay with me here, for a bit? I need to get his things, and dispose–"

Her voice broke. Cal waited. He wasn't good at personal, and he couldn't fill her silences.

"We'll burn him, if we can find anything. I know gas gels after a while, but it should still burn, right? Will you help me?"

Cal shrugged and nodded. It wasn't like he was in a hurry.

A couple of the cars in the parking lot still had gas in the tanks; gelled, as Candy had expected, but they managed to puncture them enough for the gelled gas to slip through into a container. Candy took Vin's pack, emptied his pockets, but left him clothed.

"His boots won't fit me," she explained, "and I don't want to risk his clothing. No extra risks; he said that, all the time. It's why he didn't want me inviting you along."

They brought the gas up to the body, and Cal broke a skylight with a rock after a few throws. The gelled gas heaped on the body instead of soaking in, and they lumped it inside Vin's jacket and around his legs and head.

The body burned just fine.

"I guess you should head on north," Candy said. Cal watched her in the fading light. She wasn't crying anymore, but the lines in her face had deepened. "I'd only slow you down."

Cal scribbled on the credit card pad, tore the sheet.

"I don't think you should be alone," she read. "Well, for what? I've got no chance on my own, and I don't want to get you killed too. I don't even know you."

Scribble, tear.

"I bet there's a bike or something in the mall, if we search hard enough," she read. "In a back room, or locked on a rack where the looters couldn't get to it."

Cal nodded, gestured.

"Why would you want me along?" she said. "I'm a middle manager from Orlando. The only reason I'm alive is because of Vin. I don't have any skills."

Cal thought about this. It was true; there was little reason to take an unskilled person along with him. Pragmatism ruled all in zombie territory. Finally, he wrote three words, tore the sheet, and handed it over.

"You can learn," Candy read. She looked up at Cal, and then laughed, a hard bark with no humour behind it.

"I guess you've got something there," she said. "It's getting dark, though, so we'd better hole up for the night and search at dawn."

Cal nodded.

They re-entered the mall and searched for a store with a security gate and no back exit. Many of the gates had been torn out by looters. Cal finally checked the florist, and sure enough, the security gate was still rolled up into the ceiling. There was no lock, but he laid a few chairs alongside the gate, legs stuck in so they'd fall and crash if the gate was moved.

The broken windows were another problem entirely. Cal finally settled for stacking more chairs, gathered from all over the mall, up in front, so there was no way an outside force could get past without knocking them over. It was good enough for the night. Without a travelling partner, the only way he'd sleep was in a tree or with much more security.

Cal was exhausted; he hadn't slept since the night before, but he offered – with gestures – to take first watch. To his relief, Candy shook her head.

"I'm not tired at all," she said. "You go ahead and rest. I'll wake you at dawn."

He didn't argue.

They found her a bike. It was somewhat rusty, and it took Cal several patches to get the inner tubes properly inflated, but in the end they set out on the road together. Cal kept his pace slow; he didn't know how good she was for endurance, but soon they were whipping along the coast highway at a respectable clip, slowing only to weave around the wrecks and abandoned cars that littered the highway.

They passed a massive car dealership, still decked out in holiday colours. Cal wondered if there was another dead Santa inside, wandering aimlessly among the cars, and then it was behind them and he gave it no more thought. It was the end of December, and Cal decided that anything still alive in the North could wait for warmer weather.

The road stretched out ahead along the Florida panhandle. If they continued on the coast, they'd pass briefly through Alabama and Mississippi, and then a long stretch through Louisiana. Soon enough they'd need to stop and get some serious supplies for the road, food and water and so forth. Cal had been just winging it, day by day, but he knew that the road would only get rougher.

The next town, maybe. They'd find something that hadn't been used up yet.

Candy rode beside him, stone-faced. She'd get better in time, get more experience, and wouldn't need him anymore when he decided to move on. She'd forget about Vin, and about Cal in time, assuming they made it alive. Cal lifted one hand and switched on his radio, attached to his combat vest, and set it for a cycling scan, listening for anything at all.

"Go west," Candy said, the rushing air whipping her words away. "Go west, young man." She laughed.

Cal smiled. She'd be OK.

THE END

ONE DEAD WHORE
By
Wayne Simmons

He was a gentleman.

Carla should have known that meant nothing around London's East End in 1888.

As a lady of the night selling her malnourished curves for a little bread and a lot of gin, she of all people should have worked out by now that the so-called gentlemen were, almost always, the worst. Gentlemen had frequent little 'holidays' from their prim little wives. Gentlemen clients were rare, it must be said, but those she had regularly were the most demanding. Compared to her usual scrubbers, their manners were atrocious.

Take, for example, wee Eddie from the butcher's shop. Carla's heart went out to him so much that she'd on occasion tossed him a free one. Dear little Ed, about as far from being a gentleman as England was to France, would save up his pennies for months before tripping along to the shadows of her patch, sweaty-palmed and meek, looking for nothing more than a strong-handed wank and a cuddle. It almost would have been a pleasure if the poor fucker weren't so bloody ugly.

With a gentleman it was never a pleasure. It was nothing but sick shite. Violence. Indecency. Indignity. Carla was no angel by any stretch of the imagination, but she still had good high-church values. Or would have had, of course, if her love of drink hadn't outstripped all else.

Of late, it seemed, *any* clients were rare, though, so when a gentleman came looking for her, she wasn't going to say no. She didn't know what big a mistake that was then ...

... but she knew now.

Carla, like everyone else, blamed the recent murders for the drought in business. They were the most troubling thing to hit London since the Great Fire. Everyone knew about them, and everyone was on edge. Five girls, all friends with whom she'd shared a bottle, had run afoul of her gentleman. They'd been mutilated. Bits of them had been removed and taken away. They'd been gutted like sows in seconds. Letters had been sent to the press. Authorities were taunted. It took strategy, precision and a malevolence Carla couldn't even begin to understand.

That same gentleman had decided to claim a very special part of Carla while she lay like a torn and festering rose on the bloodstained cobbles. As her vision receded into blackness, Carla felt a long, slender knife tear into an all-too-familiar place beneath her skirts ...

... he was a gentleman, after all.

Her eyes flicked open like a switch.

She was still lying where he had left her, in the cold, filthy dark of one of Whitechapel's many backstreets. Those who had happened by her corpse had wisely ignored her, probably more concerned for their own lives than her dignity. Her blood had congealed into the stones. Her heart didn't beat, and her flesh felt even colder than the scum of frost coating her dress. Carla was no longer alive, of that she was sure.

But she wasn't dead, either ...

With no heartbeat, there came no panic, and so Carla rose from the ground with relative ease and nonchalance. Her first steps were a little unladylike, her limbs refusing to shake off a certain manly shuffle she associated with ironsmiths, but soon her seductive stride returned.

Her beauty remained untouched; the same finely cut cheekbones in life, now a little paler, still framed perfect features. Her eyes, a striking bright gray, were even more piercing now. Her hair had fallen from its braided bun and now streamed in dishevelled waves down her back. Of all her charms that remained, her heartbeat was the most notable absence – that and her manners, it seemed. A deep, gnawing hunger clutched her and her lips were slick with drool. A low moaning sound escaped her, something between a burp and a growl.

She decided she needed a drink to sort herself out. Carla made her way to the pub.

She cared nothing for her peculiar appearance or predicament. As she passed through the deserted streets of London's East End, their rich cocktail of smells seemed more appealing than usual. A dense, salty mist from the fishmonger's

490

swamped her. The butcher's shop, where wee Eddie worked, offered an even thicker, more alluring stench, spoiled only by the sickly, poisonous sting of the florist's stock on Whitechapel Lane. Carla felt even more hungry than before as she battled to hold on to those more fleshy aromas that stirred the pit of her guts so magnificently. Utterly famished and still thirsty for gin, she approached the pub, pleased that its lamps still burned.

Inside, Carla could hear familiar voices. She struggled to remember things and people that once meant everything to her. The taste of gin and wine. The smell of sawdust and sweat, tobacco and snuff. The scarred wooden tables and faintly polished bar. The clinking of glasses and bottles. The sounds of laughter and voices, stained with pent-up aggression and a loathing of poverty.

Carla battled against the hunger, fearing that it would consume her completely the way her thirst for gin often did after a good night's takings. Her old self still felt pangs for merriment and joviality that her new self neither knew nor cared for. Everything was different ... yet nothing had changed.

Frustrated and hungry and angry and queasy all at once, Carla battered clumsily against the doors of the pub, desperate to get inside where more delectably-repugnant fleshy smells awaited her ...

The Gentleman in the corner sat with his head bent over the table, hat still on. A small black case lay by his side. He did not glance up as the draught from the opened door carried in the East End's distinctive fragrance. One hand was curled gently around a small glass of wine, the other rose slowly to his shadowed lips to offer a finely-scented cigar. The tip of the cigar brightened briefly as he inhaled, then darkened again as he tipped its ashes onto the floor. He was the picture of calm propriety, yet inside him burned a violent and insatiable lust for chaos.

Scattered around him, oblivious to his presence, drunken slummers talked of The Gentleman's ongoing work in Whitechapel. A rumour was circulating that another body had been spotted. Another woman, gutted. In one corner, a large red-faced man played out the latest murder with all the finesse of

Shakespeare's Falstaff, wielding his pipe as if it were the Ripper's deadly blade. The Gentleman smiled. From behind him, several older women, one speaking almost incoherently due to her rotted teeth, spat and shrieked at one another, each competing for the limelight by exaggerating their story of what had happened with greater and greater extremes of ridiculousness. They were calling him The Ripper, yet many of them talked about him as if he were nothing less than The Devil himself.

He liked that ...

The Gentleman lifted his glass as if to drink to another night's fine work. He contemplated that it might be his last, for a while, what with having gathered together most of the parts he needed. In fact, what with tonight's particular takings, he had more than enough. He drained his glass dry, patted his lips with a handkerchief, then stood.

From another table, four sets of eyes followed his every move, alert and silent, whilst another woman remained hidden from him in the shadows. He clocked them all, yet offered no reaction. He could almost smell their sexes. They were, no doubt, of the same ilk as the others. Whores riddled with equal measures of darkness and beauty. Indulgent of vice, yet still, somehow, pristine. These women held a special place in The Gentleman's heart, and he wanted to show them just how much he loved them ... but not now. Not tonight. Not for a while. He had other work to do. Dark and powerful magicks had to be called upon to create an ultimate beauty. Everything needed had been collected.

As The Gentleman stood up, one of the women rose also.

Then came the knocking on the door ...

Lisa was sweating heavily; the voices in the pub swirled around her like fog, threatening to kill her silent chant. Beneath her cloak, her face was bright red. Blood pooled in the canals of her ears and whites of her eyes. One hand shook profusely. The other left a bloody trail across the bar table as her fingers dug deep into the old wood. She was as close to death as the corpse she had manipulated was to life.

A student of the dark arts for many years, Lisa had worked

long and hard to reach this level. Every text she had studied warned of the penalty for dabbling as she had, but she had never dreamed it would be like this. Still, she persisted, digging deep within her broken heart to wreak the righteous havoc that was so desperately needed in Whitechapel.

He had to be stopped.

Four other women surrounded her, the rage and fear in their hearts mirroring the carnage ravishing Lisa's very being. Yet, they remained po-faced and discreet, supporting Lisa with nervous resilience. The bar's noise continued to swell around them; the smell of liquor and tobacco rife throughout. All four women broke out in a sweat now as their friend and colleague gasped once, then twice, before her cloaked body began to tremor in a manner most unladylike.

Then came the knock.

It was old Tom who opened the door, finally, but he didn't seem to recognise her. Carla was used to the sorry old sod grinning and drooling inanely at her every time they met, but this time, on seeing her, his face came over dreadfully pale, and a short yelp left his pickled lips before he ran into the street in a panic. Others followed suit. The normally lively pub emptied in seconds as Carla stepped inside. Even Al, the pub's landlord and all-round local heavy, made for the door screaming like a baby. Before long only one table was left occupied, and one man remained standing.

A gentleman. Her gentleman.

Carla's eyes burned a deep and dark red now, the bizarre violence filling her utterly. A gout of blood suddenly spurted from her lips and plopped onto her chin. She craved this man, this gentleman's flesh like she had never craved anything before. She craved his smell, the feel of his skin, the very taste of his heart. She longed to unwrap his body.

Like a wildcat, she pounced, but he was quicker. He side-stepped easily out of her feral reach. As Carla sprawled forward into the shadows, knocking clumsily into a table, her gentleman snatched up his little black case.

She righted herself, shaking her head like a wounded

animal, before pouncing again. The Gentleman produced a long, gleaming blade. His eyes, bright with lust, remained fixed on her. He tipped his hat then beckoned to her with one hand.

She rushed him again. This time as he stepped to the side he thrust his slender blade deep into her belly with all the grace of a matador. Carla stumbled. The gentleman wasted no time. He grabbed the knife's handle with one hand and her delicate shoulders with the other, and in one fluid motion he ripped her open from pubis to breastbone. Carla watched bemused as her innards slopped nosily onto the sawdust floor. The Gentleman looked at her contentedly as he brought the blade to his nostrils and inhaled her scent.

But Carla wasn't done.

A smile curled across her face. Her gentleman had expected her to die. She pounced again, this time taking him by surprise. His perfectly polished boots slipped in her gore, and as he lost his footing, he toppled right into her waiting grasp.

Her teeth tore into his face as if it were mutton pie, stripping cartilage and bone. He wrapped his arms around her in a perverted embrace, and she felt him reaching into her gutted torso, his hands trying to gain some kind of purchase to push her away. She could taste the ghost of his fine cigar in his blood.

The Gentleman roared. Carla silenced him when she tore his larynx from his corded throat. Thick curtains of blood spilt onto his white shirt. Carla worked her teeth and her fingernails, peeling, tearing and unravelling every inch of her gentleman. She unpeeled him in the sawdust like a palpitating artichoke, making small mewing sounds of contentment as she worked and ate.

The five women at the table sat motionless. The creature they had all known as Carla Jenkins was spread-eagled on the floor, gnawing on every scrap of flesh and bone left of the Gentleman, scraps that poured out of her torso even as she swallowed them. His black case sat useless and open on a nearby table, the surgical instruments glistening under the gaslights. The spine of a book was also visible. "*Frankenstein* by Mary Shelley," the women would have read had they been close enough to make out the lettering.

Lisa was the first to get up. She removed the cloak from her ravished face with one shaking hand. Another woman immediately rose with her, steadying her with her arm as the frail, magick-worn woman stumbled. With the help of her friend, the weary witch shuffled over to the blood-stained mess that had been Carla Jenkins. Lisa stretched her hand down to caress the feral woman's long, wet locks, feeling the dark energy from the Gentleman's blood as it seeped from her friend's hair onto her own hands.

For a moment she felt the raw evil that had raged in the Gentleman's heart surge through her own, evil she had worked so hard to purge from Whitechapel. A tear trickled down her cheek, smarting in its damp trail, and she looked again at her friend.

"Oh Carla ..." she said, her heart heavy. "Oh Carla ... why did he have to do this to us?"

The other woman whispered softly into Lisa's ear, gently trying to lead her away from the mess that had been her lover.

"Come on now, love," she said. "It's done now. It's done."

Outside, a respectful silence descended upon Whitechapel. It was as if the East End mourned in a sign of solidarity with the women of the night it knew so well. Darkness kissed and caressed the breeze, finally spitting its choked up emotion as rain gathered in the air.

Somewhere close, a tall, nervous man approached a woman standing on a street corner.

It was business as usual.

THE END

SEAHOUSES SLAUGHTERHOUSE
By
Rod Glenn

Video shop owner, serial killer and self-confessed film fanatic, Han Whitman was used to death. He had introduced quite a few to it, but even Han was somewhat perturbed by the dead rising.

Was it bad form to rise again after being killed? Han thought so. Downright bloody rude too. He prided himself in politeness and reliability. He was always polite to his victims and as reliable as clockwork at killing them. So this ... this was just bad form ...

"We're here," Han said after driving through the small shopping centre of the Northumberland coastal town of Seahouses. Shopping 'centre' might've been a slight exaggeration; it was essentially one street filled with chip shops, arcades and gift shops.

The sign read, *Seafield Caravan Park.*

"Oh, you really know how to treat a girl," Cara said with a smile.

Han gave a sideways glance of feigned annoyance. Feigned, of course, as in the six months they had been dating, he had been unable to get even remotely annoyed at her for one second. Even when the demands of the relationship clashed with the old serial killing malarkey. Bless her. And for a copper (yes, Old Mother Irony does play a cheeky hand), she was bloody hot. More than a little likeness to Uma Thurman.

This was actually their second trip to Seahouses and Cara knew damn fine that the caravan park was very nice and that it had a well-equipped spa and gym.

Han pulled up to the site office and jumped out of the Jeep Cherokee, leaving the engine idling.

The office was bright and airy and the mid-morning sunshine was pouring in through the expansive windows. No one about though.

"Hello? Anyone about? We're checking in to one of your holiday vans." He turned around and looked back at Cara waiting in the car. She mouthed, *what?* to him and his response was a shrug. He turned back to the desk to find an old woman now standing behind it. Surprised, Han said, "Hi ... erm, checking in."

The old woman seemed to stare through him for a time and then abruptly burst into a rattling cough that sounded like a cancer-ridden vagrant being strangled by a schizophrenic cat.

She finished by swallowing hard, which conjured images of a cantankerous curse-wielding gypsy from a certain Sam Raimi film. With an off-white handkerchief covering her mouth, she said, "Sorry, dear. There's been a horrible bug going round this week – seems like the whole town's got it."

Han drove through the site to their designated van, passing rows of new and gleaming vans set in perfectly manicured lawns. There were plenty of parked cars outside most of them, but very few people about. Strange for an unusually hot bank holiday weekend.

After unpacking, they took a stroll down the beach. They passed a young couple playing with a baby near the water's edge. Dad was making a little sandcastle which the baby kept smashing with a plastic spade, causing both parents to giggle at one another.

Jesus, Han thought.

"Might be us one day," Cara said, nodding towards the happy little family.

Han's first response would normally be, *I'll kill you if you get pregnant*, but that seemed inappropriate, given his hobby. He had no intention of killing Cara, whether pregnant or not. Although, it wasn't out of the question to run for the hills if she got up the duff. Instead, he muttered, "Hmm."

Cara laughed. "I'm winding you up, man. I'm just getting started in my career. I'm not looking to mess with that – or my figure, for that matter. Not for at least another five years or so."

They approached an old man who was standing in the middle of the beach with a dog lead in his hand and a blank expression.

Cara glanced quizzically at Han.

"You okay, mate?" Han offered.

497

The man continued to stare into the middle distance in the direction of the dunes, seemingly oblivious to their presence.

"I said …"

Cara cut him off. "Leave it," she whispered.

As they left the man behind, Cara glanced back. He still hadn't moved. "Maybe he's upset – lost a loved one recently or something. I've seen it before."

When they walked back along the beach half an hour later, the old man was gone. They continued into Seahouses and, after a wander around some of the gift shops, found a small pub called The Olde Ship Inn.

A couple of burly men were stood at the bar, chatting to the barman, but the place was otherwise empty.

"What can I get ya?" the young barman asked with a friendly smile.

"Guinness and a …"

"Kronenbourg," Cara finished for him.

"Pints?"

"Do they come any other way?" Cara asked.

"Hell no," he said and smiled. "My kinda people."

As the barman poured the drinks, Han said, "Bit dead for a bank holiday, isn't it?"

He nodded absently. "Seems like most of the town is down with this bug – playing havoc with trade."

As is sometimes the way with impromptu pub visits, Han and Cara ended up spending the whole afternoon and most of the evening there. They had a good craic on with the barman and the only two other customers. That was, until one of the customers broke out into a coughing fit and unceremoniously hurled the contents of his stomach onto the wood floor.

A little pissed, they swaggered arm in arm back to the caravan as the night was drawing in.

Somewhere over the other side of town, they heard shouting and breaking glass.

"Shall I go and arrest 'em?" Cara asked and found the idea most amusing.

"I'm sure local plod can handle it," Han said, giving her a squeeze.

They broke open a bottle of Jack Daniels and caned a good portion of it before Cara fell asleep in the middle of a game of Poker.

Han gently carried her to the snug bedroom, undressed her and then pulled the covers over. He then walked back into the lounge and poured himself another shot. As he sipped it, a smile played across his lips. He was a little tipsy, but still perfectly capable. How about a spontaneous slaying, eh? He was on holiday, after all.

"Why the hell not," he said to himself. He wrote a quick note saying that he had gone for a walk along the beach, just in case Cara woke up, and then collected his trusty combat knife from the hidden compartment in the boot of the Jeep.

It was a warm night, so he didn't bother with a jacket. He knew where the CCTV cameras were in Seahouses, so he'd just stay away from those areas. Too hot to wear a balaclava. And so passé.

He strolled through the caravan site, hoping for a spot of inspiration. It was all quiet, so he took a narrow lane, lined on both sides by tall hedgerows, and headed back towards the beach.

The crunch of boots on gravel was the only noise. He was nearing the end of the lane when a figure appeared at the bottom where it opened out into a large car park.

Do we have a winner? Han thought, hopeful. He kept his pace steady and quickly closed the gap, not wanting to miss a possible opportunity.

The person – a thickset man in a shabby overcoat – remained standing at the end of the lane, unmoving.

Maybe he's a would-be mugger? Han mused. *Wouldn't that be a hoot!* "You got a light, mate?" Han asked as he grew closer still.

The man remained silent and motionless.

As Han reached within stabbing distance, the Moon slipped out from behind a cloud and illuminated the man's face.

The man was missing an ear and most of a cheek and one eye was hanging by the optic nerve out of a gaping maw that used to be the socket. It has to be said that this was not exactly what Han had been expecting. The man's clothes were ripped and caked in blood and his face had the waxy pallor of a dead man (yes, he'd seen plenty of those in his time to know). So, it was doubly surprising when the creature decided to lunge at him with cold outstretched hands, one of which was gripping a dog lead.

"Wo-ah!" Han uttered, stepping back quickly and drawing the knife from behind his back. "Still not found your dog, I see. Mate, I was going to kill you for – let's say shits and giggles – but it looks like someone beat me to it."

The creature emitted a low moan that had a lonely desperation to it. It advanced on him in a slow shambling way.

Han stepped back to keep the distance between them. "Beat me to it?" he repeated. "Who do I think I am? Simon Pegg?"

It kept coming, a viscose slime drooling out of the corner of its gaping mouth.

"This is a joke, right? I know it's not Halloween, but, I don't know, is there some kind of Seahouses tradition of dressing up like the undead on bank holidays? If there is, you should be aiming it at the Goths – they love that sort of thing." Shaking his head, he added, "You're rambling when you should be rambling the hell out of here."

He had backed up nearly to the entrance back into the caravan site.

"Okay, I'm going to erm … kill you … I hope." With that, Han slashed at the creature's throat. The jugular opened up like a whore's legs, but only a small amount of congealed blood oozed out of the opening. It kept coming.

"Okay, I guess I was kind of expecting that. We've all seen the movies." As an afterthought, he said, "Christ, at least you're the Romero kind and not the 28 Days Later sort."

He hacked at the outstretched hands and saw several severed fingers plop onto the gravel. It still kept coming.

"Oh, fuck this." Han leapt at it and drove the knife deep into the gaping eye socket. After twisting it several times, it stopped thrashing and fell to the ground ... dead ... again.

Breathing hard, Han stood over the corpse, unaware that the knife was dripping gore onto his boots. After a moment, he nodded and said, "Okay ... okay, I erm ... I can see where this is going. I think I've stumbled on to the wrong film set here. This isn't my usual role. What happened to a sensible crime thriller?" He was rambling again, but to be fair, he felt that he was handling things rather well so far.

Somewhere behind him in the caravan site he heard a crash, followed by a scream.

Cara. "Shit!" As he turned to run into the site, a hand grasped his throat and a woman fell into him, sending him staggering into the hedgerow. Icy fingers sunk into the flesh of his neck and a stinking dead mouth descended, as if preparing to kiss him.

Shoving her back, he said, "Not in this life, pet. It'll put me right in the doghouse with Cara."

She came at him again, snarling and scratching. Han grabbed her by the bedraggled hair and proceeded to saw her head clean from its neck. It didn't take too much effort – Han kept a very sharp blade.

The body stopped moving, but the head had other ideas. Its mouth continued to snap at him and the eyes rolled feverishly. "Head's up, bitch," he said and kicked it into the hedge.

He was off and running into the caravan site. Two people – living ones – sprinted past him. Behind, there were half a dozen creatures lumbering towards them.

Han shouted after them, "Guys, you're only tiring yourselves out! Take your time! That's the kind of rookie error they make in the films!" Shaking his head, he headed at a more sustainable pace towards their van.

He past close to one creature and punched it across the jaw, sending it reeling. He could see their van up ahead with a creature clawing at the door. He hadn't locked it. Bugger!

The door opened and the creature stumbled inside. Han finally broke into a sprint. He reached the door in time to see the creature disappearing into the bedroom.

"Cara!" Han yelled as he rushed inside. "Wake up! Wake the fuck up!"

The creature fell onto the bed and clawed at Cara's sleeping form. The weight of the creature on the bed was finally stirring her.

"Cara!" Han grabbed its muddied shoe and dragged it away from Cara's face as its jaws snapped shut an inch from her tender cheek. It struggled in his grasp, catching her hair in an extended hand and tearing a handful out as Han wrenched it backwards.

Cara cried out and finally woke up. "For fuck's sake! What the fuck are you doing?"

Gasping with exertion, Han managed, "Cara, get the fuck up!"

Cara's eyes adjusted to the scene. She screamed, but then police training immediately kicked in (it might not have so quickly if she'd fully realised what it was that was attacking her). She untangled its hand from her hair and swiftly twisted it and snapped the wrist. She jumped free, crashing into the fitted wardrobe then fumbled around in the dark for clothes. "What the hell's going on?"

Han pulled the creature off the bed and stamped on its head repeatedly until it caved in.

Cara stopped with one arm inside a blouse. "No! What the fuck did you just do? You fucking killed him!" Tears streamed down her horrified face.

Han glanced up. "Darling, you're not grasping the situation. You've just been rudely awoken, so I can't say I blame you. That *thing* was already dead."

Cara yanked the blouse on and pulled on a pair of jeans, shouting, "What the fuck are you talking about? I know you're the fucking film freak and all, but that shit is sick!"

"I haven't got time to argue with you! We're leaving right now."

"We can't leave the scene of a crime! Are you insane? I've got to report this!"

502

"Okay, the easiest way we can do this is to show you. Put your fucking shoes on first though."

Han led Cara out onto the caravan's decking as she fumbled for her mobile phone.

One of the nearby vans was in flames. A people carrier sped past with two creatures hanging on to the rear bumper. Several creatures were shambling around and, further down towards the site office, several more were huddled over a shrieking form. They were biting and tearing at the poor woman's flesh. The air was suddenly filled with screams and the crackling and popping of the burning caravan.

Cara let the phone fall limply to her side.

"Can I assume you're up to speed on current events?" Han asked, eying several creatures that were now heading their way.

"I ..."

"I'll take that as a yes. Okay, shall we make a move, hon? Time to check out."

They piled into the Jeep as more creatures gravitated towards them from all directions. As Han sat in the driver seat, he grabbed the steering wheel then said, "Bugger."

"What now?" Cara snapped.

"I left the keys in the caravan."

"Are you fucking kidding me?" Cara yelled, hysteria stretching her vocal cords to breaking point.

Han smiled. "Of course. What do you take me for?"

Cara glared at him and managed a weak groan.

Han fired up the engine (it started immediately – we're trying to avoid clichés here!). Another mistake people make in these situations is to screech away at top speed, careening into things and inevitably crashing like the stupid cannon fodder they are. Han wasn't stupid. He pulled off the grass carefully, three-pointed and drove at a gentle pace back towards the main gates.

"Move it, for fuck's sake!" Cara screamed, finally back in the game.

"Have you seen *any* horror films at all?" Han asked, incredulous.

She opened her mouth to speak, but shut it again. A creature thumped into the side of the Jeep, causing her to shrink away.

Han slowly picked his way through the creatures and around the dismembered woman in the middle of the road and then out onto the main street.

Seahouses was aflame and in utter disarray. Living and ... not quite so living fought and ran in all directions.

Han turned left and headed away from the town, speeding up a little once on the B1340 coastal route.

Cara was mute, staring ahead.

After a time, Han finally said, "I think we'll try Bamburgh next time, eh?"

THE END

Special bonus story by the legendary co-writer of
Night of the Living Dead.

THE WALK-IN
By
John Russo

Reverend John Sutherland was inordinately annoyed by the shrill
of the tea kettle. Not that it blew his concentration. He had
been unable to concentrate even before it went off. It wouldn't
have helped if he had closed his study door; in fact, it would've
been worse. He didn't trust his wife, and always had to keep an
ear cocked for what she might be up to.

He was fifty years old, greying and balding, and Barbara
was only thirty-five. She looked about five years younger than
her calendar age. Just as beautiful as when he married her, eleven
years ago. But inside she was somebody different. He had no
real proof of this. But nevertheless he knew. If God would have
let him have a peek inside his wife's mind, he would have been
afraid to look. At times he felt guilty about feeling this way. But
he could not make the fear, the dread, the nasty, resentful
thoughts, go away.

He didn't look up when she came into his study. He
pretended to be absorbed in the writing of his Sunday sermon,
even though he had barely managed to squeak out a couple of
unimpressive paragraphs. He had already decided to dig out one
of his old sermons instead. But he still had the bible and other
treatises open on his desk, to make Barbara think he was hard at
work, so she'd stay away.

Instead, she had made tea.

She seemed to know he was trying to deceive her.

Agonizing over this, John Sutherland did not turn to face
his wife when she set down the tray, her body shielding it from
his view anyway, as she surreptitiously dropped two capsules into
his cup. His was the one with the ceramic *bas relief* of Jesus,
complete with golden halo. Hers was the one with the *bas relief* of
Mary Magdalene.

"How's the sermon going?" she asked politely.

"Just about finished," he said, pulling his notebook on top of the measly two paragraphs, and getting up to kiss her. A polite, sexless kiss, as polite and as sexless as her inquiry.

They both sat down, he at his desk, she in the big leather chair often used by parishioners who came to him with their sins, their guilt, their interminable problems.

The Episcopalian priest and his wife sipped their tea in a long, edgy silence.

Finally Barbara said, "I want desperately to be normal ... to be the 'me' that you remember, John. I don't think that seeing a psychiatrist is doing me any good."

"But, darling ..." Reverend Sutherland began.

Barbara interrupted him urgently. "I feel as if there's a war going on, in my mind or in my soul. And I'm losing. Barbara Sutherland is slowly fading to nothingness. I'm desperate, don't you see? And I've read about someone who may be able to genuinely help me."

"Who?" the reverend asked, trying to sound patient, trying to hide his doubts.

The doubts only increased as he listened to his wife telling him about a man named Dr. Steven Monroe, a so-called 'parapsychologist', who claimed to specialize in the study of 'supernormal occurrences'.

Aghast, Reverend Sutherland couldn't help scoffing. "You mean ESP, clairvoyance, stuff like that?"

"Yes!" Barbara blurted. "And reincarnation. And ... and ... possession."

John stood up slowly, came to his wife, and placed a tender hand on her shoulder. "Barbara ... darling ... please believe me; what's wrong with you has a perfectly rational explanation. You spent three years in a coma. The fact that you finally recovered physically can almost be called a miracle. But, an experience like that had to have a terrible mental and emotional after-effect. You've got to fight hard to overcome the trauma ... and then you'll be yourself again, or nearly so. But, to some extent you'll always be a changed person. You've got to understand that, darling, and we've both got to learn to live with it."

506

Pushing his hand away, Barbara argued vehemently. "Dr. Monroe says that many people who survive near-death experiences are completely changed afterwards. He believes that the human body can be taken over by an invading spirit, or aura, when its defences have been sufficiently weakened. What if something like that happened to me, John? What if I'm not ... not going insane? What if conventional psychiatry can't really help me?"

"How do you know so much about Dr. Monroe's opinions?" the reverend challenged.

"I've been reading his book on supernatural phenomena."

"He's warping your mind, what's ..."

"What's left of it?" she snapped angrily.

"I didn't say that."

"But it's what you were going to say, isn't it?"

He took a deep breath, and forced his voice to be calm and reasonable. "People like this so-called 'Doctor' Monroe are charlatans. They prey on ignorance, on superstition. All my life I've fought them and their ilk, and I'm not about to start condoning their shady practices."

"Even if it means losing me?" she said, nearly in tears. "Even if it means losing me ... to Maria Rocail?"

He took his wife into his arms, cradling her head against his chest. With stern reassurance, he told her, "Maria Rocail is dead. There's no such thing as witchcraft. The only power she can have over you is the power you give your own memories of her wickedness."

"Think about it, John," Barbara said sadly. "Think very deeply about whether or not you truly want to lose me."

She pulled herself away from him, and disconsolately left the study.

In a little while, because of the capsules in the tea, Reverend Sutherland fell asleep over his treatises and his inept scribblings.

Barbara stole back into the study. She put the Bible into a drawer. Then she removed a crucifix from its hook and rehung it upside down. Mumbling a Satanic prayer, she stared down at her drugged husband, who looked almost as if he were dead.

Several weeks and quite a few capsules later, Reverend Sutherland yielded to a growing impulse to pay Dr. Monroe a visit. As he drove downtown and parked in a cavernous parking garage, he couldn't quite believe that he was going against his own adamant principles in this way. But more and more, lately, an almost heretical rationale had begun to implant itself in his brain. He told himself he was desperate, willing to try anything that might offer hope, no matter how outwardly preposterous it may seem.

Maybe, if his wife wanted to believe in this particular charlatan, the belief would turn out to be more beneficial than reality. Sometimes it didn't matter where you got the inspiration to make changes in your life. If believing in the 'luck' of a rabbit's foot gave you hope and courage to go through hard times or attempt the seemingly impossible, could the misplaced belief be entirely bad?

With these kinds of confused thoughts churning in his head, making him question his worthiness as a man of God, he pushed the buzzer of Dr. Monroe's brownstone. The man himself came to the door, and ushered Reverend Sutherland into his Victorian-style office. There wasn't a secretary or receptionist in sight, and no desk or cubical that might have accommodated one. Dr. Monroe was quite handsome, with blonde hair and beard, wearing an impeccably tailored pinstripe suit and vest. He looked to be about thirty.

Reverend Sutherland accepted a cup of tea, sipped it, and was overcome with an uncontrollable urge to tell everything about himself and his desperate situation. He revealed that his wife, Barbara, had recently awakened from a coma caused by a terrible automobile accident. She was unconscious, on a life support system for three years. Then, she suddenly awakened, with perfectly restored physical and mental vitality. It was if Reverend Sutherland's prayers had been miraculously answered.

"Except something was wrong," Dr. Monroe prompted.

"Yes. How did you know?"

"Because you're here, talking to me. And because these things aren't unknown in the field of parapsychology. Tell me more. I think I can help you."

His words tinged with hope, the reverend recounted how joyful he had felt, taking his wife back home to his church and rectory. For a while, things had gone well, and they had both repeatedly thanked God for the miracle He had wrought. But then came the shock of discovering that all was not well, after all, for Barbara began exhibiting symptoms of a split personality.

Most of the time, during the daylight hours, she seemed totally normal, like her old self – kind, affectionate, staid and moral. But during the night, her 'other personality' would take over. She imagined herself to be Maria Rocail – the wife of a self-styled 'witch' named Simon Rocail. The Rocails were notorious for their anti-Christian beliefs and practices. They led a coven of strange, perverted people who performed the Black Mass, indulging in pagan orgies, and tried to work evil spells upon their enemies. They still were worshipped, even idolised, by their followers, even after they both died. Simon and Maria committed suicide three years ago, when they were about to be arrested for causing the death of a small child in one of their occult ceremonies.

Reverend Sutherland had been a bold, outspoken adversary of the Rocails. He had preached against them and their 'phony' worshipping of Satan. He had called their 'witchcraft' nothing but a blasphemous superstition. And he was instrumental in leading the police to uncover their ritual murder.

When Simon and Maria Rocail poisoned themselves at the foot of their Satanic alter, they left a scroll, signed in blood, which promised that they would come back as reincarnated beings to take revenge on their 'Christian Persecutors', especially Reverend John Sutherland. The reverend had scoffed at this threat, and had asked God to forgive him for being secretly glad that the Rocails were dead. He did not believe in their pathetic spells and curses or witchcraft. He was convinced that the Inquisition was a blight upon the Church, a horrible dogmatic mistake that sent thousands of innocents to agonizing torture and flaming death at the stake.

"How did this business with the Rocails' impact upon your wife?" asked Dr. Monroe.

For a long moment, Reverend Sutherland did not answer. He grappled with the ominous feeling that, in dealing with this so-called 'parapsychologist', he was giving in to temptation, allowing himself to be seduced by New Age jargon and methodology that often cleverly disguised the devil's own, insidious propaganda. But he swallowed his misgivings, telling himself that it was his own overwhelming desire to find peace for his wife that made him so willing to try a desperate approach. And he prayed that God would understand and forgive him.

Usually he had to patiently cajole and lead his parishioners toward deep personal revelations, so he could understand and help them. He was used to maintaining a careful distance from his own emotions as he listened to their tales of sexual abuse, adultery, and so on. But now he felt that he was the one who had to open his own heart to a stranger. And he found it extremely difficult.

Clearing his throat nervously, he said, "When Barbara is in the throws of one of her … uh … nocturnal episodes as Maria Rocail, she becomes more wanton, more lascivious, more sexually aggressive than she ever was three years ago. Sometimes she 'sleepwalks' down to the sacristy."

"How do you know this?"

"I've followed her. I had to know – don't you see? But I wasn't prepared for the awfulness of it. One night I heard her mumbling prayers to Satan, cursing the Blessed trinity."

"How did you feel about this?"

"I prayed for her. I asked God's forgiveness. After all, this blasphemy was subconscious. She wasn't in control of her faculties. How could she have been? She was always a good, God-fearing woman. She's been in therapy for the past six months, seeing a psychologist. It doesn't seem to be doing any good. She read some of your books, and she was impressed. I remain sceptical, to put it mildly, Dr. Monroe. I consider myself a modern, enlightened clergyman. I don't believe in the occult, the paranormal. I'm here out of desperation – a vague hope that somehow you might be able to help my wife – even if the 'help'

510

turns out to be only an ability to replace her present delusion with something less blasphemous and destructive."

Dr. Monroe leaned back in his swivel chair, pressing the tips of his fingers together. In a tone of wounded sincerity, he said, "You can trust me far more than you know, Reverend Sutherland. I have a degree in psychology. I'm a legitimate scientist, an explorer of the mind, who has found its terrain murky and enigmatic. Certain occurrences cannot be understood in conventional terms. I have come to believe that people's minds are sometimes taken over by the souls, or auras, of those who are dead." He paused, eyeing the reverend with a look of bemusement. "I see by your expression that you find this hypothesis utterly outlandish."

"I'd sooner believe that my wife is schizophrenic."

"I think that much of what is regarded as mental illness is really a manifestation of the paranormal."

Reverend Sutherland pondered this for a long time. Then he said, despairingly, "You're trying to tell me that the Rocails' curse might have had real power in it?"

"Yes, exactly."

"I have to admit that the bad luck that befell us afterwards sometimes seemed like much more than coincidence. Not three weeks after Simon and Maria were dead, I suffered a heart attack. Then my wife had the terrible accident that put her in a coma."

Leaning forward, Dr. Monroe seized upon this point and pursued it intensely. "You must realise that when a person is near death, or in a trance or coma, the body and the soul, the aura, are imperfectly joined. There is less cohesion between the corporeal self and the spiritual self, and at such times a foreign spirit may slip in and inhabit the body. These alien spirits are called 'walk-ins'."

"But it sounds like demonic possession, which I've always considered to be pure superstition."

"Or it can be a form of reincarnation," said Dr. Monroe.

Reverend Sutherland thought this over. "You're saying that Maria Rocail's spirit may have infested my wife's mind and body while she was in her coma?"

"Yes, indeed," said Dr. Monroe. "Maria's spirit may have given your wife's body the power to heal itself and regain consciousness. Now, presumably, Barbara's own spirit has grown stronger. If we can exorcise the infestation, the walk-in, we may be able to restore her to spiritual health."

"How would you do this?" asked the reverend.

"Possibly through hypnotic regression. Would your wife consent to it?"

"Yes. She would. As I said, she's the one who suggested that we come to you for help."

Two weeks later, on a Saturday night, Reverend John Sutherland and his wife, Barbara, came to Dr. Steven Monroe's office. During the past fourteen days, the reverend's wife had stirred quite a few special capsules into his evening tea; unaware of this, he thought it was his own desperate hope of making his wife better that caused him to be more amenable, more agreeable, to whatever treatment Dr. Monroe wanted to undertake.

Barbara seemed inordinately delighted to be meeting the parapsychologist and placing herself in his care. It was clear that she already idolised him and put great faith in his curative powers. There was a warmth, an invisible but tangible note of complicity between them. The complicity seemed almost sexual, and the reverend felt a spike of jealousy. Suppressing the feeling, he told himself that it was only natural that Barbara should find Dr. Monroe attractive. He was young, blonde and handsome.

He gave the reverend a cup of tea that was strangely strong and bitter. Then he asked the reverend's wife to lie down on a black leather couch. Taking out a gleaming gold watch, he dangled it on its chain in front of his patient's eyes, making arc back and forth, giving off spangles of light, as he ushered her into a deep hypnotic trance – in the trite and usual way in which this type of thing has been portrayed in thousands of pieces of fiction. The very triteness of it imparted an 'unbelievability' to the proceedings that made Reverend Sutherland feel quite distant to what was going on, almost as if he weren't in the same room. His head was groggy, and his eyes blurry, and he felt stuporous, powerless to intervene, a condition aided and abetted by the capsules that Dr. Monroe had secretly dropped into his cup of strong, bitter tea …

… and when he regained consciousness, he was still groggy, his eyes swimming, his head reeling in disbelief. At first he thought he wasn't awake at all, but in the throes of a nightmare.

He was in his own church, which had been transformed in a weird and frightening way.

The altar wasn't his altar, but a twisted satanic version in the shape of a large, red, glittering, five-pointed star made of a clay-like material. Dr. Steven Monroe, Barbara and three others, all wearing black, hooded robes, were seated at the points of the star. Black pentagrams were painted on their foreheads. Their faces appeared grotesque, demented, in the wildly flickering candlelight. At each point of the star stood a human skull, and each skull supported a tall red candle, rivulets of wax running down over the skulls' foreheads and dripping like tears from their eye sockets. The centrepiece of the altar was a huge black and red sculpture of an evil goat god with wild, curving horns and a pair of claw like hands holding a silver dagger and an ornate silver chalice.

On the wall behind the altar was a huge black crucifix illuminated by candles in silver sconces. And nailed to the crucifix was a leering human skeleton, its bones yellowish, giving off a putrid aroma from the decaying slivers of flesh still clinging to them.

From his seat in the first pew, Reverend Sutherland recoiled from the awful sight and the stench of it. He wanted to rush up there and tear it down, rip its nails out of the plaster, but he was unable to move. He just sat there, trembling, trying to make himself arise or speak, or do *something* to put a stop to the obscene proceedings.

Dr. Monroe said, "Please begin, Maria."

Reverend Sutherland squinted to see if his nightmare had truly come to life, and the witch, Maria Rocail, was truly there at the Satanic alter, her evilly beautiful face hidden in the shadow of one of those black hoods.

But, no! It was his own wife who answered to the name 'Maria', and began praying. "Lucifer, I have come before you to perform your ceremony for the reclamation of the dead. We beg you to bless our deeds, that we perform in your almighty name. Consecrate the blood that we drink to show our oneness with you, the Lord of Hell!"

What blood were they talking about? A scream pierced the church, and Reverend Sutherland's eyes darted left, as from the side door behind the altar a young woman was carried in to the church by two more robed and hooded figures. She was strapped, nude, into a chair made of rude wood, like an electric chair. The hooded men carried her, chair and all, and sat her down to the left of the altar, where she continued to scream for a while, till at last the screams subsided to weak whimpers.

"Go on, Maria," prompted Dr. Monroe.

Barbara said, "Oh mighty Lord Satan, we worship you with all our hearts and humbly submit to your desires and commandments. We believe, with everlasting conviction, that you are our creator, our benefactor, our lord and master. We renounce Jehovah, his son, Jesus Christ, and all their works. And we declare to you, Lord Satan, that we have no other wish but to belong to you for all eternity."

The girl in the chair moaned piteously as Dr. Monroe arose, taking from the alter a pair of crossed human bones and placing them at her throat, just as a legitimate priest might have used crossed candles to bless the throats of the Christian faithful on Ash Wednesday. The young girl screamed again, but her voice was weak and hoarse.

Barbara Sutherland took the silver dagger from the altar and moved in close, so that she and Dr. Monroe flanked their victim, leering down at her. Barbara said, "Lucifer, we ask you to bless her, the source of our communion. May her blood give us strength to do your bidding and grant new life to Simon Rocail., our leader."

Dr. Monroe replaced the human bones on the altar, and took up the silver chalice. Barbara laid the dagger across the

514

girl's throat, ready to slice the jugular vein, as the chalice was put in position to collect the blood. The girl emitted one last horrible scream, which was cut short by the slicing dagger. Her life gurgled out of her, and her blood was collected.

At the same instant, Reverend Sutherland felt a wrenching pain in his chest. He was having a heart attack. He knew it. But he scarcely cared. He did not want to endure any more of this horror.

His vision dimming, out of the blur he saw Barbara and Dr. Monroe coming toward him, holding aloft the blood-filled chalice. It glittered alluringly as Barbara said, "By this blood, grant our beloved leader renewed life, Lord Satan, so that he may continue to serve you!"

With a shudder and a groan, Reverend Sutherland felt his heart explode. He had always hoped to go out with a prayer on his lips, but he was unable to manage. Somehow there was no prayer left in him. At the hour of his death, thanks to its obscenely sacrilegious circumstances, he was unable to summon his faith.

Barbara approached her late husband's corpse, sat next to him in the first pew, and put the chalice to his dead lips, making him 'drink'. Most of the blood ran down his chin, but some also ran into his mouth.

In a little while, he awoke. He felt the warmth, the adoration, of the hooded figures surrounding him, in his own church.

Barbara smiled at him. She kissed him and said, "Welcome back to me, my husband, Simon Rocail!"

The hooded figures murmured appreciatively.

Reverend John Sutherland, his body now inhabited by the walk-in, Simon Rocail, put his arm tenderly around his wife, and said, "My faithful spouse, Maria. It's so good to be with you again, darling."

"Thanks be to Lucifer," said Dr. Monroe.

Simon Rocail said, "Take my hand, brother-in-law. I congratulate you on a job well done in our absence."

"You are the best brother anyone could ever have," said Maria, as Dr. Monroe bent toward her to accept her kiss on the cheek, and the other hooded figures gathered around, chuckling in delight.

THE END

Exclusive screenplay excerpt from the sequel to *Pontypool.*

PONTYPOOL CHANGES
By
Tony Burgess

EXT. FIELD DAWN
The pickup truck in the field. Mary
standing beside it. Les still having
trouble with his door. He stops, then
slides over to the open passenger door and
gets out.
Mary begins to walk as Les stands where
she had been and leans down to look inside
the truck. Mary stops and looks back. Les
straightens up and walks toward her. Mary
commences walking and Les follows, seeming
to trace her very steps.

EXT. CLUTTER DRIVEWAY DAWN
The Clutter Mailbox, in the distance, in
the dawn glow, the Clutter house. Mary and
Les walk into frame at the base of the
driveway. Cut to Les and Mary facing the
house, they stare up, the wind blowing
their clothes.

MARY
Who's that?

EXT. FRONT STOOP. DAWN
Someone, a young man, JEFFREY, is pulling
planks from the burnt stoop. Another man
walks by the kitchen window. JULIE appears
at the window looking out. Her mouth is

clearly TAPED shut. A man rises behind
her and pulls her from the window.

EXT.CLUTTER DRIVEWAY. DAWN.
Mary leaps forward.

MARY
Oh God! Julie!

Les tries to stop her but she breaks away
and runs to the house. Les pauses for a
moment and looks at his hands, surprised.

LES
No gun.

Les looks up then bolts after Mary.

INT.CLUTTER LIVING ROOM - DAWN
In the kitchen are an ELDER MAN, a YOUNG
MAN, a YOUNG WOMAN and Julie. The elder
man passes Julie to the woman and gives
her a serious look. The young man spots
something through the planks.

YOUNG MAN
There's two of 'em now. They're coming up
the driveway.

The inhabitants begin to panic. The elder
man grabs a rifle.

ELDER MAN
Why are we keeping those kids in here?

The young woman holds Julie.

YOUNG WOMAN

518

Jesus. Jeffrey's outside!

The elder man steps cautiously to the stoop door.

ELDER MAN
They come for the kids, I bet.

EXT.FRONT STOOP DAWN
Jeffrey sees Mary running towards him and he freezes.

JEFFREY
Oh God, no.

Les reaches half way up the drive way and stops.

LES
Mary! MARY!

Mary stops running. Jeffrey is frozen on the stoop. Mary a few feet from him and Les on the driveway. They all stare silently at each other.

The Elder man comes out onto the stoop to the silent tableau. He takes it in for a second.

ELDER MAN
Oh shit.

INT.CLUTTER HOUSE - LIVING ROOM DAWN
The Young Man at the window.

YOUNG MAN
They got Jeffrey!

519

He jumps for the door to help the Elder man in.

YOUNG WOMAN
Oh God! Oh God!

The Elder man is in, panting.

ELDER MAN
Shut this door. Hammer this door up. We gotta seal this place off.

YOUNG WOMAN
We can't seal this place off! They can get in the windows! They can tear those planks off!

YOUNG MAN
She's right. We can't keep 'em out forever! We're gonna have to kill 'em

YOUNG WOMAN
How many of them are there?

ELDER MAN
I saw two. But if you can see two there's two hundred you can't see.

They all stare at each other.

YOUNG MAN
Then we're all gonna die.

EXT.CLUTTER DRIVEWAY. DAWN.
Les is holding Mary tightly as she cries.

MARY

They got my babies. They got my little angels.

Mary sobs and tries to get away, but Les holds her tightly. Mary stops struggling.

MARY
What are we gonna do?

Les pulls back. There is blood on his shirt and his chin.

LES
Did I kill him?

Les looks towards the stoop. A body is barely visible in the debris. Les touches his mouth and looks at the blood.

LES (CONT'D)
That was the craziest thing I've ever seen
…

MARY
They're going to kill my children.

LES
No they're not.

Close up on Les: his eyes are cold. He looks toward the house.

LES
Not if we kill them, first.

Les looks down at Mary. Mary stops crying and takes a shallow breath.

LES
We're going to kill 'em all.

INT.CLUTTER LIVING ROOM DAWN
The Young Woman is sitting on the couch
holding Julie and Jimmy tightly. There is
a piece of TAPE across the children's
mouths. Also sitting in a chair is a
SHORT MAN with black curly hair, he is
holding a hammer. The Elder Man comes in
with a shotgun. He looks through the slats
over the TV.

ELDER MAN
I can't see nothing. We gotta be able to
see outside.

YOUNG WOMAN
What do they want from us?

ELDER MAN
Ask them kids.

YOUNG WOMAN
They can hear you.

ELDER MAN
That's right. And maybe we get sick cause
they hear what we're saying. Maybe it
works that way too.

YOUNG WOMAN
These children are as healthy as you and
me.

ELDER MAN
Well, shit. I'm not sure you and me should
be talking either.

YOUNG WOMAN
Listen, there's nothing wrong with us …

The young man bursts in from the kitchen.

YOUNG MAN
Better get in here.

The elder man gives the woman a serious
look - this is it.

ELDER MAN
We have to dispose of those kids somehow.

INT.KITCHEN DAWN
The Young Man looks through the boarded
window and waves the Elder Man to look.

The view through the slats: the barn roof
is on fire. Zombies start running from
the barn with their heads on fire. They
run in different directions into the
field.

YOUNG MAN
That's beautiful.

The scene is in fact, beautiful, with
black columns of smoke rising from the
orange heads of people running in the open
field.

YOUNG MAN
It's the kids you know.

ELDER MAN
I know.

YOUNG MAN
She's gonna let us get rid of 'em?

The men sit back in profile from the window. A CLICK. The men turn around slowly and look. The door to the basement. The door knob turns. Les opens the basement door.

He walks in, calmly looks at the men and walks over to the stoop opening the door letting Mary in.

Les walks forward, a lustful look, eyes rolling, he approaches the two men.

The two men cover their ears.

Les sees this and realizes they think he's a zombie.

LES
Hi fellas. I don't think you live here do you?

The Young man starts saying: LA LA LA LA, trying to drown out Les's voice.

Les strikes him, knocking him down. The Elder man looks up and drops his hands.

Les gives him a nasty look.

LES
We interrupting your little home invasion?

MARY

You got my children. If you've hurt them.

ELDER MAN
THEY'RE INSIDE! THEY'RE TALKING!

Les strikes the Elder man, sending him
down.
Mary runs to the living room. Les watches
her, looks momentarily confused.

INT.CLUTTER HOUSE - LIVING ROOM DAY
Mary goes to the couch and pulls the
terrified young woman to her feet.

MARY
Make your own babies.

The young woman gasps, her eyelids flutter
and she faints to the floor.

Les enters. Sees the short man with curly
hair sitting in the reclining chair with
his hammer. Les walks directly up to him.

LES
A little less conversation.

Les snatches the hammer up.

LES
A little more action.

Les raises the hammer to strike the man.

MARY
Les. No!

Mary looks at the couch. Julie and Jimmy, their mouths taped shut, look up terrified.

MARY
My babies.

Mary sits between them and holds them tightly.

Close up of Julie's face, her eyes wide with fear.

MARY
Oh my sweetheart. Oh my love. You're gonna be OK.

A frightened peep from Julie's taped mouth. Mary looks up at Les

MARY
They're terrified, Les.

Mary turns to Julie

MARY
Oh baby. Are you OK? You're OK. You're gonna be fine. Let's get this off. I want to hear you baby, I want to hear your voice.

Mary pulls the edge of the tape and Julie squeezes her eyes shut, tears rolling down her cheeks into the duct tape.

MARY
Oh Les, the tape … it's hurting her.

Mary looks up at Les. Les stares back with a look of incomprehension.

MARY
Les, help me please.

Les smiles.

LES
They're gonna be OK. Mary.

Mary smiles back as Les carefully removes the tape.

MARY
They're alive Les.

She lies her face against Les's arm.

MARY
You're my hero, Les. You're the greatest man that ever lived.

Les lowers his eyes humbly – they are uplifting words, but also painful.

The baby CRIES from outside. Les's eyes pop open.

He jumps up.

LES
I left the baby outside.

Les turns and runs through the kitchen.

The baby cries intermittently. In the silent moments the room in the kitchen is the scene Les had left. The bodies of two men and the women on the floor.

When the baby screams we see:

Les's hands pulling apart the mouth of the older man and viciously drawing the fleshless face, the bleeding teeth up to his own mouth.

Baby stops screaming, Les stands still, jolted by the vision. He looks back down at the man.

Les looks back to living room, vexed and confused.

The baby screams and we see:
The woman's headless body floating in slow motion to the wall, her neck hits and an explosion of red blood cascades down the white wall.

The baby stops crying, and Les is standing panting, he looks down at his hands, frantic.

Les moves quickly back into the living room.

INT. LIVING ROOM.
Les enters the room as the baby starts to cry again, a more distant sound.

Les slams the door shut and leans his head against it, afraid to turn around.

He squeezes his eyes shut.

LES
Mary?

A dark vision: Mary on the couch leaning
over her children. Les behind her, his
head shaking violently like a wolf ripping
prey.

Close up of Mary's face, the booming sound
of Les's insane voice. Parts of her face
gouge and split at the sound of his
illegible speech.

LES
Mary!

Les takes a breath and turns as the baby
stops screaming.
Mary is lying dead across her dead
children.

Les steps forward.

Les looks up at the wall above the couch.
The baby screams and blood flies up in an
arc.

Les sees this and is vibrating. The baby
stops crying.

Les drops to the bodies. He turns Mary
over.

He embraces her corpse.

LES
No. No. I can't … I can't … have done this

...

The baby stops crying. Les lowers Mary and strokes her hair.

LES
Did I say something? Did I say something wrong? Oh Mary … I wanted you to be alive. I wanted all of us to be alive. I'm your hero. I didn't do this.

Les sits up and lays his hand on Mary's face.

LES
I can't see myself. I can't see this. I'm a … a … thing … I'm a thing the world kills people with.

Les pulls Mary up and holds her tightly.

MARY
I wanted you to be alive. I don't care what the world does, it's stupid and it's wrong. I'm the one … I'm the one who wanted you alive. I'm so sorry.

Les lowers her slowly and stands.

LES
And I want peace on earth. I want happy babies. I want this war to be over. I want rich people to give their money back.

Les stumbles through the room.

INT. KITCHEN
Les staggers in.

LES
I want perfect, pure … air and … no …

He thinks, putting a finger to his chin.

LES
Hmmm. Disease. No more. No more and free
love. And good people.

He smiles at the simplicity.

LES
Even just one. Somebody, who's OK.
Somebody who can help me a little bit.

Les leans to the window and looks out.

Through the window: Soldiers are swarming
the front yard. One has scooped the baby
out of the barrel.

LES
And finally, what I want … since, what I
ask for, I get,

A soldier spots Les and drops to his knee
and raises a rifle.

LES
I'd like this.

BANG! The muzzle of the rifle flares. A
hole plinks through the glass and …

PONTYPOOL CHANGES COMING SOON …

531

Lightning Source UK Ltd.
Milton Keynes UK
176975UK00001B/78/P